**Two brand-new stories in every volume...
twice a month!**

Duets Vol. #45

Popular Carol Finch always "presents her fans with
rollicking wild adventures...memorable characters and
fun from beginning to end," says *Romantic Times
Magazine*. Joining her this month is mother-and-
daughter writing team Jennifer Drew with a delightful
spin-off to their first Duets title, *Taming Luke*.

Duets Vol. #46

The West will never be the same after Debbi Rawlins
serves up her first dynamite Double Duets. *Affaire de
Coeur* says "Rawlins's books are jammed packed with
witty dialogue, crazy situations, excellent characters
and a lot of laughs!" Enjoy!

Be sure to pick up both Duets volumes today!

"He's taking over the ranch. Aren't you, Mr. Bennett?"

Max blinked and took a good look at Rosie. Her hair wasn't blond. It was white. Attractive, but white. Looking a little closer, he guessed her to be in her late sixties. Was she the cook?

His gaze strayed over the other woman and he tried not to gape. She'd removed her apron and her black lace top fit her like a second skin.

"Max." Mona grabbed his hand. "I assume I can call you Max? And of course, you already know I'm Mona. Mona Lisa." Pointing to the other woman, she added, "And this here is Rosie Peach."

"Mona Lisa. Rosie Peach," Max repeated slowly, not quite able to believe what he was seeing.

Mona nodded. "Candy Kane is out shopping, but she should be home soon. There's only the three of us these days."

Max swallowed.

Mona and Rosie exchanged knowing looks. Then Rosie smiled. "Don't worry, Max," she said, patting his arm. "There may be snow on the chimney, but there's still fire in the furnace."

For more, turn to page 9

The organist started playing the Wedding March.

Taylor stepped out, tall and slim and at least a head taller than the other women. The church lights glowed off her light blond hair, making it look as though she were wearing a halo.

But there was nothing angelic about her murderous expression. She didn't even try to smile when the photographer ducked in front of her and snapped a picture. She looked as if she wanted to drop-kick him all the way to Vegas.

Clint was about to turn and face the altar when Taylor moved forward so that Mona and Candy were no longer blocking his view. His jaw dropped and suddenly his pants seemed awfully tight. Taylor's dress was...almost a dress. He drew in a deep breath and tried to compose himself. Somebody should have warned him. He could already feel a heart attack coming on.

Then she stepped up beside him. Her mysterious scent seeped into his skin until it pulsed through his veins and compelled him to turn and look at her...except his gaze went inadvertently to her stunning cleavage.

Taylor pasted on a smile. "Don't get too excited, cowboy. It's a Wonderbra."

For more, turn to page 197

HARLEQUIN DUETS

ISBN 0-373-44112-6

THE SWINGING R RANCH
Copyright © 2001 by Debbi Quattrone

WHOSE LINE IS IT ANYWAY?
Copyright © 2001 by Debbi Quattrone

All rights reserved. Except for use in any review, the reproduction or utilization of this work in whole or in part in any form by any electronic, mechanical or other means, now known or hereafter invented, including xerography, photocopying and recording, or in any information storage or retrieval system, is forbidden without the written permission of the publisher, Harlequin Enterprises Limited, 225 Duncan Mill Road, Don Mills, Ontario, Canada M3B 3K9.

All characters in this book have no existence outside the imagination of the author and have no relation whatsoever to anyone bearing the same name or names. They are not even distantly inspired by any individual known or unknown to the author, and all incidents are pure invention.

This edition published by arrangement with Harlequin Books S.A.

® and TM are trademarks of the publisher. Trademarks indicated with ® are registered in the United States Patent and Trademark Office, the Canadian Trade Marks Office and in other countries.

Visit us at www.eHarlequin.com

Printed in U.S.A.

The Swinging R Ranch

Debbi Rawlins

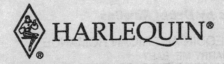

HARLEQUIN®

TORONTO • NEW YORK • LONDON
AMSTERDAM • PARIS • SYDNEY • HAMBURG
STOCKHOLM • ATHENS • TOKYO • MILAN • MADRID
PRAGUE • WARSAW • BUDAPEST • AUCKLAND

Dear Reader,

The state of Nevada is the last place I thought I'd ever set a story. It's a desert, for crying out loud! Well, not only did I set my first Double Duets in that wonderful, wacky place, but I actually bought a house there. And guess what? I love it!

Even reading the newspapers in Nevada is entertaining—and inspiring! In fact, I came up with the idea behind *The Swinging R Ranch* when I read an article about a local brothel. How could I help playing the "what if" game in my head with all the juicy material I was finding? I'm still not sure how I came up with the name of the town—Bingo. I'd never played the game, and thought I wouldn't like it. Now I'm hopelessly addicted, and on most hot afternoons, you'll find me feverishly daubing numbers in the Bingo Room of The Reserve Casino. Just don't tell my editor. She thinks I'm writing.

I hope the people of Bingo brighten up your days the way they've brightened mine.

Enjoy,

Debbi Rawlins

Books by Debbi Rawlins

HARLEQUIN AMERICAN ROMANCE
691—MARRY ME, BABY
730—THE BRIDE TO BE...OR NOT TO BE?
741—IF WISHES WERE...HUSBANDS
780—STUD FOR HIRE?
808—HIS, HERS AND THEIRS

This is for the ladies of The Reserve Bingo Room—
the best bingo agents in Nevada!

And a special acknowledgment to Carol,
"the pretty one."

1

"EVER CONSIDER WORKING for a living?"

The voice seemed to echo down a long tunnel. Max Bennett buried his head deeper under his pillow. It was practically the middle of the night. He was alone. Had to be a dream.

At a slight scraping sound, he peeked through one eye. Light flooded the room. Someone had opened the drapes.

He cursed into the pillow and closed his eye again. He'd thought he was alone. Had what's-her-name from last night come home with him? You'd think he'd remember *that*.

"Come on, you bum. Rise and shine."

Max let out a sigh of relief. It was only Taylor's voice. Rolling over, he glanced at the clock on the nightstand. His vision blurred and he had to squint. Groaning, he let his head drop back to the pillow. "For God's sake, it's only noon."

"So, you can waste just half the day for a change." She tugged at the covers he was trying to pull over his head and they landed bunched at his waist. "Did I tell you Hastings submitted his resignation? My firm will need a good contract lawyer."

All Max had on was a pair of black silk boxers but that wouldn't faze Taylor so there was no chance of embarrassing her into leaving. She'd been his best friend since their first year in law school. Although they'd dated once, they decided they made better friends. Taylor was ambitious, dedicated, serious. Everything he wasn't. Of course she didn't have three generations of blue-blooded Bennetts paying her tab.

"Very funny," he mumbled and tried to get comfortable again.

"I wasn't being funny. I'm dead serious."

Oh, man. Serious was even worse. He hated when she got serious. When any woman did.

"If you came all the way over here to offer me a job, then you just wasted half *your* day," he said, and she gave him a disappointed look. "Your time would be better spent finding a way to break into my trust fund."

He squinted at the top of the nightstand again. His gold watch sat next to an engraved lighter he didn't recognize. Where the hell was the aspirin?

"If you weren't so damn lazy you'd have read the will and already figured out that's impossible. Your grandmother was very specific about your money being dispensed in five-year increments." Sighing, she reached behind the lamp and produced a small bottle of aspirin. "Why did you bother going to Harvard? You don't need a law degree to be a vagrant."

He didn't even flinch. "Get me some water, huh?"

She stayed put and held up an envelope. "You should have told me about this."

He stared at the unfamiliar envelope. "I've got the Aspen ski trip coming up, then the baccarat tournament in Monte Carlo. I need some serious cash. So unless that pertains to me getting at my trust fund early, I'm not interested."

Shaking two white tablets out of the bottle into his palm, he contemplated trying to down them without water. A nasty thought. But so was rolling out of bed and trudging all the way across his room to the bathroom.

"You've inherited a ranch."

"Tell me something I don't know." He sank back against the pillows. "I'll give you a hundred bucks to get me some water."

"Did you know it's located in Nevada?"

"Yeah, I even know that's a state. I checked."

"Hope you didn't strain yourself," she said as she walked toward the bathroom. She returned with a crystal goblet of water and handed it to him. "This is only because I want you alert and concentrating. Now, who in the world is this Lily McIntyre who left you the ranch? Surely not one of the Bennetts. I doubt they've ventured west of Boston. Too uncivilized for them."

He wasn't offended by her remark. It was true. "Lily's my great-aunt on my mother's side."

"Have I met her?"

"Nope. Neither have I."

Taylor frowned. "I always thought you had a pretty close family."

"Ah, but we like to leave the skeletons in the closet."

Curiosity sparkled in her eyes as she sat at the edge of his bed. "I can't wait to hear this."

He grinned, then grimaced. His head still hurt like hell. "Okay, I confess...I don't know anything about Aunt Lily. But she's gotta be the family skeleton because everyone has suddenly developed acute hearing and speech losses. Then there's the fact she was stuck out on some small ranch in the desert."

"Think again. This 'small' ranch sits on over three hundred acres."

Max sat up, alert suddenly. "You think it's income producing?"

"Don't get too excited. Nevada is still the desert." She frowned and shook her head. "There's something strange about this letter. Did you even bother to read it?"

"Yeah, most of it." Taylor could be so damn annoying at times. Who wouldn't have been interested in an inheritance? Even if it was a ranch. Cash would be better, especially when he had three more years before he'd be solvent again. "But it doesn't make sense. A ranch is supposed to have cows and horses and chickens...stuff like that, right?"

She shrugged. "That's what I thought. I don't know about chickens though. Aren't they raised on farms with pigs?"

One side of Max's mouth lifted in wry amusement. They'd both lived their entire lives in Boston, he on Beacon Hill, Taylor in Roxburry.

She frowned thoughtfully as her gaze scanned the letter. "It's near a town called Bingo. All that acreage should be worth something."

He snorted. "I wouldn't count on it."

Her cell phone rang. "So you're just going to roll over and play dead?"

Max smiled. "No, I'm going to let you look into it for me."

She glanced up before taking the call. "God, you're so predictable."

He was about to make a crack when she answered the phone, her tone crisp and businesslike. If he knew Taylor, he wouldn't be getting rid of her soon, so he thought about hopping into the shower. And then he heard her mention Nevada.

He shook his head with a half smile. Of course she was already on the case. Probably had had her calls forwarded. She was efficient, if nothing else.

"Isn't there anyone besides Mr. Southby who can help me regarding a letter he sent out on the fifth?" she asked into the receiver. "When do you expect him?"

After a brief pause, she said, "It's the middle of the week. He can't just go fishing and not say what day he'll be back." Taylor's expression tightened. "That's not good enough. I need someone to help me now."

Max checked a grin. It was really too bad about Taylor and him. There was so much to like about her. Yet the lack of chemistry was the least of their problems. As an attorney she could be a pit bull, which was good. But as a life partner, he needed someone who wasn't so ambitious, someone more fun-loving and adventurous, like himself. And if she had her own trust fund, all the better.

"Yes, regarding the Swinging R Ranch. I'm Mr. Bennett's attorney, and we're somewhat confused about the lack of inventory outlined in Mr. Southby's letter, or maybe livestock is a better word. Anyway—"

Her sudden silence drew his wary attention. He looked up at her stunned face.

"Would you please repeat that?" Color slowly tinted her cheeks. She visibly swallowed. "I see." Then she cleared her throat, and he could tell she wanted to laugh. "I'll be sure and tell him. Uh-huh. Yes, I will. Oh, I suspect he'll be arriving in Bingo within a few days."

He frowned as their gazes met. She couldn't mean him.

Her sudden grin told him otherwise. "Thank you for your help, Mrs. Crabtree." She hung up the phone, not even trying to hide her amusement.

Whatever foolishness she was up to, he wasn't in the mood. Only one thing interested him. "Is the ranch profitable?"

"Oh, I suspect it might be."

"And?"

"Congratulations, Mr. Bennett." Taylor struggled to stifle a laugh. "You're the proud owner of an honest-to-goodness, legal-as-a-copper-penny brothel."

"GOOD EVENING, ladies and gentlemen, and welcome to the Abby Cunningham for Mayor dinner. Of course, as you all know, I'm Cabby Anningham." Letting out a shriek of disgust, Abby made a face at her tired reflection in the bathroom mirror.

She'd known most of the people who'd be at the dinner since she'd started toddling around Bingo twenty-five years ago. How she could still get so nervous and tongue-tied was beyond her comprehension.

Her stomach in knots, she padded out of the bathroom, into her bedroom and headed straight for the dish of peanut M&M's sitting on her dresser. Chocolate wouldn't cure her nerves. In fact, she'd probably end up with a face full of zits for the dinner tomorrow night, but right now, those little suckers were the only things that would get her through this rehearsal.

She still had to decide whether to wear her hair up in a more sophisticated style, like maybe a French twist, or leave it long and loose to her shoulders the way she always wore it. The people of Bingo tended to favor familiarity, but Abby wasn't sure how much her age was a deterrent. Twenty-six was awfully young to be mayor. Even if her father had held the office for three terms, as did his father before him.

After carefully sorting four red candies from the rest of the colors, she sank to her bed, leaned back against the pillows and started popping the M&M's into her mouth. She'd eat the green ones next, and then the rest in no particular order. It wasn't that she was superstitious exactly, but she saw no point in changing her habits now.

"Abby...yoo-hoo. Abby, I'm home."

At the sound of her grandmother's voice, Abby bolted upright and slid the dish of candy into her underwear drawer. She swallowed the last M&M whole, then cleared her throat. "I'm in my room, Gramms."

Estelle Cunningham instantly appeared in the doorway. Her smile faded, her gaze narrowed, and she sniffed the air. "I smell chocolate."

"In here?" Abby laughed. "You're imagining things. Do you think I should wear my hair up or down tomorrow night?" She twisted it up and sent her grandmother a questioning look.

Gramms brushed past her, sniffing, and went unerringly to the dresser drawer. Abby's only hope now was that the ill-favored peanut variety she'd purposely bought would discourage Gramms.

"Really, Abby, you shouldn't mix these with your unmentionables." Estelle sat on the bed with the dish on her lap, scooped out an orange-colored one and carefully nibbled the coating and chocolate off the nut. "You know, maybe that's how someone thought to invent those edible panties. Do you suppose? I think they're called Candies, or some such thing."

"How do you know about that?" Abby frowned. "You've been hanging around those women at the Swinging R again, haven't you?" She grabbed the dish of M&M's. "And no more of these. Doctor's orders."

"You have no business talking to my doctor, Abigail. No business at all. You forget who's the grandmother here." She shook her snow-white head and briefly eyed the candy before directing her stern blue gaze at Abby. "And don't let me hear you referring to the ladies of the Swinging R as *those women* again. Shame on you. Why,

Rosie, Mona and Candy have all contributed handsomely to your campaign fund, young lady.''

Sighing, Abby sat beside her grandmother and patted her age-spotted hand. ''I've been meaning to talk to you about that. It's not that I don't appreciate their support, but I don't think it's appropriate for them to be passing out gift certificates for future services at the Ranch.''

''Why not? The gift certificates are separate from the 'Vote for Abby' flyer. They're stapled together but we were very careful not to make it sound like a bribe.''

''We? You haven't been... Oh, Gramms.'' Slumping, Abby dug into the bowl and popped candies into her mouth without regard to color. Why bow to superstition? Her career was probably over anyway.

Estelle chuckled. ''You young people think everything is such a big deal, that the whole world is going to come to an end if one little thing goes out of whack in your life.'' Her smile gentled, reminding Abby so much of her father that it made her chest ache with fresh grief. At forty-eight, her parents had been too young to die. But the driver of the speeding semitruck hadn't taken that into consideration.

''I know you disapprove of the Swinging R,'' Estelle continued, ''but brothels are legal in this county and the place is practically an institution. Folks don't mind having the ladies around. They've always contributed to the community just like everyone else.''

Abby decided to keep further comment to herself. There was no point in upsetting her grandmother. Besides, she really didn't have anything against the Swinging R, as long as her grandmother didn't start hanging around there too much. ''I know,'' she said, passing her two M&M's. ''And I'll welcome each of their votes.''

Gramms frowned. "Don't be stingy with those. You weren't raised that way."

"You know what the doctor said—"

"Abigail, you're only twenty-six. How can you be such an old fa—?"

The phone rang, cutting off their conversation. Just as well, Abby thought as her grandmother pushed off the bed to get it in the next room. Abby had heard the admonishments before. Many times, in fact. She was too serious, too responsible, too staid for a person her age. Baloney. All of it.

Even if it were true, it wasn't as if Abby had a choice. She was all Gramms had and someone had to look after her. Next month she'd be seventy without a hint of slowing down. That's why Abby never bothered to get the phone anymore. It was always for Gramms.

"Some of the girls want to go play bingo tonight," Gramms said as she breezed back into the room. "We're going to grab a bite to eat on the way."

Abby smiled, tucking her disappointment away. "No fries or cheeseburgers, and definitely no cheesecake."

Her grandmother made a face. "I was going to ask you to come with us, but now I'm not so sure." Her gaze strayed to the clothes spread out across the bed. Then her eyes met Abby's. "Did you have plans for us tonight?"

"No." Abby shrugged off the lie. "I'm just trying to decide what to wear tomorrow night."

Gramms frowned at the selection, then went to the closet and pulled out the short red dress she'd given Abby last Christmas. "This is what you should wear. Not one of those old fuddy duddy navy or gray suits. Now let's go."

Abby took the dress and gave her grandmother a kiss

on the cheek. "Go have fun. I'm still practicing my speech."

Gramms waved a dismissive hand. "You don't have to do that. You'll beat old man Cleghorn just by showing up. No one wants that antiquated fool back in the saddle." She put a finger to her temple, and lowered her voice even though there was no one else in the house. "His chimney's been clogged for some time now, and he wasn't the sharpest tool in the shed when he was in his prime, if you know what I mean."

Abby wasn't sure she did, but she knew better than to ask. "I don't want to win by default, Gramms. I want to win because I'm the best person for the job."

Estelle's eyes widened. "Everyone from here to Las Vegas knows you care more about this town than a bear loves honey. Even when all your friends flew the coop after college, you came right back here. Not that I agree with your decision, mind you." Gramms gave her that gentle smile again that made Abby's heart constrict. "No one here doubts your ability or your loyalty, Abigail. And when you win, it isn't going to be by default or because your name is Cunningham."

"Thanks, Gramms." Abby sweetly smiled back. "But you still aren't getting any more M&M's."

Estelle's smile faded and she snorted. "Don't buy the peanut ones anymore. They get in my dentures."

"Good. Don't eat them. Now, outta here. The girls are waiting for you."

Gramms hesitated. "You're sure you don't want me to stick around and help you?"

"Nope. I'm just going to putter around a bit. Maybe take a nap before dinner. I made a casserole. Enough for three nights. Later maybe I'll have time to bake a batch of cookies for your bridge club meeting on Sunday."

Estelle frowned. "There's something very wrong with this picture. It's Friday night. *You* should be going out."

Abby gently took her grandmother by the shoulders, faced her toward the door and walked her out of the room. "I'm doing exactly what I want to be doing."

"Taking care of me?"

Abby grimaced at her grandmother's weary tone. "Don't say it like that. You hardly need a baby-sitter. I'm just a homebody, Gramms—I always have been. You know that. Now, go have fun. But don't stay out too late."

She hesitated again, and Abby had to give her another nudge before she grabbed her patchwork purse off the hall table. "You know I've loved staying with you here in your daddy's house, don't you, honey? And how much I've treasured our time together?"

Abby reared her head back at her grandmother's serious tone. "You're not leaving me and getting married or anything, are you?"

"Oh, good Lord, no."

Abby had been teasing. Sort of. Gramms could be awfully impulsive at times. "Nothing's going to change," Abby assured her, realizing she was probably worried about their time together being upset by Abby's job. "You're not losing a granddaughter. Hopefully you'll be gaining another mayor in the family."

Oddly, Gramms didn't look pleased. She merely stood motionless for a long moment, staring back with an uncertainty that made Abby uneasy. "Well, I'd better go. You know how I hate being late."

"Gramms? Is there anything you want to tell me?"

She pushed open the front door and paused. "Just that I love you. And there's nothing in this world I wouldn't do for you."

Despite the lingering summer heat, Abby walked out onto the porch, watched her grandmother climb into her car and waited until the blue sedan had disappeared behind the hedges of pink oleander that lined the end of their driveway.

The feeling that something wasn't right stayed with her long after she'd returned to her room, selected an outfit, decided on a hairstyle, taken a nap and had some dinner. But it wasn't until she went into Gramms's room to get her laundry basket that Abby understood why she'd felt uneasy.

Gramms's closet was half empty. So were her drawers. On the center of the handmade quilt that covered her bed was an envelope.

Heart pounding, Abby lunged for it.

She tore half the note along with the envelope and had to piece it together. When the message became clear, Abby let out a shriek that shook half of Bingo.

2

IT HAD ONLY BEEN AN HOUR since Max stepped off the Bennett family's private plane and onto Nevada soil and already he hated Bingo and everything associated with it. The desert was not his idea of a good time. It was hot, dusty and he didn't give a damn what the pilot said, Max *knew* he saw a friggin' scorpion. So what that they'd still been forty feet from the ground. A scorpion was pretty damn hard to miss.

From the back seat of the hired car, Max eyed the passing landscape with disdain and suspicion. Scorpion or not, he had no use for anything smaller than a kitten that had four or more legs. He shook his head. How could Aunt Lily have left Boston for this place?

Of course Boston didn't have legal brothels.

He smiled, thinking of the events of the past twenty-four hours. The Bennetts had gone bonkers over Aunt Lily's bequest. Normally when he asked for use of the family plane, he'd get a lecture. Not this time. His parents had coughed it up so fast it was a joke. They wanted him to hurry and wash his hands of the place. He'd really have hated telling them that he was thinking about keeping it to supplement his trust fund. So he hadn't.

"How much longer before we get there?" Max asked the driver, and like the two other times he'd asked, the man sighed.

"About fifteen minutes." The man muttered something under his breath, then added, "Don't they teach you boys how to tell time back east?"

At the man's insolence, Max gave a startled laugh. "Yeah. They even teach us manners. What's your name?"

"Herbert Hanson." The man shook his head and from under the battered tan cowboy hat he wore, his black eyes met Max's in the rearview mirror. "You must be one hardheaded son-of-a-gun."

Max snorted. "I'd ask how you arrived at that conclusion except I have a feeling that's unnecessary."

"If they taught you manners, you weren't listening too good. I introduced myself to you when I picked you up, son. But you were too busy shooting your mouth off about how you'd ordered a Lincoln Town Car."

Very few people could render Max speechless. Herbert Hanson's brassy dressing-down had him dumbstruck.

"I'm sure you're used to getting what you want," Hanson continued, "but out here in Bingo, folks are plumb grateful to get what they need. This old Caddy will get you there safe and sound," he winked into the rearview mirror, taking some of the sting out of his words, "in the next thirteen minutes. You can count on that."

A dozen sarcastic remarks flew through Max's head, including one that would make old Herbert think twice about getting a tip. But the man had hit a nerve and Max decided to leave it alone.

He stared out the window in silence, wondering how long it would take to get his business wrapped up and get the hell out of Dodge. There was only one motel in town and he certainly wasn't expecting much there. He'd had a difficult enough time getting picked up. There was no limo service in Bingo. Herbert was the motel manager's uncle and he'd agreed to run Max around to supplement his retirement income.

A good reason not to tick off the old guy, or Max could end up without wheels. And scorpion territory was not the place to be hotfooting it around.

Of course he could always stay at the Swinging R Ranch. After all, he owned the place. The thought made him cringe, and he had to remind himself that brothels were legal here in certain parts of Nevada. Hell, it probably boosted the local economy, supplied jobs, kept women off welfare, provided college tuition.

He shoved a hand through his hair. None of this reasoning made him feel better. He'd never been forced to evaluate his position on prostitution, legal or not, and he sure as hell didn't want to do it now. Not when he was almost broke. Still, the idea that a woman ever had to make a living on her back made him squirm. Great time for him to develop a conscience.

On the near horizon, the flat dusty terrain gave way to a handful of buildings. He glanced at his watch. That had to be Bingo. Taylor had warned him the town was small, but he'd figured a population of nine-hundred-and-two required more than a ghost town.

From behind his dark glasses, he squinted at the sign coming up on the right. It said, Welcome To Bingo, and below it, Population nine-hundred-and-two. Except the two was crossed out and five was etched in.

"What do you people do? Count cows and horses?" Max asked.

Herbert glanced at the sign just as they drove past it. "Nope. The Hoover boys left for college this fall and we don't expect they'll be back. But Alma Hopkins just had triplets. Six months ago Louise Jenks had only one, but we suspect there's another bun in her oven."

Max stared at the back of the man's head. He could see enough of his somber profile to see that the guy was serious. Max slumped back in his seat. This was definitely not his scene. The sooner he figured out how much money the Swinging R could make him and got out of here, the better.

"I changed my mind about going straight to the motel. Let's swing by Chester Southby's office instead."

"We can do that," Herbert said in that annoyingly lazy drawl of his. "But that ol' boy is going to be fishing on a nice day like this, not sitting cooped up in his office."

"It's Friday afternoon. Somebody has to be there."

"Why?"

Max frowned. Valid question, he supposed. He himself never kept normal hours. He sighed. "Just drive."

"Happy to oblige, son. I get paid by the mile and I could sure use the money. I got me a big purchase in mind."

Herbert couldn't be a day under sixty-five, probably closer to seventy, and Max had to admit he was curious about what the man was so hot to get his hands on. Probably a new car. In fact, eyeing the worn vinyl upholstery, Max hoped that was it. But he wasn't about to ask. So far the old guy hadn't pried into Max's business here in Bingo and he wanted to keep it that way.

That he was the new owner of a bordello had nothing to do with his desire for anonymity, he told himself. It wasn't as though he was ashamed. He just liked his privacy, that's all.

"Yup, just what I thought." Herbert slowed down and pointed to an ancient building that leaned slightly to the left. "See that sign on the door? It means he won't be back for another couple of days."

Max squinted at the sheet of white paper tacked to the red door. "It looks like a giant smiley face."

"That's right. Getting away from his wife for two days makes Chester real happy. You want we should head back for the motel?"

Max let out an exasperated sigh. The last thing he needed was to have to hang around for an extra day. He frowned suddenly. "Wait a minute. You said head *back* to the motel? We already passed it?"

"Yup. Four blocks behind you on the right."

Max slowly turned around. Was he kidding? The entire town was only three blocks long. At least by normal city standards. Four only if you counted the five-car parking lot adjoining Edna's Edibles.

"It's got that dang purple roof. You can't miss it."

Not even with his eyes closed. Max shook his head at the ill-shaped monstrosity that hovered near the other side of town. Several add-ons in varying shades and types of wood sent the building sprawling into the desert. It wasn't very big. Just weird. "I've changed my mind. Take me to the Swinging R Ranch."

Herbert slammed on the brakes. Good thing they'd been crawling. Twisted in his seat as he was, Max's seat belt could have done some serious damage otherwise.

"You wanna go *where?*" Herbert turned around to give Max a steely-eyed glare. The old man had done a lousy job of shaving and sunlight glinted off missed spots of gray beard. One side of his mouth drooped, probably from too many years of pipe-smoking. "What in the hell for?"

"What do you think?"

"It better not be for what I'm thinking."

Max held onto his temper. No way was he going to

get in a scuffle with this crazy old coot. Then he stopped, frowned. "Wait a minute. What are you thinking?"

Herbert eyed him for a long uncomfortable minute. "There ain't too many reasons why a fella goes to the Swinging R."

Max took a deep breath. "Yeah, I see what you mean. Actually, I have *other* business there."

"I'm listening."

This got tricky. Max hadn't decided yet if he wanted anyone to know who he was. But the look of murderous intent in Herbert Hanson's eyes pretty much decided things. Of course if the guy had a daughter who worked there Max might be in even deeper trouble.

Damn, he wished Taylor were here. "I'm Lily McIntyre's nephew."

Herbert's bushy salt-and-pepper brows shot up. "No kidding. You the new owner, huh?"

"So it seems."

"Well, why didn't you say so?" Herbert grinned and whipped the car around in the direction from which they'd come. "We'll be there in ten minutes, tops."

Herbert was apparently anxious to visit the Ranch. Seven minutes and two ignored stop signs later, they pulled up in front of a sign that announced the Swinging R Ranch.

Max's heart sank at the sight of the old rambling blue house. The wraparound porch had probably been attractive once, but right now the outside railing had more slats missing than were in place. The surrounding white picket fence was half down and large scabs of peeling paint hung loosely from the portion still standing.

"Well, aren't you going to get out?"

Max snapped out of his trance and realized Herbert

had actually gotten out and come around to open his door. "What happened to this place?"

Herbert frowned at the house, studying it for a moment, then shrugged. "Poor old Lily. She done the best she could but she was getting on in years and sorta just let the place go."

"Didn't she have any help?"

"Oh, yeah, but she was headstrong. Tried to run everything herself anyway. Let me help you with that bag, son."

A ray of hope filtered through Max's gloom. Maybe the disrepair was a result of Lily's eccentricity and not a failing business. "No, thanks. I can—"

"Herbie! You old scoundrel." A booming feminine voice coming from the side of the house cut Max off. "You didn't tell me you were coming today."

Max turned around to see who had lit Herbert's face up like a Vegas neon sign. But it was hard to get a good look when she ran past him and flung herself at the older man. To his credit, Herbert caught her and spun her around a couple of times before putting her back on the ground.

She was slim, petite even, with a head full of flaming red hair. When she aimed her charcoal-lined blue eyes at Max he was surprised to find that she was near Herbert's age.

The housekeeper probably, judging by her age and the full white apron she wore. Flour smudged her left cheek. Or maybe she was the cook. Max smiled. Things were looking up if the place could still afford help.

"Well, hello, Sugar," she said, running a lazy gaze over him. "Who might you be?"

"Come on, Mona." Herbert drew her attention. "Don't I get more than a hug?"

She slapped his arm, but her lips curved. "You old rascal. I've a good mind to leave you standing out here in the hot sun for not warning me you were coming." She patted her hair. "I must look a mess."

"Hell, no, Mona. You always look good to me." Herbert picked her up off the ground again. Laughing, she gave him another smack on the arm and he put her down.

Max eyed the other man with new interest. Maybe the guy wasn't as old as he thought.

"Come on in, and bring your friend. Rosie just made some fresh lemonade." Mona led them up the path toward the front door, Herbert panting behind her like a lovesick puppy.

Max didn't like the looks of the porch stairs but the other two didn't seem worried so he followed them into the house.

It looked fairly normal. From the foyer, he could see part of the living room. Tan carpeting, an overstuffed blue plaid sofa and two recliners. No red velvet or black lace easily visible. Maybe they saved those sorts of things for the bedrooms.

That he was in a real-life brothel struck him suddenly and he had the most unnatural urge to shiver. This was all legal, he reminded himself, but it didn't help.

"Hey, Mona, have we got company?" a voice asked from the kitchen.

"Herbie and a young man," Mona called back. "Are you decent? We're coming in for lemonade."

Max laughed. They both gave him odd looks. He'd assumed Rosie was the cook, or some other help. Maybe she was one of the...

He cleared his throat. Taylor was his attorney, dammit. He should have insisted she come and handle this. "Is there a place I can wash up?"

"Sure, the kitchen sink." Mona reached behind to untie her apron as she led them through the dining room.

So much for trying to stall. Following beside Herbert, Max couldn't help but notice the rhythmic sway of Mona's hips but he straightened in disgust when he realized he was admiring a woman old enough to be his grandmother.

"Either of you boys want some rum to go with that lemonade?" Mona asked over her shoulder.

"None for me," Herbert said. "I'm working."

"Working?" Mona laughed. "Standing here jawing with us?"

"Nope. Driving this young fella around."

They reached the kitchen, and with open curiosity, Mona turned to give Max the once-over. "You still haven't told me your name, Sugar."

"Max Bennett." He offered his hand.

She frowned. "Now, why does that name sound familiar?"

"Maxwell Bennett?" A surprised high-pitched voice came from somewhere in the corner.

He looked past Mona and Herbert to find a well-rounded, platinum-blond woman balancing on a step stool in the walk-in pantry.

Mona looked from Max to the other woman. "Rosie, you know this young man?"

"For goodness sakes, Mona, this is Lily's nephew." She came out of the pantry, dusting her hands, and sending up a mist of flour. "He's taking over the Ranch. Aren't you, Mr. Bennett?"

Max blinked. When the air cleared, he got a good look at Rosie. Her hair wasn't blond. It was white. Attractive, but definitely white. The lines etched around her mouth and fanning from her brown eyes put her in the late sixties category. Was she the cook? Which made Mona...what? The housekeeper?

His gaze strayed over to her. He tried not to gape. She'd removed her apron and now he knew what they did with black lace. The fabric fit her like a second skin, clinging and diving to a deep V between her sizable breasts.

"Max." Mona grabbed the hand he'd offered earlier. "I assume I can call you Max? And of course you already know I'm Mona. Mona Lisa. And this here is Rosie Peach."

"Mona *Lisa*. Rosie Peach," Max repeated slowly. This couldn't be what he was thinking.

Mona nodded. "Candy Kane is out shopping but she should be home soon. There's only three of us these days."

Oh, man. Max swallowed, not sure what to say.

To his further embarrassment, Mona and Rosie exchanged knowing looks. Then Rosie smiled. "Don't worry, Max," she said patting his arm. "There may be snow on the chimney but there's still fire in the furnace."

"WHERE IS SHE?" Abby stood on the porch of the Swinging R and planted her hands on her hips, waiting for Mona to deny that Gramms was here.

"I presume you're talking about Estelle." Mona folded her arms across her chest, keeping the screen door open with one hip. "She's not here."

"I knew you'd say that."

"She's out shopping with Candy."

"Oh." Abby hadn't been prepared for the admission. "Well, what time will she be back?"

"How should I know, Abigail? I'm not her mother."

Mona narrowed her dramatically made-up eyes. "And neither are you."

Abby lifted her chin. It didn't take a rocket scientist to figure out what this show of rebellion was about. She knew Gramms thought she was too bossy. But Abby sure wasn't about to discuss their personal business with Mona. "I'll wait."

"Don't you have campaign things to go worry about?"

Abby was about to reply when she heard a deep rumbling laugh coming from inside. She'd already seen Herb Hanson's car parked alongside the house. No surprise. Everyone knew he and Mona had been an item for a number of years. But that wasn't his laugh she'd heard. Curiosity elbowed her and she shifted to get a look inside.

Mona shifted, too, blocking her vision. "Abigail, you know we like to protect the privacy of our gentlemen callers."

Everyone knew the Swinging R had been closed to *that* kind of business for nearly twenty years. Mona was just trying to be a pain. Abby sighed. "Are you going to make me wait out here?"

"I'm thinking about it. Unless you promise to leave Estelle alone. She'll go home when she's good and ready."

Abby tried to keep her chin up. But it hurt to think that Gramms was trying to get away from her. They'd always been close, and after Abby's parents died, they'd gotten even closer.

"Ah, shoot. Come on in, honey," Mona said, and Abby stiffened at the trace of pity in her voice. "Rosie made some fresh lemonade a little while ago."

Abby was about to refuse, upset that she'd somehow revealed too much of her thoughts. But Mona's eyes were kind, and that deep rumbling laughter coming from inside called to Abby again.

"Thank you," she said a little more stiffly than intended, and followed Mona inside.

As soon as she crossed the threshold she saw him. He had his back to her. A very nice back. Medium brown hair a tad too long. Broad-shouldered, tapered waist. And his jeans fit him...extremely well.

"Nice buns, huh?" Mona whispered.

"I wasn't looking there," Abby shot back, obviously in too loud a voice.

Both men turned.

Heat blossomed in her cheeks. "I guess I'll go find Rosie," she muttered.

Before she could slip away, Mona grabbed her arm. "Not so fast. There's someone we want you to meet."

Abby had no choice but to stop and look up.

Oh, no.

Green eyes. She was the world's biggest sucker for guys with green eyes. She'd made two huge mistakes over green-eyed men—one in high school, one in college. Both disastrous. And this man's eyes were gorgeous, especially the way they lit up with his smile.

"Hi, I'm Abby," she said, disgusted at how tongue-tied she felt.

"I'm Max Bennett." His perfectly shaped mouth curved slowly, a faint dimple appearing in one cheek.

"You certainly are," she murmured, astonished by the sheer beauty of him. She cringed. Had she really said that out loud?

"Did I tell you I'm Abby?"

His green eyes gleamed with amusement and she found she couldn't look away. When he started to nod slowly, she found herself absently nodding along with him. Horrified, she snapped out of the trance.

This was not at all like her. The clammy palms, the speeding pulse. Sure, he was gorgeous but…she wanted to be mayor. She had to focus on her campaign, concentrate on her career, on bringing Bingo into the twenty-first century. Her future had been too meticulously planned. It did not include a man. Or a family. For now, anyway. Maybe later…

She took a deep breath, trying to rein in her wildly galloping thoughts. For heaven's sake, she was only being introduced to the guy. Campaign jitters, that's all.

She stuck out her hand. "Abby Cunningham. I'm running for mayor."

Surprise flashed in his eyes. "Mayor? I assumed you worked here as one of the…" He shrugged.

Abby's mouth opened but nothing came out. He thought she was a… She couldn't even think it, much less say it.

"Nah, Abigail's been to college and everything," Mona said. "She's going to be our next mayor just like her daddy was."

"Good for you." Max's slow grin had her getting all rubbery again, and she forgave him for mistaking her for an employee here. The warm feel of his palm pressed to hers just about finished her off. "When's the election?"

She quickly withdrew her hand and inconspicuously rubbed her tingly palm down the front of her jeans. "In two months."

"Pity I won't be here to help celebrate your victory."

He didn't mean he would really celebrate with her, of course, but at the low intimate timbre of his voice, Abby got all shivery inside.

"What do you mean?" Mona asked. "Who's going to

run the place if you're not?'' At Abby's puzzled frown, she added, ''Max is the new owner of the Swinging R.''

Abby gaped at him. ''You're the new owner?''

He nodded.

The warm fuzzy feeling instantly vanished. What the heck was he doing here? If he had even a passing notion of reopening the place...or allowing Gramms to stay on...

Abby got so worked up she could barely sustain the thought.

''You're right, Mr. Bennett. You won't be here in two months. I'm going to shut you down.''

3

MAX WATCHED the pretty brunette go from warm and friendly to cool and scowling in two seconds flat. Too bad. She had dynamite brown eyes and a great smile...when she didn't look as though she wanted to see a noose around his neck.

Max gave her a big grin. "Excuse me, but isn't the Swinging R legal in this county?"

"Oh, don't pay her any mind." Mona tugged at Abby's arm. "Go to the kitchen and get yourself a glass of lemonade and quit stirring up trouble."

Abby wouldn't pull her gaze away from him. "For now. But that's going to change real quick."

"When you're mayor?"

She lifted her chin. "That's right."

Mona reared back her head. "Abigail Cunningham, what kind of foolishness is this? I never heard you say any such thing before now. Does your gramma know about this nonsense?"

Abby turned red and looked away.

"Seems I bring out the best in Abigail," Max said, which earned him another glare.

"Ah, shoot, she's just joking." Herbert slid an arm around Mona's shoulders. "Aren't you, Abigail?"

"She's got her nose out of joint because Estelle spent the night here," Mona said before Abby could respond.

"Let's go have some lemonade and forget this crazy talk."

"Estelle spent the night *here?*" Herbert frowned, glancing briefly at Abby before returning his attention to Mona. "Why?"

Abby's entire body language changed. No longer looking defensive, she turned toward Mona, her light brown eyes turning dark and uncertain as she waited for the answer. Something so raw and vulnerable in Abby's expression caught Max off guard and triggered an odd flutter in his gut.

No one said a word for what felt like an hour. Mona's nervous gaze darted to Abby, then back to Herbert. She fiddled with the fake string of pearls around her neck. She was stalling, thinking of something to say.

Max glanced again at Abby. A crestfallen look dulled her eyes, and Max had a strong and strange urge to comfort her—which was of course absurd. Not just because he wasn't the nurturing type or because he didn't even know this woman. Not even because he had no idea who Estelle was or what the hell was going on. But the trace of longing and disappointment that lingered in Abby's face, even as she bravely lifted her chin, struck a chord so deep inside him that he wanted to climb back into Herbert's car and drive straight to the company plane and get as far the hell away from Nevada as he could.

"I'll answer that question, Herbert." Abby gave the older man a tight smile. "My grandmother is trying to get away from me."

"Oh, hogwash." Mona shook her head. "That's not true. She wants to give you some breathing room."

"Of course it's true. She thinks I'm too overbearing just because I'm concerned about her welfare. But this isn't the time or place to discuss it." Abby took a step toward the door. "So please tell her to give me a call when she gets in."

Max straightened. To his amazement, he didn't want her to leave. "You running away from a fight?" he asked, and she glanced at him, looking a little startled, as though she'd forgotten he was there. "I never knew a successful politician who tucked their tail between their legs and ran."

"What on earth are you talking about?" She made a face. "Mona and I aren't fighting."

"Now you sound like a politician—evading the question."

Abby wrinkled her nose. "I think you've been out in the heat too long."

"You boldly tell me you're going to shut me down, then without a word of explanation you're running off." Max shook his head. "When you take a stand, you'd better be prepared to back it up if you want to be taken seriously."

She folded her arms across her chest and looked at him with tolerant amusement. "Really? And you know all about this sort of thing?"

"More than I care to," he said, and when she raised her brows, waiting for him to explain, he shrugged. "Let's just say my family has some history in the political arena." A small understatement, considering he came from several generations of senators. But he didn't like to think about that.

"Oh? And what do they think of you owning a brothel?" she asked, her tone so sticky sweet he was surprised she wasn't swarmed by flies. "One that's made money off of helpless women."

Max kept as straight a face as he could. From the looks of things, it had been a long time since this place had turned so much as a dime. And helpless? Mona looked like she was ready to take a switch to somebody's behind.

"What's the deal, Abby? You sound like a disgruntled ex-employee or something," he said seriously. At her wide-eyed indignation, he started to crack, but his poker face lasted long enough for him to add, "Or maybe you were turned down? If that's the case, I'm sure we can reevaluate your application."

Abby obviously had a temper. He could see she was trying to squelch it by pressing her lips together and taking deep breaths, but her eyes had that unmistakable glint of malice.

"How generous of you, Mr. Bennett," she said with remarkable aplomb. "But I assure you that had I chosen to seek employment here, I would have had no trouble whatsoever."

Herbert chuckled.

Mona gave him a warning look and placed her hands on her hips. "Okay, you two. That's enough."

"He started it," Abby blurted, and promptly turned red again.

A grin tugged at Max's lips. She really was cute. Refreshing, too. The women in his circle never blushed. In fact, a few of their ribald comments had made him squirm a time or two.

"Okay, this is last call for lemonade," Mona said, motioning Herbert to usher Max into the kitchen. "You're still welcome, Abigail, if you promise not to bring up any more sore subjects." She slid a glance to the door. "Otherwise I'll have your gramma ring you later."

Abby gave the older woman a conciliatory smile. "I'm going to pass on the lemonade, but I would like a few minutes alone with Mr. Bennett."

Mona chortled. "When pigs fly."

Max held up a hand. "It's okay, Mona. I think I can handle her."

Before Mona could voice another protest, Herbert slipped an arm around her shoulders and steered her toward the kitchen.

"We'll be lapping up some of Rosie's lemonade while you two are pow-wowing," he said. "Come join us when you're done."

They waited until the other couple disappeared, and then Max gestured toward the living room. "Why don't we sit down?"

Abby smiled. "Didn't take you long to make yourself at home, did it?"

"I do own the place."

Rolling her eyes, she walked stiffly past him toward a frilly pink love seat beneath a velvet painting of Elvis Presley. So much for the room being furnished normally. Max didn't follow her right away. He was too taken by her scent. It wasn't anything immediately recognizable, not flowery exactly. Maybe a hint of cloves. Whatever it was, he liked it. Almost as much as he liked the gentle sway of her hips and the way her worn jeans hugged her fanny.

She sat down, crossed her legs and primly folded her hands on her lap. When he still hadn't moved, she gave him an odd look and uncrossed, then recrossed her legs. He moved toward her, bypassing the couch and the antique Queen Anne chair. The only seat left in his path was beside her and her eyes rounded in disbelief.

When he settled in next to her on the love seat, she let out a sound of exasperation and shifted closer to her corner. "Don't you understand the concept of personal space?"

He pursed his lips as if giving the question consideration. "This seat is built for two, right?"

She narrowed her gaze on him and he noticed how long her lashes were, yet there didn't seem to be anything artificial about them. It was an odd thing for him to notice. Hell, choosing to sit here next to her was pretty damn odd. He had no idea where that idea had come from. It certainly hadn't been conscious.

"I know what you're trying to do." Their gazes made contact and she paused. Her tongue briefly darted out to moisten her lips and he realized this had been a bad idea. "But it's not going to work."

"What isn't?"

"You're trying to intimidate me. I don't care if you'd sat on my lap, I'm not backing down."

"Good. I like a woman with backbone."

"That's another thing. I don't give a hoot about what you like or don't like."

"Don't give a hoot," he repeated, thoughtfully. "Now that's one I haven't heard before. Is that a local saying?"

Abby smiled. "Trying to provoke me won't work either."

"What? I'm serious."

She stared at him for a long, silent moment, and he knew what it felt like to be a bug under a microscope. Her expression never wavered as she studied him, as though she were truly interested in what he was thinking. Her frankness surprised him and unnerved the hell out of him.

So did her mysterious feminine scent...the chocolate brown of her eyes...the crisp tart smell of green apple on her breath.

Abruptly he stood and glanced at his watch. "I haven't got all day. What is it you want to talk about?"

She started a little at his sudden move. "I want to know what you intend to do with the Swinging R."

Her question took him aback, although it really shouldn't have. What else would she want from him? But he really had no clue how to answer her. Considering the circumstances, he'd probably sell it, if he could find a buyer. "I don't know yet."

"Then what are you doing here?"

"Trying to figure out how to generate some income."

Her eyes widened and she stood, too. The top of her head didn't even meet his chin, but that didn't stop her from backing him up. "You're not serious."

"Why not? This is a business. Businesses are supposed to make money." He stood his ground and she stopped two feet away, her eyes ablaze with outrage and disbelief.

And then she blinked, and a slow smile softened her expression. Damn, but she really was cute, pretty even. Nothing striking, but the kind of woman a man eventually wanted to come home to every night. Other men. Not him. Marriage was for guys with nothing better to do.

"I see," she said nodding. "You're teasing me. I guess I deserve it for being so pushy. But I really am interested in your plans for the place."

"I wasn't teasing."

Her smile vanished and she glared, lips tight with disapproval. When she suddenly lowered her gaze to his body, he shifted uncomfortably wondering what she found so interesting down there. And then he realized she was studying his watch. Next, her attention fastened on his shoes.

She looked up. "You obviously don't need the money. Why bother with this place?"

He snorted. "You know that much about me in just twenty minutes?"

"A gold Rolex and five-hundred-dollar Gucci shoes pretty much disqualifies you from welfare."

The watch was pretty distinctive but he was surprised she recognized his designer shoes. Snobby of him maybe, but Bingo wasn't exactly the shopping Mecca of the west. No upscale neighborhoods or large luxury cars. These were obviously plain people with simple tastes.

He chuckled to himself at the irony of his thoughts. After twenty minutes, here he figured he knew all about her. He had a feeling that if he stuck around long enough, he'd find that there was a lot about Abby Cunningham he would never have guessed. But it wasn't going to happen. He was out of here by tomorrow.

"Stalling isn't going to discourage me," she said, when he'd apparently been quiet too long. She folded her arms over her chest. "And for your information, my question is purely personal, and not political."

"Right."

Uncrossing her arms, she glanced over her shoulder toward the kitchen. Herbert and Mona were long gone. Abby took a step closer to him and lowered her voice. "I'm sure you can see that this place is no longer operational. The, uh, ladies are in retirement, so to speak, but they still need a place—"

A loud squawk cut her off and made them both jump. Mona came marching toward them, her face reddened with anger, a raised frying pan in her right hand. "Retirement, my fanny. It'll be a cold day in August before you put this old mare out to pasture. Now, Abigail, I suggest you *get* before I really lose my temper."

The frying pan was one of those old cast-iron ones that had to weigh a ton, and it did, judging by the way it kept inching down, causing Mona to pitch forward slightly, teetering. Max was about to relieve her of it before someone really did get hurt, when Herbert surprised her from behind and lifted the pan out of her hand.

"For cryin' out loud, Mona, have you stopped taking your pills again?" Herbert set the pan on top of a tall bookcase out of her reach.

"Dammit, Herbie, whose side are you on?" Mona smacked him on the upper arm. "How's a body supposed to make a living?"

With a weary sigh, Herbert slid Max a helpless look. "Come on, Mona, you haven't done that for almost twenty years."

"Viagra, honey, Viagra is changing everything. We'll be open again. You'll see." She looked at Max. "You're a businessman. Tell him."

Everyone turned to Max, Herbert with an expression of dread, Abby with amusement glittering in her eyes. Max cleared his throat. "I hadn't really thought much about that."

"What's there to think about?" Mona put her hands on her hips. "You get a supply of the stuff and we'll pass them out. There won't be enough hours in the day once all those old goats from Bingo start lining up."

Max took a deep breath. He was a worldly, laid-back guy. He could handle this conversation, even if Mona did look like she could be his grandmother.

He made the mistake of looking at Abby for help. A grin tugged at the corners of her mouth and her eyes sparkled with mischief.

"Yeah, Max," she said, her forehead wrinkling in a thoughtful frown. "You could order Viagra by the bushel, pass it out like candy and put all these ladies back to work. After all, it is legal in this county."

Max gave her his best smile. If she thought he would cower, she was wrong. He was a Bennett. Made of strong New England stock. He could handle anything.

"Yoo-hoo! Anybody home? I have a surprise."

Everyone turned toward the high-pitched voice coming from the kitchen.

"In here, Candy," Mona called out.

Two women appeared at the door. Both seventyish. Both grinning. One holding her hand behind her back.

"I have a surprise," the shorter one drawled, glanced behind and tugged on a leash.

The world's ugliest lizard lumbered forward and stuck out its very long tongue.

"Her name's Tami," Candy said. "Isn't she adorable?"

Max told himself he wasn't going to faint. But he put a steadying hand on the couch just in case.

4

"WHAT IS THAT?" Max asked, relieved his voice hadn't cracked.

"An iguana," the short blonde said, her artfully made-up face scowling at Max's abruptness. "Who wants to know?"

"Okay, Candy, don't go getting your knickers in a twist." Mona stepped between him and the other woman. Not that Max had any intention of getting closer. Especially not as long as the overgrown lizard's tongue kept swiping the air. "This here is Maxwell Bennett, Lily's nephew."

"Well, I'll be damned." Candy looked him up and down. "You came all the way out here yourself, did you? Figured you'd send some fancy lawyer to take care of things all neat and tidy."

God, Max wished he had. "Nice to meet you, Candy. Now about this thing..." He gestured to the iguana, then took a hasty step back when it moved. "Tell me it isn't some sort of pet."

Candy narrowed her gaze. "She's a she, not an it, and I already explained her name is Tami."

Mona sighed loudly. "You haven't met Estelle yet, Max." She inclined her head toward the other woman with short silver hair, much more conservative in her blue shirtwaist dress next to Candy's tight jeans. "Estelle?"

She was smiling at Herbert and paying them no attention.

Mona looked from Herbert to the silver-haired woman, and she planted both hands on her hips and started tapping one foot. "Estelle?" Her tone was sharper this time.

"Hmm?" Estelle turned an absent gaze toward them.

"I am *trying* to introduce you to Mr. Bennett." Mona's hands remained on her hips, and with her fiery blue eyes she issued Herbert a brief warning before forcing a smile for Max.

He checked out the position of the iguana before stepping forward to offer his hand, and caught Abby's smirk out of the corner of his eye. She'd been so quiet he'd almost forgotten about her. She was obviously aware of his discomfort and enjoying it far too much.

Trying to ignore her, he smiled at Estelle. "Pleased to meet you. How long have you been, uh…" to his annoyance, he stumbled for a suitable word "…working here?"

A shriek coming from Abby startled them all, drawing their attention. Even Mona stopped scowling at Estelle and frowned at Abby. "What in the hell has gotten into you?"

But Abby's anger was clearly reserved for Max alone. She marched up to him, stopping only inches away, then tilted her head back and glared. "That is my grandmother you are speaking to," she said through gritted teeth. "She does not work here."

"Oh, get off your high horse, Abigail." Mona huffed. "You saying she's too *good* to work here?"

Abby blinked, but she kept her attention on Max. "I'm just saying she doesn't. And she has no business staying here."

The tension in the room raised the temperature by ten

degrees. And Max had no intention of fanning the flames. He looked away from Abby and stared at the iguana. It stared back. "I'll tell you who has no business here. It's that disgusting tongue-wielding reptile."

Candy gasped. "Disgusting? Tami is not disgusting. She's my new pet." Her face softened as she looked at the creature. "Aren't you, sugar baby?"

"You think you're keeping her here?"

"Why not?" Candy's overly plucked eyebrows arched in challenge. "Where do you usually keep a pet?"

"One like that?" Max snorted. "In a zoo."

"Over my dead body." The blonde folded her arms across her chest, the movement giving the iguana's leash more slack, and the animal took two steps toward Max.

Hell, it was his dead body he was worried about. He backed up, and stepped on Abby's foot.

"Ouch!" She gave him a light jab to the ribs.

He grunted, more in surprise than anything else. "For crying out loud, I didn't do that on purpose." When their eyes met, she tried to signal something he didn't understand.

"I don't get it," Candy said. "What's it to you if I keep Tami here? None of you girls mind, do you?"

Mona shook her head. "She's gotta be better than that tarantula you had last year."

"Or that monkey who kept hiding our garters," Rosie added.

"He was a mean-spirited little thing."

Were they putting him on? Max looked at Herbert who had sat down, pretty much ignoring everything, and picked candies out of a blue glass dish.

"What about you?" Candy turned to Estelle. "You helped me pick Tami out so I assume you vote she stays."

"Uh, excuse me." Abby cleared her throat. "Gramms is coming home with me."

At this point, Max didn't give a damn what anyone did. Maybe it was time to cut his losses. He was a minute away from telling Herbert to take him back to the airstrip. These people were all nuts. He eyed the iguana who stood between him and the door.

And then he caught the look on Estelle's face. Of course he didn't know her, so perhaps he was wrong, but she looked awfully close to tears. He glanced at Abby. Fear clouded her eyes.

Oh, hell, it was probably his imagination. He didn't know her either. Nor was this domestic dispute his problem. His gaze reluctantly shifted to Abby again. He hated seeing her beautiful brown eyes so panicked.

"What's wrong with your grandmother staying here a while?" he asked, knowing he would regret it.

Disappointment spread across Abby's face. "She has a perfectly fine home she shares with me. Not that it's any of your business."

"What I'd like to know," Candy cut in, "is why keeping Tami is such a big hairy deal."

"Because I don't like reptiles," Max said, his patience gone.

"What difference does that make? You're not living—" Candy stopped, her gaze narrowing in suspicion. "You're not moving in here."

Max reacted with a short bark of laughter. "Don't be ridiculous." He shook his head. He was still packed. If he had half a brain he'd head back to the plane right now. But then he briefly caught a glimpse of Abby's shiny brown hair. "Look, I'll only be here a couple of days to take care of business. I'm thinking about staying here instead of the motel. But that—'' he stared pointedly at the iguana ''—has to stay outside until I'm gone.''

Candy opened her mouth to protest, but Rosie stuck an oatmeal raisin cookie in it.

''That seems reasonable,'' Mona said, ''now how about you tell us what kind of business you'll be doing?''

He gave her a censuring look. ''*My* business.''

Mona chuckled. ''You remind me of Lily. Stubborn as an old mule.''

''If Mr. Bennett will be staying here, obviously there isn't enough room for you, Gramms.'' Abby locked gazes with Estelle. ''I'll help you get your things.''

''Now, hold on there.'' Candy's voice was a little garbled until she swallowed her bite of cookie. ''We have three extra rooms since Misty got married and Ginger went back east. And, of course, since Lily, God rest her soul, headed for the great beyond.''

''Don't forget the sewing room,'' Herbert chimed in. ''You gals never use it. I could even fix it up some if you like.'' Mona's suspicious gaze swung from Herbert to Estelle. ''How come you never offered to help us fix things up before?''

Herbert rubbed the side of his chin, looking slightly sheepish. ''Now, that's not true. I repaired the back steps twice. Plus you know I'm pretty busy most days.''

''Yeah, running down to the Vegas strip and betting on those damn fool Dallas Cowboys and Denver Broncos.'' Mona sniffed and cast another piqued look at Estelle. ''At least that's what you been telling me.''

Max was about to put an end to this ridiculous conversation when Abby's expression caught his interest. She had an unusually expressive face, and it wasn't difficult to see how her thoughts had unraveled. She was just as worried about anything going on between her grandmother and Herbert as Mona seemed to be. He wondered what that was about, and his interest surprised him. God knew he had many faults, but curiosity wasn't one of them.

Abby's gaze slowly swung his way, as if she'd felt him watching her. An unexpected pink tinted her cheeks and she looked really cute. Not his type, but cute.

"I could use some help in the kitchen," Rosie said, breaking the brief silence as she headed down the short hall, "especially if everyone is staying for supper."

"I'll go change my clothes and be right in," Estelle called to her, carefully avoiding Abby's gaze.

"I need to talk to you, Gramms."

"In a minute." The older woman waved a hand and hurried down the opposite hall.

"And you," Mona said, pointing a scarlet-tipped finger at Herbert. "Outside. I have a thing or two to say, and I don't think you want anyone hearing it."

Worry puckered the man's brows. "Gee, I'd really like to Mona, but I told you, I'm working." He turned a pleading look to Max. "Maybe we should go see if Southby is back from fishing."

"No rush." Max's slow grin met with Herbert's squinty-eyed threat. "Go visit with Mona. And take your time."

"Come on, Tami." Candy tugged the leash but the iguana seemed preoccupied with Max. It stuck its long tongue out again as if trying to see if it could reach him. It couldn't but Max inched back anyway.

"Go. Scat." He tried to shoo it, but it kept staring at him like he was dinner.

Behind him, Abby giggled.

He growled in exasperation.

"We're going already." Candy jerked on the leash and

this time Tami obeyed, and they started down the same hall Estelle had taken.

"I hope there's a back door through there," Max called after them.

Candy didn't so much as look back, and Max pretty much figured she planned on sneaking the little beast into her room. The motel was beginning to sound awfully good.

He turned to Abby. "What are you grinning at?"

Lifting a shoulder, she pressed her lips together and slowly shook her head.

She hadn't smiled much but when she did her entire face changed. It lit up like sunshine on crystal-clear water. Her bow-shaped lips were a natural pink. Perfect. Tempting.

"Didn't your parents ever take you to the zoo when you were a kid?" she asked, letting her mouth curve again.

"Yes, they did. In fact, I like zoos. They have bars and cages."

She shook her head at him.

He snorted. "I didn't see you running up to give it a scratch behind the ears."

"Touché."

Max's curiosity stirred again. Her response surprised him. What he'd expected was a more down-home word or phrase, but not something Taylor or one of his other friends would say. "Tell me the truth. You don't think it's weird that Candy has pets like tarantulas and iguanas?"

"You want the truth? I think it's weird that any state would legally sanction brothels in this day and age."

"Oh, brother." Max scrubbed at his eyes. He'd gotten up too damn early. "So, back to lecturing."

"Wrong." She shook her head. "I'm not, really." She studied him for a moment. "Truth time again. If you hadn't inherited this place, would you have bought it?"

"What kind of question is that?"

"It's my devious way of trying to find out what you really think of a place like this."

He smiled. "I think it needs a couple more cushioned rockers."

She smiled back, a truly terrific smile. "You're dodging the subject."

"Damn right I am. You already told me that if you become mayor you're shutting us down."

"Oh." She frowned. "Sounds like you're considering reopening the place."

"I might."

"Really?" Her expression didn't waver. "It would take an awful lot of money."

"Hell, it'll take a lot just to keep it standing." And that was no joke. He'd obviously wasted his time flying out here.

"Probably. But you have to do something."

He shrugged. "I could just walk away. Leave the place as is."

Shock registered in her eyes. "No, you can't. The house isn't safe."

"Then they should move out."

"And where do you suggest they go? These women live on social security, not fat pensions."

"Not my problem."

She stared in disbelief, then in disgust. "You own the place. It's your responsibility."

"Excuse me, but I didn't sign up for this headache."

"Too bad. You've got it."

He shrugged again. "Like I said, I could walk away."

Abby growled—literally, and convincingly enough that he glanced over his shoulder to see if the iguana was back.

"I can't believe you could be this…this heartless." Abby went to the plate of cookies Rosie had left, picked out a ginger snap, sat on the couch, then took an enormous bite.

Most women he knew took small nibbles. Not Abby. Obviously this was a woman not afraid to tackle anything. She started to say something else but her mouth was full.

Max jumped in while he had the chance. "I'm not heartless. This is business. Maybe I *should* reopen it." Sighing, he raked his fingers through his hair. "I don't know what I'm going to do with it. Last week it was bad enough when I thought I'd inherited a brothel. Today I find out it's a retirement home."

"I heard that."

They both started and turned to meet Rosie's disapproving frown. "Better not let Mona hear you spewing that stuff. Me, I know better. And I like things just the way they are, but you heard her earlier, she and Candy have this idea that Viagra is gonna change things around here."

At the mention of Viagra again, Max almost lost his cookies. Except he hadn't had any. Surely Mona had been joking earlier.

Rosie picked up the plate. "I don't want you two spoiling your supper."

Wordlessly, he watched her carry the cookies back to the kitchen. Abby hadn't said anything either. She probably blamed the whole idea on him. He reluctantly looked her way and realized she was trying to keep from laughing.

He relaxed a little. Abby wouldn't think this was funny if it were for real. "She's joking, right? About Mona and the Viagra?"

"I doubt it. Mona is always talking about the good old days."

"And you think that's funny?"

Her eyebrows drew together in a thoughtful frown, all traces of amusement gone. And then her lips tilted slightly. "Good for you, Max."

"What?" Something was wrong. She called him Max.

"You have no intention of reopening the Swinging R."

"I never said that."

"You didn't have to." Her smile grew more triumphant. "The expression on your face just said it all. You looked traumatized by the thought Rosie isn't kidding."

"Traumatized?" He snorted. "What are you smoking? There is nothing in this little hick town that could traumatize or surprise me."

Abby's expression fell, then it tightened. He'd hurt her feelings, and ticked her off, too. "I'm sorry our *hick town* doesn't meet with your approval. Amazing, you've been here all of one day and you're able to pass judgment already."

"I didn't mean to insult you."

"We already settled that fallacy. In order for me to be insulted, I'd have to value your opinion."

"I believe you're right. Let's see... Oh, yeah, you don't give a hoot about what I think."

"Exactly." She folded her arms across her chest. It wasn't a big chest, but nicely proportioned, well-rounded.

Apparently he'd taken too long to make that determination because when he raised his gaze to hers, she seemed ready to bite his head off. He cleared his throat, loosened his collar, checked his watch.

"Are you staying for dinner?" he asked, trying to change the subject and hoping a chunk of his hide wasn't on her menu.

She stared at him in thoughtful silence for nearly a minute. "I'll make you a deal."

"What?"

"I can get rid of the iguana while you're here, if you tell my grandmother she can't stay."

That was unexpected. He rubbed his jaw, noting he needed a shave. "What's wrong with her staying here?"

Abby let out a low exasperated groan. "She doesn't belong here. She belongs at home with me."

"She lives with you?"

"Yes."

"Anyone else? Husband, kids, boyfriend?" He shrugged when he saw the storm clouds gathering in her face. "Cats? Dogs?"

"None of your business. But no. It's just Gramms and me."

"So how come she ran away from home? You ground her or something?"

Sighing, she rolled her eyes toward the ceiling. "Why do I bother?" She got up from the couch, dusted the cookie crumbs from her hands over an ashtray, then faced him with a phony smile. "Wish I could say it was nice meeting you, Mr. Bennett."

"What are you getting all bent out of shape for? I can't agree to throw an old lady—" he grimaced "—your grandmother out without understanding why."

She stared at him again, in that measuring way, as if trying to come to a decision. "Apparently I'm just not enough fun for her. She thinks I'm a fuddy-duddy."

"Well, you probably could loosen up a bit."

"Here we go again." She threw up her hands. "Did I ask for your opinion?"

Max grunted in disbelief. What happened to the old Bennett charm? Women didn't treat him like this. They smiled and giggled and asked his opinion all the time. "Wouldn't matter if you had. You're obviously too stubborn to listen to anyone."

"Ooh, I'm all Jell-O inside you have me so rattled with that snippy tone."

Damn independent career women. This is why he stayed clear of them. They were too mouthy, too…immune. "Guess you know my answer. Estelle stays."

Her smug expression wavered. "I'd hoped you could put our personality conflict aside and see reason."

"Present me some reason to see. You haven't told me a thing."

She blinked, and visibly swallowed. "It's sort of complicated. Part of it has to do with my involvement in the town, running for mayor…" she shrugged, shifted from one foot to the other, reluctance showing in her every movement "…even being a Cunningham."

"She doesn't agree with your running for mayor?"

"Gramms didn't think I should come back to Bingo after college at all."

Uneasiness crawled down his spine. This was personal stuff, none of his business. He should stop her. "Why *are* you here?"

"Do you still live in the place you grew up?"

"Well, yeah, but that's Boston."

"And you think Bingo is inferior, so why would anyone stay?"

He winced at the way she made it sound. "Guilty."

"At least you're honest." Her smile was wry. "And at times I may even agree, but if we all, the townspeople here, felt that way, the town would just shrivel up and die."

Max didn't see what would be so bad about that but he decided to keep that gem of honesty to himself.

"I know what you're thinking," she said without censure. "But Bingo isn't a bad place to grow up. In fact, it's a pretty damn good place to raise kids. And if anyone feels the need for bright lights and partying until dawn, Las Vegas is less than two and a half hours away."

"But Estelle feels differently?" he asked, not sure how this information all fit together.

"No, of course not. She just wants someone else other than her granddaughter to carry the banner."

"Or be the town martyr."

Abby's lips thinned. Anger glittered in her eyes. "No one is twisting my arm. I chose to come back of my own free will. Bingo needs me, so does my grandmother."

Max mentally cringed. That would be good enough reason for him to get the hell out of town. He looked into Abby's earnest eyes. Not her. She seized responsibility with eager arms. It finally hit him. Only twenty-six and she wanted to be mayor.

He took an uneven breath. Estelle was probably right. Abby needed to get a little selfish, go out and have fun, trudge through a couple of hangovers, get a life.

"Now," she said with a weary sigh, as if she'd just spilled her guts, which to some degree she had. "Do you understand why I want my wonderful but misguided grandmother to come home? Why she *needs* to come home?"

Max rubbed the back of his cramped neck. He did not

intend on getting in the middle of the women's personal squabble. Nor could he kick the older woman out against her will. Which meant Abby was about to hate him forever.

5

ABBY WAITED until the waiter removed her plate of uneaten roasted chicken, mashed potatoes and buttered corn before she excused herself from the head table and made tracks for the bathroom.

Just like every other candidate in Bingo's history, Abby and her volunteers held her fund-raising dinner at the community center, a modest room which her two campaign volunteers had crowded with tables and chairs, and a podium under which three tacky orange balloons floated. Behind that was the "Vote for Abby for Mayor" banner.

If you squinted you could see the crease in the fabric after *Abby* where *Cunningham* had been cut out and the banner had been taped back together. Someone had misspelled *Cunningham.* When one of the volunteers said it didn't matter because everyone knew who Abby was, Abby didn't miss the irony.

As she neared the bathroom, she swept her gaze over the room one last time in hopes of seeing her grandmother. She prayed she was here. Abby thought she had seen her briefly while dinner was being served, but she couldn't figure out where Gramms was sitting, or why she hadn't taken her place next to Abby at the head table.

Then again, maybe her mind was playing tricks on her and she hadn't seen Gramms at all. Having gotten only three hours sleep last night was doing strange things to Abby's concentration.

"Well, Abigail, don't you look…" Mrs. Bacon took Abby's hand, then stepped back to size her up "…different."

Abby patted her hair and smiled at her boss, the middle school principal. "I thought the French twist would make me look older."

Mrs. Bacon's critical eye roamed Abby's face. "You're wearing more makeup, too. Don't start looking too sophisticated or folks will think you're clearing out just like every other young person who graduated from Bingo High in the past ten years."

Abby frowned. She hadn't thought of that when she'd decided to go for the more mature look. In truth, she hadn't thought of much more than her grandmother and Max Bennett, the new thorn in her backside.

"I think most people know me better than that, Mrs. Bacon. I did come back to teach seventh grade just like I said I would."

"That you did," the older woman said, nodding her head, her gray, wiry hair barely contained in her customary bun. "And we're all the better for it."

Pride swelled in Abby's chest. Mrs. Bacon's compliments were few and far between. But more than that, such affirmations reassured Abby that coming back had been the right decision. Not that she ever doubted it, not really. Today had been an exception, a low time. It was one of the reasons she'd put her hair up, and worn makeup—to remind herself she was a grown-up. She hadn't felt much like one today. All she'd wanted to do was curl into a ball and hide under the covers.

She missed Gramms.

Max Bennett, she wanted to tar and feather.

"By the way, where's Estelle?" Mrs. Bacon peered around the room. "I thought she'd be sitting at the head table with you."

"Abby! You have to speak in five minutes!" Trish, one of the volunteers, headed toward them, weaving in and out of the mob of tables and chairs.

"Please excuse me, Mrs. Bacon. If I don't hurry to the rest room, it's going to seem like an awfully long speech." Abby smiled her apology and took off before she had to answer Mrs. Bacon's question.

Trish hurried after her. "Have you seen your grandmother yet?"

Geez, Louise. Abby sighed. "What is this? Does everyone think she's gone missing?

"Of course not. She's here."

Abby put on the brakes, and turned to Trish. The tall blonde stopped a hair short of running into her. "You saw Gramms?"

"Well, yeah." Trish blessedly quit chomping her gum for a second. "That's why I asked if you'd seen her yet. I want to know who the hunk is with her."

Abby nearly choked. "Max is here?"

"You know him?" Trish's eyes widened and she started to chomp her gum with a vengeance.

It had to be Max. He was the type of guy women reacted to like this—the bugged eyes, hair patting, lip-licking. Not her, of course. Disgusted, she turned away from Trish and pushed through the rest room door.

"Uh, I think that's the wrong—"

Trish didn't have to finish. The exact instant Abby realized she was entering the men's room, she ran into Max Bennett on his way out.

Surprise flickered across his face, but he recovered quickly, and grabbed her upper arms when she stumbled backward. "Looking for me?" he asked, flashing a megawatt smile.

"Not even for an emergency lifeline." She shook away from him, glaring fiercely to counteract her boneless legs.

Trish popped her gum loudly. Out of the corner of her eye, Abby saw the younger woman's mouth drop open, prompting Abby to glance around to see if anyone else had overheard. They were in a remote corner, and fortunately, no one else was in sight.

Abby quickly stepped out of the men's room doorway. "Trish, why don't you go make sure everything is ready for my speech."

Trish nodded, backing away, her gaze shooting from Abby to Max—especially Max.

"You look terrific," he said, before Trish was out of earshot, and he lifted a hand to touch a stray tendril of hair at Abby's temple.

She ducked away from him. He looked better than terrific in a perfectly fitted dark blue suit. Clean shaven, tanned, disgustingly even white teeth. And those beautiful green eyes... It would be a miracle if any of the women paid one second of attention to her speech. "What have you done with my grandmother?"

"What have I *done* with her?" One eyebrow lifted in amusement. "You give me way too much credit. Estelle has a mind of her own. Must run in the family."

"Okay, here's a simpler question. What the hell are you doing here?"

"My civic duty."

"You're not a resident of Bingo."

"No, but I do own a business you've threatened to shut down."

Abby's breath caught. "This is only a speech, not a debate."

"I understand."

"I didn't even plan on mentioning the Swinging R."

Max smiled. "You sound nervous, Abby, maybe you ought to splash some cold water on your face before you have to get up on that podium."

Cold water. Great idea. Right down the front of Max's perfectly tailored suit.

"That would be a very bad move, Abby." He shook his head. "It would look like poor sportsmanship at the very least."

He couldn't know what she'd been thinking... "I don't know what you're talking about," she muttered. "Now, if you'll excuse me."

"Hold on." He grabbed her arm when she turned to go. "Someone should have caught this before now."

She froze when he touched the back of her neck, his warm fingers grazing her skin and threatening an on-slaught of goose bumps. The soft sound of a closing zipper startled her.

"There." His hands fell away.

A tad disoriented, she took a deep breath and slid him a glance. "Thanks."

"No problem. Call me later if you need help undressing."

The haze evaporated. Abby snorted. "Now who's giving you too much credit."

He laughed. "Give 'em hell, Abigail," he said softly, then sauntered away as if they'd just discussed the weather.

Abby took three deep breaths, then hurried into the correct rest room. She stared in the mirror at her flushed face. Her lipstick had worn off, certainly not from eating, as she hadn't been able to do that all day. Her nose was shiny, her eyes too bright and she'd forgotten to bring her purse to tackle the repairs.

Topping it all off, she was late for her speech. Folks wouldn't like that. They went to bed early in Bingo.

Quickly she checked her teeth and was about to turn away from the mirror when the stray tendril Max had touched caught her eye. It fell in a loose flattering curl on her cheek. When she turned slightly, golden highlights captured the light.

She did look nice tonight. At least better than usual. Certainly not on a par with Max's standard, but nice. It annoyed the heck out of her that she gave a single hoot what Max thought, but there it was. His compliment had made her pulse speed and her heart had fluttered like a trapped butterfly.

Good thing she could at least maintain perspective. Guys like him didn't go for girls like her. And the truth was, she wouldn't be happy with someone like him. Not for the long haul, anyway. Of course she didn't really know him, but she had some college experience with men like him. Good-looking, used to getting their way, never having to carry their fair share of the load because some poor smitten sap was willing to do it for them.

She straightened, feeling better about putting life back into perspective. Sure, she was still late, but she wasn't feeling so rattled anymore.

As soon as she left the rest room, she heard the disgruntled murmuring of the crowd, and she hurried toward the podium. Halfway there she saw Gramms trying to get her attention, and all her newfound composure dissolved like a puddle of melted chocolate.

Abby had never been more glad to see her and she waited, in spite of the nosy looks and whispers, as

Gramms got closer. Her familiar lilac scent reached Abby first, comforting her, making her feel a little emotional. Lack of sleep always made her a little sappy.

"You look beautiful," Gramms whispered as she kissed Abby's cheek.

"Where have you been? I was worried." Abby ushered her away from straining ears to a spot near a deserted table.

"Mona couldn't decide what to wear, and Candy misplaced Tami for an hour so we got here late. I'm sorry, honey. But surely you knew I'd come."

"Mona and Candy are here with you." Abby scanned the room without success. In fact, she couldn't see Max either.

"Of course. So are Rosie and Herb and Max. He's such a nice young man, don't you think?"

Abby made a face. "Why are they all here?"

"To support you, of course."

"Even after I threatened to shut them down?"

Gramms's lips curved in a patient smile. "They know you didn't mean it."

"The place is a firetrap," Abby murmured. "And it's a wonder no one has broken a leg on those front steps."

"Abigail." The warning in her grandmother's face and voice should have subdued Abby.

"If I'm mayor it'll be my duty to review the condition of all public property. It's nothing personal."

"The Swinging R isn't public property, young lady, you're just being stubborn and manipulative."

Abby gasped. "Gramms, I can't believe you're accusing me of being manipulative. Stubborn, I can see."

Several heads turned, and Gramms said in a lowered voice, "Promise me you'll leave the Swinging R out of our dispute."

"Dispute? We're not having a dispute. It's just a tiny misunderstanding. Come home tomorrow and everything will be back to normal."

Gramms sadly shook her head.

From the podium, Trish tested the microphone with an earsplitting gum pop.

Torn between saving potential constituents from Trish and pleading with Gramms, Abby looked from one woman to the other. The decision was made for her when Gramms kissed her cheek, wished her good luck, then headed toward the back of the room.

"ABBY SEEMS NERVOUS," Mona commented to Estelle and Max. "That isn't like her."

Max studied Abby's body language. Even sitting way back in the armpit of the room he could see Mona was right. He hoped he hadn't said anything to upset Abby. He laughed at himself, thinking about how she would react to that notion. She'd say he was giving himself too much credit again.

"I'm afraid that has something to do with me," Estelle said, sighing. "I hope I'm doing the right thing."

To his disgust, Max's curiosity was piqued, and he looked at Estelle, hoping she'd explain. Not that this crazy nosiness was new. After all, here he was at a sad excuse for a fund-raiser, sitting in the far corner with four older women, only one of whom, he suspected, didn't have her receiver off the hook.

"Maybe we should sit up closer," Mona said. "Being able to see you might comfort her."

Max shuddered at the thought. He liked sitting back here in the semidarkness where he didn't have too good a view of the ladies' dresses, especially Mona's. The plunging neckline and short tight red silk skirt were almost indecent. Well, not on a twenty or thirty-something, but on someone old enough to be his grandmother?

He glanced around the room, grateful that the rest of the audience sat in front of them and hadn't seemed to notice.

"Weren't you listening to Estelle?" Across the table, Rosie stopped fanning herself and frowned at Mona. "If Estelle thinks she's the one who's upset Abby, why in the hell would she sit in clear view and upset her some more?"

"Was I talking to you?" Mona angled her face away from Rosie, and in a loud whisper to Estelle said, "Guess she remembered her hearing aid."

"You're the one who needs a hearing aid. You obviously weren't listening to Estelle." Rosie lifted her chin, faced the podium again and resumed her fanning.

There had been an argument over who got to wear the last pair of black lace garters. Apparently, they hadn't reached an amicable agreement.

"Ladies, I think Abby is about to start speaking," Max said quietly, and received three conciliatory smiles.

Candy hadn't bothered to enter the conversation at all, or even look at him. He figured she was still ticked at him for making her tie Tami to a pole in the garage. Tough. Just thinking about the critter gave him the willies, especially after today's episode of hide-and-seek. No way that thing was sleeping in the same house with him.

The tall thin blonde who'd been with Abby earlier seemed to be having trouble with the microphone. She called a man from the audience up to the podium to help, while Abby stood aside and fidgeted with a small stack of index cards.

"Oh, dear, she is nervous," Estelle whispered, leaning

toward him. "She normally doesn't need notes to speak."

Max patted her hand. He liked Estelle, and frankly couldn't figure out why she wanted to hang out at the Swinging R. The rest of the ladies had their good sides, too, but the place was definitely bordering on becoming a loony bin.

"If she's prepared notes, then it must mean she was nervous before this evening and it has nothing to do with you." He watched Estelle's expression sag, and wondered again why the devil he was sitting here, and why he cared about what happened to Abby and her quest for public office.

Maybe it was his advancing age prompting his interest, like women who followed soap operas for half a lifetime, or retired men who sat around diners and barbershops retelling old war stories. God, the thought was depressing.

His gaze drew to Abby. More likely it was because she'd gotten under his skin, made him wonder about her, and what made her tick. He'd been disappointed when she hadn't stayed for dinner, even though he'd hardly expected her to after he suggested she butt out of her grandmother's business just as he intended to do.

"I'm afraid it does," Estelle said, breaking into his preoccupation.

He hesitated, having lost the thread of their conversation. "Does what?"

"Abigail's nerves. It has everything to do with me. She doesn't understand why I've moved out."

"Have you?" He heard himself ask the question, but he couldn't believe it. Stay out of this, he told himself. "Permanently?"

"That depends." She gave him an embarrassed look. "Oh, you don't want to hear our problems."

He shrugged. "If it would help to talk about it, I don't mind listening."

"Oh, that's so nice, but no, really…"

He straightened. "No problem. Honest."

A shrewd smile slightly curved her lips. She tried to hide it. Too late, he'd seen it. She'd baited him, dammit, and he'd fallen for it like a two-ton drunk elephant.

"Abigail thinks the town is going to fall apart without her. Not in a vain sense, of course, but she has this silly idea that Cunninghams are the glue that keeps Bingo together. And she feels she needs to do her share."

He frowned. It wasn't like the place was called Cunninghamville, nor did he see evidence that the family controlled the town.

Estelle smiled as if reading his mind. "There has been a prominent civic servant in our family for several generations. Prominent by Bingo standards, anyway. But it really goes deeper than that." She paused, and glanced over at Mona and Rosie who were busy arguing over who needed glasses.

He thought it odd that she was willing to tell him something she didn't want her friends to hear but he gave her an encouraging smile and leaned closer.

"Abigail was already leaving for college when her parents died but she took it very hard. We all did. They were too young to die in that senseless truck accident, but for Abby, the sense of abandonment seemed to be the straw that broke the camel's back, if you pardon the old expression.

"People had started leaving Bingo about ten years before, and one by one, all her little friends began moving away. She'd no sooner find someone new to play with when the child's father would find a job in Las Vegas or Reno and off the family would go. Not a single one of her high school friends returned after college, either. Only Abby." Estelle sighed. "I fear, mainly, to watch over me."

"Ah, so you feel guilty."

"There's that, but equally upsetting is that Abigail has tied herself to this town for no good reason. There aren't enough jobs here, so of course people will continue to leave. She can't take it personally and she can't save everyone. I don't think she can divorce herself from her image of what the town used to be. But she can't recreate the past. And she certainly isn't responsible for trying to do it."

The blonde suddenly called for everyone's attention via the now working microphone, and grateful for the distraction, Max slumped back in his chair. Estelle had warned him it was complicated. She wasn't kidding. Simply having listened, he felt as weary as if he'd just run a marathon.

With new interest, he watched Abby smile at everyone and begin her speech. It seemed more like a pep rally, he realized as she got deeper into it, her nervousness apparently forgotten. She must have been a cheerleader in high school.

It tired him out just watching her enthusiasm gain momentum as she talked about her vision for better classrooms, developing sports teams to occupy the youngsters and enable them to compete with neighboring schools, and eventually, the prospect of building a community college just outside of town.

When someone asked where they were going to find the students to fill the college, Abby smiled serenely and explained how she had a plan to attract more businesses to the area.

Max thought she'd gone off the deep end. No sane businessman would move his concern way out here no matter what the tax advantage, but no one questioned her. Instead, there was lots of head-nodding and satisfied smiles. Obviously she was well-respected and trusted. And Max got the most peculiar feeling in the pit of his stomach. A kind of strange mix of anticipation and longing and helplessness, almost like when he was a kid and he'd wanted something really badly but it was just out of his reach.

He didn't know what it meant to have that same peculiar feeling now. He would have blamed it on the strange-looking chicken they'd served for dinner except he'd missed that dubious pleasure.

His gaze drew to Abby. It had something to do with her, although what, he had no idea. He couldn't even identify with her. It was impossible for him to understand welcoming someone else's responsibility, much less asking for it. Hell, it was sort of like begging for a migraine.

Abby not only took responsibility in stride, she embraced it. What must she think of him?

He felt raw suddenly, exposed. It made no sense, made him want to sink low in his chair.

Until he thought he heard someone yell his name.

6

ABBY SCANNED the sea of smiling faces. The speech had gone well. She'd quickly shed most of her nervousness. And as expected, the roasted chicken from Edna's Edibles was a hit. Everything was going fine until she thought she heard a man's gruff voice yell out Max Bennett's name.

She glanced around the room again, but she didn't see Max, nor anyone who might be calling to him. Most of the people were facing her, still chuckling over the little joke she'd made about everyone getting home before acting mayor Cleghorn had the streets rolled up. A few others were looking around, mostly just distracted, probably by the lateness of the hour. Nothing unusual.

Great. Now her overtaxed brain was playing tricks on her. No one here even knew Max, and anyway, the people of Bingo weren't so impolite as to holler over her speech, even if she had just wrapped things up.

"Okay, anyone have any questions?" she asked, more as a friendly gesture than anything else. Ida Brewster and Tommy Lee Smith had already fired two at her earlier. She expected everyone wanted to go home by now.

"Aren't you going to answer mine?"

At the same gruff voice Abby thought she'd heard earlier, everyone twisted in their seats to see who it was. She herself squinted, trying to see past the last grouping of tables but she still couldn't identify the speaker. It hadn't helped that his voice was somewhat garbled. Heaven help her, she hoped Fritz Walker hadn't crawled into his moonshine again and wanted to pick a philosophical fight about today's mores.

"I'm sorry," she said, still unsuccessfully scanning the room. "I didn't hear the question."

"I wanna know about the Swinging R, what that Max Bennett plans to do with it."

Mention of the Swinging R started the murmuring again. Abby's patience slipped three notches. She shaded her eyes against the lights' glare and strained for a better look. "Fritz, is that you?"

No one answered.

Something was fishy. The Swinging R wasn't an issue. She had made it a personal one, but politically, no one had questioned the existence of the brothel in her entire lifetime. Why would someone bring it up now?

"I'd like to see whom I'm addressing before I answer the question," she stated firmly, and the few people who hadn't already craned their necks for a look, turned around to see who it was.

Herb Hanson stepped out from behind a large fake ficus plant. "I guess that would be me." He shuffled forward a couple of feet, his face redder than the bandana around his neck.

"Why you wanna know? You finally gonna marry Mona?" someone shouted out, and everyone else laughed.

"That ain't none of your business," Herb said, and headed for the far corner of the room, grumbling under his breath. Something made him stop, or someone.

He slowly turned around and faced Abby, his reluctance as obvious as white icing on a chocolate cake. He stuck a finger in between his neck and bandana and tried to loosen it. "Well, Abigail, what's your answer?"

Someone clearly had put Herb up to this to rattle her, but she wasn't giving in easily. Maybe she could even embarrass him into sitting down and keeping his mouth shut. "I'm sorry. Could you repeat the question?"

"Oh, come on, Abigail, you heard me."

"With all the commotion, I forgot," she said with a sweet smile and a small shrug.

He just stood there for a moment, and she hoped he was reconsidering allowing himself to be a puppet for whomever was pulling the strings. Not that it was too hard to guess who that would be. Mona, probably. Except that didn't make any sense. Why would she want to put the Swinging R in the spotlight?

A sudden thought struck Abby. Viagra. Was Mona serious?

"Did you say you want to reopen the Swinging R?" she asked and received exactly the reaction she wanted.

While the audience issued a collective gasp, Herb's cheeks colored with outrage, and he whipped off his tan Stetson and slapped the side of his leg with it. "Are you loco?"

She raised her brows in innocence. "I'm not really sure what you're getting at."

Herb glanced over his shoulder. Abby tried to see whom he was looking at but a row of silk trees in the back of the room blocked her view. When she moved her head slightly to the right, she saw him.

Max Bennett.

What the dickens did he have up his sleeve?

"Tell me exactly what you want, Herb." Her patience was gone, the sharpness in her voice vibrating into the microphone and bouncing off the walls.

"Gosh darnit, you're getting me all confused."

"Why? Don't you know what you want? Or maybe you're speaking on someone else's behalf? Mr. Bennett's, perhaps? Did he ask you to do his dirty work for him?"

Herb started stammering, and regret pricked Abby for picking on him. She started to let him off the hook when Max stepped forward.

"That's enough, Abby," he said, holding her gaze. "I assure you I don't know anything about this."

The room grew absurdly quiet as everyone gawked at him. Then like dominoes, the younger women started putting their heads together and whispering. The older ones seemed to all turn their avid attention to Abby.

She cleared her throat, then gritted her teeth when the sound echoed through the microphone. "Fine. Then if there aren't any more questions, we'll wrap this evening up."

"Come on, Abigail," someone from the audience yelled. "Who is this guy?"

She'd brought this on herself, she realized with disgust, by trying to provoke poor Herb. Her only comfort was that Max looked about as happy as she was over this situation. "This is Maxwell Bennett. Mr. Bennett is Lily McIntyre's nephew, and the new owner of the Swinging R."

The silence lasted only a moment, and then the collective murmur grew to a roar. Obviously, few if anyone had seen Max before now, although how they could have missed him was beyond her. He was taller than almost anyone here, his shoulders definitely broader. He was only one of three men who wore a suit. Plus, he had green eyes.

Finally, Virgil Mayflower, who owned both the gas

station and the general store, stood and approached Max with an extended hand. "Welcome to Bingo, son. We're sure glad to see you."

Max smiled and shook Virgil's hand, but Abby could tell he was uncomfortable. No one else could possibly detect his unease, he was too polished, and it puzzled her that she was able to see it. She didn't know him well enough, yet she had no doubt she was correct.

"You just get into town?" Virgil asked, stepping back to appraise Max, frowning as he slicked back his dark straight hair.

Virgil took pride in the fact that he was always the best-dressed man in Bingo, and generally he was, but his dark brown western-cut suit didn't hold a candle to the custom Italian design Max wore.

"Yesterday."

"Good, good. Glad you could make it tonight. Wish you'd spoken up sooner."

Max swept a glance around the room. Everyone's gaze was glued to him. "I leave tomorrow."

"What?" Virgil reared back his head. "Then what did you decide to do with the Swinging R?"

"Don't know yet."

Abby smiled to herself. If Max thought he could get away with that answer, he was in for one heck of a surprise. Virgil was also the richest man in Bingo but he was always looking for ways to increase his business, and probably the only one who'd like to see the brothel restored to its glory days to provide more traffic through town.

"When are you gonna know?" Virgil demanded, his legendary impatience sharpening his tone. "That old place has been run-down for years. You look like you could afford to put quite a few bucks in the place."

Max reacted with a bark of laughter. "You seem to have a strong opinion. Care to buy the place?"

Some people gasped, others laughed. Abby leaned on the podium, enjoying the fireworks and being off the hot-seat.

"Well, maybe I just might." The telltale vein popped out along Virgil's receding hairline. He was both angry and flustered, not a pretty combination for him.

"Ah, shut up, Virgil, and let the young man speak," Mabel Salazar said, crossing her arms over her enormous bosom. "We all know you wouldn't put a plug nickel into the place. You're just interested in making money, not spending it."

Other than a murmur or two, no one said anything. Virgil had both influence and a temper, and people didn't like having to drive to the next town for groceries when he got steamed.

"Hey, Virgil." Max surprised the older man by shaking his hand again, distracting him from the menacing look he was giving Mabel. "No hard feelings, huh? I had a rough flight, and I'm pretty tired. I'm still trying to decide what to do with the place."

Virgil gave a grudging shrug, but he still looked peeved when he slid Mabel another look. "No problem."

"If it's not too much of an imposition, and if you have some time tomorrow morning, maybe we could have coffee and you could give me some ideas."

The way Virgil's chest suddenly puffed out was almost comical. "Sure, son, I can probably fit you into my schedule."

"Terrific. I'll call your office and check with your secretary."

That startled laughs out of half the audience. Virgil had neither. He had a desk in his garage.

"If I'm not there my wife will know where I am," he mumbled and went back to his table.

Abby silently shook her head. Amazing. Max had even charmed that old goat Virgil. But she'd eat her day planner if Max had any intention of giving Virgil's opinion a passing thought. What the heck was he up to?

Maybe she wasn't giving him enough credit. Maybe he'd just wanted to help defuse the situation. And maybe Candy's new pet iguana would learn to fly.

"Sorry for the interruption." Max gave her a slight bow of his head. "Abby."

The way he'd said her name sent a shiver down her spine. It sounded entirely too familiar, intimate almost. And it wasn't her imagination, judging by the exchange of knowing glances among the women.

She straightened and gave him a tight smile. "No harm done. We're through here." Her smile broadened for the audience. "Thank you all so much for coming."

"Not so fast."

Oh, no. Abby briefly closed her eyes. When she opened them again, she watched Mona and her grandmother march toward the podium. Behind them, Mona dragged Herb, who'd slunk off earlier.

"We still want to know why you want to close down the Swinging R." Mona stopped beside Max, who looked like he'd rather be on the front line of a pie-throwing contest.

Big mistake, Mona, Abby thought with a smug lift of her chin. The townspeople would probably be on Abby's side...

Her chin came down and her jaw slackened as her gaze bounced from one face to the next. Everyone stared at her in such indignant shock as if she'd suggested they all get naked.

"What?" She turned up her palms. "I didn't say that," she muttered, and Mona snorted. "Not exactly, anyway."

"You mean, you wanna board up the doors and windows?" Mabel Salazar asked in a scandalized voice.

"That's not—" She got cut off by several people speaking at once.

"You going to tear it down?" someone called out.

"She can't do that. The place is practically a national landmark."

"Where would all the ladies go?"

"That's a horrible idea, Abigail. Your mama and papa would turn over in their graves."

Everyone kept talking until Abby wanted to clamp her hands over her ears. Instead, she glared at Mona, who had the audacity to grin and wink. Beside her, Gramms shifted from one foot to the other, looking distraught.

Abby felt no pity. This was supposed to be her big night and it was turning into something horrible. How could her grandmother have participated in this calamity? "Would everyone please calm down and listen?" she began. If only they understood…

When the noise only grew louder, Max picked up an empty water glass and hit the side with a spoon. It made enough of an odd tinkling noise that he got most everyone's attention.

"Ladies and gentlemen," he said with one of his charming smiles, "perhaps I can help clear up this misunderstanding." The women all smiled back, and some of them started fanning themselves. The men waited rather patiently for him to continue.

Mixed feelings plagued Abby. She was glad he got them to settle down, but she didn't want to be rescued by him, or feel obliged to him in any way.

"Yesterday I arrived to a couple of surprises." He glanced at Mona, and then smiled at all and sundry again. "You see, Aunt Lily's will wasn't all that specific."

He paused, and a brief silence followed, until comprehension dawned and the crowd started laughing. Mona looked a tad put out, and Abby didn't mind that one bit.

Max gave a good-natured shrug. "To make a long story short, Abby was teasing me when she mentioned something about shutting down the Swinging R."

His eyes found hers, daring her to contradict him.

Virgil turned to her. "So you don't really have some foolish idea to close those gals down."

She hesitated, stewing over the corner Max had backed her into. "Close those gals down? We were talking about a place, a building, not the ladies."

"Same thing." Virgil waved a dismissive hand. "The Swinging R is practically an institution and so are them gals."

A chorus of "yeahs" made her teeth grind together.

"So, what is it, Abigail?" Virgil had gone to stand next to Max and Mona. Wasn't that just cozy?

She glanced at Gramms. Their eyes met for a second, and then Gramms looked away. That hurt.

Abby sniffed. "Weren't you all listening to what I said tonight? I have enough on my plate to worry about without expending my energy on the Swinging R."

Virgil frowned, along with several others. "That means you're leaving the Swinging R alone?"

She glanced at Max. He pressed his lips together, trying to suppress a grin, and she gave him a look that told him how delighted she was to provide him with all this entertainment.

He let the grin take over, then mouthed, "Just cry uncle."

That did it. She tapped the microphone, and assured that it still worked, she leaned toward it and said, "Okay, everyone, if you have a few more minutes, let's talk about the Swinging R. How many of you have been out there lately?"

The men all sat there stone-faced, while some of their wives waited for their answers.

After a long silence, Herb held up a hand, and said, "I have."

Everyone roared with laughter.

Mona gave his arm a light smack with the back of her hand. "They already know that, Herbie."

Abby waited until the crowd settled down. "All right, I have a question for you, Herbert. What sort of shape is the place in? Do you think it's safe?"

He started loosening his bandana again, glancing at Mona and looking as though he wanted to hightail it out of the hall. "Well, I'm not sure."

"What about the back steps? There were a few rotting boards you had to replace, weren't there? And didn't a couple of others come loose. Aren't you afraid Mona, or one of the other ladies might fall and hurt themselves? Didn't you ask them to avoid using the back door if possible?"

"For crying out loud, you sound like a prosecutor," Mona said. "You want to be mayor, or are you looking to take over Chester Southby's law practice?"

"Sounds to me like she's the one doing the avoiding—the issue, that is." Virgil narrowed his gaze on her. "Maybe you need some competition, young lady. Someone besides old Cleghorn."

Abby couldn't believe what she was hearing. She waited for someone to come to her defense, to tell Virgil he was crazy, but most of the women were too busy ogling Max, and the men didn't want the place shut down.

She looked at Gramms for support, but she turned away. Abby sucked in a breath. Geez Louise, if her own grandmother wasn't on Abby's side...

Boy, was she screwed.

7

ABBY HAD JUST FINISHED her lesson plans for next week when someone knocked at her classroom door. For the first time ever, she'd closed it, having no desire to talk with anyone. Last night had ended in a disaster and she needed time to lick her wounds.

But, of course, closing her door, something she never did, probably invited more speculation, more curiosity, more trouble. She didn't care, not as long as she had some peace and quiet. And didn't have to hear the name Swinging R. Or Max Bennett.

She hesitated a long time before forcing herself to get up from her desk and head for the door. It was probably Mrs. Bacon, demanding to know what Abby thought she was doing closing a door in Bingo, Nevada. Sometimes she truly didn't know why she ever came back. Max was right. It was nothing but a hick town.

Cringing at her own thoughts, she opened the door, and sighed with disgust. "What the hell are you doing here? Trying to finish me off?"

Max frowned. "You can't possibly blame me for last night."

Wordlessly, she turned and went back to her desk. When he followed, she snapped, "Did I invite you in?"

He shut the door behind him. "How can you think last night was my fault?"

That made her a little nervous. If she were speaking

to him she'd tell him to leave it open. But then he was likely to get the wrong idea. Good thing she wasn't speaking to him.

She picked up a Walkman lying on her desk, adjusted the headphones on her ears and cranked up the volume before she slid a stack of tests to correct in front of her. Before she could grab her red pen, Max lifted the headphones off her head from behind.

"Hey!" She twisted around and scowled at him. "Ouch!"

"Don't move. It's caught in your hair. And turn the damn volume down."

She turned it up. He jerked the headphones which pulled her hair. "Ouch!"

"Gee, sorry."

She caved in and lowered the volume before it caused her permanent hearing damage, then tried to take the headphones from him. "I'll do this."

"Keep still." He swatted her hands away.

When she made a second attempt, he grabbed both her wrists with one hand. Then, to her utter and complete astonishment, leaned down and kissed the side of her neck, his lips warm and firm against her skin.

She froze, but her pulse went bonkers. Heat filled her cheeks and belly and lower. She swallowed hard, not sure what to say, what to do.

He released her hands and extracted the headphones from her hair. "There." Stepping back, he looked at her as if nothing had happened.

Should she ignore the kiss? Yell at him?

Kiss him back?

No, that was out of the question. Definitely out of the question. She'd have to be an idiot.

She stared up into his beautiful green eyes.

As calmly as possible, she got up and opened the door. "I thought you were leaving today," she said, and returned to her desk, her gaze lowered, carefully avoiding the amusement in his face.

And then it hit her. He really was supposed to leave today.

Was he on his way to the airstrip now? Her panicked gaze slid his way. He wore jeans and a white polo shirt. That told her nothing.

"Well?" she asked, her voice sounding oddly calm. To her amazement, she didn't want him to go.

"Why do you want to know?" He flashed a grin and sat on the edge of her desk. "You going to miss me?"

"Like I would an ulcer."

He made a disbelieving sound. "Seriously, you know I had nothing to do with last night."

"I seem to recall you being right in the middle of things."

"Hold on. I only stepped forward to keep you from pounding on poor Herb."

"I wasn't pounding on him." Frustrated, she moved a stack of books with too much force and one of them went flying off her desk. "And who do you think you are barging your way in here and kissing me?"

He'd stooped to retrieve the history book, but he paused for a second, a smile spreading across his face. Then he scooped up the text, laid it on her desk and sat on one of the students' chairs, facing her. "Is that what has you in such a delightful mood?"

She forced herself to meet his gaze just because he probably figured she wouldn't. "What do you want? Another piece of my hide?"

"Sounds too painful. How about lunch?"

"It's three o'clock."

"Your point is?"

"Normal people had lunch hours ago, not that I consider you normal." She smiled. "Or that I would ever think of having lunch or anything else with you."

His gaze had strayed to the wall clock, and he was frowning slightly. "Three, huh?"

She took a closer look at him. He was unshaved, and his too-long hair was a little disheveled. "Did you just wake up?"

He lifted a shoulder. "Not exactly."

Appalled, she sank back in her chair and stared at him. "You did."

"Did not. I've already stopped by Chester Southby's office and everything."

"He's still away fishing."

"So, I only said I stopped by."

"That took all of two minutes."

Max grunted his annoyance. "What are you? My social secretary all of a sudden?"

Abby did little to hide her smile as she relaxed in her chair and folded her arms across her chest. "Sorry. I'm sure you spent your day deciding what you'll do with the Swinging R."

"You're not mayor yet, sweetheart. I don't need you poking your nose in my affairs."

"But it was okay for you to kiss me?"

"You're still fixated on that?" Amusement lit his eyes. "That wasn't even a real kiss. I just did that to get you to keep still."

"You presumptuous..."

"It worked."

Momentarily speechless, Abby stared at him in indignation. When she finally opened her mouth to give him a good dressing down, she caught some movement out of the corner of her eye.

"What are you two arguing about now?"

Abby glowered at Virgil, standing at the door, his arms crossed above his big, round belly, the snaps of his red western shirt ready to pop. "Put out that cigar."

She'd sounded more terse than she meant to, but her nerves were shot. She was afraid he'd heard too much, and by the time the story made its rounds, they'd have her and Max french-kissing in the back seat of her car.

With a bulldog frown, Virgil pulled the stogie out of his mouth. "Don't get your bowels in an uproar. I haven't even lit the damn thing yet."

Abby glanced at all the papers she had yet to grade and sighed. "What is this? Grand Central Station?"

Max stood, and nodded to the older man, then looked at Abby. "What do you know about Grand Central?"

"Probably from going to that fancy school back East," Virgil said, and proceeded to make himself at home on one of the students' chairs.

Abby winced inside, waiting for the chair to break. Of course the upside would be getting rid of Virgil. Max, she didn't know what to do with yet. She wanted him to leave, yet she wanted him to stay.

Reluctantly, she slid him a glance. He was looking at her, curiosity making his green eyes glitter.

What she really wanted was for him to give her a real kiss.

Dammit. The thought added salt to her raw nerves. "What do you want, Virgil?"

He frowned at her. "You're not still miffed over last night, are you? We were just having a healthy discussion, is all."

"No, I'm not miffed. But I do have a lot of papers to grade."

Virgil glanced at Max, then pointedly looked at Abby, and grinned.

"Mr. Bennett was just leaving," she said. "Hopefully, not just my office, but Bingo—even better, Nevada."

Virgil chuckled. "I sure hope not. We have a proposition for him."

"Proposition?" Max looked nervous.

Abby felt a flutter in her stomach herself. "We?"

"A bunch of us from last night had coffee this morning and we were thinking—" Virgil looked around the classroom. "You got any water in here?"

"Virgil," Abby warned between clenched teeth.

A confused frown clouded Max's face, as though he were trying to wade through the undercurrent, make sense of what was not being said.

"He doesn't want any water," she explained. "He just likes to build suspense. Virgil, you always do this, and for your information, no one in town likes it. They think you're a drama king."

Virgil scoffed and looked at Max for support.

Max only shrugged. "She could've called you a drama queen."

Abby immediately looked down at her desktop blotter to keep from laughing out loud. It was enough to imagine Virgil's inevitable bug-eyed expression at that remark.

"Your grandmother's right, Abigail," Virgil muttered. "You're just no fun."

Her gaze flew up to the older man's face, the laughter instantly dying inside her. "Is that what she told you?"

Virgil shifted in his seat, suddenly not so eager to meet her eyes. "Not in so many words. In fact, Estelle didn't mean—'' He scratched his belly. "Oh, hell, I ain't getting in the middle of you two hens.''

Her gaze flickered to Max. The trace of sympathy she saw on his face only fueled her anger. "Did Gramms put you up to something? Is that why you're here?''

Dread coiled like a snake, making her stomach cramp as she waited for the man's answer. If he lied to her, she'd know it. Whenever he spun tales, his left ear wiggled. As children, she and her friends used to laugh about it.

She wasn't laughing now. It seemed as though the entire town was in on some sick joke, except her. She was the punch line. This was all so unlike Gramms.

Abby hoped there wasn't a medical reason behind her grandmother's odd behavior. The thought subdued her anger, but stoked her fear. She was going to call Doc Sawyer, whether Gramms liked it or not.

"Don't go getting all paranoid. My being here hasn't got anything to do with Estelle.'' Virgil turned to Max, obscuring her view of his ear. "I hear you're planning on staying a spell.''

"Who told you that?'' Max asked, his mouth tightening with annoyance.

"Herb Hanson. And being as he's your driver, I figure he ought to know.''

"He ought to know to keep his mouth shut, too,'' Max mumbled and glanced irritably at Abby.

"Why are you staying?'' she asked in such a curt tone that both men stared at her. "Surely our hick town can't interest you that much.''

"It doesn't. You forget I have a business concern here.''

Virgil started stuttering, his gaze on Abby. "Wh-who are you calling a hick?''

"Don't look at me." She moved her chin in Max's direction. "He's the one who thinks Bingo is some backwoods town."

Max steadily met her gaze. "I knew you were looking to pick a fight from the moment I walked in here."

"Then you should've turned right back around."

"I sure should have."

"It's not too late."

Virgil made a sound of disgust, then struggled to get up from the chair, but his belly got in the way of the traylike student desk attached to the arm. When his face started reddening, Abby took pity and showed him how to lift the desk up and slide it down to the side of the chair.

"Darn it, Abigail, you could have told me that contraption was movable." Virgil rubbed his butt. "Those chairs aren't fit for midgets." His frown cleared. "At least you two banshees have stopped your sniping."

"Don't count on it," Max said. "Looks like she's winding up for round two."

"Says you." Abby lifted her chin. "I'm more mature than that."

"So why'd you make a big deal over the kiss?"

She let out a low shriek. That smile was going to get wiped off his face if it was the last thing she did.

"What kiss?" Virgil looked from one to the other. "You two been necking in the classroom? You can't do that."

"Oh, please." Abby's cheeks heated. "You know me better than that, Virgil Mayflower."

"Then why is your face stained with guilt?"

"Yeah, Abigail, why is that?" Max's slow grin was anything but charming right now.

"Can't you tell he's goading you, Virgil?" She leaned

back in her chair, trying to look relaxed. Thank goodness for the desk blocking their view of her shaky legs.

Nervous energy ricocheted through her. Why was Max staying all of a sudden? Why had he stopped by to see her? Darn it, she hadn't even given him a chance to explain. Of course he'd been too busy kissing her. Not real kisses, as he'd pointed out. But, geez, was she ever itching to…

Feeling prickly and warm suddenly, she looked over at him. He was watching her, his brows drawn together in undisguised interest as though he were trying to trespass into her thoughts.

She averted her eyes, and found Virgil watching both of them. He had a horribly interested, almost excited look on his face, and Abby knew she wouldn't be showing up at the diner for a long while. She hated being the subject of gossip, one of the few things she despised about small-town living. But that had never been a problem for her until now. Until Max.

"Look, you two," she said, standing abruptly. "I'd love to sit here and trade barbs with you but I have to work for a living."

"Don't you want to hear our proposition?" Virgil asked, a shrewd gleam entering his eye. "It involves you somewhat."

She'd almost forgotten about that, and so had Max judging from the way he straightened and peered warily at the other man. Tempted to tell him she didn't give a hoot what he had to say to Max, she simply couldn't. Her curiosity was piqued all over again.

"Now that I have your attention." Virgil looked from one to the other. "The committee feels that it would be beneficial if—" He stopped short and snapped his fingers. "Darn it. I forgot something."

One look from Abby, and he added, "It's not what you think. I'm not trying to draw this out, so don't start pounding on me." He quickly looked at Max. "Tell me, son, what do you do?"

"Do?"

"How do you earn a living? Besides running brothels."

Max gave Virgil a threatening look. "I do not run brothels."

"Okay, okay. Forget I said that. What else?"

Max shrugged. "I dabble in the family business."

"What would that be?"

"Why?" Max frowned and slid Abby a questioning glance. "What are you getting at?"

"Is it that top secret?" Virgil chuckled, and withdrew the cigar from his pocket. "The Bennetts aren't drug runners or moonshiners, are they?"

"Yeah, right." Max grunted and shook his head. "Worse, they're politicians."

Virgil's eyes got rounder than two silver dollars. "You don't say?"

"I sure as hell wouldn't lie about something like that," Max said with an absence of fondness.

Abby didn't see herself as a politician so she didn't take offense. She was more interested in who he was talking about. A couple of Massachusetts' senators were named Bennett. There was even talk that one of them may run for the presidency.

"Excellent!" Virgil grinned at Abby. "Perfect, isn't it?"

"You said you work in the family business," Abby said, ignoring Virgil. "Does that mean you campaign for them?"

Max shook his head, his expression suggesting he

found the idea amusing. "The Bennetts own a chain of clothing stores."

He seemed so detached, it took Abby aback. He hadn't said "the family business" or "we." It was clearly a subject he didn't like discussing, and she wondered why he hadn't simply told Virgil to kiss off. Even more odd was the way Max kept studying her, as though looking for a reaction.

"I swear to high heaven, getting information out of you is worse than talking to my seventeen-year-old," Virgil grumbled. "Would you just spit it out?"

With obvious reluctance, Max tore his gaze away from Abby and frowned at Virgil. "What are you talking about?"

"Your position with the company. What do you do for them?"

Impatience darkened Max's eyes. "Nothing. Okay?"

"Nothing?" Virgil sent Abby a confused look. "Nothing?" Then his narrowed gaze swung back to Max. He thought Max was pulling his leg. Abby wasn't so sure. "Where did you go to school?"

"Harvard."

"Well, now..." Virgil started smiling again. "What did you study?"

"Law." Max kept his attention focused on the other man, and Abby got the feeling he was purposely trying to avoid her gaze.

He needn't have bothered. Her mind had already raced ahead, and she had a sudden sick feeling she knew where this conversation was destined.

"You a lawyer?" Excitement sizzled in Virgil's voice.

"Technically."

"Excellent!" Virgil looked as though he were ready

to burst. He started to say something else, but Max held up a silencing hand.

"Oh, I don't have any more questions," Virgil said, and lit his cigar. "You're gonna make the perfect candidate to oppose Abigail for mayor."

8

MAX DECIDED his initial assessment had been correct. These people were all nuts. He glanced at Abby. She didn't look happy. Hell, he wasn't happy either.

"I can't wait to go tell the others." Virgil puffed on the cigar. "A lawyer. You can't hardly get more qualified than that."

"Put it out, Virgil. I don't need my classroom stunk up by that thing." Abby's normally expressive face was an unreadable mask.

"Oh, yeah, sorry. I guess I got carried away with all the excitement." He snuffed it out on the bottom of his shoe. "You must be pretty excited, too, Abigail."

"Ecstatic." She stared off for a moment, lost in her thoughts, and then set her sights on Virgil. "You said you had to go tell the others. Who would that be?"

"The usual crowd," Virgil said, and edged toward the door.

Max hadn't said a thing yet. They were crazy, and he had no intention of staying in Bingo. End of story. But there was definitely something happening here, something subtle that he didn't understand.

"Hold it, Virgil." She rose from her desk and went to stand face to face with him. "Who decided I needed opposition?"

"For Pete's sake, we thought you'd be pleased, Abigail. You said yourself you didn't want to win the election by default. It sounds as though Max here could give you a good run for your money.''

''Ah.'' Abby started nodding, her controlled expression still giving nothing away. ''Gramms told you that, huh?''

Understanding dawned, and Max realized he should have guessed. This was about Abby and Estelle. Virgil was a fool to get involved. No way would Max get in the middle.

But he didn't like Abby's body language. She was upset, and it bothered him to see her like this. ''What's the matter, Abby? Can't stand the heat?''

She stared blankly at him.

His teasing had missed the mark. He hadn't ignited the fire he hoped would ease the tension and divert the conversation. But her control had slipped somewhat, and she stood there beginning to look glum and helpless.

Her apparent lack of fighting spirit burned a hole in him. He wished he could read between the lines. It was clear he was no threat to her candidacy, even if he wanted to be. The people obviously loved and respected her, while he was nobody to them. In fact, if they really knew him, they'd have a good laugh over having even hatched the idiotic idea. Abby understood all that, which eliminated her feeling threatened as the reason for her mood.

''Okay,'' she said finally, calmly. ''If that's the way you all want it...''

Max grunted. ''They're obviously pulling your leg, Abby.''

''No, they aren't.'' Her gaze hadn't left the other man, who looked a little red in the face.

''Virgil?'' Max waited until he had the guy's attention. ''Tell her this is a joke.'' Virgil's didn't respond. ''Or are some of you still sour grapes over last night? Is that what this is about?''

"I don't need you defending me, Max." Abby returned to her desk and started straightening stacks of papers. "There's nothing more to say here."

"Defending you, my foot. Virgil just wasted a chunk of my time. They don't want me as a candidate. They only—"

"Now, hold on there." Virgil pulled a piece of paper out of his pocket. It was folded in quarters, so Max couldn't see what it was, but Virgil handed it to him. "This here is all the proper paperwork for your nomination. This is no joke, son."

"You people *are* crazy." Max shook his head. "You don't know a thing about me."

"Sure, we do. You come from a family of politicians. You're a Harvard lawyer. Seems to me this election is going to be real interesting, especially with Abby being a Yale graduate and all. Aren't those two schools rivals?''

Max shot her a surprised look. Yale? She went to Yale and came back to Bingo?

"What's the matter, Max?" Her eyebrows arched in challenge. "Can't stand the heat?"

At the first sign of life he'd seen in her, relief cushioned him. It probably had just occurred to her she had nothing to worry about. "The French Riviera in June is the only heat I'm interested in."

"Wimp."

He shrugged at her taunting. "That's me."

Disappointment stole the sparkle from her eyes. "Too bad. It would have been fun to beat you."

Seeing the renewed spunk in her made it almost worth

accepting the nomination. "Look out. Your overconfidence is showing. Bad move for a politician."

"Guess there are those who are doers, and those who just talk about it."

Virgil watched them spar, his gaze bouncing back and forth as if he were watching a tennis match. "Maybe you two ought to set up a debate. Save us from driving all the way to Las Vegas for entertainment this weekend."

Max grunted. "Okay, the fun's over."

Virgil narrowed his eyes. "What do you mean?"

"Whatever you and your cronies were up to—"

"Hold on there." Virgil's face creased in a frown. "We're serious about this. Bingo is small, but we're a civic-minded town with lots of caring people. We want a strong mayor who can lead us into the future."

Max gestured to Abby who remained stoic. "You have one."

"No dispute there. We're lucky to have Abigail. She cares about Bingo as much or more than anybody here, so I think she would agree that we'd all benefit from an honest-to-goodness race." Virgil looked at Abby for confirmation, and she slowly nodded. "There…you see?"

Max saw all right. On the outside she was as cool as a mint julep, but something was simmering below the surface. Something that made her eyes a little too bright, her faint smile strained. It probably had to do with Estelle. Nothing he could do about it, but he still hated seeing Abby deflated like this.

"So…" Max rubbed his chin. He hadn't even shaved yet. Of course this was way too early for him to be out and about. "You're making me your token candidate. Think I'll pass."

"Token, my rump." Virgil drew back his head. "If anything, you're overqualified."

Max yawned. He needed a bite to eat, and he needed a nap. Maybe he could still talk Abby into going over to the diner. "A family of politicians and a law degree don't automatically make a good candidate."

"For Pete's sake, we know that. We aren't yokels." The older man started to stick the cigar in his mouth again, but glanced at Abby and slipped it into his breast pocket instead. "The law degree is just gravy, son. We made up our minds last night after Abigail's speech. We liked the way you handled yourself."

"I didn't do anything."

"Of course you did. When things got heated, you stepped right in, cool as they come, and got everyone settled down."

"You call that heated?" Max laughed. "That was nothing."

"My point exactly." Virgil waved a hand at Abby. "You didn't get rattled. Now, this young lady can have a mighty hot temper at times—"

"Hey." Max cut him off. "This *young lady* went to Yale and could have had her pick of jobs. But she chose to come back here. I think a little gratitude might be in order."

"Don't go getting all worked up. Look at her...she's smiling. She knows I don't mean nothing."

Max blinked, surprised at his small burst of temper. Normally, he was more laid-back—too laid-back, according to Taylor. He cast a brief sideways glance at Abby. She *was* smiling—at him.

"It's just that Mona and Rosie told us about some of the suggestions you made around the Swinging R," Virgil continued, "and how you settled things with Candy and her iguana. You've got a good head on your shoulders and we want you to run."

Max switched his attention back to the other man. These people weren't impressed because he was a Bennett or had a Harvard law degree. They thought he had a good head on his shoulders. Imagine.

He studied Virgil's impatient but earnest features for a moment. "You're serious about this?"

"Of course we're serious." He looked grumpily at his watch. "Why else would I be missing *Judge Judy* to woo you? Isn't that right, Abigail?"

Max looked back at her, and she nodded, her eyes remaining carefully noncommittal as they met his. Of all times for him to be unable to guess what she was thinking.

He really did need more sleep. A bunch of strange stuff was churning inside him and tipping him off balance. He didn't belong in Bingo, nor did he have any intention of staying for an appreciable length of time, but damn if he didn't have a sudden longing to stick around, to go ahead and make a play for mayor.

It was merely a nomination they were asking him to accept. Of course he had no chance of winning. Didn't want one. The people wanted Abby, just as it should be. But that didn't mean he couldn't hang around and play in her sandbox for a while.

ABBY STARED at the overflowing laundry basket, then pushed herself up from the chair and forced her feet to move. It was difficult to care about grading papers or making dinner or doing wash after the day she'd just had.

If the people of Bingo wanted to punish her, a slap in the face would have been far kinder...certainly more direct...and quicker.

She carried the basket into the laundry room and stared at the empty shelf over the dryer. Out of detergent. Out of fabric softener. And she was pretty nearly out of patience.

How many times had she put her life on hold to be of service to the community? How many nights had she stayed up too late, grading papers, making and freezing casseroles, because she'd spent the entire week on civic business?

But did the people of Bingo give a damn? No. They wanted a stranger for mayor. A rich gadabout playboy who wouldn't care if a new middle school was built, or if Wal-Mart opened a store within the city limits.

Max didn't even care about the Swinging R. He'd all but admitted that to her the first day she met him. Couldn't Virgil hear himself? He'd referred to the suggestions Max made for the brothel. Well, big whoop-de-doo. Suggestions were easy. Taking responsibility wasn't.

Maxwell Bennett cared about one thing: himself.

And the sad truth was, she wanted him to stay.

She was hurt, but it wasn't his fault. He hadn't asked to be nominated. The good people of Bingo had deemed that action necessary. Maybe she should give up. Max was right—she could have her pick of jobs. A company in New York had given her an open-ended offer, so had one in Houston.

But she wouldn't do anything rash, not when the sting of rejection was so fresh.

"Abby!"

She poked her head out of the laundry room. Who the heck had come to see her at this hour?

"I know you're home, Abby." It was Max. Probably at the open front door where she'd left only the screen locked. "I saw your car in the garage."

She hopped over the dirty laundry and went to the door. "Good for you. What do you want?"

"Why didn't you answer?" He ran a slow gaze down her body, and she realized what a complete mess she was.

Tough. He shouldn't have come unannounced. "I didn't hear you. I was doing laundry." She tugged at the hem of her stained pink T-shirt. It was cropped to a couple of inches under her breasts, leaving part of her stomach exposed.

"Are you going to let me in?"

"Why?"

"Because it would be the neighborly thing to do."

She pulled up her sweatpants with the stretched-out waist. It slid down to her hips again, showing her navel. "No, why do you want to come in?"

He smiled. "So I can be neighborly."

She closed the heavy wooden door.

"Come on, Abby." He knocked—hard. "I'm not going away, so you might as well let me in."

She groaned. He was probably stubborn enough to stand there all night, perfect fodder for the rumor mill. She opened the door. "What do you want? I was getting ready to go to bed."

"I thought you were doing laundry," he said, and she started to close the door again. But he'd already opened the screen door and stuck his foot inside.

She glanced down at his Gucci loafer. Boy, was she tempted. Except Max seemed to be one of those guys who had everything go his way, and she'd probably end up with a dented door.

"You can come in, but make it snappy."

"Wow, I think I might have heard that phrase from a movie once."

"If you want to be mayor of this little hick town, you'd

better get used to our quaint sayings.'' She preceded him into the living room, and when she turned to face him, she caught him looking at her butt.

Great. She knew darn well what it looked like in sweatpants. Two heads of cabbage.

He didn't even look sheepish when he met her accusing gaze. "What did you say?"

She rolled her eyes toward the ceiling and folded her arms across her chest. "What do you want, Max?"

"If I tell you, I'll probably get a slap across the face." He made no attempt to conceal his meaning, but boldly captured her gaze. And then he lowered his to her lips, lingering for what seemed like forever, before his attention drew to her bare midriff.

Abby wasn't sure what to think. Men like Max didn't go for women like her. But this was Bingo, a little low on eligible or sophisticated females, and maybe he needed a temporary distraction.

She, however, didn't need or want the blunder of a one-night stand. Although she had friends who'd succumbed to the temptation and remained unscathed, Abby knew she wasn't built that way. Besides, she had the unnerving feeling that one night with Max would haunt her for a very long time.

Even knowing nothing would happen, the intense way he stared at her made her nervous. She plopped herself down at the far end of the sofa, as far away from him as possible. The action didn't discourage him from keeping his gaze on her, his eyes making her warm and sensitive and, God help her, needy.

She wanted Max to kiss her. She'd thought about it a lot since this afternoon. Too much. Maybe if she simply got it out of her system…

"I've been thinking about you today," he said, and

sat on the sofa. Not too close, but she still preferred he'd chosen one of the chairs.

The low timbre of his voice sent a shiver down her spine. "Ah, feeling guilty for interloping, huh?"

"Yeah, right." He grunted. "You know better than that. I need another obligation like I need a root canal."

"So, why accept?"

He shrugged, looking restless all of a sudden. "I don't know. I like aggravating you."

"Gee, what a mature reason to run for office."

A slow smile curved one side of his mouth. "You're right. The truth is, I don't know why I accepted, but I thought you'd be kind of glad once you thought about it."

"Why? Because I'd have the privilege of you hanging around Bingo longer?"

His genuine look of surprise startled her. Was it her sarcastic tone? Did he expect her to fall all over him like other women did?

He shook his head. "I figured you'd be glad because you know you don't have any competition."

Confused, she made a face.

"Virgil said they thought you needed an opponent. Eventually they would have found someone else. Someone legitimate. With me, you don't have to worry."

"Because you don't intend to stick around." With mixed emotions, she nodded, his logic making some sense to her. It chafed that he thought she couldn't stand up to another opponent, that she would need his help in eliminating any possible competition. He really was a smug son-of-a-gun.

And still, on a personal level, she hated the reminder he'd be gone soon.

"Well, yeah, there's that, too."

"What else is there?"

He looked taken aback. "I'm not a good candidate."

"What?" She laughed...except he looked serious. "What do you mean, exactly?"

"Come on, Abby, we both know I'd make a lousy mayor."

She thought he was kidding at first, but when he started to shift uncomfortably under her scrutiny, she realized he wasn't. "That's ridiculous. You have excellent credentials. You may not know the town right now, but you could learn everything you need to know in a week."

Max pursed his lips in silent amusement. "You don't understand."

"Then explain it to me."

"Forget it." He was about to get up, but Abby reached over and took his hand, and he settled back down, his gaze warily finding hers.

"Is it because of me?" Abby asked, releasing his hand, and wishing she didn't have to. It was big and warm and it felt good having her palm pressed against his skin. "Are you afraid you'll hurt my feelings if you run for real?"

"No. This has nothing to do with you."

He paused for a moment, and Abby shrunk back to her corner, feeling foolish. Of course it had nothing to do with her. Max lived in a different orbit. One where there were beautiful and sophisticated and competent women who intrigued him. Why would he give her or the campaign a second thought?

"Credentials don't mean a thing," he finally said. "If they did, my family would be bugging the hell out of me to run for office. They know better, so they don't."

"You mean, they know you better. They know you aren't interested, so they leave you alone."

He shrugged, that restless energy returning. She saw it in the way he abruptly stood, the way he rammed a hand through his hair. "Yeah. You're probably right." He paced to the window and stared out at the half moon for a moment. "My sister wasn't so lucky. The day she graduated from law school my father and uncle grabbed her and set her up in an office on Newbury Street in Boston."

Abby blinked, her heart growing a little heavy. There was the slightest hint of longing in his voice, just enough to make her understand there was a whole lot more to Max than she'd ever considered.

He turned away from the window and looked at her, a sheepish cast to his features. His gaze quickly flicked away. "Poor kid. It happened so fast, she didn't know what hit her. I think she wanted to work for Greenpeace or something."

It took Abby a moment to remember he was talking about his sister. "Is she younger than you?"

He nodded. "Her name's Victoria. I call her Tori. She's two years younger."

"Shame on you."

Max narrowed his gaze. "What do you mean?"

"As her big brother, you should have given her some lessons in being a stubborn jackass."

He smiled. "When you're right, you're right. Maybe she could have stayed out of Father's clutches."

Abby wanted the subject reverted to him running for mayor, and why his confidence seemed to be lacking in that area. She was dying to learn more about him and his relationship with his family, but he seemed to relax again and she didn't want to spoil their rapport, or chase him off.

"I'm glad you stopped by," she said suddenly.

He sent her a skeptical frown, and she could almost

see the tension coiling in his shoulders again. Maybe he thought she was going to play psychiatrist. Make remarks about his family. About him.

"Didn't mean to shock you." She lifted a shoulder in a flippant shrug. "I was thinking about having a glass of wine and I hate to drink alone."

He looked unconvinced.

"Or I could make us some tea if you prefer." She uncurled her legs and stood, afraid he would leave. Except other than to tackle him, she didn't know what she could do about it if he did. "I have red and white wine, or Oolong tea."

A faint smile touched the corners of his mouth and he took a step toward her. "I thought the phrase went something like, coffee, tea or me?"

Her breath caught in her chest. "I don't have coffee."

He stopped inches in front of her, slid an arm around her waist and hauled her up against him. "No problem. Coffee isn't what I want."

9

IN THE MOMENT it took Max to lower his mouth, Abby was convinced she was having a heart attack. Her entire chest would explode at any minute.

His fingers dug lightly into the bare skin at her waist and heat surged through her like wildfire. If he didn't hurry and kiss her, she was likely to throw herself against him and tumble them both to the couch.

By the time his lips finally touched hers, Abby had no bones left in her legs and she sagged against him. He apparently took her weakness as encouragement, or maybe surrender, and his arm tightened around her, holding her steady for the exploration of his lips on hers, his tongue in her mouth.

Hundreds of thoughts swirled in her head. A series of reasons why she shouldn't be standing here, kissing him, feeling heat and need envelop her, hoping he'd move his hand up her shirt and cup her breast.

She ignored them all when he nibbled the corner of her mouth, trailed the tip of his tongue along her jaw, lightly bit her earlobe. Her deep shuddering breath caused a pleasant friction between his chest and her breasts, and to her horror, she found herself rubbing greedily against him.

He groaned and put his mouth over hers again, grabbing a handful of her hair and pulling her head back so he could drive his tongue inside her eager mouth. Moisture gathered between her thighs. Her breasts ached for his touch.

He pulled back a little and when he looked down at her, his eyes were dark and glazed. Or maybe it was just her. She couldn't see all that well, could barely stand.

"Abby?" His voice was ragged, coarse sounding. It made her want him more. "I didn't come here for this. I swear to God I didn't."

She couldn't speak. Words got lost between her brain and her mouth. She only stared at him, wanting him so badly it scared the hell out of her.

"I hope you believe that." Uncertainty entered his eyes, and she sensed his withdrawal even before his hand fell from her waist.

She did believe him. She knew he'd started the seduction to distract her from the issue, but she didn't care. She took his hand and placed it back on her bare skin. Not in back, but on her stomach, where his fingers slid under her shirt and grazed her breast.

The startled look in his eyes lasted a second, and then satisfaction gleamed as sure as sin. He worked his hand up until the weight of her breast was in his palm, and she closed her eyes, relishing the incredible experience of Max's talented fingers.

A few more seconds and he unsnapped the front of her bra. She smiled when he impatiently pushed the cups aside and kneaded her breast. Her hardened nipple begged for his attention, and when he finally took it between his thumb and forefinger, she thought she'd collapse with pleasure.

"Open your eyes, Abby," he whispered, his breath a balmy breeze caressing her chin. "Look at me."

It took every bit of her strength to do as he asked, and

when she finally lifted her eyelids she was rewarded with the beginning of a beautiful smile.

"You feel so damn good, baby," he whispered, steadily holding her gaze, slowly running his hand over her breast until her nipple prodded the center of his palm.

Then he dipped his head and suckled her through the T-shirt, dampening the fabric with his liquid heat. When he moved to her other breast, she looked down and saw the erotic way the wet material molded to her nipple, and she had the frightening and thrilling desire to pull the shirt over her head and bare herself to him.

He raised his head, but put his hand where his mouth had been before she could feel the loss. He didn't let go while he drew her closer, but kneaded with just the right amount of pressure, and when his lips covered hers again, she eagerly opened her mouth.

His amazing technique and obvious experience should have warned her off. She was no match for him in the sex department, but when he pulled her so close that their hips became one, and his arousal pressed hard and insistent against her stomach, she couldn't think about anything except how much she wanted him pushing inside her.

This time he briefly closed his eyes, a low, guttural sound coming from deep in his throat. His hand left her breast to cup her rear, the other one already there, fingers digging into her flesh, pulling her against him, until he stumbled backward.

Abby grabbed hold of his shirt, barely keeping them steady and upright. A breathless laugh escaped her. A weak grin curved Max's mouth. It faded as his gaze traveled down her body, then fixed on her chest, his jaw tightening, the hand at her waist flexing.

She glanced down. Her shirt had slid down her shoulder and most of her right breast was bared. Only the nipple was hidden by the T-shirt, but he tugged the fabric down another inch and the pearled tip sprung free.

At his sharp intake of breath, her knees went weak. He grasped her tighter around the waist, drawing her up as he slid down until his tongue touched her.

Outside, a car horn blared.

Max ignored it. He took her nipple into his mouth, and suckled her. Hard. Hungrily. And she closed her eyes, giddy with the knowledge she was in his arms, and that the entire night lay ahead of them.

Tentatively, she reached for his top shirt button. It was already unfastened and she trailed her fingers to the next one. She undid it and slipped her hand inside his shirt, his skin warm and firm against her palm.

A horn blared again.

Max cursed under his breath.

She stilled her hand.

He slid back up and kissed her hard on the mouth, started to pull away and kissed her again. "That's Herb," he said, slowly rearing back and looking at her, his voice raspy, his eyes dilated until they were almost black.

Abby took a deep shuddering breath, trying to clear the fog from her brain. Still confused, she gazed back helplessly.

"He dropped me off," Max said, running his palm over her breast, spreading the moisture from his mouth there across her heated skin. "I told him to come back in an hour."

"Oh." She blinked. "I could take you home later."

He stared at her in silence for a moment, his hand stilling. "Don't tempt me."

She gave a small shrug. They both knew what she was

suggesting. Was she insane? She swallowed her pride. "I don't mind driving you home."

A slow, sad smile curved his mouth. "Herb's got a big mouth, Abby."

"Not really."

"The whole town would be talking by noon tomorrow." He brought his hand back down and cupped her breast. Gently he pinched her nipple between his thumb and index finger, and she sucked in a breath. "God, Abby, I want to stay. I just don't think it would be wise."

He was right. Somewhere in her addled brain she knew that, but it was so darn hard to think straight, much less verbalize a coherent sentence. So she nodded, and tried to step away.

Somehow she ended up a step closer.

Max cursed again. He grabbed her upper arms and hauled her against him, kissing her so hard she thought her neck would snap. Then he put her away from him and shook his head. "I've got to go."

"I know," she whispered.

"Before Herb comes to the door."

She pulled up the neckline of her T-shirt, and covered her breast, her shoulder. The fabric was so stretched out that the shirt no longer fit very well, and the neckline drooped.

He helped her adjust it, then tipped her face up to his. "You have to live in this town. I don't want you to do anything you'd be ashamed of tomorrow."

"You're right, of course." Abby moved away, wanting to kick herself for sounding so curt. Why couldn't she sound glib and sophisticated, like this was no big deal?

Except it was a big deal. A huge deal. And, too late,

she already felt ashamed for practically begging him to stay.

"Abby." He reached for her.

She ducked away. "No, I'm okay. I didn't mean to sound so…" She hugged herself, feeling a slight chill. "I don't usually do this sort of thing," she murmured.

He sighed. "I know that."

The horn blared for the third time.

Max hurried to the door and opened it. Just when she thought he was going to leave without saying goodbye, he waved at Herb, then turned back to her. His eyes were so beautiful they made her ache. "I'll call you tomorrow. Okay?"

"Sure."

A wry smile tugged at his mouth. "Could you possibly sound less enthusiastic?"

"Possibly."

"You're damn lucky this door is open and Herb can see me."

"Why?" she asked innocently, amazed she could sound so calm. Because she knew, her entire body knew. His eyes told her the wicked things he wanted to do to her, and the knowledge sent a white-hot thrill through her that scorched her nerve endings.

Max smiled. "I'll show you tomorrow." He stepped outside, but before he closed the door, he said over his shoulder, "Sleep well."

She stayed right where she was long after she heard the lock click into place. Nothing would happen tomorrow. By then she would have regained her wits. Given herself a good talking to. Recalled a hundred times what he'd said earlier—that she had to live in this town. That he didn't—and wouldn't—was left unspoken.

Abby didn't need to hear it aloud to know the truth.

Before long, Max would be gone. At least she'd still have her dignity.

"TAKE ME SOMEPLACE where they have good booze and loud music," Max told Herb as soon as he got in the car.

"At nine-thirty? In Bingo?" Herb laughed. "You got a couple loose screws in your head?"

"Probably." Max sighed, and stared out at the darkness. Not even a streetlight shone. He was in a restless mood, a reckless one. It would be wiser to go back to the Swinging R and go straight to bed. "There's got to be something open."

"You keep picking at that leather," Herb said, glancing over at Max's fidgeting hands, "and you'll be digging deep in your pockets for new upholstery."

Leather? It was some kind of cheap vinyl. Max folded his arms across his chest. "Where do you go when you want a couple of brews?"

"Well..."

"I'm buying."

Herb grinned. "The Watering Hole. It's over in the next county. It'll take us twenty minutes. But don't tell Mona we went there."

Max eyed him with interest. "Why?"

"She doesn't like me drinking."

"Is that why you go all the way to the next county?"

Herb shrugged sheepishly. "No point in getting her riled. Besides, folks wouldn't like seeing you bellying up to the bar either."

"I didn't say I was going to get smashed. Just have a couple." He thought of Abby. Then maybe again, he might get good and plastered.

"Doesn't matter. They wouldn't like their new mayor drinking in public."

"You're kidding?"

"No, siree."

Max shook his head. What did Abby see in this place? Whatever it was, he should be glad of it. Yet one more mark of how different they were.

He needed the reminders. Strange feelings and ideas were making him a little crazy.

"What's the altitude here?" Max asked, and Herb reacted with a bark of laughter.

"Oh, I'd say about a hundred." He laughed again. "This is the desert, Bennett."

Max sighed. He knew that, but he wanted a quick and dirty explanation of why he felt light-headed around Abby. Why he wanted her so much. Too much. Almost an aching need. Like something inside him would be left undone for the rest of his life if he didn't have her.

It scared the hell out of him.

He rolled down the window and let the pleasant desert air hit his face. It was cool and refreshing, though not nearly as cool as it should be for fall, at least not like it was in the East.

But the weather was the least of what made Nevada so different. Attitudes, goals, lifestyles—all vastly differed. Man, they even had scorpions and iguanas. Living out here would be a challenge, not an altogether pleasant one. Yet there were definite advantages...

Why the hell was he even thinking along these lines? He liked his life just the way it was. Pathetic as it sometimes was, it suited him.

Dammit. He'd never once thought of his life as pathetic before. That was a description Taylor would use, and probably Abby if she knew him better.

The thought sliced to the bone.

Sighing, he rammed a hand through his hair. Three days ago life was pretty damn simple. Today it stank.

"You worried about the campaign?"

Max turned to Herb. "What are you talking about?"

His wrist dangled over the steering wheel as he sprawled back, relaxed, as though he'd left the driving to someone else. Max glanced at the speedometer. It was broken, but they had to be going around eighty. Of course there was nothing ahead or behind them. Just acres and acres of moonlit cactus and tumbleweed.

"Your campaign. Coming in this late must have you nervous some. You need any help, just holler."

Max laughed, letting his head thump back against the headrest. "It's a sham, Herb. No one wants me for mayor. They're trying to provoke Abby for some reason, although why, I have no idea. They're damn lucky to have her."

Herb looked away from the road long enough to make Max squirm. "You're wrong."

"Hey, watch the road, will you?"

"I got the Caddy on cruise control."

"That only monitors the speed, which by the way is a little fast. It's not like autopilot."

Herb chuckled and flipped a switch. The car slowed. "Here I thought you were one of those guys who liked fast cars and faster women."

Max stared out his window. He used to be. What had changed? When the hell had it happened?

"Mona tells me you ordered some building material to fix the old porch."

"Yeah, it should get here by the end of the week."

"That must have cost you a pretty penny. Guess that means you're going to—"

"It means," Max cut in, "the porch is unsafe and I

don't want anyone getting hurt. That's it. I still don't know what I'm going to do with the place.''

"But you bought the girls a new refrigerator, too."

Max shrugged. "The old one wasn't working properly. I didn't want them getting food poisoning or something."

Herb slid him a skeptical look. "You wouldn't be dumping money into the place unless you were thinking of keeping it. You're too smart a fella for that."

"Drive, Herb." Max slouched down in his seat and closed his eyes, wishing he could catch a quick nap. Even ten minutes would make him feel better, maybe straighten out his wayward thoughts...about Abby.

She was dangerous for him, more hazardous than the fastest car he'd driven, or the steepest hill he'd skied. She made him want to feel things he wasn't ready to feel.

For God's sake, she had him half thinking he could live in Bingo, Nevada.

"Hey, you know how to two-step?" Herb asked. "They've got a great country-and-western band at The Watering Hole."

Max groaned and slumped lower. Next he'd probably have to learn to square dance. "I've changed my mind."

"What?"

"Take me back to the Swinging R, Herb. I don't need a drink. I need sleep, lots of it." Drinking never once solved a problem. Created some, though.

"Well, hell, we're almost there."

"With the way you drive, you can drop me off and still be almost there."

Herb grunted, slowed the car and made a U turn in the middle of the two-lane highway. "Guess I got you figured wrong."

"How so?" Not that Max really wanted to know, but listening to Herb beat listening to his own crazy thoughts.

"I thought you were one of those big city swingers. Someone I could stay out late and party with."

Max smiled at the thought of "partying" with Herb. "You ever been married?"

"Nope."

"Ever want to?"

"Sure. As soon as I save enough money for a ring, I'm gonna ask Mona. I think."

Max stared at the man's serious profile. "You've been waiting all these years just to save up for a ring?"

"Yup. And because of Estelle. I'm not sure she'd like me getting hitched to Mona."

Max laughed, hard enough that Herb gave him a dirty look. Was this what was in store for Max? Driving around in a beat-up old car, alone.

Nah, Max would at least be driving a Porsche. But he'd still be alone. Looking for the next watering hole. Wondering where he'd gone wrong.

10

"I'LL SEE YOUR BLUE garter and raise you my pink feather boa." Mona leaned back, puffed on her cigar and studied her cards with the keen-eyed precision of a jeweler.

From the doorway, Max scrubbed at his weary eyes. She was the best poker player he'd run across in a long time. That's why he stayed clear every time she or Candy got the cards out. Mona had already taken him for a pair of gold cuff links. "If you're bluffing again, Mona, I'm gonna strangle you with that boa." Candy stared at her cards in indecision, shaking her head, cursing under her breath.

"You're not going to know until you see my bet." Mona smiled, then puffed.

Rosie waved the smoke away as she set down a plate of steaming biscuits on the table. "Better get this table cleared if you all want any breakfast."

Max yawned, and they all turned around to look at him.

"What are you doing awake at ten in the morning?" Rosie's puzzled frown was echoed by all three women.

Mona set down her cigar. "Something wrong?"

Max plowed his way to the coffeepot. "No. I went to bed early." While he poured himself a cup of the strong brew, he caught Mona and Rosie exchanging funny glances. "I know that's no crime here in Bingo," he said, eyeing them suspiciously.

Candy grunted. "I'd get myself back in bed if I were you, then try getting up on the opposite side." She took another look at her cards, muttered something a woman her age shouldn't, then laid her cards down and glared at Mona. "I fold. Let's see what you got."

Mona's laugh was more a cackle. "Bull hockey. I don't have to show you my cards."

"I'm not playing poker with you anymore, and this time I mean it." Candy got up from the table and stormed out of the room.

Mona gathered up her winnings—a couple of garters, several lace hankies and a dollar-off coupon for prunes. "You lie, sister. You'll be begging me to play when our social security checks get here."

Rosie shook her head and wiped her hands on her apron before opening the refrigerator. "I won't. You've cleaned me out for the last time."

Mona smiled at Max. "Wanna play?"

"Yeah, right." Funny how four days ago this scene would have seemed unbelievable to him. But this was life at the Swinging R. And damn if he wasn't getting used to it. "You're a card shark, Mona. I'm not getting bitten twice."

Her gleeful laugh made him smile. "How about we play three out of five hands? If I win, we get a new television."

Max swallowed the hot coffee too fast. The TV they had now really sucked. It took half a day just to warm up. Of course everything around here was in dire shape. He could bankrupt himself without even trying.

Leaning a hip on the counter, he stared into his mug. There wasn't a heck of a lot to do way out here, and surely a modest-sized color TV wouldn't set him that far back…

"Oh, before I forget…" Mona said around the cigar. "Abigail called for you."

Max's head shot up. "This morning?"

Mona had been looking past him, but she met his eyes. "I was talking to Estelle."

Behind him, he heard someone walking across the creaking floor. Estelle had obviously just entered the kitchen.

"Oh," he mumbled.

"Good morning, Max." She touched his shoulder as she passed. "I already spoke to her a few minutes ago. She's on her way over."

"Now?" Max straightened.

"Better get a shirt on if you want breakfast at the table, young man," Rosie said as she set down a plate of crisp bacon.

"Right." He started to put the mug down, but instead poured more coffee and took it with him into his bedroom.

He didn't want breakfast. It was too early to eat, but he didn't want to look like a slob for Abby. While he shaved, he thought about last night and how soft her skin was, and about her utterly perfect breasts.

"Ouch!"

He cringed at the blood trickling from the nick on his chin. A cold shower would have been better, he thought as he blotted the tiny wound, then continued shaving.

Ironically, thinking about her physical attributes got him in a lot less trouble than thinking about the woman herself. Not only was she smart and pretty, but her capacity for caring was beyond anything Max could comprehend. His family of hotshot senators all liked to think of themselves as civil servants. They couldn't hold a candle to Abby.

She had passion, too, and enough enthusiasm to set Bingo on a progressive track. The night of her speech he'd laughed to himself over her grandiose plans for attracting new business to Bingo. He wasn't laughing now. If it could be done, Abby would be the one to do it.

He hurried with his shower and put on the last of his clean clothes. And then he brushed his teeth a second time. His hair wouldn't take long to dry, one of the good things about the lack of humidity in the desert.

By the time he returned to the kitchen, Mona and Rosie had already eaten and gone outside to wait for the UPS man. They'd been in a tizzy all yesterday waiting for their overdue Victoria's Secret shipment. Max hoped he was gone when it got here. There were some things he just couldn't stomach to watch.

Estelle had just sat at the table with a biscuit and homemade strawberry jam in front of her. "What are your plans for today?" she asked, then took a dainty bite.

Max shrugged. "I haven't thought about it yet."

"You have to start planning your campaign, I'd imagine."

He refilled his mug, then grabbed a plate from the cupboard, and took it to the table. The blue glaze around the rim of the dish was chipped, damaged, just like everything else around here. He was tempted to put it back, look for another plate, but he knew better. He wouldn't find one that was in any finer shape.

What the hell was he going to do with this place? With these women? Abby was right. He couldn't turn them out in the cold. He had some sort of responsibility toward them.

Responsibility.

God, he hated that word.

Depend. Rely. All of those words gave him a rash, made him itch to get moving again. Hit the road without looking back.

"Whatever is going on in that head of yours, Maxwell?" Estelle pushed the plate of biscuits toward him. "You look like you're ready to explode."

He sighed, then gave her a weak smile. "You could say that."

"Want to talk about it?"

"Nope." He opened a jar of peach jam. He'd had the strawberry yesterday. "Shouldn't Abby be here already?"

"She had to run over to Ganesville and pick up some posters she had made."

Max frowned. "For her campaign?"

Estelle nodded. "She takes running very seriously."

"I know, but it's not like she has any competition. Voting day will practically be a formality."

"Not since you're running against her. Pass the butter, please."

He handed her the small earthenware crock. "Okay. I can understand Herb and Mona and Virgil thinking my nomination is for real, but you know better, Estelle."

She narrowed her gaze on him. "You'd better be running in earnest. Abby deserves a fair battle, and you—" She looked down at her half-eaten biscuit.

"Yeah?"

"I should've had peach jam, too."

"Estelle."

She smiled and looked shrewdly at him. "I think you have to run—for your own benefit. You need a project to show yourself what you're capable of."

"Running for mayor of a hick—a town like Bingo? I don't think so."

She lifted a shoulder and took a small bite. "No, I think I do like the strawberry better."

Max was definitely not a morning person, and she was trying his patience with this cat-and-mouse stuff. "Why would you say something like that?"

"Because I've been watching you for the past three days."

The uncharitable remark he'd summoned died on his lips when he heard the back stairs creak.

"Gramms?"

"In here, Abby," Estelle called out. "The door's open."

He wiped his palm down his jeans, surprised at how nervous he was suddenly.

Abby opened the door. "Max? What are you doing here?" She looked confused, and then gave Estelle a dirty look.

Obviously the older woman had told her he wouldn't be here. Would Abby not have come if she thought otherwise? That thought rankled. Why would she be hesitant to see him? Last night, she'd wanted him to stay.

His mood plummeted. "Hi, Abby." He didn't answer her question. He figured it was rhetorical.

"Morning, Max." She cleared her throat and stepped into the kitchen with a white box in her hand. "I brought some of those eclairs Mona and Candy like from that bakery over in Ganesville." She sounded funny, nervous. "There's some apple strudel for you and Rosie, Gramms." She set the box on the counter. "Mind if I help myself to coffee?"

Estelle waved a hand. "Of course not. Go right ahead."

"What did you bring me?" Max asked, and he saw the pink seeping into her complexion right before she turned to get a mug from the cupboard.

She got her coffee and turned around, only a trace of color still in her cheeks. "A poster."

"What does it say? Vote for Abby Cunningham?"

She took a seat near Estelle. "How did you know?

"Lucky guess."

They sat in silence for the next few minutes, and not even Estelle tried to revive the conversation. She just kept nibbling at her biscuit. Abby glanced at the wall clock a couple of times, checked her own plain silver wristwatch once.

Max stretched the tension out of his neck, then picked up his mug and plate. "Well, I'll leave you two ladies alone."

"We don't mean to chase you away," Estelle said. "We don't have anything private to discuss."

The look Abby shot her said otherwise.

"I've got a few things to do anyway." Max set his plate in the sink, then refilled his coffee. He was about to put the pot down, but lifted it toward the women instead. "Anyone else?"

Estelle beamed at him. "I'd like a little warm-up."

Strange behavior for him. He usually did for himself, or someone did things for him. But here at the Swinging R, everyone pitched in. Kind of one big happy family, like on the old television series *The Waltons*. Small courtesies seemed to be rubbing off. Wouldn't his family be horrified.

He topped off Estelle's coffee, then moved the pot over Abby's mug. "I'm fine," she said, quickly covering the top with her hand. It trembled slightly.

His eyes met hers. She blinked and looked away.

The knock at the door was a welcome distraction. He saw a short, bald man he didn't recognize through the screen.

Both women turned, and Estelle said, "Come on in, Zeke. Is Martha with you?"

"She's at home." The man stomped his feet so hard on the outside rug, Max prayed the porch wouldn't collapse. "We have a couple of sick chickens she's tending."

Max quickly glanced at Estelle and Abby. They didn't laugh so it obviously wasn't a joke. How the devil did you know when a chicken was sick?

"If you're looking for Mona or Rosie, they're out front. Candy's sulking in her room." Estelle rose and got the man a cup of coffee.

Zeke chuckled. "Mona wipe her out at poker again?"

"Some things never change." Estelle motioned him to a chair. "Did you meet Max?"

"Can't say that I've had the pleasure. Saw you at Abigail's party the other night, Mr. Bennett. I'm Zeke McAllister." He shook Max's hand before taking a seat at the table. "In fact, it's you I come to see."

"Me?" He looked at Abby. She stared at Zeke, her expression troubled.

"Yup. You said you're a lawyer. Am I right?"

"Yeah. I mean, no." Max drew a hand over his face and blew his frustration into his palm. He should have gotten out of here while he could. "I'm a lawyer. At least I went to law school."

"That's good enough for me. I want to sue Tom Sawyer."

Max squinted, waiting for the punch line. When no one spoke, he asked, "The fictional character?"

"No, my neighbor."

Max looked at Abby again. This time she looked back. "His neighbor's name is Tom Sawyer?" he asked her, trying to gauge the guy's mental health.

She nodded, her eyes gleaming with amusement.

"Why are you asking her? Didn't I just tell you Tom's my neighbor?" Zeke muttered under his breath, then took a noisy sip of coffee.

Ignoring him, Max smiled at Abby, relieved to see her acting normal again.

"Aren't you going to ask me why I wanna sue Tom?" Zeke stared at him. "Being as you're my lawyer, I'd think you wanna know."

Max blew out an exasperated breath. "I'm not your attorney."

"You have to be. Southby is fishing, as usual. And there's no other lawyer around for over fifty miles." Zeke's face creased in a frown. "Besides that, you fixed Jed Hinkley's problem. You can't be showing favorites if you're running for mayor."

"Jed Hinkley?" The name sounded familiar to Max.

"He runs the drugstore and post office."

Max nodded, remembering. "I didn't do any legal work for him. He was worried about keeping the required postal hours and still being able to run his store. I only suggested he move the post office to a spare counter near the pharmacy section."

"See, that's what I mean. You handled it all nice and tidy. That's all I'm asking." Zeke took another sip, then waited for Max to respond.

He was tempted to point out the difference between common sense and legal work, but he didn't want to insult the old guy. Looking to Abby and Estelle for help proved vain. They just sat there with blank looks on their faces, waiting for him to answer.

Man, he was going to hate himself for doing this, but he pulled out a chair and sat down. "What's the problem?"

"It's like this…" In contrast to his bald head, Zeke's bushy eyebrows drew together over his suddenly animated face. "Tom and me share the same oleander hedge separating our driveways. For thirty-four years we've taken turns trimming it in a nice round shape. Now he's got this darn fool idea to make it square."

Max waited in silence for the rest of the story, but it seemed none was forthcoming. Zeke got up to refill his coffee, then sat down again and stared expectantly at Max. "And?"

"And?" Zeke stiffened. "And he's gonna start cutting it into a square tomorrow morning no matter what I say. It's up to you to stop him."

Max wondered what horrible thing he'd done in a past life that was making this one seem like a bad cartoon. "Let me get this straight. You want to file a lawsuit over this."

"I have no choice. When he came up with this harebrained idea three years ago, I was able to talk him out of it. This time he says he's having things his way."

Max massaged the back of his neck, and sighed.

"Zeke, this isn't a legal matter," Abby began, but Max gave her a sign he'd handle it.

Which was probably a mistake. She knew these people. She'd know what to say. But he always passed off his problems—to his attorney, Taylor, to his accountant, or to anyone else who was willing to clean up after him. This time he wanted to handle things himself. God help him.

"Are you and Tom friends?" Max asked.

"Used to be," Zeke muttered.

"This is important. Do you consider Tom Sawyer your friend?"

"Well, of course. I've known him for forty-three years. Been living next to his ornery hide for most of them."

"How important is your friendship?"

Zeke pursed his lips, his forehead creasing in thought. "It's important—unless he touches those hedges."

Max shook his head. "No 'unless,' and no 'buts'. Either the friendship is important to you or it isn't. I advise you to decide before you take any kind of legal action. Because once you do, I've seen more than friendships go straight down the tubes."

The older man's expression remained petulant but he seemed a little rattled, too. "Why does he have to have his way?"

"Didn't you say he'd brought this up three years ago?" Max asked, and Zeke nodded. "Seems to me you've had your way for a while now. Maybe it's his turn?"

Zeke glanced at Abby and Estelle, then leaned back in his chair and folded his arms. The stubborn glint in his eye was still there but he seemed to be mellowing.

"It's all a matter of what's more important—people or things," Max said, and Zeke's expression immediately softened. "It's your call."

"Guess I never thought of it that way before."

"I can file papers today, if you like. Serve Tom with a summons by tomorrow, have him thrown in jail if he doesn't comply," Max said with a straight face. Not only did he have no legal grounds to execute any of those threats, he wasn't even licensed to practice law in Nevada.

"Jail? What the hell is the matter with you?" Zeke unfolded his arms and rubbed his pudgy jaw. "I don't want him in jail." He glared at Max for a moment, and then he blinked and a grin curved his mouth. "You're a pretty cagey fella, you know that? You knew I didn't want him in jail."

"I hoped you didn't." Max slapped both hands on the table, prepared to get up. "Can we consider the matter settled?"

"Not so fast." Zeke reached into his back pocket and pulled out his wallet. "How much do I owe you for your legal advice?"

Max laughed. "You don't—" The look he got from Abby made him falter. He had no idea what she was trying to tell him with the peculiar faces she was making.

Finally she said, "Zeke, why don't you just let him bill you? That's how it's usually done."

"Not with me." The man shook his head, his expression proud and stubborn. "You know I pay what I owe."

Max looked at Abby for a cue. She simply gave a slight shake of her head. He was on his own. "Tell you what, Zeke. I don't accept money for my services because I'm not that good with numbers, but I could use a good arm with a hammer. You know anything about carpentry?"

"Built two of my own chicken coops."

"Well, if you're not doing anything Saturday, we'll be getting a shipment of lumber and we could use some help repairing a couple of things around here."

Zeke grinned and stood. Max also got to his feet so he could accept the hand the older man offered. "I'll be here, right after sunup."

Sunup? "Great," Max said, his lack of enthusiasm undisguised.

"You're a mighty damn fine lawyer. Of course you already know that."

Max snorted. The poor old guy didn't know what he was talking about. Still, Max had solved the problem, and he had to admit it felt pretty good. Damn good, actually.

Zeke went to the bakery box and pulled out an eclair. "Jed's right. You'll make a damn fine mayor, too."

Max frowned and automatically looked at Abby. She tried to hide the hurt caused by Zeke's thoughtless remark, and she did a good job, sitting there without so much as a twitch. But Max had seen her eyes before she'd shuttered them. He'd seen the pain of betrayal.

Anger boiled in his gut, and he used every ounce of willpower he possessed to keep his mouth shut. She wouldn't appreciate him speaking up or defending her. Abby liked standing up for herself. But this was her town, dammit, they should be on her side.

Afraid he would say or do something he'd regret, he promptly headed for the back door. "Good luck," he said over his shoulder to Zeke. He forced a smile for Abby and Estelle, and left without a clue as to where he was going.

Feeling numb, Abby sat silently while Gramms and Zeke exchanged a few pleasantries. Funny, how she'd been worried about seeing Max again after last night. She'd been excited, scared, anxious. Now, she was glad for his abrupt departure. She wished Zeke would leave, too.

Almost as if she'd willed it, he got up, said his goodbyes and left. After several minutes of silence, she looked up.

Gramms watched her with a troubled frown. "You know Zeke didn't mean anything, honey. He's just tickled Max paid him some attention."

Abby managed a weak smile. "The thing is, he's right, Gramms. Max was really good. I would never have been that patient. I'd have sent Zeke back home to fight his own battle.''

''And that would have been okay, too. You have a history with these people. You know their quirks. Zeke would have gone home and argued with Tom a few more days, then everything would have blown over.''

Abby nodded, not because she agreed, but because she wanted to drop the subject. ''Let's discuss why you asked me out here. You said you're thinking of coming home.''

''Not exactly.'' She had the good grace to look sheepish because that was *exactly* what she'd implied. ''I said I hoped to not be staying here much longer.''

Abby raised her brows. She should have been furious that Gramms had dragged her out here under false pretenses when she had so much work to do, but her mind kept straying to Max.

''You might as well know...'' Gramms hesitated, and started fidgeting. ''I'm going to just come out with it. I'm sweet on Herb Hanson, and if he asks me to marry him, I'm accepting.''

''What?'' Abby gaped. ''Herb! What about Mona?''

''Oh, Mona doesn't want to marry him, or anybody else. Or she'd have done it long ago. Me, I mean business. Haven't I already buried two husbands?''

Abby groaned and laid her head on the table. She knew she shouldn't have gotten out of bed this morning.

11

ABBY PAID for her barely touched English muffin and hot chocolate, then paused at the window of Edna's Edibles and stared out at the banner being strung across Virgil's general store. It urged people to "Vote for Max Bennett for Mayor."

Her stomach cramped and she was glad she hadn't finished her breakfast. Of course she hadn't had much of an appetite since going out to the Swinging R yesterday and discovering her life had gone to hell in a handbasket.

"Hey, am I glad I ran into you. You just get here?"

She stiffened at the sound of Max's voice, then slowly turned around. "No, I'm on my way out." She frowned. "I was at the counter. I didn't see you."

Max smiled, a special smile that reminded her he'd kissed her senseless. He'd seen her bare breasts. He'd like to see them again.

She swallowed and started toward the door.

"Wait a minute." He laid a warm, caressing hand on her arm and she nearly jumped through the roof. "I just got here. Through the back door. Can't you stay for a cup of coffee?"

"The back door, huh? Gee, aren't we getting cozy? Edna is very particular about who she lets use the back."

He shrugged, his mouth still curved in a grin. "Maybe it's because I told her she makes the best peach pie I've ever had."

"I'm sure you're right." Abby made a soft sound of resignation. All Max had to do was smile and half the women in Bingo would give him the key to their chastity belt. She didn't blame them. Even she was tempted to cavort with the enemy.

"What's with the long face?" he asked, his expression sobering. "I know I didn't do anything. I'm not the one not returning phone calls."

She raised her brows in innocence. "Did you call? My answering machine hasn't been working very well."

The way he studied her, his eyes full of confusion and doubt, it was obvious he knew she was lying. "You could have called me. After the other night I thought—"

Abby grabbed his shirt sleeve and pulled him toward the only empty booth in the corner. The small diner was crowded and too many eyes and ears were tuned in their direction.

"I take it this means you'll have coffee with me." Max gave her a wry smile as he took a seat across from her. When their knees touched, she angled hers to the side. He noticed, and frowned.

"Half the town is staring at us. The other half have their antennas up."

"So?"

"So?" She made a face. "Duh, what do you think?"

"We're adults."

"At least one of us is."

Max chuckled. "Okay, so I don't want to grow up. Sue me."

Abby stared down at a heart etched on the table top. "You think this is a big joke, don't you?"

"Are you referring to the other night? I swear I tried to call—"

"Shhh..." Abby glanced around. At least eight pairs

of eyes were trained on them. "Are you bound and determined to let the entire town know what a sucker I am?"

She pressed her lips together. She hadn't meant to say that. And he sure hadn't expected it, judging by the sudden grim expression on his face.

He stared warily at her until Edna came to take their coffee order, and then he flashed the older woman only a brief smile before returning his somber attention to Abby. "I hope you plan on explaining what you meant."

"Nothing." She straightened and let her gaze stray around the diner. People were starting to leave, some of them probably late for their jobs after lingering to watch her and Max.

He hadn't said a word in the past minute, and when she tentatively looked his way, his troubled gaze awaited hers. "Nothing? That doesn't wash, Abigail."

Edna brought their coffee to the table prompting another stretch of silence. Even the usually talkative owner must have sensed the tension, because she turned away so quickly she almost forgot to leave the cream for Max.

After she set it in front of him and scooted to the next table, he said quietly, "We can go someplace else and talk about this, if you like, but we *will* talk about it."

Abby sighed. She knew he meant business. There was little evidence of his normally easygoing disposition. "Look, about the other night." She glanced around. No one was near enough to hear. "I don't usually do that sort of thing."

"I know that, Abby." He looked disappointed, maybe even hurt. "What is going on in that head of yours? I didn't take anything we did lightly, either. I want to see you again."

"You're seeing me now."

"Abby."

She took a sip of coffee, trying to stall. "Look, let's discuss it after the election. I don't think we should socialize while we're running against each other."

He laughed. "Come on. Get serious."

"I am serious. I don't think it looks good for us to be doing anything but discussing business."

"Abby, I'm not a serious candidate."

She stared at the genuine astonishment on his face and didn't know what to think. "Everyone else thinks you are."

"Of course they don't. They're just trying to give you a hard time, and create a little excitement, make it seem like a real election," he said, and she gave him a blank look. "You know what I mean. I'm not even a good prospect."

That wasn't the first time he'd discounted his credentials and it bothered her. "I'd say they think you are. Have you seen Virgil's store lately?"

He frowned. "Why?"

She inclined her head toward the window. "Have a look."

Max eyed her with suspicion, as if he thought she was playing some sort of prank on him. He didn't get up, but he leaned way over to the left and craned his neck for a look. He blinked, then an expression of horror crossed his face. "Are they nuts?"

"I wouldn't suggest you ask them."

He kept staring out the window at the banner. When he finally straightened and brought his attention back to her, he said, "These people seriously need to get lives."

"You're not going to get votes making cracks like that."

He snorted. "You must think this is all pretty hilarious."

"I don't follow you."

"You know you have this election all sewed up, and all you have to do is sit back and watch everyone make fools of themselves."

"Now, I really don't follow." She shook her head in confusion. "I admit, I had been somewhat smug a week ago, but that was before I had some real competition."

"You can't mean me." He slumped, shaking his head. "Okay, I realize, they all might not know better, but you do." He ran a hand through his hair and glanced nervously around the diner. The place had mostly emptied out. "I haven't done a single worthwhile thing in my life, and I don't see me changing my pattern anytime soon."

"You big fraud."

"Yeah." He scrubbed at his eyes. "Guess that about covers it."

"No, that's not what I mean. What do you call what you've been doing around the Swinging R? You're replacing appliances, getting repairs done, and Mona told me about how you're using your broker to invest their social security savings in order to get a better return on their money."

He sent her a wary look. "So?"

"They may not know that most brokers couldn't be bothered handling the piddling amount of money they have to invest, but I do—which means you pulled strings. And from the amount of return Mona's expecting, I'd guess maybe you even sweetened their pot with some of your own funds?"

He shifted uncomfortably. "So? You said yourself they were my responsibility."

Abby smiled. "Not exactly. But I do admire what you're doing. I'm sure everyone else does, too."

"Yeah, well, Mona's got a big mouth. She shouldn't be telling people our business out at the Ranch."

"Get used to it. Not too much is private in this town. Anyway, that kind of concern and action is what people look for in a mayor."

Surprise flickered in his eyes, and then pride. It was fleeting, but she was certain she saw it before Max exhaled loudly and turned toward the window, his expression blank.

She gave him a few moments of silence, then asked, "Why are you so hard on yourself?"

His gaze shot back to hers. "You are so far off the mark it's a joke. If there's an easy way out, believe me, I take it. I am never hard on myself."

Abby pressed her lips together. She was tempted to nail him for deliberately misunderstanding her. But something in his voice, the tension in his eyes, warned her to back off. She was getting too personal, possibly even hitting a nerve, and he didn't like it. Or maybe she was provoking a thought he'd rather not pursue.

"I have a question for you." He leaned forward, his eyes narrowed. "Why aren't you royally pissed off at these people? They shouldn't even be thinking about another candidate with you willing to be mayor."

Caught off guard, she struggled for a retort. His gaze grew more speculative and she looked away, fearful of what her eyes might reveal. "I already told you I want the best person to be mayor. If that means you..." She swallowed, and forced a smile. "Then I'll fully endorse your win. I won't take it personally."

"You should, dammit."

Abby relaxed. He looked so ready to slay a dragon for

her, it wasn't hard to smile after all. It was a heady feeling, seeing him look so fierce in her defense. Made her mind go in a direction it shouldn't. "Where would it get me?"

His lips curved in resignation, and he reached across the table for her hand. "Well, I'm not so noble. I'm pissed at them. Hell, I'm not even going to stick around, and they have to know that."

She left her hand beneath the warm reassurance of his, even while Edna gawked. Abby didn't know what felt worse—the reminder that he'd be gone soon, or the fact that the people of Bingo had betrayed her. Both thoughts hurt like hell.

Max brushed his thumb across the inside of her wrist and smiled at her, his eyes riveted to hers. "We're making progress. You didn't jerk away."

"And Edna's already headed for the telephone."

"Then you might as well have dinner with me since the damage is already done."

"I don't know..." She tried to pull away, but he wouldn't let go. "We could always claim you were merely reading my palm."

"That wouldn't be a lie. I can do that. I learned in Budapest about a year ago," he said with such a straight face as he turned over her palm, she wasn't sure if he was serious. "An old gypsy woman traded me the secret for a solid gold lighter."

"You don't smoke."

"You're ruining my story."

"Sorry."

"Let's see." He stared down at her palm, his forehead creasing in concentration. "Hmm, that's interesting..."

"What?"

"Keep still." He pulled her hand closer, forcing her

to lean across the table. His gaze stalled on her mouth for a moment, his naughty thoughts as clear as a crystal ball, before he refocused on her palm. "Looks like you're going to have a long life. A very public one."

She bit back a grin at the mock seriousness of his tone and expression. "As in political?"

"Wait." He peered closer, then looked up in awe. "You didn't tell me you wanted to be president."

"Right. I can't even get my neighbors to vote for me."

Her voice cracked, and her joking remark fell flat. Embarrassed, she yanked her hand back.

"Abby?" Concern wiped the humor from his face.

"That was a joke."

Raucous laughter came from somewhere near the cash register, and they turned to see Virgil and Zeke entering the diner. Virgil spotted them immediately and headed straight for Max.

"We've been looking for you, son." Virgil stopped halfway to snuff out his cigar. Everyone knew Edna would have his hide if he stunk up her diner. "Got something to show you."

Max sighed and glanced at Abby. "Save me and I'll be your slave for life," he whispered urgently.

"Don't forget," she murmured back, so darn glad for the interruption she could kiss Virgil. "I'm going to be around for a very long time."

He gave her a smile that warmed her all the way to her peach-tinted toenails. "Is that supposed to be a threat?"

"Okay, you two, enough of this goo-goo eyes stuff." Virgil stopped at their table, not quite close enough for Abby to give him a swift kick but she still fantasized about it. "We need to get down to business. You done with that coffee, Bennett?"

Max sprawled back in the booth and gave Virgil and Zeke a lazy grin. "Yup, done with the coffee. But not done making goo-goo eyes, so why don't you two be good boys and scram?"

Virgil's sagging jowl sagged another inch and he gaped at Max. "What do you have a burr up your butt for? We only wanted to show you something."

"Rudeness rarely gets my attention."

"Rude?"

"You were pretty darn rude, Virgil," Zeke said, shaking his head. "I gotta agree with Max on that one." Zeke leaned closer to Max. "It sure worked out swell with my neighbor, Tom. Glad you talked me out of that foolish lawsuit. Thanks again."

The admiration in the older man's face and voice brought a gleam of pride to Max's eyes and warmed Abby's heart. She sat back and listened to Virgil murmur a grudging apology, then embark on his version of how Max's campaign should be run.

It was interesting to watch Max interact with the other men. His guard was relaxed and his reactions were often quite unexpected, especially when compliments or praise were involved. It was obvious that although Max may have grown up with wealth and privilege, he sure hadn't received a lot of strokes to his ego.

"What do you think, Abigail?"

At the sound of her name, she looked at Virgil. So busy analyzing Max, she didn't have a clue what the older man wanted. "I've got to be running along. My first class starts soon." She rose and smoothed her skirt. "Thanks for the coffee, Max."

"Don't forget about dinner," he said, oblivious to the annoyingly curious interest of Virgil and Zeke. "I'll call you."

"I'm pretty tied up tonight..." She squeezed between two chairs to get to the door, and noticed Edna wiping the same clean table over again.

"I'll call," he repeated, watching her intently despite Virgil's attempt to claim his attention.

She gave him a tight smile, waved and slipped out the door. It was a cool morning and she gratefully breathed in the crisp air. When she looked up and saw the big bold banner with Max's name on it, she had to take another breath.

It was like a slap in the face to see the town so excited over the prospect of a newcomer, a stranger they didn't know, running against her. Abby could half understand why the women were all atwitter and eager to welcome Max as their new mayor. With Max's megawatt smile and sexy green eyes, it was no surprise the female population gravitated toward him.

And then there was Max himself. A guy as good looking and rich and smart as him should have had an ego the size of Hoover Dam. And in some respects he did, but there was still that little boy in him who glowed with pride every time someone sought his advice, or he was able to help in some way.

Abby had seen it several times now, and that was the only reason she hadn't come unglued. A perverse side of her wanted Max to win, wanted him to have tangible proof that he was worthy of the town's confidence. The other part of her hurt so badly she wanted to drop out of the race, childishly let them all drown in their ignorance when they realized Max wasn't a long-haul kind of guy.

Ironically, the last time she'd felt this conflicted was right after college when she'd had the fleeting desire not to return to Bingo. The turmoil had only lasted a couple of days before she made her final decision. Foolishly, she'd thought Bingo needed her.

She dragged her gaze away from the banner, and glanced around, afraid someone would see her feeling sorry for herself. But she wasn't really, she thought as she hurried down the street toward the school. Because she was beginning to think that Max needed to win this election. And she'd just decided to do everything she could to help him.

MAX FELT LIKE A HEEL. No, he felt more like the scummy stuff that sometimes got stuck to the bottom of his shoe.

Virgil rambled on while Max watched Abby dash down the street, *after* she'd taken a long tortured look at the newly hung banner over Virgil's store.

She was hurt over the town's cavalier attitude toward her, no matter what she said, and Max was kidding himself if he thought otherwise. The problem was, he hadn't thought too much at all. He knew Abby's future position as mayor was secure. He was no threat. These people were morons. Incredibly naive, anyway, and he didn't expect he'd change that, but somebody had to stop them from hurting Abby, and show them some gratitude was in order.

"Bennett?" Virgil's bark snapped Max out of his preoccupation. "Are you listening to me?"

"As a matter of fact, I'm not," Max said, already distracted again, as he got up from the table. "I have something I need to do. I'll see you boys later."

Virgil sputtered. "This is important."

"Right," Max said absently as he laid some money on the table, then left the two men sitting there with stunned looks as he exited the diner.

First he had to call Taylor, and get her to liquidate some of his assets. Next he had to figure out what to do about Abby. She needed to win this election. And he was going to do everything he could to help her.

12

ABBY GRADED yesterday's homework papers, prepared lesson plans for the next two weeks and vacuumed every room in her house. It was eight-forty, and still Max hadn't called.

She shouldn't care, and she didn't, really. In fact, she'd already rehearsed her refusal to his dinner invitation. Except he hadn't called in order for her to refuse him. The rat.

After flipping on the television, she settled on the sofa with an industrial-sized package of peanut M&M's. She hoped it was enough. Self-pity required lots and lots of chocolate, and a good swift kick in her behind. She figured she'd save the kick for tomorrow.

Abby had just popped two candies into her mouth when the phone rang. She didn't know if she should swallow them whole or spit them out. She chewed as she dashed to the phone, then took a quick time-out, taking two deep breaths, so she wouldn't sound breathless. She picked up the receiver, but before she could answer, she heard Mona's voice.

"Abigail? Abigail? Are you there? We need you here quick."

The panic in the other woman's voice waylaid Abby's disappointment. "Mona? Calm down. Is it Gramms?"

"No, it's Max. You gotta come right away."

"Max?" Abby's heart took a dive. "What's wrong?"

"You're wasting time, Abigail. Get down here."

"Okay." She took a deep breath and glanced at her parents' grandfather clock. "I can be there in fifteen minutes."

"Oh, we aren't at the Swinging R. Come to Birdie's." Mona hung up before Abby could ask her what the dickens they were doing at Bingo's only bar, which usually closed about now.

Fortunately, Abby already had on a decent outfit, which had nothing to do with the fact that Max might have shown up unexpectedly. So she grabbed her purse and keys, and jumped in her car. All the way to town she told herself nothing was seriously wrong, that Mona had probably overreacted to something Max had said. Still, Abby arrived at Birdie's five minutes later when it would normally take nine.

Five cars were parked in the small lot, which was unusual for this time of night. Everyone knew Birdie closed promptly at eight-forty-five so he could make it home in time to watch reruns of *The Beverly Hillbillies.*

The door was unlocked and Abby slipped quietly inside, hoping to get her bearings and maybe a quick assessment before everyone started talking at her at once. It was easy to remain undetected. A crowd of about a dozen people were preoccupied with something happening at the bar. To her relief, no one seemed panicked or distraught, so it couldn't be anything too awful.

Virgil had one of his bulldog frowns on his face, and Zeke just kept shaking his head with a look of dismay. Mona and Rosie both looked somewhat upset, but probably more stunned than anything else. Abby couldn't see Gramms or Herb.

She lifted herself on tiptoes but still couldn't see what was going on. Then Zeke leaned toward Virgil, and said,

"You think this has to do with Abigail standing him up for dinner?"

"Could be," Virgil said. "Damn shame, ain't it?"

"Bartender! Where's that whiskey I ordered?"

Abby blinked at Max's loud, garbled voice. He sounded...drunk.

"I already told you, buddy, we're closed." Birdie had never been Bingo's most patient resident, and he sounded as though he was about ready to string Max up. "Now, get out!"

"Whoever heard of a bar closing this early? What kind of hick town is this?" Max's words were slurred.

As soon as Abby could feel her legs again, she stepped forward. One by one, everyone turned to look at her, and the murmuring started.

"Thank goodness you're here," Mona said. "Maybe you can talk some sense into him."

Abby stared at the back of Max's head. His hair was a mess and he was slumped over the bar. "What happened?"

"What the devil do you think happened?" Virgil asked with disgust. "The idiot got stinking drunk."

"Probably because you stood him up," Zeke muttered, sending Abby a peevish glance.

"Who you calling an idiot?" Max turned around with a thunderous look on his face. He saw Abby, and grinned. "Hi, baby, when did you get here?"

"Oh, Max." Sighing, she slowly walked toward him.

"What's the matter, honey? You don't look too good." He squinted at her as if he were having trouble seeing. "Hey, Birdie," he yelled, "get Abby a whiskey, too."

Birdie Weaver pulled the towel from around his neck and threw it on the bar. "Abigail, I'm giving you three minutes to get him out of here," he said, then started furiously scrubbing the top of the old scarred oak bar that had been in his family for three generations.

Max pounded a fist and almost landed on the floor when he missed the bar. He righted himself, then swayed to the left. "Get me out of here? Is that any way to treat your next mayor?"

Birdie howled with laughter. "Next mayor, my foot. No one's gonna vote for you, buddy, not now." Birdie looked at Abby. "You got two minutes." He hitched up his pants. "Or I get to throw the bum out myself."

"Now you're calling me a bum?" Max leaned over the bar toward the much bigger man.

Abby grabbed his arm and pulled him back. "Come on, Max, let's go get some coffee."

He smiled down at her. "Hi, Abby."

She slipped an arm around his waist and urged him away from the bar. "Can you make it to my car? It's right outside."

"Of course I can, honey." He stopped and didn't budge when she tried to drag him. "You smell good," he said, then lowered his head and kissed her in front of everyone.

She pulled her head back, but kept hold of him. "Knock it off, Max. Now, walk."

"Here, I'll give you a hand," Virgil said, stepping forward.

"You wanna help?" Max winked at him. "Go get Abby and me a bottle."

"Max?" Abby waited for him to look at her. "Shut up."

He widened his eyes. "You're not mad at me, are you, honey?"

Virgil started to take his arm, but Abby waved him

away. "No, Max, I'm not mad, but I will be if you don't go to the car with me right now."

She spoke to him as if he were a child, and obediently he nodded his head. He didn't make another sound all the way outside except to yawn. When they got to the car, she had to hold him up with one hand, while opening the door with her other.

Everyone had followed them outside, but they hung back without saying a word or offering any help, which suited her just fine. She wanted to get Max out of here, sober him up, then find out what the heck had gotten into him.

She got Max settled in the passenger seat, then went around the front of the car to her side when someone yelled, "Where you taking him?"

"Not to your house," Virgil said, his voice a warning.

"She's taking him to the Swinging R, you big bozo." Mona pushed through the crowd toward the car, then motioned Rosie to follow. "Can we get a ride with you, Abigail? Herbie is supposed to pick us up but no telling when he'll show."

Abby hesitated. She actually had planned on taking him to her place, but that was probably a bad idea. "Sure, come on."

The women piled into the back, and amazingly, said not a word all the way to the Swinging R. Max alternated between mumbling and snoring. And Abby kept thinking how unreal this whole night had turned out to be. If she hadn't seen Max in this pathetic condition with her own eyes, she'd never have believed it.

The porch light was on, and Candy came out in a frilly pink robe as soon as Abby cut the engine. The iguana was nowhere in sight, and thank God for that. In his present state, Max probably would have had boots made out of the poor critter.

"Is he all right?" Candy asked, her hands on her hips, a worried frown on her face.

Mona got out first. "He will be, after the nasty hangover he's sure to have."

"We probably ought to start forcing some water down him." Candy ducked to peer into the car her expression still one of concern. "That'll keep him hydrated and help ease some of the sting later."

Abby climbed out of the car, and glanced at Candy with interest. The woman had made no bones about not liking Max and his attitude toward her pet iguana, but obviously something had shifted.

"Rosie, why don't you help Abigail?" Mona stopped on the bottom step and pulled her crocheted shawl more snugly around her narrow shoulders. "I'll go make sure his bed is cleared off in case we have to dump him quick like. Candy will hold the door open for you."

Candy nodded, and Rosie already had Max's door open. Abby wasn't about to turn down the help. She didn't think she could get him inside by herself, especially if she couldn't wake him up entirely.

She took a deep breath, then shook his shoulder. "Come on, Max, we're home. Wake up."

He mumbled something unintelligible but didn't move a muscle. She shook him again, and this time he slid to his left and ended up sprawled across the center console and the driver's seat.

Abby groaned, leaned into the car and grabbed his shirt. She tugged, but he wouldn't budge. "I ought to let him sleep it off out here."

"I don't know, Abigail." Rosie shook her head and

rubbed her hands up and down her arms. "The temperature is starting to drop."

"Good. It would serve him right." But that didn't mean Rosie had to suffer in the meantime. "Go on inside, Rosie. I'll take care of Max."

"You're going to need help getting him out of there."

"I'll just go get Tami and put her in the driver's seat. I figure that'll motivate him to get his butt out."

Max stirred.

Rosie chuckled. "I imagine that would. Now, if you're sure you don't need me..."

"Nah, I'd rather you go make a pot of coffee, if you don't mind."

"Good idea." Rosie paused on the porch steps, and Abby noticed that thick redwood boards now replaced the rotting wood planks. Had Max replaced them himself? "You want me to bring you a sweater?" Rosie asked.

"No, thanks. One way or the other, I won't be long." Abby leaned in and shook his shoulder again. When he didn't move, she added, "Want me to bring Tami to keep you company?"

He sat up abruptly and mumbled, "Where are we?"

"At the Swinging R. You can get up while I'm here to help, or you can sleep in my car all night."

He muttered a curse, then said, "Give me a hand."

Abby gripped his upper arm, and he swung one of his legs out of the car. It took him another couple of minutes to get the other one out. And then he rested his elbows on his thighs and cradled his head in his hands.

She stepped back and folded her arms across her chest, tapping her foot, waiting for him to pull himself together. She sincerely hoped he felt like crap, and had a headache like a marching band. He deserved it for pulling such a juvenile stunt.

"Is he okay?" Candy called out anxiously from the porch.

Abby had forgotten the woman was still there. "I hope not." At the alarm on Candy's face, Abby relented. "He's fine. You don't have to wait out here. We'll be in shortly."

Candy said nothing else, but she stayed put and continued to look on with concern.

Max looked up through bleary eyes. "Where's that whiskey I ordered?"

Abby let out a low shriek. "If I get you a whiskey I'm pouring it over your head." She grabbed his arm again with a rough jerk. "Up. Right now."

He stood, unsteadily, then took small uneven steps with her prompting. "Hi, Candy, don't you look pretty in that fluffy pink thing." He gave the older woman a big goofy grin.

Candy smiled sadly back and came to the top of the steps in her fuzzy house slippers to help him up. "You big silly lug. What'd ya go out and do this for?"

Abby tried to concentrate on safely guiding Max, instead of on the other woman's surprising turnaround in attitude. "Watch your footing, Max."

He leaned more heavily on her, slipping an arm tighter around her waist and pulling her against him. Rubbing his chin on the top of her hair, he sighed. "Thanks, Abby."

His voice sounded so normal suddenly that she almost stumbled. She briefly glanced at him, then returned her attention to navigating the steps.

She heard a car pull up just as they crossed the threshold, but she didn't look back, not wanting to lose momentum as she propelled him toward the hall leading to the bedrooms.

"He's in Lily's old room," Candy said. "The first one on the right."

The door was open, and even with him plastered against her, Abby managed to turn the corner without incident. Mona had just turned down the bed. She picked up a pillow and fluffed it before propping it up against the ornately carved antique mahogany headboard.

"I heard a car," Mona said. "Is it Herbie?"

"I don't know." Relieved to see the end in sight, Abby paused to catch her breath. Boy, was she out of shape. Of course, Max was pure muscle and not easy to haul around.

He brought his head up and squinted as though he had trouble seeing. "Hi, Mona, when did you get home?"

Mona rolled her eyes. "I'll get the coffee."

"I'm having second thoughts on that," Abby said. She dragged him the last few feet and let him topple to the bed. All but one of his legs made it. "Maybe we should let him sleep. He'll come to soon enough."

She yanked off his loafer and lifted his leg onto the peach satin sheets. From the other side of the bed, Mona pulled off his other shoe, then drew the cream-colored lace quilt up to his chin.

He looked so out of place in the feminine bedroom, especially such a flamboyantly decorated one. The women hadn't changed a thing since Lily passed on. The eccentric madam had always been one of Bingo's most colorful characters. Until tonight, it had been hard to believe Max was related to her.

Abby almost reconsidered giving him coffee. She was too darn curious to wait until tomorrow to find out what had happened, why he'd made such a foolish spectacle of himself. It didn't make sense. This was not at all like him.

"Seems to me he'll be out for a while. I'm gonna go see if that's Herbie." Mona frowned. "You wouldn't happen to know where Estelle is, would you?"

Abby shook her head. "I assumed she was here. What time did she go out?"

"Don't worry. I have a feeling she might be home now." Mona left with a long face, which made Abby guess Gramms's absence had something to do with Herb.

Just what Abby needed. A feud between Mona and Gramms on top of her drunk...

Her errant thoughts made her pulse skid. What was Max to her? A friend? A colleague of sorts? Or a...

She bit her lip, and stared down at his unshaven face. His beautiful, unshaven face. Her heart and stomach got all fluttery. How could she feel this way about him in less than a week?

Tentatively, she reached out a hand and smoothed back his hair. She let her fingers lightly trail down his cheek, the roughness of his day-old beard sending a shiver through her. "Ah, Max, what happened to you today?"

He startled her by grabbing hold of her wrist and tugging her toward him. She sat awkwardly on the edge of the bed, and stared at his still-closed eyes.

He slowly opened them, smiled, then closed them again. She'd thought he'd dozed off, but his grip was still surprisingly firm when she tried to disengage her hand. Instead of releasing her, he drew her toward him.

"Max?"

He kept his eyes closed but continued to tug her hand until she was almost lying across his chest. Poised awkwardly over him, she braced herself with one hand on the pillow beside his head. Their faces were only inches apart. She could kiss him and he probably wouldn't even remember.

She stared down at him, moistening her lips, and trying with all her willpower to let go of the crazy thought. It wouldn't be fair. It would be immoral to take advantage of him this way, not that she thought he'd actually mind, but still...

The decision was removed from her when he slipped a hand around her nape and drew her mouth to his. He slid his tongue between her surprised lips and dove so deep she couldn't breathe. Still reeling from the startling kiss, she barely noticed that he'd unfastened two of her buttons and slipped his free hand inside the front of her blouse.

For a man who was supposed to be drunk, he wasted no time in dipping his fingers inside her bra and finding her nipple. He squeezed lightly, and kissed her deeper, making her want to crawl under the covers with him.

"Max," she whispered against his mouth, her voice so breathless and garbled she barely understood what she'd said. "Max, you're drunk. You don't know what you're doing."

He groaned and cupped her breast, and then moved his mouth lower, letting his tongue trail down her throat, to the valley between her breasts.

Abby closed her eyes as the pleasure washed over her. They shouldn't be doing this in his condition. It wasn't right. But it felt damn good...

"Ah, Max..." She forced herself to pull back a little. Even with the sheet draped over him, she could see he was hard. His grip around her waist tightened and he tried to tempt her back to him. But he released her when someone at the door cleared their throat.

"Everything okay?" Candy asked when Abby turned to see who it was.

She nodded, feeling the heat climb her face.

Thankfully, Candy didn't react or seem put off. She merely asked, "Could I talk to you a minute?"

"Sure."

"Privately."

Abby looked at Max. His face and body had relaxed again and he was starting to snore slightly. She slowly got up, careful not to disturb him, not that she thought anything short of an atomic blast would jolt him to a coherent state.

She followed Candy out to the living room, and heard raised voices in the kitchen. Conflicting curiosity nagged her, but she sat across from Candy and gave her full attention.

"I know what's eating at him," Candy said, her expression grim. "I overheard a phone call he made this afternoon."

Abby shifted, torn between honor and a strong desire to find out what was troubling Max. "Should you repeat it?"

The other woman shrugged. "I'm gonna, anyway."

"Guess I can't stop you." Abby cringed at herself. Okay, so she was a pathetic excuse for a human being. "Well?"

Candy stared down at her shiny red-tipped fingers. "Part of it's our fault. We've been pushing Max for new appliances and furniture and repairs." She looked up with sad eyes and shrugged. "We thought he was rich. Figured he'd pour some money into the place for some kind of tax write-off, or something."

After allowing silence to lapse, Abby offered, "For the

record, I think Max is rich, but I still don't understand—"

Candy started vigorously shaking her head. "He may have been rich at one time, but he isn't now. The phone call he made was to a stockbroker or someone who he told to liquidate his assets. I'm not totally sure what that means, but I do know what 'get me some fast cash' means."

Abby frowned, more curious than ever. "That doesn't mean it has anything to do with you ladies. Maybe he wants to use it to make another investment."

"He found out there's a bunch of back taxes owed on the property. If it's not paid, the state can take the Swinging R away."

Abby sank back in her chair, her head reeling with the events of the night and this new information. "Do the others know?"

"Not yet. Max made the phone call about an hour before he went and got himself shit-faced. I'm gonna tell them, though. They've gotten real fond of him and they're gonna want to know."

Exhaling, Abby stood. "I understand, although I wish you wouldn't tell the others. Besides upsetting them, what you heard is Max's private business."

"I didn't hear you trying to stop me from telling you."

Abby's cheeks burned. "No, I guess I didn't." She felt her pocket for her keys, then remembered she'd left them in the car. "Well, I figure he's going to be asleep for a long time so there's not much I can do here."

"I'll make sure there's a bottle of aspirin and some water by his bed in the morning."

"Thanks."

"No need to thank me." Candy shrugged. "Guess I've kind of grown fond of the young fellow myself."

Abby smiled. "Yeah, me too." Then blushed at Candy's knowing look. So much for even thinking about going back to Max's room tonight.

In the brief silence that followed, she heard Gramms's voice in the kitchen, and debated ducking in to say hi before leaving. But she just didn't have the energy. If Mona was still in a tizzy, Abby knew staying a minute longer was asking for nothing but trouble.

She said a quiet good-night to Candy and slipped out the front door. Herb was on the porch, sitting on one of the new rocking chairs Max had bought for the ladies, staring up at the star-filled sky.

"Sorry I wasn't there to help you with Max," Herb said softly, shaking his head. "I can't believe he went and did a fool thing like that, especially after I told him how the folks would feel about their mayor drinking in public. Hell, there's liquor here. If he wanted to get plastered he should've done it without witnesses. Dumb kid."

Abby frowned. That was the thing. Max was far from dumb. He also wasn't a drunk. In fact, now that she thought about it, when he kissed her, he didn't smell like he'd had a lot to drink. "When did you tell him about not drinking in public?"

"The night I picked him up at your place. He wanted to go straight to a bar. I told him the nearest one open was the Watering Hole. Halfway there he changed his mind." Herb shrugged. "Somehow I didn't figure him for much of a drinker."

Neither did Abby. "Well, it's over and done with now." She patted his shoulder as she passed him and headed down the stairs. "Why don't you go home and get some sleep? Your boss won't be wanting a drive anywhere tonight."

Herb grunted. He didn't say anything more, and Abby

knew he was feeling badly over the incident, just like everyone else who knew Max. Funny that he'd been here only a week or so, and everyone was so genuinely fond of him.

Weary to the bone, she climbed into her car and patted the seats, looking for the keys. She found them and was about to start the car when she caught a glimpse of Max through his open window. He was talking on his cell phone, pacing the room, looking as sober as a judge.

13

"YOU HAVE A remarkable appetite for someone who drank half the liquor in Bingo last night," Mona said as she set down a plate of blueberry pancakes in front of Max.

He'd already devoured a three-egg ham and cheese omelet and three slices of buttered wheat toast that Rosie had fixed him. It was amazing how nice everyone was being, considering what an ass he'd been last night.

"Thank you, Mona." He winked at her. "Nothing could keep me from your blueberry flapjacks."

She eyed him with suspicion before turning back to flip pancakes in the ancient cast-iron skillet.

Miraculously, she didn't say another word, although Max didn't much care what anyone thought this morning. He'd accomplished his mission last night. There wasn't a soul in Bingo who'd vote for him now.

He glanced at the wall clock. It was nine-thirty. He figured Abby had a lineup outside her door by now, most of the ingrates on their knees, begging her to be mayor. They should've been more appreciative in the first place.

"Has Herb been by yet?" he asked between bites. "I need him to run me to town."

Mona glanced over her shoulder with arched brows. "I'd have figured that's the last place you'd want to go today. Anyway, he won't be back for another hour. Rosie and Candy had business in town. He took them about fifteen minutes ago while you were on the phone.''

He pushed his plate away and sighed. ''That reminds me, if I get any phone calls, I'm not here—unless it's Abby.''

''I don't expect too many people will be anxious to talk to you today.''

A weird sensation burned in his chest. She was right, of course, and he was surprised he cared. But he'd gotten used to people dropping by, asking for a piece of advice, legal or otherwise. That they wouldn't vote for him after last night didn't bother him at all, but he'd miss the small votes of confidence they'd demonstrated over the past week.

''Something wrong with my flapjacks?'' Mona poured more coffee in each of their mugs.

He shook his head. ''Guess I'm not feeling all that terrific after all.''

She hesitated, and he braced himself for a lecture on the evils of drunkenness. She set down the coffeepot. ''If you ever need to talk, I can be a pretty damn good listener.''

''What?'' He gave a casual shrug. At the concern darkening her eyes, he felt pangs of guilt sting him. ''Because I had too much to drink last night? I assure you I don't make a habit of doing that, and no, I don't have some deep dark problem which prompted my behavior.'' He shrugged again. ''I was just letting off a little steam. That's all.''

She looked as though she wanted to say more, but she pressed her lips together and picked up the coffeepot. As she turned back to the stove, she said, ''By the way, I canceled that order for the new washer and dryer. We decided we don't need them.''

"What?" Max stared in disbelief. "Half the time you use a washboard because you're worried that old washer will shred your things. Of course you need them."

She waved a dismissive hand. "We just don't like using machines for our finer unmentionables."

"That's not what Candy said the other day."

"Since when do you listen to her?"

The phone rang, and Mona rushed to get it.

"I'm not here, especially if it's Taylor." He called out the reminder, then stared at her retreating back. Why hadn't she picked it up in the kitchen? Something sure seemed fishy.

And now, suddenly, they didn't want a washer and dryer? He hated watching them scrub their clothes with torn rubber gloves. After he reinstated the order, he was going to find out what the hell was going on.

ABBY SAT at a window table, sipping coffee and watching Virgil and his son tear down Max's banner. She'd almost stayed away from Edna's today, knowing what the buzz would be, but she'd decided she'd rather hear it now than later.

Everyone had been exceptionally nice to her today, and she had the unusual and uncharitable desire to tell them all to go to hell. Maybe because she'd been away at college and graduate school for so many years, or because she simply hadn't been back long enough to adjust, but, oddly, Bingo didn't seem the same.

People were different than she'd remembered through a child's perspective. The ones she recalled would have been concerned for Max. They wouldn't have turned their backs on him...as quickly as they'd turned their backs on her.

She set down her cup and sighed. He'd gone through

an awful lot of trouble for nothing. She now realized she didn't want to be mayor either.

"Abigail? I didn't expect to see you here."

At her grandmother's voice, she turned in surprise. "Me? I come here all the time. You're a ways from the Ranch. What are you doing here?"

"I'm just picking up some sandwiches for the girls and me. I'll sit with you while Edna's making them up."

"You came to town for sandwiches?"

Gramms's guard immediately went up. Abby knew the signs—the furrowed brows, the thinned lips—and she could kick herself for sounding so inquisitive.

"Rosie and Candy had business in town, and I stopped at home to pick up something. They're still over at the...they're still tending their business, so I thought I'd surprise them with some ready-made sandwiches. Is that all right with you, Abigail?"

Now Abby knew there was trouble, and that she better tread lightly if she wanted to find out anything. "What's the matter? Getting tired of Rosie's cooking? Starting to miss mine?"

At her teasing tone, her grandmother relaxed and smiled. "Well, she does use an awful lot of grease." Then she frowned slightly. "I'm surprised you haven't asked about Max. Or did you already call him today?"

"No, but I'm sure he's fine." She took an unhurried sip of coffee.

"Well, yes, I guess a hangover isn't fatal."

"Oh, he doesn't have one. Trust me."

Gramms's brows shot up. "Not from what I heard about last night."

"He wasn't drunk. He was faking."

"Faking? Why on earth would he do that?"

"So that everyone would vote for me."

Gramms shook her head. "I can't believe he would make himself look like such a donkey just to get people to vote for you. Honey, you're already the leading candidate."

"I wouldn't be too sure."

Gramms's face brightened. "Well, if he did, isn't that the most chivalrous and romantic thing you've ever heard?"

Abby rolled her eyes. "Don't get any ideas. He probably just didn't want the hassle of running a campaign and putting up with Virgil."

"Abigail, you don't believe that. We all see how he looks at you."

Abby quickly lifted her coffee and sipped the lukewarm liquid. Gramms was right. Abby didn't believe that, or at least she didn't want to. She'd rather think that Max had tried to defend and protect her, and part of her truly did. But she didn't want Gramms to know about her foolish thoughts.

When she looked at Gramms again, she realized she needn't have worried about giving away her reaction. Gramms was too busy craning her neck at something out the window.

She looked at Abby suddenly and gave her a nervous smile. "Well, I'd better get those sandwiches. I'll call you when we get back."

"Get back? Where are you going?"

Gramms stopped, looking as guilty as a fox in a henhouse. "We're just going back to the Swinging R. I meant I'd call you later."

"Oh, well, okay." She didn't believe her for a minute. As soon as Gramms turned her back to pay for her sandwiches, Abby twisted in her seat and peered out the window. Candy stood across the street near the corner, talking to Herb who had just pulled up to the curb with Mona. Behind Candy, Rosie walked out of the bank, smiling and waving a large envelope.

Quickly, Abby turned back around, pretended to be interested in reading Edna's specials, then waved at her grandmother as she left the diner with her sandwiches. Abby waited a couple of minutes before turning around again. Gramms had just approached the car. The other two had already climbed in, and as soon as Gramms joined them, Herb's old Cadillac sped off—in the opposite direction of the Swinging R.

Abby leaned back in her chair and thought for a moment. What had they been doing at the bank? She knew it wasn't time to cash their social security checks. And Gramms had looked awfully guilty about something.

She took some money out of her purse and left it on the table. Enough to cover her coffee for the entire week. She didn't care. She had to hurry to the bank and talk to the manager, Mr. Whipple. One good thing about a small town, there were no secrets.

"I SAY WE PLAY roulette for a while, build up some cash, then go to the blackjack table." Mona flexed her fingers. "That should get me a good enough stake to clean up at poker."

"Roulette? You talking about playing the numbers, or wagering on black or red?" Candy fiddled with her silver dangly earring. "The money can sure go fast if we're not careful."

A cocktail waitress in a skimpy black-and-white uniform taking drink orders from two slot machine players blocked Abby's view and drowned out Mona's answer.

As much as she wanted to edge closer, Abby stayed

hidden behind the Megabucks machine and hoped the cocktail waitress would hurry and move on.

Once Mr. Whipple had told her the ladies were headed for Las Vegas, it wasn't too difficult to find them. They had two favorite casinos they patronized occasionally, and Abby had been lucky enough to find them at the first one she checked. In fact, Herb's poor old beat-up car had chugged into the parking lot only seconds before Abby. Good thing they hadn't spotted her.

"I still think we ought to at least play a couple of games of keno," Rosie said. "It's possible we could get lucky."

"Worst odds in Vegas," Mona answered. "A fool's game if you ask me."

"I only said it's possible," Rosie snapped. "And for that matter, the thousand-dollar bingo coverall isn't chump change."

"It is to Max." Mona's voice rose slightly. "How's he gonna pay back taxes and the bills for all that stuff he's been ordering for us?"

"Mona's right," Candy said quietly, so quietly that Abby almost stumbled into view while trying to hear. "We ought to bite the bullet and let Mona do her thing. No one's beat her at poker in a long time."

"Long time? You name the last person to beat me."

"Okay, Mona, we all know you're the best poker player in all of Nevada, except I still think we should drop a few dollars in the Megabucks machine. The jackpot *is* up to nine million."

Gramms's voice startled Abby, even though she knew she was there. That they might suddenly converge on the megabucks machine she was using for cover had Abby in a mild panic. She wasn't ready to show herself—yet.

"All right, all right," Mona said, "but let's wait until

we see how much money we can round up from the table games.''

''Hey, I want to play the quarter Wheel of Fortune machine, too. There's a progressive jackpot of six hundred and fifty thousand. And you know how good I am at the one on television,'' Rosie said, which met with several sounds of exasperation. No one bothered to point out that the slot machine version had nothing to do with guessing words or phrases.

They just all turned and silently walked toward the long row of tables offering games of blackjack, craps, roulette and two poker and blackjack variations Abby didn't even recognize.

Her heart swelled at the thought of what these women were willing to do for a man they barely knew. A man in whom they obviously saw what she saw—compassion, generosity, selflessness. But she couldn't let them do it. She couldn't allow them to risk their meager life savings, even if it was to help Max.

Although it was the middle of the afternoon, like in most casinos, you couldn't tell. Overhead lights were dim, the slot machine lights bright and gaudy, the clang of coins dropping, hitting metal, heralding another winner.

Excitement ricocheted and spiraled throughout the building. Like some sort of living thing, it bounced off the walls, rode on the joyous shouts of jackpot winners, and promised to change lives. In spite of herself, even Abby could feel it pulsating within her. She had to get to the ladies and reason with them before they did something irreversible, especially with Mona leading the pack.

They had just made it to the roulette table when she caught up with them. Still arguing over whether to bet black or red, they hadn't yet placed a wager.

Rosie noticed her first, her eyes getting rounder than two silver dollars. "Did you follow us?"

The rest turned to Abby.

Mona muttered a creative curse. "Estelle, you have a big mouth."

"I didn't tell her. Abigail, what are you doing here? I thought it was your turn at the library today."

"Gramms didn't say a word to me." Abby folded her arms across her chest. "If she had, I wouldn't have let you get this far."

"Your bossiness doesn't work around us, Abigail, so save it." Mona pulled out one of her poker cigars from her straw purse. She didn't smoke normally, only when she played poker. "Ladies, we'll just ignore her."

Abby plucked the cigar from her hand. "This isn't about me being bossy. I know what you're doing here, and—" Her voice broke. She cleared her throat. "I think it's wonderful that you care this much for Max, but he wouldn't want you to do this. You can't gamble your savings away."

"Who says we're doing that?" Mona had lost some of her bluster. "Estelle, you haven't been filling the girl's head with stories, have you?"

"I swear Gramms didn't tell me anything, Mona. I saw Rosie coming out of the bank and I did some investigating. I'm begging you all to think this through. If Max really does owe back taxes, and he doesn't have the money, you're all going to need your savings more than ever."

Rosie and Candy exchanged glances. Gramms bit down on her lower lip. Mona frowned with a touch of uncertainty.

"Ladies," the dealer called for their attention. "Please either place your bets or step away from the table."

"Keep your pants on, buddy," Mona barked.

"Excuse me?" The dealer's courteous smile disappeared. "I'd really hate to have to call security."

"That won't be necessary." Abby grabbed Mona's arm and dragged her several yards from the roulette table. The others readily followed.

Abby frowned thoughtfully. "Actually, I probably should have let them throw you out."

Mona glared. "Very funny."

Abby hadn't been joking, but she decided to drop the subject. "Why don't we all go have some coffee or ice cream sundaes? How about that?" Rosie and Candy showed immediate interest. "My treat. Then you can think about what I said before you do anything else."

"I don't want to think about it. I just want to play poker." Mona snatched back her cigar. "And I don't think coffee or ice cream's going to change a thing."

After a brief silence, Candy said, "Mona's right. I know I won't be changing my mind." She looked directly at Abby. "I don't expect you'll understand, but no one has really done anything like this for us before. We owe Max."

Touched by the woman's sincerity, Abby couldn't say anything at first. Finally, she said, "I think I do understand. But I know Max doesn't feel you owe him. He wouldn't even want that. Whatever he's done, he's done because…because he's a good person and he genuinely cares."

"I know," Mona said, stepping forward. "And I agree with Candy." She put a silencing hand up to ward off Abby's budding protest. "Hear me out. We've always felt a part of the town. Heck, we've all been around longer than most folks in Bingo."

Candy and Rosie exchanged startled glances. Mona

never acknowledged age in any way, shape, or form. The topic was downright taboo around the Swinging R.

"Everyone's always been nice to us, offering smiles and a few pleasantries when we're in town," Mona continued, oblivious to the others. "No one ever shunned us. But you know what? No one's ever offered to help us. They all know the place is falling down around our ears. But not once did anyone come out with a hammer in hand, not even our old customers."

Abby blinked, then looked at the others. They stared back, their eyes carefully unreadable. Mona was right. Abby herself had been guilty of turning a blind eye. She wasn't good with her hands, or at using a hammer or anything like that, but she could have done something...

Mona took her hand and gave it a small shake. "I know what you're thinking, and if you feel one lick of guilt, I'll take you over my knee. Hell, even Herbie, God love him, hasn't swung a hammer once without me asking, and that's okay. We aren't looking for pity, or for someone to take care of us. Besides, no one has that obligation, not even Max. But he's trying anyway."

Abby shook her head, helpless to think of anything rational or clever to say. Not that she could offer anything to change their minds. That was clear on each and every serene face. And they were right. Max had stepped up to the plate.

"Oh, hell." She threw up her hands. "I can't believe I'm doing this," she said, then lifted her purse strap off her shoulder, set her bag on a stool in front of a Wheel of Fortune machine and started digging for her wallet.

She pulled it out and looked up into four stunned faces. "What? You're going to tell me I can't pitch in?"

A nervous laugh broke out, and they all started hugging her and each other, and laughing raucously—until a man in a dark suit with a name tag came by and told them to break it up.

They quieted down while Abby counted her cash. She had only fifty dollars. "I passed an ATM machine on the way in," she said. "I can only withdraw a couple of hundred, but it'll help."

Mona rubbed her hands together. "We can skip roulette and go straight to the poker table."

"No, you won't," a deep, angry voice said from behind a bank of slot machines. "Ladies, I strongly suggest you put away your money," Max added as he stepped into view.

14

MAX DIDN'T KNOW what else to say. From the looks on their faces, they thought he was angry. Good. Better they think that. The truth was, he was too overcome with emotion to do anything but stand and glower.

"What are you doing here, Max?" Abby shoved her wallet back into her purse and straightened. She tried to look casual. She looked guilty as hell.

"Herbie brought you here, didn't he?" Mona narrowed her gaze. "That no-good son-of-a-gun—"

"Herb couldn't have brought him," Abby said calmly, her gaze dueling with Max's. "He didn't have enough time after dropping you off. May I talk to you in private?" she asked Max.

"No. I'm going back to the Swinging R now. If any of you loses so much as one penny on my behalf, I will sell the place. And I won't be picky about the buyer."

He started to turn away, but Abby grabbed his arm. She lifted her chin in challenge. "How much did you hear?"

"Enough." He gave her a long hard look, jerked away, then left without looking back.

His insides burned, and so did the back of his eyes. All this caring about people was too damn overrated. First you start giving a little bit of a damn, then you find yourself doing something nice for someone, and then they're doing something nice back for you. Independence was easier. Lonelier, perhaps, but definitely easier.

Exhaling loudly, he stopped at the bar. While the bartender waited on someone else, Max decided he didn't need anything to drink, after all, and left. He had a long drive back to Bingo, and he had some serious thinking to do. Except he needed something to wash down the lump in his throat.

He pushed through the heavy glass doors into the sunlight, away from the glitter of neon and the cloud of smoke that seemed to hover over the casino floor. He used to love places like that, the energy, the excitement, even the gaudy unnaturalness. Today it sickened him...though not half as much as knowing the ladies could have lost their life's savings over a worthless bum like him.

ABBY, ROSIE, CANDY and Gramms drove back in silence. Mona had decided to wait for Herb who was supposed to pick them up at four. She still didn't believe he had nothing to do with Max finding out about their plans. Abby didn't care. She was more interested in Max's reaction.

At first she'd thought he was furious, and to some degree he probably was angry, but she saw the look of fear and confusion in his eyes, too. She wasn't sure what it meant, but she aimed to find out.

"Are you coming in?" Gramms asked as they turned down the dusty dirt drive and the house came into view.

"Darn right I am," Abby confirmed. "He has to talk to me sooner or later. If he's not home, I'll wait."

"On a scale of one to ten, how mad would you say he is?" Rosie asked, then hiccuped, something she often did when she got nervous.

"Ah, his pride's probably just bruised, is all. He'll come around," Candy said. "Hey, isn't that Zeke's truck parked beside the garage? What's he doing here?"

"Maybe that's how Max got to Vegas. He borrowed Zeke's pickup." Abby hoped so. She wanted Max to be here. Now. She had quite a few things to say to him, whether he wanted to hear them or not.

She parked the car near the porch, but no one seemed to be in a hurry to get out. Abby sighed, and climbed out first, then headed up the steps. She paused at the door, took a deep breath, then marched inside.

A noise came from down the hall, and assuming he was in his bedroom, she kept right on going. His door was open, and she paused to knock on the wall before showing herself.

He looked up from the open suitcase he was packing. His eyes briefly met hers, and then he picked up a semi-folded shirt and threw it in the bag.

Her heart plummeted. "You're leaving."

"It's time." He wouldn't look at her.

"Why?"

He shrugged and threw in another shirt. "There's not much else for me to do around here."

"What about the Swinging R?"

"The back taxes will be paid, enough repairs made to insure the place is safe, and then...I guess life will go on."

She rubbed the sudden chill from her arms. "Why did you pretend to be drunk last night?"

He shot her a resentful look. "Pretend? Why would I do that?"

"Maybe you thought that was the only way I could be mayor—by default."

"Abby." He looked genuinely appalled. "That isn't

true. You're going to be a terrific mayor." He sat on the edge of the bed, a defeated look on his face. "That wasn't about you. I swear it wasn't."

She sat beside him, but said nothing, hoping he'd keep talking.

He rubbed wearily at his eyes. "You're going to be the best mayor Bingo has ever had. I would've been the lousiest. I prefer they didn't figure that out, so I'm hitting the road. Satisfied?"

"Not on your life. If you say you wouldn't be a good mayor one more time, I'm going to..." At a momentary loss for words, she stood suddenly, uttering a sound of disgust. "Knock you senseless."

"Abby, you don't understand—"

She stood in front of him and forced his chin up. "Stop putting yourself down."

He smiled at her, a sad, resigned smile that nearly broke her heart. "I'm not putting myself down. I merely know my limitations." He cupped her hips with his hands and drew her closer. She rested her palms on his shoulders, trying not think how tight and warm her body was growing.

When she started to protest, he silenced her with a warning look. "My grandmother adored me. It was pretty obvious I was her favorite grandchild. It wasn't fair to the rest of the kids, but obvious nevertheless. When she died, she left each of us a trust fund. My sister and cousins all received the total sum of their trust on their twenty-fifth birthdays, no strings attached. Know what the terms of my trust were? That the money be distributed in five-year installments until I'm forty."

He stared at Abby without bitterness or resentment, only acceptance, and her heart broke a little more. She cleared her throat, and shrugged. "So?"

"So…" His hands fell away from her and he leaned back. "Even my wonderful grandmother, who loved and adored me, knew what a worthless, lazy bum I am."

Abby saw red. She let go of his shoulders, took half a step back and stared at him.

"I'm not looking for pity," he said quickly, and started to get up. "I chose the course of my life. And I like it just the way it is."

She pushed him back down. "Pity? Why in the hell would I pity you? You're smart, good-looking, charming, and guess what Mr. Bennett? You have heart. Lots of it. I don't know how your family measures success or defines a person, but making lots of money or inheriting it doesn't mean squat."

The corners of his mouth started to curve.

"Get that patronizing look off your face. I'm dead serious. You care about Mona and Rosie and Candy when you don't have to. You could have walked away and you didn't." She cupped his face in her hands when he started to look away. "Tell me something, how would your family have handled this situation? Considered it simply business and cut their losses? Kicked the women out? Walked away?"

He looked startled, then annoyed. It gave her pause, but only briefly. She had too much to say, too much to lose. When he tried to draw back, she forced him to look at her.

She took a deep breath. "I happen to have excellent taste, Buster, and I would not fall in love with a worthless, lazy bum. Got it?"

He blinked. To say he looked stunned would be an understatement. And then he smiled. A magnificent smile that lit her heart and soul.

He placed his hands on her outer thighs, guiding her

closer, between his spread legs, then he slid his palms up her hips and cupped her bottom, pulling her closer still. His face was level with her breasts and her nipples tightened, imagining his breath on them, his hungry mouth.

"Finished?" he asked.

She shrugged, nodded, her knees weakening at the smoldering intensity in his eyes.

He stretched up slightly, at the same time running a hand up her back to her nape, and she knew he was going to kiss her. Her knees gave and he hauled her against him, their mouths meeting roughly, eagerly. His tongue parted her lips and entered her mouth. She lost her balance and fell so heavily against him he sprawled back on the bed, with her on top of him.

They almost didn't hear the knock at the open door. And then Rosie loudly cleared her throat.

Abby jumped up and straightened her blouse.

Max leisurely came to a sitting position. "This better be good, Rosie," he said, his breathing ragged.

"I suspect it is." She looked uncertainly from Max to Abby, then back to Max. "You have company."

He frowned. "Me?"

"Yup. Shall I bring her back here, or you want to come up front?"

Before he could answer, a tall striking blonde in a navy blue suit appeared in the doorway. Her blue eyes widened on Abby.

"Taylor?" Max straightened. "What the hell are you doing here?"

The woman slowly dragged her gaze away from Abby, and leveled it on Max. "Good question. What's going on, Maxwell?"

He shoved a hand through his hair and took a deep,

shuddering breath, and Abby automatically shrunk back, away from the bed...away from him.

Rosie mumbled something unintelligible, then disappeared.

Taylor walked into the room, eyeing Max's open suitcase, and Abby, with the familiarity of a woman who knew him well. *Very well.*

Abby swallowed. She wanted to shrivel up and die. This was Max's kind of woman—tall and leggy, blond, beautiful, elegant. Her purse and shoes matched, so did her nail polish and lipstick.

Max stood, and Abby expected him and the woman to embrace, but they didn't. He merely gestured toward Abby. "Taylor Madison, this is Abby Cunningham. Abby..." Looking uncomfortable, he nodded toward the blonde. "Taylor."

Unexpectedly, the other woman gave her a slow smile, and extended her hand. "Nice to meet you, Ms. Cunningham. Or may I call you Abby?"

"Abby, of course," she said, surprised at the woman's firm, warm handshake. "Nice to meet you, too." Abby stepped back, feeling awkward. "I need to be going. I've got a lot of things to do, and I..." Shrugging, she moved toward the door.

"Abby, wait," Max called, and she reluctantly hesitated. Their gazes met, and for an instant an emotion so intense flashed in his eyes it made her knees weak again. Maybe she was wrong about Taylor. Maybe... "I'll talk to you later, okay?" he said, his tone noncommittal, almost flip.

"Sure." She forced a smile, but she needn't have bothered. He'd already turned to the beautiful, sophisticated Taylor.

Abby choked back her disappointment and humiliation, and fled down the hall and out the front door before anyone could see the pain on her face.

"Is ABBY THE REASON you're still here?" Taylor set down her briefcase and purse, then sat on the only chair in the room and calmly looked at Max. "Why you've gone off the deep end?"

Max shoved his suitcase aside, sprawled out on the bed, and stared at the ceiling. "Maybe."

Taylor laughed. "Well, that's progress. No outright denial." She let a lengthy silence lapse, then asked, "How serious is this?"

He briefly thought about sugarcoating the situation, making light of his feelings for Abby. But he kept hearing her voice in his head, telling him she loved him.

He swallowed hard. "I'm in love with her."

"Whew! I'd say that's serious. Have you told her?"

"Not exactly."

"Oh, Max."

"Well, you picked one helluva time to show up. We were just getting around to that part." He met Taylor's skeptical gaze. "We were."

He looked away, the new feelings simmering inside petrifying him. Never before had he told a woman he loved her. He'd had plenty of relationships, a couple of them lasting nearly a year. But they'd turned out to be physical infatuations without substance, and their natural deaths hadn't fazed him.

It was different with Abby. Sure, she appealed to him physically, but more important, he liked the way she made him feel about himself. Her confidence in him boosted his own faith in his abilities, his humanity. She helped him to see things, qualities about himself, he never knew existed.

No, it wasn't going to be difficult to tell her he loved her, not one bit.

"Okay, what's going on in that head of yours?" Taylor stared at him with concern. "I can almost see the wheels spinning."

He gave her a healthy dose of teasing silence, then said, "Guess what, Taylor? I'm a pretty good guy. And I'm going to make a damn fine lawyer someday."

Her surprise gave way to a wide grin. "I like Abby already. After we take care of business, I hope I can spend a little time with her."

Max chuckled. "Always worried about taking care of business. We're going to have to find you a distraction, too."

"Don't even think about it." Her expression tightened as she lifted the briefcase she'd left beside the chair onto her lap. "I don't have to point out that your family is going to flip when they find out what you're doing."

He shrugged. "I never could please them. Why try now?"

Taylor studied him for a long uncomfortable moment, before a delighted smile lifted her lips. "Growing up right before my eyes. Wow!" She snapped open the briefcase. "How many shares of stock do you want to sell?"

"Enough to pay the back taxes and fix up the place. Oh, and make sure you set up an escrow fund to cover future taxes." He rubbed his eyes. "They're going to need new beds, too. It's amazing anyone can sleep on these relics— What?"

She was staring at him again, her brows creased in bewilderment. "You realize you're pretty much going to be wiped out of cash, and any means of getting your hands on some, until your next trust fund installment."

He slowly nodded.

"What are you going to do?"

"Well, let's see…" He smiled. "I *could* work for a living."

15

ABBY ORDERED a cup of coffee and English muffin even though she knew she wouldn't be able to choke down any food. Her appetite had fled yesterday afternoon when Max's girlfriend had shown up. Unfortunately, Abby's common sense had deserted her, too, just in time for her to make a big fool of herself.

She closed her eyes against the memory of Max's incredulous look when she blabbed that she loved him. He and Taylor must have had a good laugh over that one. Plain Jane Abby of Bingo, Nevada, falls for the smart, stunningly gorgeous Maxwell Bennett. Who wouldn't have a laugh?

She shook her head suddenly, which earned her several curious looks from Edna and two other diners. No, Max wouldn't laugh. He wasn't like that. He'd probably even feel bad that he'd led her on—which, of course, he hadn't. She was the one who'd lost sight of reality.

No, he *had* led her on, dammit. If he had a girlfriend, he had no business kissing Abby the way he had, or doing anything else, for that matter. Memories of the night in her living room had her reaching for a glass of cold water. The sloppy sip helped little. Her body remembered every touch…her lips, every kiss…

She forced her gaze out the window. If she didn't stop torturing herself, she was going to go crazy.

Looking out on Main Street did nothing to soothe her

wounded spirit. The loss of connection she'd once felt
with the town and people threw her into deeper mourn-
ing. But at least she and Gramms had ironed things out.
Gramms had only been trying to force Abby into enjoying her freedom. And, after all, her roots were still here
and she loved teaching her students, and she supposed in
time her old feelings would be restored.

In truth, the hurt from the town's rejection had already
faded some. It was Max who she couldn't shake from
her thoughts. Who caused the acute ache in her heart, the
hole in her being.

She blinked.

Ice-cold realization shot through her.

The town hadn't truly rejected her, at least not like
Max's family had rejected him, no matter how subtly.
How much hurt had Max suffered over the years? No
wonder his eyes had lit up with the town's belief he'd
be a good mayor.

Yet he'd been willing to throw it all away, even make
a fool of himself, in order to protect her feelings.

Abby took a deep, steadying breath. He deserved to be
mayor, whether he wanted the position or not. She
drummed her fingers on the table. She could do it—make
sure he was elected—as long as she personally stayed
uninvolved. Her heart couldn't take it otherwise.

The diner's door creaked open and Abby looked up
like everyone else. Today Taylor Madison wore a smart
gray suit as she walked briskly toward the counter and
stood impatiently waiting for someone to take her order.

Not wanting to be spotted, Abby slid down in the
booth, hoping Edna would hurry to the counter so Taylor
wouldn't start looking around.

Too late. The blonde turned, her eyes widening when
her gaze connected with Abby. Taylor smiled and headed

straight for Abby, calling an order for black coffee to Edna along the way.

"Hi, Abby, mind if I sit?" She slid into the opposite bench chair before Abby could open her mouth. "Max just dropped me off. He's on his way to your house."

Abby straightened. "My house? Why?"

"He tried calling you last night but you obviously weren't home, and he about blew a gasket waiting to talk to you."

She'd been home, eating M&M's. She simply hadn't answered her phone.

"Anyway," Taylor continued, "I'm glad I have this chance to talk to you alone."

Oh, no. Abby braced herself while Edna brought Taylor's coffee. Edna didn't seem in any hurry to leave, and Taylor stubbornly kept silent.

Abby squirmed in suspense.

Finally, Edna moved on to wipe down the next booth, and Taylor leaned across the table. "I've known Max for almost ten years and I have never seen him so happy."

Great. Abby was so glad she was able to warm him up for her. "Ten years, huh? You've stuck around a long time." She realized how awful that sounded when Taylor frowned. "I mean, a lot of women would have expected a ring by now."

A startled look crossed the other woman's face, and then she laughed. "I'm his attorney, and his friend. Strictly platonic. We met our first year in law school."

Abby's mouth opened. Nothing came out.

"Oh, my." Taylor made a face. "You thought—"

She cut herself off when nosy Edna nearly fell over the booth trying to hear their conversation.

"I've had enough coffee," Taylor said, pushing her cup aside. "Care to take a walk?"

Abby grinned. Edna was going to have a cow at any minute. She hated missing out on anything. "Sure."

Both women pulled out their wallets. Abby put down money first and led the way outside. Thoughts somersaulted inside her head like cheerleaders on steroids. If Taylor and Max were just friends, then maybe...

She abruptly turned to Taylor who stopped just short of running into Abby. "You said you've never seen Max happier?"

"That's right."

"Did he tell you the people want him to run for mayor of Bingo?"

Taylor blinked. "Ah, no, he left out that part." She frowned thoughtfully. "How did he react?"

"You said yourself, he's never been happier."

The other woman chuckled. "I have a feeling his high spirits have a lot more to do with you."

Abby's heart lurched. "Really?"

Taylor started to answer, but her lips parted without sound as she stared at something behind Abby.

"Abigail Half-pint Cunningham, what the devil are you doing back here in Bingo?"

Abby recognized Clint's voice immediately and spun around to give him a piece of her mind for using her old nickname. As soon as she laid eyes on him, she started laughing instead.

"Are you growing a beard, or did you forget to wash your face?" she asked, and he wrapped her in a big bear hug and picked her up off the ground.

His dark hair was much longer than she remembered it ever being. It made him look dangerous, sort of mysterious, even though she'd grown up with him.

"Clint Southwick, put me down. You're making me dizzy."

He spun her around once more. "You forgot to cry Uncle."

"All right. Uncle, already." Her feet hit the ground and she smiled up at him. "When did you get into town?"

He shrugged, his interested gaze straying to Taylor, who was busy dusting off her skirt. "About an hour ago." He lifted his Stetson off his head and nodded toward Taylor. "Sorry about kicking up so much dust, ma'am."

Abby bit back a smile at the lazy drawl Clint used. Like Abby, he'd gone away to college and then law school. He later joined the navy as an officer and earned quite a reputation as a successful JAG lawyer. She knew he'd recently been discharged. She couldn't wait to catch up and find out what he was up to.

She glanced at Taylor, who didn't looked amused or charmed by Clint's country-boy routine. She swatted one last time at her skirt and mumbled through tight lips, "No problem."

Abby cleared her throat. "Clint, this is Taylor Madison."

He immediately offered his hand, and Taylor finally accepted it, although she looked loath to do so.

"So, how long are you staying this time?" Abby asked.

He shrugged again and set his hat back on his head. "I don't know. We'll just see how it goes. What about you? You visiting?"

"Nope, I moved back."

"No kidding. Things sure have changed around Bingo," he said, his gaze again drawing to Taylor.

"She doesn't live here," Abby said and grinned at both their dirty looks. "Just thought I'd share that."

"Gee, thanks, Half-pint."

She laughed. "You staying at the ranch?" she asked, and he nodded. "I'll call you."

"I'll be waiting on the edge of my seat." He picked her up and spun her around one more time, ignoring the whack on the arm she gave him. "Good to see you, Half-pint." He set her down and tipped his hat to Taylor. "Ms. Madison."

Abby noticed the way Taylor watched Clint saunter away, and her chest tightened at the guarded interest in the blonde's eyes. Abby wanted to tell her to forget it. Clint was as unavailable to someone like Taylor as Max was to Abby.

They were as different as wine and beer, roses and dandelions, apples and oranges. Why had Clint suddenly shown up? To remind Abby that no matter what Taylor had to tell her, no matter how happy Max seemed, it would never work between him and Abby?

"Who is that guy?" Taylor finally asked.

Abby sighed, her spirits drooping again.

"That's what I want to know," a deep voice rumbled from behind.

Both women turned to Max. He was frowning in Clint's direction.

Abby's pulse fluttered. Her heart skipped two beats. She told herself to wise up. "His family has a ranch about twenty miles outside of Bingo. Clint and I practically grew up together. He was kind of like a big brother to me."

Max silently sized up Clint's retreating form, and Abby realized Max looked jealous. Her pulse went nuts again.

"Why haven't I seen him around before?" Max asked, leveling his troubled gaze on Abby.

"He's been out of town." She shrugged and waved at Herb, who had just walked out of the drugstore and was sorting through his mail. "Looks like your ride may be ready."

He studied her for a moment. "We have to talk."

"Guess this is my cue." Taylor smiled, then gave Max a look Abby couldn't interpret.

Abby watched her walk back into the diner on high heels that seemed as natural to her as breathing. It made Abby shudder. Heck, panty hose made her shudder. She absently shook her head. There may be no chemistry between them, but Taylor was still Max's kind of woman.

"Abby?"

"Taylor is so beautiful." She hoped that didn't sound wistful as she slowly brought her gaze to his.

"Yeah, if you like the stuffed shirt type." He stared directly into her eyes. "Me, I like the shorter, more down-to-earth type."

For a week or two, maybe. "Liar."

He smiled. "I'll promise not to beat myself up anymore if you admit you're beautiful."

Now he'd pushed too far. After a scorching glare, she turned away and headed for her car. If he was going to leave, she wished he'd just go. It was inevitable. If not today, then next week. There were too many other Taylors in the world.

He caught her hand and drew her toward him.

"Stop it, Max."

"Stop what? Stop trying to make you see reason? I don't think so."

She sighed. "I saw reason. She told me to quit being a fool."

Inexplicably, he looked hurt. When she tried to free

her hand, he held tighter and drew her closer. "Abby, are you going to let me talk?"

"No."

"Sorry, I phrased that wrong. Abby, you *are* going to let me talk."

She avoided his gaze and stared down Main Street. Virgil was standing at the door of his store. Every customer at Edna's had their nose pressed to the window.

"And you *are* going to listen." He hooked a finger under her chin and forced her to look at him.

"I thought we were at least friends," she said. "Can't you leave me with a little dignity?"

That wounded look again. He exhaled slowly. "Open your hand."

She hesitated, eyeing him with suspicion, then slowly uncurled her fingers. What the heck was he up to? "Is this something we should be doing in the middle of Main Street?"

One side of his mouth lifted. "I hadn't finished reading your palm the other day."

She blinked, disappointed suddenly. What had she expected? A ring?

"See this line here?" He lightly ran the pad of his thumb along her palm to her wrist. "See how it parallels this other one? It means that not only are you going to have a long life, but you'll be sharing it with someone."

Their eyes met. "Someone you already know," he continued. "Someone who loves the way you look, the way you care so much for others. Someone who admires your loyalty."

Her breath caught. She knew what he was saying, or at least assumed she did. So why was disappointment nudging her? And why didn't he just come out and say he loved her?

"Oh, look at this." He traced a pair of small lines by her thumb. "Two kids. I wonder what that means?"

She swallowed as their eyes met again.

He smiled.

She tried to return it. She couldn't. "Good question. What does it mean, Max?"

His smile faltered. "What do you think?"

"I think you're still holding back. You can't quite take responsibility by the horns, can you? Let someone else take the last step, make that final move."

His expression tightened, and he dropped her hand. "Is this payback, Abby?" He nodded toward the gawkers in Edna's window. "I just opened up my heart to you, and you try to humiliate me."

"You don't believe that," she said.

But he had already turned away and headed toward the drugstore where Herb's Caddy was parked. His clothes were half packed. He estimated he could be ready to leave before noon.

The thought was like a blow to the gut.

He saw Herb stooping down to look at himself in the car's side mirror. Dammit, Max didn't want to talk to anyone. He wished he'd kept Zeke's truck another day.

"Hey, Max, what do you think?" The man straightened suddenly, grinning, cocking his ear toward Max. "I just got it special delivery."

On his earlobe, a small diamond gleamed.

Max squinted for a better look at the earring. "Is it real?"

"Yup. I've been saving up for it."

Max frowned at him. "I thought you were saving up for a ring for Mona?"

"I was, but I didn't want to make Estelle mad." Herb shrugged, and ducked down to admire his earring in the mirror again. "Besides, what does an old guy like me wanna get married for?"

Max stared in disbelief. Herb would rather have an earring than companionship, laughter, someone who believed in him? He cursed under his breath and turned around.

Abby was still standing where he'd left her.

Had she been waiting for him to come to his senses? Did she know him better than he knew himself? She was right. He'd been a coward. But no more. No way was he going to end up like Herb.

Kidding himself through life. Lonely. Missing Abby.

Max headed back toward her, and when it looked as though she might bolt, he started to run. She didn't move again, but he didn't slow down until he got within a yard of her.

"You're not getting rid of me that easy," he said, a little out of breath.

"Really?" She folded her arms across her chest and smiled.

"I love you, dammit, and—" Out of the corner of his eye, he saw that everyone in Edna's diner had moved from the window to the door so they could hear. Exasperated, he turned to them and spread his hands, palms up. "I'm trying to ask Abby to marry me. Do you mind?"

They all shook their heads, and stayed put.

Sighing, he turned back to Abby.

She was laughing. "They're my witnesses, so you'd better make this good."

Max nodded. "Okay." He got down on one knee.

"For goodness sake, I was kidding." She uncrossed her arms and tried to pull him up.

"Nope. I'm staying right here until you promise to

marry me. Have my children. Whip me into shape when I start getting stupid.''

"Can we start now? You're being stupid. Get up."

"Is that a yes?"

A smile tugged at her mouth.

"For crying out loud, Abigail," Virgil hollered. "Put that man out of his misery!"

Max smiled and took her hand. "Yeah, Abigail, put me out of my misery."

"Okay, already, I'll marry you," she said with a growing smile.

He stood and slipped his arms around her waist. "I expect a little more enthusiasm during the honeymoon."

"What honeymoon?" She slid her arms around him. "We have a town to run."

"We?"

"We share the office of Mayor. That's part of the deal."

He drew his head back in mock horror. "You mean, you really do want me to work for a living?"

She gave him a dry look.

Laughing, he hugged her again. "I'm going to make you so proud of me."

"I already am," she whispered. "Bingo is lucky to have you. So am I."

"I love you, Abigail Cunningham, more than I thought I could love anyone."

"I love you, too, but if you make me cry in front of all these people you'll have to be Mayor by yourself."

"You drive a hard bargain, lady," he said, then sealed their deal with a kiss.

Whose Line Is It Anyway?

Debbi Rawlins

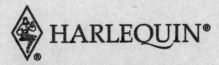

HARLEQUIN®

TORONTO • NEW YORK • LONDON
AMSTERDAM • PARIS • SYDNEY • HAMBURG
STOCKHOLM • ATHENS • TOKYO • MILAN • MADRID
PRAGUE • WARSAW • BUDAPEST • AUCKLAND

1

"WHO'D WANT TO WEAR that ratty old garter?"

Taylor Madison eyed the petite older woman with the teased red hair and gaudy green sequined dress who was speaking.

She continued, "It's supposed to be 'something borrowed,' not something Goodwill wouldn't even want."

"Oh, and that leather bustier you wanted her to wear would have been better?" The disdain on the blonde's face emphasized the crows' feet around her blue eyes. "Give me a break, Mona. You're still PO'd because I thought of the temporary tattoo."

Taylor brought two fingers to her throbbing temple. The flight from Boston to Las Vegas had taken three hours longer than it should have, almost making her late for Max and Abby's wedding, and she did not need to listen to the ludicrous squabble of the bridesmaids, if you could call them that, over wedding traditions.

Not that the ladies from the Swinging R knew the meaning of the word *tradition*. The dresses they'd chosen for the bridesmaids, including Taylor's, looked more like Halloween costumes.

She squeezed between the two women to get to the full-length mirror. The back room of the old white stucco church barely had enough space for three people much less six, especially when two of them spent every spare minute sniping at each other.

Taylor wondered if her friend Max knew what he was doing, getting married and living in Bingo. He'd only known Abby for three months, after all, and this town had more than its quota of crackpots.

"Now, now, girls, let's not ruin Abigail's wedding." Rosie smoothed back her gorgeous white hair. She seemed the most normal of the trio from the Swinging R Ranch. At least she acted more her age, except for the penciled-in mole high up on her left cheek, a kind of Miss Kitty look from the old western TV series.

Abby stood before the mirror, adjusting her veil, and she turned to give Taylor a wry smile. "Are you sure you want to look?"

"I beg your pardon?"

Taylor watched Abby's gaze lower to the peach spandex-and-chiffon dress Taylor had poured herself into. It was way too short and the low neckline arrowed toward her navel. If she didn't end up with pneumonia she'd eat the dyed-to-match spiked heels.

Taylor still couldn't believe she was wearing the awful thing. If anyone at her law firm saw her dressed like this... She shuddered at the thought, and decided she'd karate chop the first person with a camera that came near her. She hadn't taken that defense course for nothing. At twenty-nine she was about to become the youngest partner in the prestigious Boston firm...if she played her cards right.

"Max told me you're the Armani suit type. I hope he explained I had nothing to do with picking out your dress." Abby reached over and repinned a strand of Taylor's hastily rolled French twist. "In the excitement of the moment, I agreed to let Mona and Candy choose the outfits." She turned back to the mirror and sighed. "You should have heard how much I had to beg and barter for this.''

Taylor eyed the slit that reached Abby's thigh. It wasn't a *bad* dress, but as far as wedding gowns went, it was certainly different. Too form-fitting and low-cut for one thing.

Taylor squinted at the bride's cleavage. Well, now she knew what the woman had been referring to when she mentioned a temporary tattoo. At least Taylor *hoped* the purple rose wasn't permanent. In a way, it was a good thing Max's family had refused to attend the ceremony.

Abby sighed. ''Candy promised it would wash off in two days.''

''It's...different. Quite becoming.''

Abby laughed. ''Tactfully spoken, like a true attorney.''

Taylor's lips twitched. ''That bad, huh?''

''I meant that in the nicest way,'' Abby said, and bent forward to adjust her cleavage. She straightened and tugged her sweetheart neckline back up, covering half the rose. ''According to Max, your highly regarded reputation as an attorney is surpassed only by your loyalty to your friends. Wearing that dress for our wedding cinches it.''

''Yeah, well, if I fall on my face trying to walk in these heels, the friendship is over.''

With a sympathetic frown, Abby stared at Taylor's four-inch spikes. ''You should have drawn the line at those. I would've backed you up.''

''I didn't know I had the option.'' Taylor sighed. ''Frankly, when Mona called me in Boston—'' She glanced at the redhead. ''Mona, right?'' Abby nodded. ''Anyway, I gave her my size and measurements and didn't think any more about it. I guess it's fortunate everything fits."

Abby pressed her lips together, but eventually broke into a grin. "You're being very gracious. Max told me as soon as you saw that dress you'd tell us where to stick it."

"Remind me to thank him for that charming characterization." Jealousy pricked Taylor. She wondered what else Max had told Abby. Although they had no romantic feelings for each other, Max was Taylor's best friend. Their relationship was almost like a marriage without the complications, or the messy sex part. He knew her past, and all her insecurities. She knew his, and they regularly traded confidences. Now he'd share his with his wife.

Abby turned back to the mirror and moved the lacy white veil back an inch. "I didn't have the heart to refuse when the ladies asked to plan the wedding. Nothing very exciting happens around Bingo and this is a big deal to them."

"But it's your *wedding.* One of the biggest events of your life." Unease needled Taylor when the other woman gave her a peculiar look.

"What about you?" Abby asked with a casual shrug of one shoulder. "Any marriage plans in your future?"

Taylor shook her head. "I'm married to my career for now. Maybe later. But I'm not anxious."

"To tell you the truth, I wasn't either. But then Max showed up." Abby shrugged, but the glow on her face gave Taylor an odd tightness in her chest.

"Max is a great guy, and I'm really happy for both of you," Taylor said, impulsively grabbing Abby's hand. "I think you're perfect for him."

She meant it. Abby's selflessness in letting the ladies plan her wedding raised the woman several notches in

Taylor's esteem. It also made Taylor a little melancholy. She'd been that kind of person once, skipping dinner even though she was hungry so that her little brother would have enough to eat. She'd come a long way since then, depending on how you looked at it.

"Thanks. I'm glad you're here for Max. It means a lot." Abby smiled. "Now, back to business. You can ditch the shoes if you want. Clint nixed the white patent leather ones Candy chose for him. God only knows what he's wearing."

Taylor immediately stiffened. "He's in the wedding party?"

"Yeah. So you remember Clint Southwick? I think you met him outside of Edna's Edibles, right?"

Oh, yeah, she remembered him all right. Three months ago, when Max had called her to liquidate his assets, Taylor had flown in for a day to see if Max had lost his mind. She ended up losing hers.

After briefly meeting the dark-haired, scruffy cowboy, the rest of the day she kept imagining that she'd caught glimpses of him, first in the Las Vegas McCarran airport, and then during her layover in Dallas. Ridiculous, of course…

Taylor blinked at the bewildered look on Abby's face and realized she was waiting for an answer. "Yeah. I, uh, I didn't realize you were such good friends."

"Clint and I grew up together. We went our separate ways after high school, but since he's been back in town, he's spent a lot of time with Max and me. He's good people. You'll like him. In fact, he's your partner."

"My partner?" Dread slithered like a snake up her spine.

"For the ceremony. You know, like when you go down the aisle to the altar."

"Of course." What was it? A one, two-minute trip? She could handle Clint Southwick for that long.

"And for the reception. Max asked him to entertain you."

"Great. Something else I need to thank Max for," she muttered, and Abby gave her a quizzical look. "You can tell Mr. Southwick that I really don't need a baby-sitter."

"I have a feeling I'm going to be a little busy for the next few hours so you might want to handle that yourself."

Taylor's cheeks burned. "Of course."

Abby gave her a mischievous smile before turning back to the mirror. "But don't count on getting rid of Clint that easily. When Max asked him to be your escort, he seemed mighty anxious to oblige."

IT WAS WARM FOR DECEMBER, even for southern Nevada, even standing on the shady side of the church lawn. Just Clint's luck. He stuck a finger between his clammy neck and the starched shirt collar in hopes of loosening the sucker. Today was probably the only time in his life he'd have to wear a monkey suit and Bingo topped off at a record-high temperature for December.

Shoot, if it had been anyone else but Abby and Max tying the knot, Clint would have spent the evening sitting in front of the tube with an ice-cold beer.

He checked his watch when he saw Max and Herb Hanson pull up in Herb's 1960 Caddy. Countdown time. Thank God. The sooner he could get out of these duds the better.

Max jumped out of the car before Herb turned off the engine. On him the white tuxedo looked good, even though his tie hung loose around his neck. "Have you seen Taylor?"

Clint shrugged. "Not yet. Why?"

"Her plane was delayed, and then the guy I sent to pick her up at the airport couldn't find her. I hope she made it."

Ah, hell. Clint had been looking forward to seeing her again. Tall, blond, eyes the color of the Caribbean Sea...she was just his type. Physically, anyway. But that was it. He'd heard too much about her from Max. Ambitious, obsessed with being the best, she was too uptight for him. He'd left all that behind for a simpler life here in Bingo.

"The church is packed so I could've missed her. But I bet she's here," he said after he thought about it for a second. "Otherwise, you know Mona would be out here hollering for her."

"Good point." Relief eased Max's features. "Taylor's resourceful. I'm sure she managed to get here on her own."

Clint grunted. That was the trouble with women nowadays. They didn't want guys coming to their rescue anymore. It wasn't that he didn't like competent, independent women, but when they did everything themselves, it took a lot of fun out of the courtship. Not that he was looking to date anyone. He had his hands full trying to get the ranch back in shape.

"You about ready to go in?" he asked, checking his watch again. "It's time."

Max took a deep breath. "Ready."

Herb moved in beside him, tugging at his cummerbund, fidgeting with his diamond stud earring. He looked more nervous than Max. Probably should be, too. From what Clint heard, Abby's grandmother Estelle had a mind to drag him down the aisle.

"Don't forget that." Clint pointed to Max's loose tie.

"Thanks." Without having to look in a mirror, Max deftly tied a perfect bow.

That was the difference between them, Clint thought. Wearing a tux was natural to Max. He'd be as at home on an African safari as he was at a Nevada roundup. Not Clint. He had never gotten used to all the formal dinners, cocktail parties full of silly small talk, the pomp and circumstance of his other life.

"What about Zeke? Is he here yet?" Max asked as they made their way around to the front of the church.

Clint nodded. "He helped seat the guests so he should already be inside."

They entered the church and quickly took their places at the back, where they would pair up with the bridesmaids to walk them down the aisle. To his annoyance, Clint found himself scanning the doorway to the back room, hoping to see Taylor. Mona and Candy stood outside arguing about something. They wore the strangest frilly pink dresses, which made him appreciate the monkey suit more. Beside them, a beaming Estelle waited to walk her granddaughter down the aisle.

The organist started playing the wedding march and the back room door opened. Taylor stepped out, tall and slim and at least a head taller than the other women who stood in front of her. The church lights glowed off her light blond hair, making it look as though she were wearing a halo.

But there was nothing angelic about her murderous expression. She didn't even try to smile when the photographer ducked in front of her and snapped a picture.

She looked as if she wanted to drop-kick him all the way to Vegas.

He was about to face the altar when Taylor moved forward so that Mona and Candy were no longer blocking his view. He did a double take. Taylor's dress was...almost a dress. He squinted at the hem, her legs. Or were those shorts? No, it was a dress. A really short dress. And she had great thighs. Lots of long shapely leg. Spiked heels. Man, somebody should've warned him. His heart might not be in good enough shape.

He tried to concentrate on the organ music, considered vaguely how he should be looking for the cue to start down the aisle, but the deep V of her dress beat out the competition for his attention.

Herb nudged him. "Are we supposed to start already? Reverend Manson is looking this way."

"What? Yeah, let's see... Who goes first?"

"I think Zeke and Candy."

When the organist started the music over again, and everyone turned toward the back of the church, including Max, Clint gave Zeke the eye and signaled with a jerk of his chin to get started. Zeke and Candy quickly paired up and began the trek to the altar. Herb and Mona linked arms and followed.

Taylor stepped up beside Clint. Her mysterious scent seeped into his skin until it pulsed through his veins and compelled him to look at her...except his gaze inadvertently went straight to her cleavage, before it raised to her eyes.

"Don't get too excited. It's a WonderBra." She pasted on a smile, slipped her arm through his, and took a step before he was ready.

He recovered his footing in time to keep from making a total fool of himself. Briefly he considered a payback remark that would make her blush the rest of the way to the front but he decided to take the high road. For now.

Her heels made them nearly the same height, and giving her a sideways glance, he was struck by the flawlessness of her skin, the perfect definition and proportion of her jaw and chin. The only fault he could see was that her nose was a little crooked. It gave her character.

They got to the front and she wasted no time in breaking contact and taking her place in the opposite pew with the other bridesmaids. Abby and Estelle had started down the aisle and everyone turned to them. Max's smile was bigger than the Grand Canyon as he waited for his bride, and Clint's chest tightened with an odd yearning.

The feeling had nothing to do with Abby, personally. She was like a sister to him. Maybe he was just getting old. Not that being thirty-three qualified him for social security, but the family house seemed bigger and emptier these days. He missed his mother's laughter, his younger brother's antics, yet he was glad they had both found happiness, his mother at a retirement community in Florida and David at an accounting firm in Los Angeles.

It was up to Clint now to keep the ranch going, and produce enough income to pay off the remaining mortgage. Although ranching was a far cry from his short-lived naval career, he'd decided this was where he belonged. Where there were still wide open spaces and a man could raise a family without worrying about violence and destructive peer pressure. He just hadn't gotten around to the family part yet.

Clint watched fondly as Abby got closer, her gaze glued to Max and her eyes bright with excitement. She looked beautiful and happy, and Clint was glad for her. He genuinely liked Max, and as different as the two of them were, together they made a great team. When Max got too full of himself, Abby kept him down to earth. And when she got overzealous, Max reined her in.

The ceremony started and Clint forced himself to concentrate on what was happening. It was hot and crowded, and he could barely think about anything besides getting out of his jacket.

Fortunately, the service was short, but touching, most of the wording chosen by Abby and Max. The looks of love and admiration they trained on one another brought more than one sniffle from the packed pews. Both were popular and well-respected, and the people of Bingo had looked forward to the day when their co-mayors would tie the knot.

When it was time to make the return trip down the aisle, he caught Taylor staring at him. She quickly averted her eyes, but dutifully took his arm as soon as the bride and groom had started down the aisle. For good measure, he laid his free hand on the one Taylor had draped over his arm, and then smiled when she tensed.

By the time the entire wedding party got outside, the sun had sunk behind the two-story red adobe school across the street, providing the front of the church with shade and a soft pink glow. While everyone talked and laughed at once, and threw handfuls of rice at Max and Abby, Taylor disengaged herself from Clint and shrank back.

It irked him that she didn't participate. Disappointed him, too, because he'd been looking forward to spending some time with her. But obviously she thought she was too good for the simple people of Bingo. He'd met plenty of her kind during his stint in the Navy. No thanks.

"That could have been us, you big lug." Mona elbowed Herb as she stared wistfully at Abby and Max being showered with congratulations. "Instead, what do you do? You buy that damn fool earring."

"Let's not get into that again, Mona." Herb glanced at Clint, and then heavenward, as if seeking divine intervention.

She made a sound of exasperation, then turned to him, but her gaze snagged on Taylor standing away from the festivities, her arms folded across her chest.

"What is that girl doing way back there? Why aren't you entertaining her, Clint Southwick? Shame on you."

"Entertain her? What do you want me to do, strip?"

Mona chuckled. "Do that and you'll get all of our attention."

Clint shot Taylor a look of disgust. "Hey, if she'd rather hide in the corner than mix with the local yokels, then the heck with her. Give her a piece of cake to go and I'll take her to the airport."

Rosie sidled up beside him with a reproachful arch of her brows. "Stop it, Clint. Taylor isn't like that. She's a very sweet girl. If she seems standoffish it's because of that floozy dress Mona made the poor girl wear. I'd hide in a corner, too."

Mona's red-tinted lips parted in disbelief. "Floozy dress, my fanny. I saw one like it in one of those sophisticated French magazines." She turned toward Taylor. "Look at her. I don't know a single other woman who could pull off wearing that dress like she can."

Herb scratched his jaw. He'd missed shaving a big patch of gray stubble near his ear. "Well, I don't know, Mona. She is showing an awful lot of skin."

Mona glared at him. "I'm still steamed at you. I suggest you keep your opinions to yourself."

Rosie leaned toward Clint. "She had a birthday last

month. You'd think she'd mellow out, but she's still as bossy as ever.''

"I heard that.'' Mona put a hand on her hip and rattled off a list of complaints she had about Rosie.

Clint wasn't listening. He watched Taylor with new interest and a wave of sympathy. That dress was something Mona would've worn in her heyday when the Swinging R was open for business as a legal brothel. Taylor had to be pretty mortified. Maybe he'd jumped to conclusions about her. He hoped so.

Max and Abby were surrounded by well-wishers and Clint figured they wouldn't miss his congratulations right now. Mona and Rosie were still at it, so he quietly left the group and approached Taylor.

"What are you doing way over here?'' He motioned with his chin toward Mona and Rosie. "There's a lightweight match going on over there. Don't you want to know who's going to win?''

That got a smile out of her. "I'd put my money on Mona. But I think all three of them live to pick on each other.''

"Well, ma'am, I do believe that is a fact.'' Smiling, he reached to tip the brim of his Stetson, then remembered he wasn't wearing one, and raked his hand through his hair instead. How quickly boots and a hat had become a part of him again, after being home for only three months. His mother had warned him it wouldn't be easy to take the country out of the boy. She was right.

"You cut your hair.'' Taylor blinked. She'd obviously surprised herself as much as she had him.

"My hair?'' He pushed a hand through it again, wondering what prompted that observation. He hadn't cut it recently... And then he nodded. "It was long when you met me. I'd been bumming my way across the country and let it go. But I prefer it short.''

She nodded politely, and then let her gaze stray toward Max and Abby. A small wistful smile lifted her lips. "I never thought Max would bite the dust.''

"So what do you really think about marriage?''

She looked blankly at him, and then chuckled. "I don't have a thing against marriage.''

"It's just not for you.''

Shrugging an almost-bare shoulder, she pursed her lips. "Maybe some day. It's too soon to think about it.''

The satiny smoothness of her skin distracted him, the way the fading light gave it a golden glow. He brought his gaze back to hers, so clear and blue, not many secrets could hide there.

"You one of those career women who's going to wait till she needs a cane to chase her babies around?''

"There's nothing wrong with women having children later in life. Do you know what the average age of the expectant mother is these days?''

Clint laughed. "No, can't say that I do.''

She gave him a sheepish look, then stared past him. "Never mind.''

"No, tell me. I'm interested.''

"Right.''

"I am. I'm not getting any younger and if I want to start a family I'd better be informed,'' he said, and she looked with skeptical curiosity into his eyes. "I need to know if I should stick to young fillies or if it's okay to go after an old mare.''

Her look of outrage was worth anything she was about to dish out. "You are the biggest—''

He couldn't keep a straight face a second longer and he started laughing.

She cocked her head to the side, her arms still folded. "I'm glad to see you're enjoying yourself."

"Tremendously. Come on. Let's go join the party."

Her expression tightened. "I-I'll be along in a minute."

"Hey, I was only joking."

"It's not you." She shifted and inched further back into the corner. "I have a small problem."

Clint frowned, but when she adjusted the neckline of her dress, understanding dawned. He shrugged out of his tuxedo jacket. "It is a little chilly."

Wariness drew her eyebrows together.

He smiled. "Allow me."

He held up the jacket to her, and her expression relaxed, a small smile of gratitude curving her lips. "Thanks."

But he didn't surrender the jacket when she reached for it. Instead, he draped it around her shoulders, breathing in her seductive scent. He eased the lapels together, and she automatically moved toward him.

"Thanks," she said again, a little breathless this time, her eyes darkening with the same heightened awareness that pumped furiously through his veins.

"My pleasure." He gave the lapels an extra tug.

She stumbled forward a step and they got so close her tiny gasp fanned his chin with warm minty breath. It took all his willpower not to pull her against his chest and kiss her. One of those deep lingering kisses that would keep them both up, tossing and turning all night.

He exhaled slowly and shifted away. "Shall we?"

She stared at the arm he offered her, moistened her lips, and then met his eyes. Her gaze widened a fraction and then she simply nodded before linking her arm with his.

As they started toward the others, she cocked her head slightly toward him, and in an amused voice she said, "By the way, I like your boots."

He glanced down at the scuffed toes of his gray cowboy boots. At least he'd dusted them off. "You should have seen what Mona wanted me to wear."

"I can imagine."

"Yeah, I bet you can. How long do you suppose we have to keep these clothes on?"

"Traditionally, throughout the reception." She lowered her voice as they approached the rest of the wedding party. "But I have a feeling Abby and Max would understand if we wanted to change much sooner."

"Guess we'll at least have to take pictures first."

She groaned, and then hope lit her eyes. "Maybe not. People in the wedding parties usually wear matching dresses and tuxes, and since we all have on something different and Abby didn't personally choose any of these outfits..."

"Ah, good point." He grinned. "I say we duck out now. Go someplace and get naked."

She gave him a disdainful look. But then her expression changed when something caught her eye behind him. He turned to look but she grabbed his arm.

"Good idea," she said to his surprise, and pulled him toward the parking lot.

2

AS GOOD AS IT FELT to give Clint a taste of his own medicine, to see shock register in his eyes, Taylor's primary objective was to get away from the photographer. She ignored the man when he called out to her as she hustled Clint off toward the parking lot. She sure hoped he had a getaway car handy.

"Hey, that guy's calling you." Clint stopped, but she managed to pull him another few feet.

"Don't turn around. Just keep going."

"He's only the photographer." He stopped again, and this time she couldn't budge him. The muscles in his forearms bunched and tightened. "Has he been bothering you?"

The deadly glint in Clint's eyes startled her, then gave her a foolish thrill when she realized he wanted to defend her.

"No, nothing like that." She glanced over to see that Mona had intercepted the man. "He probably wants to take a picture."

Clint frowned. "And?"

"I'll strangle myself with your tie before I have a picture taken in this dress."

His roving gaze started at her throat, strayed to her chest and down further. She realized his jacket had parted and she drew the lapels together to cover herself. The appreciation in his gaze was hard to miss, and she struggled to take a breath.

"I think you look fantastic," he said in a low quiet voice that made her skin prickle with excitement. "But I understand. Why don't you go have a private talk with Abby? I know she'll understand, too."

She sighed. "I suppose that would be the adult thing to do."

He smiled and winked. "I'll go keep the shutterbug busy."

Taylor absently watched him walk toward Mona and the photographer. He was patient and understanding, especially considering she hadn't told him the entire story. From tugging on the hem of her dress so much, a rip had started in the back. Right now it was only about two inches long, but there hadn't been much skirt from the start. A safety pin could take care of the problem, but it was also a darn good excuse to change.

Surprised, she realized she'd grabbed hold of his jacket sleeves and was unconsciously pulling them tighter around herself—as though they were his arms embracing her.

It was easy to imagine him holding her as she breathed in the musky scent that clung to the fabric. *His* scent...rugged and masculine and entirely too alluring. She liked him. More than that, he appealed to her in a very primal way. Primal enough that if he asked her to get naked again, she just might take him up on it. Good thing she'd only be here for two days.

THE RECEPTION WAS HELD at the community center, most of the tables set up inside, with a few out in the courtyard near the makeshift stage where a band played country music. Occasionally they'd play something by Andy Williams or Tony Bennett, but then the songs were usually off-key and the singer mumbled the parts he didn't know.

Standing outside near a crooked desert palm, Taylor accepted a second glass of champagne and told herself that was it, no more. She'd had a long tiring day running through airports and sitting on planes next to wailing children. She hadn't even been able to work on the brief she needed for court next week.

And now, she couldn't change her clothes because the airlines had yet to find her luggage. Too bad everyone around here was so short. She couldn't even borrow anything. If it weren't for Clint's jacket, she would've wrapped herself in one of the red checkered tablecloths by now.

"I wondered where you'd run off to." Clint walked up with a beer in one hand and a plate of cheese in the other.

"Why, do you need your jacket back?"

"Nope. Not even if it were ten degrees." He offered the cheese. "I heard dinner isn't for another half hour. Want some?"

Taylor shook her head. "I thought the meal was catered. Why is everything so late?"

"This is Bingo, darlin'," he said with a slow smile while setting the plate on a nearby table. "People get to it when they get to it."

"But a wedding is a special occasion. Shouldn't they at least be…" she waved a hand, "trying to make sure things go smoothly?"

"Maybe, but no one seems to mind. They're all having a good time."

He was right. She followed his gaze toward the four couples who'd just lined up on the large hardwood squares serving as a dance floor. Their moves were foreign to her and she figured they were doing the two-step or line dancing or some such country thing. Other guests were laughing and talking and drinking out of paper cups or beer bottles.

Even Max seemed amazingly relaxed as he stood with his arm around Abby's waist, talking with Estelle and Herb. The idea that Max had just gotten married was staggering enough, but that he seemed oblivious to the checkered tablecloths, the smell of barbecued meat coming from smoking barrels near the playground, and the plastic utensils waiting at the end of the buffet table was almost inconceivable.

Taylor had attended several Bennett family weddings in Boston with Max. They had all been grand affairs with no expense spared. The kind of sparkling white weddings little girls fantasized about. Even Taylor had indulged in a fantasy or two. Not when she was little because that kind of opulence hadn't existed in her world. But this...

"Why the frown?" Clint startled her by nudging up her chin.

She blinked, then met his eyes. Tiny flames of green and gold danced against the light brown, making them hazel, she supposed. Only she'd never seen a color that remarkable before.

"What kind of dancing is that?" she asked, embarrassed to reveal her true thoughts. This was Clint's town, his people. They had a right to their own ways.

"Are you kidding? Where have you been?"

"Boston," she said wryly.

"Hey, even people in Boston know what line dancing is. Hell, they even know how to do it in Paris."

"Oh, you've been there?"

Ignoring her mocking tone, he said, "Twice, as a matter of fact." And then disregarded her start of surprise and added, "You must've been under a rock." He motioned with his long-neck beer bottle toward the dance floor. "Even yuppies started getting into this a few years ago."

Several other people had joined the line, some young, some old, all of them laughing and having a good time. Was Clint right? Was this another craze she'd missed because she'd kept her nose in law books so much?

"You really don't know, do you?" He was staring at her, his dark brows drawn together in a frown.

"About this type of dancing?" She shrugged and pulled the jacket tighter around her, nearly spilling her champagne. "I work long hours. I don't have a lot of free time."

She didn't know why she sounded defensive. It was none of Clint's business how she spent her time. Besides, she loved her job. Her salary paid for a BMW she'd never thought she'd own in a million years, and clothes she hadn't even dared dream about as a kid. Life was darn good.

His troubled gaze stayed on her for a minute, as if he were analyzing her. She didn't like it. "Come on," he said, taking her champagne glass from her and setting it down next to his beer and the plate of cheese.

"What?" She jerked her hand behind her back when he reached for it.

"Let me show you how it's done."

"You mean, dance?"

"Sure." He tried to grab her again.

Once more she evaded him. "No, thank you."

He caught hold of the jacket sleeve and tugged gently. It started to slide off her shoulders. "No one's going to laugh."

"That isn't my concern."

"Ah, the dress."

"Try the heels. They're lethal."

Clint smiled. "Kick them off."

"And go barefoot?"

"Sure. Tell you what…I'll take my boots off if it'll make you feel better."

Taylor laughed. "You would, wouldn't you?"

He looked surprised. "Why not?"

She shook her head, still chuckling over the image of them dancing barefoot like a couple of kids, and he took advantage of her weakened moment by capturing her hand and drawing her closer to the dance floor.

The music changed as soon as they got to the edge. It slowed down to an Andy Williams tune as best she could tell. "Gee, too bad. Maybe you can teach me next time."

The patronizing smile she gave him faded like an old photograph when he slipped an arm around her waist and hauled her up against him. Her breasts flattened against his chest.

"You didn't think I'd waste this song, did you darlin'?" he whispered near her ear, his breath gliding down her neck, skimming her spine and sending waves of longing that drowned her resolve.

She didn't resist, didn't say a word as he led her to the middle of the floor. He let her go, momentarily breaking the spell. Slowly, he buttoned the top of the jacket, his fingers brushing the skin above her breasts, as he made sure the tux stayed on her shoulders. Then he slipped an arm beneath the jacket around her waist, and brought her closer against him, his free hand finding hers.

His palm wasn't nearly as callused as she might have expected, the discovery distracting her when he brought her hand down against his thigh instead of extending it in the traditional manner.

Under the cover of the jacket, his fingers dipped into the low back of her dress and stroked her waist, his thumb massaging deep into her tired muscles. She wanted to close her eyes and lay her head against his chest, to let the erotic feelings building inside wash over her.

But there were so many people around, and having had a glass of champagne on an empty stomach was already flirting with disaster. She glanced around to find that not a single person was paying them any attention. More couples had crowded the dance floor, surrounding them and affording them ample privacy.

If Taylor tilted her head the slightest bit back he'd probably kiss her. And she'd let him. The realization that she'd thought about him once too often since meeting him months ago stung. It was so uncharacteristic of her. Not just because he was totally not her type, but because she had so little time for personal relationships.

Sadly, the main reason she saw Max so much was that he was also her client and not just her friend. The thought hadn't occurred to her until this evening, and it chafed because she'd never foreseen her life going this way. Family and friends had always been important to her. Now her career devoured her time like a ravenous beast.

But she wasn't in Boston now. She was far away from court deadlines and pending litigation and her barely manageable calendar. She was in Bingo, in Clint Southwick's strong arms, and if he tried to kiss her, she might even invite him back to her motel...

Almost as if he read her mind, he pulled her closer until no air separated them. Under the jacket his hand roamed the bare part of her back, molded the curve of her fanny. The fact that he was hardening against her, and that she could obviously feel it, didn't seem to bother him.

He hummed softly in her ear, rubbed his clean-shaven chin against her temple and lightly kissed her hair. Part of her French twist came loose and a thick lock of hair fell to her shoulder. Had he unpinned it?

She pulled back to look at him and he brushed his lips across hers. It was a fleeting kiss. Certainly nothing potent enough to make her heart pound and her knees turn to jelly, but she was suddenly having trouble keeping in step with him.

"Maybe we should take a walk," he whispered, his lips trailing the shell of her ear.

"I don't know." She glanced around. The other couples were either dancing close or laughing and talking. Abby, however, looked directly at them. She smiled when she caught Taylor's eye. "I don't think that's a good idea. They may start serving dinner and won't know where we are."

Clint laughed, the sound a deep seductive rumble in her ear. "In Bingo, someone always knows where you are."

"Great."

"A big-city girl like you worried about what people think? You surprise me."

She put a little distance between them and started to deny it, but it was the truth. "Don't you care?"

"Nope."

"Not even a little?"

"Why should I? If I bow to other people, do what they want me to do, are they going to pay the mortgage on my ranch? Take care of my horses and cattle if I can't? Hell, no. So tell me darlin', why should I concern myself with their opinions? As long as I don't bother them, they've got no call to bother me."

She wrinkled her nose. "I suppose if you work for

yourself, or aren't involved with the public much, it would be easy to have that attitude.''

"Maybe."

"I work for a very prominent, high-profile law firm," she said, annoyed by the patronizing lift of his lips. "I can't be as blasé about my appearance or conduct as you apparently are about yours."

"Too bad."

"I'm not complaining."

"Well, then what's got you so prickly all of a sudden?"

The music stopped, and Taylor was glad. There was no point in talking to this cowboy about things he simply didn't understand. Other than bumming around the country, Clint had probably only worked on a ranch. Things were different out in the real world. He didn't get it. And Taylor didn't want to interrupt her little holiday fantasy by explaining.

"Where are you going?" He caught her hand when she started to leave. "They'll play another song."

"I think I'll go...powder my nose."

He studied her face. "Your nose looks fine to me. Even that little bump. How did you get that? Old football injury?"

Taylor gasped. "How kind of you to notice, and point it out."

She turned, but he caught her hand again. "I'm not criticizing you. I'm just curious."

"I'm getting it fixed." Self-consciously, she brought a hand up to cover the flaw. "As soon as I have some time."

"Don't." His expression and tone were serious as he took her hand away from her face and held it. "It's a part of you. You're beautiful. Haven't you ever heard the term *Don't fix what isn't broke?*''

"That's the point. It *was* broken."

"See? It's part of your history, part of what made you who you are today. Tell me how it happened."

She stared at him, not sure what to say. Amazingly, he was serious. The last two guys she dated had urged her to correct the imperfection. She agreed she should. She shook her head. "You're crazy."

This time when she turned to leave he didn't stop her but followed her off the dance floor. "When did it happen? When you were a kid?"

Groaning, she stopped at the table with their drinks. "Why is this so important to you?"

He shrugged. "Just trying to get to know you."

"Let me give you a tip. Next time you try to pick up a woman, do not point out her ugliest feature. Call me crazy, but it takes the fun out of the evening."

"Taylor," he murmured and ran a hand up her arm, "don't penalize me for seeing things differently from you."

He'd already had her when he said her name in that lazy drawl of his, but when his palm created that pleasant warm friction on her skin, she was ready to forgive him anything.

But she wasn't ready to explain how she'd broken her nose as a young teenager, or why there'd been no money to fix it then. A janitor's salary didn't go far, especially not with five mouths to feed. Not that she blamed her father. Never. He did the best he could for his family.

"Taylor?"

She blinked. His hand was still on her arm and she had trouble focusing for a moment.

He gestured with his chin toward a white plastic chair. "Is that your purse? It's ringing."

"What?" She frowned. "Oh, my cell phone." She scrambled to grab her purse before the caller hung up. As if she didn't know who it was. It had to be Howard. It was almost always Howard. Her boss didn't believe in personal time.

"Hello?" She covered her other ear. "Yes, there's a party going on. I'm at a wedding, Howard. Max Bennett's wedding. Remember?"

She met Clint's quizzical gaze and mouthed that it was her boss, although why she'd felt compelled to do that she had no earthly idea. Annoyed with herself, she turned away so he couldn't hear her conversation.

Howard asked for some details on the case she was litigating, and then reminded her that she had a deposition on Tuesday. She patiently listened, knowing this recap was more for his own benefit than hers, but for the first time she could recall, his controlling nature needled her.

"I'll take care of everything, Howard. Don't I always?" Her tone came out sharper than intended. "I'll see you on Monday."

She disconnected the call and slipped the slim phone into the pocket of Clint's jacket. If she knew Howard, that would not be the only call he made to her today. Sighing, she turned back to Clint. He was sipping his beer and watching the band.

"Everything okay?"

She rolled her gaze toward the cloudless sky. "My boss wanted to remind me I had a deposition on Tuesday."

"This Tuesday?"

She nodded.

"When are you leaving?"

"Tomorrow night."

Disappointment clouded his features, darkened his eyes...made her heart flutter. "Why so soon?"

"I have a busy schedule."

"You flew all this way and you can't even stay for more than one night? Lady, anybody ever tell you to slow down?"

"Yeah, Max, but he's never had to work for a living," she said dryly.

"Working for a living is one thing, killing yourself for one is another."

"Ah, you know that much about me, huh?"

He gave her such a long odd look it made her think twice. Maybe Max had talked about her. The idea chafed.

"Everyone, may I have your attention?" Mona stood on one of the chairs, waving her arms, trying to get people to stop talking and listen. When the noise didn't settle down, she put two fingers between her lips and let out an ear-piercing whistle. That did the trick.

"Thank you," Mona said, smiling coyly. "Edna says the food is ready, so after the wedding party has loaded up their plates, you all can start getting in line." People started clapping and howling good-naturedly. Mona held up her hand for silence again. "But before you all start stuffing your faces, we're gonna have a toast to the bride and groom."

Mona bent down to listen to something Herb whispered in her ear, then called for everyone's attention again. "Change of plans. We're gonna eat first, and toast later."

Several people cheered, while Mona stepped down from the chair with Herb's help, and Taylor turned to Clint. He was grinning at her.

"What?" Her lips automatically lifted in response.

"I wish you could have seen your face when Mona gave her little spiel."

Taylor lost the smile and raised her eyebrows. "What do you mean?"

"Bet you've never been to a wedding like this before."

"Well..." Taylor narrowed her gaze. "Are you calling me a snob?"

He frowned in thoughtful silence for over a minute.

"You have to think about it?"

Amusement gleamed in his eyes. "I figure you'd expect lace and linen, maybe even real china?"

She shrugged a shoulder, eyeing a huge pot of baked beans being carried to the buffet table. "Well, I've never been to a reception that was a barbecue, if that's what you mean."

"What will you have for your wedding?" He looked earnest enough, but what an odd question.

"I don't know. I—"

"Come on, you two." Mona barged in between them and took them each by the arm. "Get your fannies over to the food so everyone else can eat, too. The head table is over there with the flowers and balloons."

"Yes, ma'am," Clint said, winking at Taylor. "I hope Edna made enough food. I've been thinking about her honey-glazed ribs all day."

Great. Ribs. Taylor sighed to herself. That was going to be fun and easy to eat. Now she wished she'd eaten the airline food after all. She was starving.

Clint picked up plates for both of them—white plastic, platter-shaped with a white-on-white trim. Obviously Edna had gone all out. Clint didn't seem to mind. He piled on half a rack of ribs, and a chicken leg drenched in a sweet red sauce that Taylor could smell from where she was. Space was already at a premium when he crowded in a giant scoop of beans and another of coleslaw, then added a big flaky biscuit on top. The amount of food alone made her slightly nauseous.

"Here you go." He offered her the plate. "I'll make mine and join you at the table."

She stared at the loaded plate. "You made that for...?" She gave him a dry look and chuckled. "Very funny."

She scanned the trays of food, ignoring the beans, opting for a little coleslaw and a biscuit, then fished out a small chicken breast she figured she could reasonably cut up with a plastic knife.

Clint was still beside her when she turned around. He frowned at her plate. "Is that all?" He shook his head. "Since you have room, bring me a couple more biscuits, will you?"

She nodded, startled at his familiarity and the realization that he probably really had made that plate of food for her. After choosing two plump buttery-looking biscuits, she followed him to the table, and was surprised when he automatically pulled out her chair. She supposed she really was a snob because she hadn't expected a cowboy to have such good manners.

"Taylor?"

She leaned forward to see Abby two seats down.

"I asked Rosie to keep tabs on the airlines to see if your luggage made it. If it's here and they can't deliver it tonight, Herb said he'll run out and get it."

Taylor had totally forgotten. "For goodness sakes, don't worry about my suitcase. You just have a good time."

Abby's smile spread across her glowing face. "I am having the time of my life."

"You'd better," Max growled from beside her and nuzzled her neck, sending her into peals of laughter.

Taylor quickly sat back and picked up her fork. It was still hard to see Max in this new role, to see him as part of a couple. For some reason, it gave Taylor a panicky feeling she couldn't explain.

"Were you ever romantically involved with Max?" Clint asked quietly.

"No." She shook her head, smiling. "We had one very platonic date after meeting our first day in law school. That was it. We've been great friends ever since."

His gaze roamed her face and then the corners of his mouth lifted slightly. He was apparently satisfied with her answer. Not that it was any of his business. Or that she cared what he thought.

"You really should try the ribs," he said after a brief silence, and she was relieved at the subject change.

"I'll stick with the chicken. It's less messy."

"So that's the problem." He pulled a piece of meat off a bone and held it to her lips. "You don't even have to get your fingers dirty."

"Uh, no thanks."

"Open up."

"I prefer chicken, really."

"Just one bite, Taylor." His gaze fastened on her, searing, intense, hypnotic. "Just because it's different doesn't mean you won't like it."

"I believe Eve made a similar comment to Adam. Look where it got them."

He gave her a lopsided smile. "Yeah, naked."

She sighed. "Just put the meat on my plate, please, and I'll taste it."

"Taylor." He shook his head in mock disappointment.

"Where's your sense of adventure? This is the wild west. Last of the untamed—"

She gave him a bland, unimpressed look. He smiled and did as she asked, and then licked the honey glaze off his fingers, slowly, methodically, until she found it impossible to look away.

He was clearly doing it on purpose, disconcerting her with his suggestiveness, making the heat erupt in her belly, rendering rational thought hopeless, and she seriously considered dumping her iced tea onto his lap. Except then he'd probably make her give up his jacket.

She thought about it for a moment, and decided she had a better idea. She'd give him exactly what he wanted.

3

"ARE YOU SURE you want more of that stuff?" Clint eyed the glass of champagne Taylor took off the tray. It wasn't as if she'd had too much to drink—as far as he knew she'd only had two glasses all evening. But she was acting mighty strange. She had been ever since dinner ended.

"Why?" She gave him a puzzled look as they walked back to the table they'd claimed earlier, away from the crowd near the crooked palm. "Don't you like champagne?"

"Nope. Never have."

"But you have tried it?"

He nodded. "A long time ago."

"Sometimes our tastes change. You should give it another try." She sat first, and when he took the seat across from her, she picked up the arms of her chair and scooted closer to him.

Things were getting stranger by the minute. He warily watched her bring the drink to her lips. Her tongue darted out to lick the rim of the glass before she took a leisurely sip, her eyes closing briefly as she savored the sparkling wine.

She set down the glass and smiled. "I wish you could see the look on your face right now."

"Huh?"

Taylor laughed. "I moisten the rim of the glass so my lipstick won't stick."

He straightened his back. "I knew that."

She laughed again. "So, you ready to give champagne another try?"

"No, thanks." He held up the beer he'd been nursing for the last half hour. "I'll stick with this."

"Oh, Clint, where's your sense of adventure?"

He gave her a wry look.

"Come on, just one little taste."

He narrowed his gaze on her. What was she up to? Throwing his words back at him, acting all coy and pouty. No doubt she was headed somewhere with all this. He'd know it even if the hair on the back of his neck wasn't standing straighter than a branding iron.

"All right," he said, finally. "One sip."

"I have something better." She dipped her index finger into the glass, letting only the pale pink-tinted tip trail through the bubbly. Then she brought it to his lips. "Here."

Clint's mouth went so dry, his chest burned like a Mexican chili pepper. Composing himself, he let her drag her finger across his lower lip. When she withdrew, he grabbed her hand. Her eyes widened slightly but she didn't struggle.

He licked the champagne off his lip, and then put her finger in his mouth and sucked it dry. "Hmm, you're right." Letting her go, he leaned back in his chair, but kept eye contact. "I like it better than I thought. I'll probably want more later."

Taylor blinked, sank back, and quickly took another sip. "Honestly, I like it mixed with orange juice better. It's an actual drink, called a mimosa, served at brunch. Ever had one?"

Her voice was slightly higher, her speech a little more rushed, and her cheeks had pinkened—subtle changes. Overall she still looked relatively cool and collected. Good, solid courtroom experience did that for a lawyer.

"Yeah, they're not bad." He leaned toward her again and captured her hand. "But I prefer my champagne like this." He took her finger and dipped it in her glass and brought it to his lips.

Ignoring her sharp intake of breath, he drew her finger into his mouth again.

"What's going on over here?" Mona walked up and planted her hands on her hips. "Don't tell me I have to plan another wedding so soon."

Taylor flew back so fast, her chair scraped the concrete with a horrible screech. "Why on earth would you say something so ridiculous?"

"Ha!" Mona's eyebrows, a perfect match to her red hair, rose in indignation. "I suppose you were just feeling for his tonsils."

"Mona, you old rascal, come here." Clint stood and gently pulled her toward his seat. "You've been working hard all day. Get a load off."

"Who you calling old?" Her gaze narrowed threateningly, but she accepted the seat, her face drawn and tired. In the next second she pulled a cigar out of the neckline of her low-cut dress. "While you're up, I'll take one of those glasses of champagne. In fact, make it two. I've never seen such puny glasses."

"Yes, ma'am." He gave her a mock salute. "How about you, Taylor? Can I get you anything?"

A paper bag to pull over her head, judging by the humiliation coloring her face. She cleared her throat. "No. Thank you."

"Okay, be right back."

"Take your time," Mona said. "Taylor and me will have a nice little chat."

Taylor looked less than pleased, and her eyes pleaded with him to hurry. The thought that he shouldn't leave them alone had crossed his mind, but hell, Taylor could handle Mona…although he wouldn't take any bets on that.

Unfortunately, the nearest watering hole had run out of champagne and he had to go clear across the courtyard. It wasn't all that far, but Mona's mouth could do one heck of a lot of damage in those extra two minutes.

Gloria, one of Edna's waitresses, was working behind the makeshift bar, and moving slower than a turtle crossing Main Street. She kept having to stop and push up her oversized glasses that were Scotch taped at the bridge. He hoped this extra job would make her enough money to finally fix the darn things, except he knew better.

Folks around Bingo were content to let things be; they avoided change no matter how much it improved their lives. After living away for so long, he was having trouble getting used to that attitude.

"Hope you're not planning on drinking all of those by yourself." Max eyed the lineup of champagne and beer Gloria had set in front of Clint. "You wouldn't be trying to get Taylor drunk, would you?"

"Nah, we're trying to get Mona to pass out."

Max laughed. "Good luck. But I have a feeling she might be meaner drunk."

"Man, I didn't even have chief petty officers as demanding as that woman."

"That doesn't surprise me." Max's expression sobered. "Does Taylor know about your naval career?"

"I doubt it, unless Abby said something. But there's

no reason Taylor should know." Clint grabbed two of the champagne glass stems in one hand. "Why do you ask? Has she got a thing against the military?"

"No, I just figured she'd be interested in you being a lawyer."

"Ex-lawyer. I'm a rancher now."

"Right."

Clint frowned as he snatched the beer. "*You* went to law school. Do you consider yourself a lawyer?"

Max snorted. "No way."

"The way I see it…" He shrugged, not sure what he was thinking, or what any of this had to do with Taylor. Except that it'd been an enormous decision to leave the career about which he'd been so passionate at one time. But had he stayed, the emotional toll would have been too high. That didn't mean the itch to return didn't nag him. Best he didn't think about that phase of his life. "My JAG career is past tense. I'm just a cowboy trying to make a living."

"Good enough." Max clapped him on the back. "Just one more thing. Taylor isn't as tough as she seems. Go easy."

Clint stared at him for a moment, not knowing what to say. Max had left a lot more unsaid; it was in his eyes. A warning, maybe? He liked and respected Max, and Clint didn't blame him for looking out for his friend, but still, it was easy to take offense. Did Max think Clint wasn't good enough for her?

Max and Taylor came from that other place across the tracks where people used too many forks for one meal. The same kind of place the other officers Clint had served with had come from. But Max was different, he reminded himself, he'd shunned his family, married Abby, started new roots in Bingo. Clint was probably being unfair assuming Max didn't approve.

"Why don't you come back with me and say hi to Taylor?" Clint asked. "She'd like spending time with you."

A slow knowing grin curved Max's mouth. "It seems she's been having a good enough time with you."

"Uh…yeah…well…"

Max chuckled and held up his hands in supplication. "Hey, it's none of my business, but don't let Abby or Mona see you getting chummy. They'll plan the wedding first and ask questions later."

Clint just laughed as he ambled back toward the women. There might be some truth to that, but he didn't have to worry. Taylor would be gone before he could blink an eye.

AS SOON AS CLINT had left, Mona had leaned closer to Taylor. "So what do you think?"

Taylor lifted her brows. "About?"

"Don't play coy with me, missy. I'm talking about Clint, of course. Handsome devil, ain't he? And he has a real nice spread just east of town. It's the second largest ranch in the county."

"How nice for him."

Mona gave her a steely-eyed stare. "You've got that same smart mouth Max used to have, but we'll see…"

"Smart mouth?" Taylor slumped back in her chair. "Mona, I just met the man and you're practically giving me his portfolio."

"His what?" The older woman stopped in the middle of lighting her cigar. It wasn't even one of those slim ladies' cigars. It was big, ugly, hand-rolled and probably stank worse than it looked.

"You're not going to smoke that here, are you?"

"You see a remote control attached to this thing? Where else am I going to smoke it?" Mona lit a match.

Taylor blew it out. "Not here."

"That was rude."

"No ruder than you lighting up under my nose without asking if I minded."

Mona glared at her. "You're too sassy for Clint. He needs a nice girl. Someone who isn't mouthy and has good manners. A real lady."

"Good luck. I hope you find her." Taylor folded her shaky hands on her lap so Mona couldn't see the effect of her words—which was so insanely ridiculous Taylor could hardly stand it. What did she care what Mona thought?

Taylor did not aspire to be a "nice girl" or a "real lady." She'd already been a nice girl, the one who sacrificed for others, who studied hard to please her parents. But Mona's remark still stung.

Barracuda. The Shark. The nicknames her colleagues called her were mostly in fun. They were a tribute to her winning trial record. But the implied images made her cringe. She'd never wanted to be the kind of lawyer who pushed and pried at all costs, even to the point of drawing blood.

After staring at Taylor in a thoughtful and uncomfortable silence, Mona asked, "Where are you staying tonight?"

"A motel."

"The Lazy Susan? Bah. Why not the Swinging R?"

Taylor half smiled. "I didn't think you'd want a mouthy broad like me around."

Mona's lips twitched. "You should stay with us. Max has made a lot of changes. The place is looking real nice.

The girls and I were thinking it might make a fine boardinghouse, or even one of those fancy bed-and-breakfasts.''

"Sounds interesting." But impractical with no customers way out here. However, Taylor kept that thought to herself.

"Yup, we figure with them finding silver so close to Bingo, we just might start getting tourists, maybe even prospectors."

"What silver?"

"You didn't hear about them finding silver in that old abandoned mine? Max must have been too busy thinking about the wedding. Of course I would have expected it to make national news, Nevada being the leading producer of silver." Mona squared her shoulders with an air of self-importance. "I heard that tidbit on the local six o'clock."

"Great. I know Abby and Max are interested in bringing more industry and jobs to town. Maybe this will help."

"Help?" Mona grunted. "This is big news. Why, this could change everything—"

"Here you go." Clint set two glasses of champagne on the table. Half the wine sloshed out of one glass onto the table, and Mona's cigar. "Hope you didn't get too parched waiting for me."

"For crying out loud, look what you've gone and done." Mona picked up the soggy stogie and stared balefully at it.

"You shouldn't be smoking anyway." Clint winked at Taylor. "Besides, I thought you reserved those things for poker nights."

"And special occasions." She muttered a curse. "And since no one will play poker with me anymore, I guess

I won't be smoking another one until the babies start coming."

Taylor looked at Clint, then back at Mona. "What babies?"

Mona frowned as if Taylor were dimwitted. "Max and Abby's babies, of course."

"Is there something I don't know?" Taylor looked to Clint for help.

He shrugged. "Beats me. I think Mona may just be speculating, huh, Mona?"

"It'll happen." Mona stood, shaking her head. Her hair was so teased and sprayed, nothing moved. "Sooner or later, there'll be a parade of those little critters running around underfoot. You'll see."

Taylor idly watched Mona down a glass of champagne, then meander toward Herb and Estelle, her second glass in one hand, her ruined cigar in the other. It was unnerving to think of Max as a father, holding a baby or changing a diaper. Mind-boggling, really.

"Man, it's weird to think of Abby being a mother," Clint said, a mystified expression wrinkling his brows. "I've seen her with the kids she teaches, and she's great with them and all that, but man..." He shook his head. "I don't know. It's just weird."

"I know." Taylor made a face as her gaze sought out her friend. He was dancing with his bride. "I was just thinking the same thing about Max. What a scary thought."

"Why?" Clint stared at her quizzically. "Because you think he wouldn't be a good father? Or is it more personal?"

She hesitated. "What do you mean by personal?"

"Scary because you're thinking it's time for you to settle down, too?"

"No!" Her response came out too abruptly.

"Whoa!" He reared his head back. "Guess you know what you want, or don't want."

"Time for a subject change." She picked up her champagne and took a sip. She was tired from the long flight and feeling more emotional than usual. Part of it was because her best friend had just gotten married. She didn't want to think about what the other part might be.

"Okay," he drawled, a hint of mischief in his voice. "Where were we when Mona interrupted?"

After a moment's reflection, she nearly spit out the champagne.

"Ah, I remember." Clint moved closer. "You were trying to sell me on the merits of sparkling wine."

"No, I believe we got past that part."

"Hmm, I must have missed something." He took a loose tendril of her hair between his fingers and played with the tip. "How long is your hair?"

She jerked her head a little but he didn't let go. "That's an odd question."

"I've only seen it up in that twist thing."

"So?"

"So, take it down and let me see."

She laughed. "Now?"

He pursed his lips, the expression casual, and then he looked directly into her eyes. "Or we could go to my place."

Taylor stared back, uncertain what to say, or how to react. Isn't that what she'd decided she wanted just over an hour ago? To have a little harmless fling? She'd be getting on that plane tomorrow no matter what, so why not get Clint out of her system?

There was a strong physical and chemical attraction between them. She knew enough about body language and certain male nuances to know he was as much a victim to the attraction as she was. What would be the harm of one night together?

She turned away and stared at the crowded dance floor. Oh, God, this was so not like her to even vaguely consider a one-night stand.

"Taylor?" He lightly touched her hand, and she met his eyes—warm, infuriating, irresistible. "Let's just enjoy the rest of the evening and see what happens."

She nodded, and he smiled, picked up her hand and kissed the back of it.

The music changed from country and western to something slow and moody. Taylor was about to ask him if he wanted to dance, when he tugged at her hand and inclined his head toward the dance floor.

She stood, tempted to shuck his jacket, the hell with the skimpy dress. But then she remembered all the wonderful things he'd done to her back under the cover of that jacket.

Keeping hold of her hand, he led her to the dance floor. She stepped in close and put both her arms around his neck. He slid his hands beneath the jacket and pulled her even closer. Her heart started to pound so hard he had to feel it. Her breathing had also quickened, and when she tried to regulate it, the air seemed to clog her throat.

It was astounding how a man she barely knew could affect her this way, especially one that wasn't even remotely her type. But heaven help her, if he tried to kiss her right now she wouldn't care, not even if everyone stopped and watched. She'd kiss him back with everything she had to give.

"Taylor?"

She didn't want to break the contact, to lose the pleasant friction of her breasts rubbing against his muscled chest, but she reluctantly pulled back slightly to gaze at him.

It was a mistake...depending on how you looked at it.

Their eyes met for only an instant, and then his gaze lowered to her mouth, lingered for several seconds before his head started to slant and come closer. She took a quick breath and met him halfway.

He had incredibly malleable lips, covering every millimeter of hers with a gentleness that was almost frustrating. She didn't know how he'd managed it, but he tasted of butterscotch. Sweet, addictive...making her want more...of his mouth, of him.

Astonished at her own boldness, she touched the tip of her tongue to the seam of his lips. His hands tightened on her back, his fingers digging into her bare skin, making her bolder. She put more pressure on his mouth, until he opened to her and their tongues met.

He immediately hardened against her belly and she suddenly wanted to be rid of the jacket, her dress, wanting no barrier between them. But she had to stop herself, tone things down. She'd regret her foolish behavior later.

Clint must have been having similar thoughts because they both cooled it at the same time. Their lips parted, touched briefly again, and then they pulled back and stared at each other with glazed eyes. At least she thought his were glazed. She was practically seeing double.

After a few steadying moments, he said, "Looks like Max and Abby are getting ready to head out."

That meant it was their opportunity to leave, as well, and Taylor's nerve shriveled like a raisin.

Maybe nothing serious would happen. Maybe they'd kiss and cuddle and talk all night. Stay up to see the sunrise. She met his eyes again—dark, mysterious, intense.

Nothing serious? Yeah, right.

She swallowed. "I guess we'd better go say goodbye."

"Yeah, we should. Just give me a minute."

Taylor swallowed again when she realized why he needed the time-out. Her gaze fell to his damp lips and the perverse desire to get him excited again made her snuggle closer. "Do you know what time they leave for the Caribbean tomorrow?"

Clint shifted. "Uh, darlin', you're not helping my condition."

"Sorry," she mumbled, and one side of his mouth lifted. He obviously didn't believe her apology for a second.

"They aren't leaving until tomorrow evening. A bunch of us are supposed to go to the Swinging R for brunch tomorrow and watch them open presents. Mona's idea, I believe."

"That's right. I remember now." She sighed, hoping she had at least a few brain cells left in her head. That's why she'd scheduled an evening flight home.

"Well, shall we?" He motioned her ahead of him.

She straightened the jacket around her shoulders, and tugged down the hem of her dress, which had ridden up considerably. The song hadn't yet ended and she had to weave her way through the dancing couples.

Max and Abby already had a crowd around them, and Taylor stood back to wait her turn. Clint moved in beside her, his shoulder touching hers, his fingers lightly drawing patterns on the back of her hand. When she slid him a shy glance, he smiled, such a tender, sincere, reassuring smile, she no longer had any doubt what she wanted...at least for tonight.

An older couple moved away from Abby, and Clint motioned Taylor ahead of him. Before she reached Abby, her cell phone rang. She gave Clint an exasperated look and shrugged as she reached into the jacket pocket for it.

He gestured toward an empty bench off to the side. "It's quieter over there. I'll be talking to Abby and Max." He paused. "Tell your boss to get a life."

Taylor smiled, and as she moved away, she flipped open the slim phone. Before she could say hello, a gruff voice barked, "It's about time you answered. Where the hell were you?"

It wasn't Howard. She had no idea who it was. "You have the wrong number."

"Come on, Maggie, you don't think I recognize your voice? Put him on the line."

Taylor was about to disconnect the call, but instead asked, "Who did you want to speak to?"

The man muttered a curse. "Put Clint on. Now."

Confused, Taylor didn't respond right away. Why would someone call for Clint on her cell? Maybe... She took the phone away from her ear and studied it. It looked like her phone.

"Maggie, I'm losing my patience."

She'd faintly heard the caller speak and brought the phone back to her ear, while she felt inside the other jacket pocket, and withdrew another phone.

Her phone.

The two were identical, except for the tiny dot of red nail polish near the Send button she'd never been able to remove. Apparently this other phone belonged to Clint.

"Okay, Maggie, you tell him something for me—"

"Uh, sir, if you'll just hold on a minute—"

"I ain't holding on. You just tell him I want in on that Swinging R deal. At least fifty percent of anything that's dug up, or I'm blowing the whistle on his silver mining scam."

Stunned, Taylor sank down on the bench. "Who is this?"

But the man had already disconnected the call.

The word *scam* echoed in her head as her gaze sought Clint. He was standing next to Max, talking and laughing, as if the two were great friends.

Except now Taylor wasn't so sure. Who exactly was Clint Southwick? Friend or foe? She suddenly had no idea.

Heaven help her, a minute ago she'd been ready to sleep with him.

4

"TAYLOR, ARE YOU all right?" Max narrowed his gaze with concern. "You look pale."

Beside him, Abby nodded. "In fact, maybe you should sit down. Did you have enough to eat?"

Taylor could barely concentrate on the conversation. Thoughts scrambled inside her head as she tried to make sense of the phone conversation, but kept coming up with more and more questions.

She dismissed their apprehension with a casual wave of her hand. Thank God it didn't shake. "I'm fine, really. It was such a long flight, and you forget I'm still on East coast time."

"Probably been working too hard." Max shook his head at her. "You've got to slow down, Taylor."

"Cut it out," she said, giving herself a shake. She punched him playfully in the arm. "I came over here to congratulate you again, not get scolded. So, where are you headed for the night. The Vegas strip?"

"Sorry, it's a secret."

Abby laughed. "We can tell *them*." She turned to Taylor and Clint. "We don't want Mona to know. We're just going to Mesquite, which is probably silly since we have to be back at the Swinging R by noon."

Taylor's insides constricted. What the hell was she going to do now? She had to tell them about Clint, that he could be out to swindle them in some way, but she didn't want to ruin their honeymoon. Nor could she toss around accusations without more evidence. She could wait until they returned. As long as Max was out of town he couldn't sign anything that would jeopardize his property.

"By the way," she said casually, "have you decided what to do with the Swinging R? Mona said something about making it into a bed-and-breakfast."

Max gave her a funny look, then chuckled. "As much as I'd love to discuss business and the Swinging R with you, I have something a little more pressing on my mind." He slipped an arm around Abby. "Like getting the hell out of here."

Everyone laughed, and Max leaned forward to give Taylor a peck on the cheek. "We'll see you tomorrow, right?"

She nodded. "I have a late flight."

Max slapped Clint on the back with a sly look Taylor's way. "Then I know we'll see you tomorrow."

Her heart sank when she saw the exchange. She'd made a total fool of herself over this...this scoundrel. And everyone would know it once she exposed him.

"YOU'RE AWFULLY QUIET." Clint tried to take her hand.

Taylor moved it away and pretended to scratch her chin. When she was through, she laid her hand on her lap, under the table where he couldn't get to it.

"Like I told Max and Abby, I'm tired." She glanced at her watch. Only ten minutes since they'd left. Ten minutes she'd sat here with Clint, trying to figure out what in the heck to do. Her brain was pure mush. "I think I'll go find Rosie and see if she's heard anything about my luggage."

"If she hasn't I can run you out to the airport." He

held her gaze. "Or I have a shirt you can sleep in tonight."

"I'm sure they've located my bag by now." She stood, and hoped he stayed put. She needed some thinking time. Away from him. Away from the suggestion in his eyes, his voice. He still thought they were on for tonight. This was going to be sticky.

He got up from the chair, and her stomach rolled. "I'm going to go say hi to a couple of guys I haven't seen in a while. Shall we meet back here?"

Relief calmed her. "Sure."

"Say, fifteen, twenty minutes?"

"Sure."

He gave her a troubled look. "It was the phone call that upset you."

Her knees wobbled. "What phone call?"

"That last one before we saw Max and Abby off. Was it your boss again?"

"Oh, yeah." She sighed. "He's uptight about a case I'm trying in a couple of weeks. It's one of our firm's major clients."

He whistled. "You must be their star."

"I'm very good at what I do," she said looking meaningfully into his eyes. "I investigate my facts thoroughly. I make sure I know exactly who my opponent is, and I don't like to lose."

He grinned. "Remind me never to oppose you."

"It would be an extremely bad idea." She turned to go in search of Rosie, but not before she caught the bewilderment on his face.

Good. Let him make himself crazy wondering what she meant. Tempting as it was, she didn't look back. She saw Rosie right away, her snow-white hair making her easy to spot in a group of women talking near the bar.

Taylor wasn't half as anxious about her lost luggage as she was to learn more about the new silver discovery. Mona had mentioned it, but Taylor figured Rosie would be a more reliable source of facts.

Seconds before she reached the group, the phone rang again. Taylor stopped, took a deep breath. It was the right pocket, which meant it was Clint's phone. As she reached for it, she ambled off to a private area on the grass before she answered.

"Uh, I think I have the wrong..." It was a woman. She had a soft youthful voice, probably in her twenties. "Is Clint Southwick there?"

Damn. Damn. Damn. "He's around somewhere, but I can't locate him at the moment."

"Oh." After a long pause, she asked, "Could you give him a message?"

Taylor held her breath. "Sure."

"Tell him Sheila's waiting up for him."

Taylor gritted her teeth and briefly closed her eyes. If Clint were in front of her right now, she'd think about doing some serious bodily harm to him. She'd assumed the woman was another of his scam pals. Obviously she had a more personal arrangement with him. He had some nerve asking Taylor to go home with him. What a snake!

"That's all," the woman said when Taylor hadn't responded.

"Fine. I'll tell him." She quickly disconnected the call before the woman demanded to know who Taylor was, although she hadn't really seemed curious or upset. Clearly she was used to Clint being a philanderer.

She slipped the phone back into the jacket and continued toward Rosie, counting to ten under her breath so that she didn't blow it as soon as she opened her mouth.

As cool as she could be in the courtroom, right now, she wanted to scream.

"I was going to go find you," Rosie said when she saw Taylor approach. "I talked with a very nice woman from the airlines and she assured me your bag is coming in on the next flight from Salt Lake City."

"Utah? That wasn't even one of my stops."

Rosie gave her a sympathetic smile. "At least you know they've found it."

"When is the next flight?"

"Tomorrow morning."

"Great."

"Don't worry, honey, we have everything you need at the Swinging R." Rosie briefly glanced past Taylor, and lowered her voice. "But maybe I shouldn't assume you're coming back with us." She winked.

Terrific. For one of the few times in her life, Taylor was speechless. Had everyone seen her make a fool of herself with Clint?

"That happened to my grandson just last month," said one of the women who'd been talking to Rosie. "Except his suitcase ended up all the way in Quebec, or another one of them foreign countries." She waved a hand, withered from too much desert heat. "I can't remember."

"That happened to Zelda Sorrenson's nephew, too, but they never did find his bag," another woman said, her dentures clicking with every other word. "And I heard they only reimbursed him a hundred-and-fifty dollars." Straightening, she lifted her double chin. "That's a crying shame, ain't it?"

The two other women in the group promptly had to tell their lost baggage stories, too, and Taylor sighed to herself. She hated to be rude and pull Rosie aside but...

A better idea came to mind.

One of the women got distracted by a passerby eating a slice of chocolate cake, and Taylor knew she had to act fast to keep the grapevine intact.

"You know," she said, butting in and promptly getting everyone's attention. "I sure hope the situation at McCarron Airport improves before tourism picks up out here."

The women all stared at her as if she'd polished off one too many glasses of champagne. The one with the clicking dentures snorted. "Tourists? Out here?"

The tiny bluish-haired woman who'd been relatively quiet until now asked, "Why on God's good earth would tourists come to Bingo?"

"Oh." Taylor blinked. "Maybe I misunderstood."

"Misunderstood what?" two of them said together, all eyes on Taylor.

"About the silver mine."

They all seemed confused and looked at each other.

Rosie groaned. "You've been talking to Mona."

Taylor nodded. "She said something about an old mine being rediscovered."

"Ida, did you hear anything about that?" The blue-haired woman turned to the denture clicker.

Ida frowned. "Not a peep."

"Hold on, girls." Rosie waved a hand to get their attention. "Mona overheard something that's got her convinced there's still silver around here. Don't pay that rumor no mind. You know Mona. She's been bored senseless since no one will play poker with her anymore."

Disappointment registered in everyone's eyes. "Shoot, I thought we'd finally have some excitement around here," Ida said. "But since I do all the recording work for the land office, I would've heard something, even if it was a rumor."

"What about the old Swanson mine?" someone asked. "Didn't Clint Southwick just buy that parcel?"

Ida nodded. "Yeah, but he didn't want the mine, only the land. Some of it's still good for cattle grazing."

Taylor's pulse quickened. She wasn't so sure of that. "You mean like the Swinging R?"

Rosie frowned. "What are you talking about?"

"The land north of the Swinging R." Ida nodded. "I hear Wilson's Creek has kept some of that gully green enough to feed a couple of herd."

Concern left Rosie's eyes. "Now that you mention it, I think I may have heard Maxwell talking about selling some of that land to Clint."

"Might as well." Ida shrugged her plump shoulders. "It's not doing anybody any good as it is."

"Maybe Max will use the money he gets to fix up the Swinging R some more." The blue-haired woman leaned in a little, as if she had something important to pass on. "I heard he just ordered a new living room suite from Floyd Merriweather's store over in Saunder's Bend."

"Why didn't he get Virgil to order him furniture?" Ida grunted. "I bet that old cheapskate Floyd charged him twenty percent over retail. He did my sister Bertha."

"Why, he gave me a real good deal two years ago—"

"He wasn't such a cheapskate two years ago. Ever since his wife ran off with—"

"This is all so fascinating," Taylor broke in, hoping to rewind the conversation. "We don't have silver mines and such back east."

Ida stared at her. "What's so fascinating about dead silver mines? There's nothing more depressing if you ask me. We all depended on those mines at one time. Our fathers and husbands worked there to put food on our tables."

The thought deepened Taylor's worry. If there was silver, it belonged to these people whose sweat was used to mine it. Was Clint really so heartless and mercenary? "Maybe there's still silver that hasn't been discovered. Maybe Bingo will—"

"Lordy, but you have a vivid imagination." Ida turned back to her cronies. "Let me finish telling you about Floyd's wife and that phony Indian chief she ran off with..."

Taylor sighed when she saw that even Rosie's attention was glued to Ida. Since Taylor had no interest in Floyd or his two-timing wife, she quietly moved away from the group. She saw Clint immediately. He stood only several yards away, watching her.

A shiver skimmed her spine and she pulled his jacket tighter around her shoulders. Had he heard her prod the women for information? Not from where he currently stood, but he could have been closer. No, the ladies would have spotted him and called him over to join them. Everyone seemed to love Clint. Could he have everyone fooled? Even Max? No way was she leaving Bingo before she found out.

He started in her direction. "Any news on your luggage?"

"It's coming from Salt Lake City tomorrow morning."

He smiled, shaking his head. "Hope it gets here before you leave."

Her return smile wasn't so pleasant. "Anxious for me to leave, are you?"

"Why would you say a thing like that? Darlin', I'd keep you here for a month if I could."

"I bet," she muttered under her breath. Of course, he didn't know that she was onto him.

He glanced at his watch. It was gold, and although she

couldn't tell if it was real gold, it was an awfully nice piece for a cowboy to own. "You about ready to leave?"

"What time is it?" She ignored her own watch, and moved closer to get a look at his.

A smug smile curved his lips, and he immediately put an arm around her waist, drawing her against him. "Time to get out of here."

She squirmed out of his hold. "Stop it."

His brows drew together in a puzzled frown, and he promptly dropped his arms to his side. His confusion was genuine and she realized he'd actually thought she'd moved closer to be embraced.

"What's wrong, Taylor?"

She shrugged. "I'm disappointed about my bag."

He didn't say anything, nor did he make a move to get close again, and it occurred to her it wouldn't be smart to distance him. If she wanted to find out what he was up to she'd better be a little nicer. The idea galled her.

She took a deep breath. "I'm sorry," she said, making big cow eyes at him. "My makeup and everything is in there. I usually keep some key items in a carry-on, but I brought my briefcase and it was heavy enough..." She gave a helpless, feminine shrug, and hoped she wouldn't make herself gag.

The corners of his mouth lifted in sympathy, and he slid an arm around her shoulders. This time she didn't shake him off. "I know someone who could lend you some things until a store opens tomorrow morning."

Sheila? It took every ounce of her self-control not to utter the name. Seeing the shock on his face would almost be worth it. The man on the phone had called her Maggie. She wondered how Clint would react if she mentioned that name.

"Like I said earlier, I have a shirt you can sleep in. I even have a spare toothbrush."

"How convenient."

He gave her a funny look.

She smiled coyly. "I guess I should tell Herb I don't need a ride. I don't want him hanging around looking for me."

They'd already started walking and he guided her toward the parking lot. "Don't worry. He knows you're with me."

Only he doesn't know the real you either. She left the words tucked safely inside her head. "Thanks for shuttling me around."

He stopped and turned her to face him. They were closer to the cars than to the wedding guests, and there were more shadows than lights. "You think I'm hanging around just to do Max and Abby a favor?"

"I didn't say that."

He tipped her chin up and lowered his head. His warm breath dancing across her cheek was an invitation she didn't want. Intellectually anyway, but her mouth had moved a fraction to meet his, and before she could remind herself he might be the enemy, their lips melted together, his tongue demanded entry.

She allowed her traitorous body another moment of gluttony before she pulled away. "I think we've given everyone enough of a show tonight, don't you?"

"No one's watching." He slid the jacket off her shoulders. "They're all trying to finish off the free booze."

"What are you doing?"

He answered by lowering his head and kissing her bare shoulder, and then her collarbone.

"Clint?"

He trailed his tongue down her cleavage, nipped with his teeth at her sensitive skin.

She briefly closed her eyes, disgusted with herself for being so turned on. "Clint?"

"I've thought about you so many times since I met you on Main Street," he murmured, his voice hoarse, gravelly. He worked his way back up, kissing her collarbone again, her neck.

His declaration startled her, rendering her momentarily helpless to speak or reason. He sounded so sincere. That fact would only complicate matters if she allowed it. He was still a man, and his physical attraction to her had nothing to do with his ethics, with his lack of conscience.

"We can't—" Her voice caught when he let the jacket slide down her back to her waist, and then used it to trap her against him.

"Taylor, kiss me."

She held her breath. His arousal thrust against her belly, rock-hard, insistent, and God help her but she wanted to kiss him. She wanted to feel his warm flesh rubbing against hers, his tongue teasing her nipples. But there was a very real possibility that he was a swindler, a thief. How much more pathetic could she be?

The disheartening reminder gave her enough strength to push him away. To his credit, he swiftly loosened the jacket around her, allowing her to step back.

He looked confused, wary. "Taylor…"

A cell phone rang. She stood, staring at him, paralyzed, wondering how she should handle the situation if it was his phone again. Should she pretend she didn't know it was in his other pocket? Hoping it was hers this time, she scrambled for the jacket. He readily let it go, but irritation marred his expression.

The ringing phone was his. She made a quick decision and answered the call.

"I need your help," the man on the other end said before she even spoke. He was obviously a heavy smoker, his voice coarse and raspy. "I'm in the Saunder's Bend jail. I need you to bail me out."

She hesitated, not sure if she should reply, hang up, or hand Clint the phone. She cleared her throat. "I think you have the wrong number."

A pause on the other end. "Where's Clint?"

"Just a moment." She widened her eyes at Clint, trying to look innocent, bewildered. "It's for you."

He frowned, looking genuinely baffled, and then the fog seemed to lift. "It's mine. Just bought it a week ago." He took the phone from her. "I forgot I had the damn thing."

Staying right where she was, she folded her arms, expecting him to slink off to privacy, especially when he found out one of his fine, upstanding friends needed to be bailed out of jail.

"Clint Southwick," he stated into the phone, surprising her with his businesslike tone, and by staying beside her. He listened to the caller, then sighed with disgust. "I ought to leave you there. This is the second time this month."

She studied him, mystified that he seemed unconcerned she was present. Of course he didn't know his friend had already told her what he wanted.

Clint listened a while longer, then said, "I'm not going out there tonight. Tomorrow morning I'll see what I can do." At something the caller said, Clint mumbled a mild curse. "None of your business." He disconnected the call, and shook his head.

"Problem?"

"Nothing that can't wait until morning. Now where were we?"

"On our way to your car."

A slow grin curved Clint's mouth as he dropped the phone back into the tux pocket and then draped the jacket over his arm. "Right. This way."

Grateful he didn't resume their intimacy, she followed him to a shiny new red pickup truck. He opened the passenger door for her and she noted the inside was as spotlessly clean as the outside. She stepped up, ignoring the hand he offered, and slid into the black leather seat.

She'd never ridden in a pickup truck before and she hadn't expected it to be so state-of-the-art. The dashboard had lots of strange gadgets, and a CD player. Once they'd gotten on the highway, she was further surprised at the smooth ride.

"Do you want to pick up some things now or wait until tomorrow? I'll give you a shirt and toothbrush for tonight."

She swallowed, took a deep breath. "I won't need anything. I've decided to go to the Lazy Susan."

Although she kept her attention straight ahead, she knew he'd turned to look at her. Silence fell, loud and awkward.

"Okay," he finally said. "We'll be there in five minutes."

The silence continued until they passed through town and the ugly motel came into sight—except everything was dark.

"What's your room number? I'll shine my headlights until you get your key in the door."

Taylor blinked. "I don't have one yet. I went straight to the church."

Clint chuckled. "Darlin', this is Bingo. Everything closes by nine, including the Lazy Susan. Hector is sleeping by now, and since he's as deaf as a post, looks like you're stuck with me."

5

OH, HE WAS SMOOTH, Taylor thought as she glanced from his country-style living room to his sprawling den. She'd bet his place looked just like any other rancher's in the valley with the quaint needlepoint wall hangings, the handmade quilts casually thrown over the leather chairs.

A couple of things really surprised her, though. The house was huge, at least five times larger than her little thousand-square-foot apartment, all one level, with several double doors from the bedrooms and living room, leading outside to the surrounding deck. It was too dark to see what the house overlooked, but they seemed to be sitting on a small hill and she guessed there was some sort of scenic view below.

The other thing was, Clint had lots of books, walls of books. Shelves on either side of the fireplace in the den were crowded with hardbacks on one side and paperbacks on the other.

From her cursory glance it appeared the books covered a wide range of subjects from modern ranching to Nevada state law. That didn't surprise her. He was probably trying to figure out how much time he'd get in the state pen when he got caught trying to swindle his neighbors out of their land, or mineral rights, or whatever he was up to.

"You want anything to drink?" Clint called from the kitchen.

She wandered in that direction and saw him peering into the refrigerator. Like the rest of the rooms, the kitchen was large...with blue gingham curtains, of course.

He pulled out a jug of milk, and when he saw her he smiled. "I've got orange juice, milk, cola, beer and water. That's it."

"Water would be fine."

He set the milk jug on the butcher-block island, and then got down two glasses from the hickory cabinet to the right of the sink. Everything was spotless; even the cupboards had been polished to a high sheen and the brass accessories gleamed.

"Do you live here alone?" Taylor poured his milk while he got her water from a built-in dispenser on the freezer door.

He looked surprised that she'd performed the reciprocal courtesy, which irked her. "No, Maggie lives here."

Maggie. Taylor straightened as he handed her the glass. She left his on the butcher-block island.

He picked up his milk, and made a motion with his head toward the den. "Let's go sit for a few minutes, and then I'll show you where the bedrooms are. I think you'll have a choice of three. I'm not sure, though. I don't like Maggie working all day so I told her not to bother keeping the rooms all ready."

They both sat, him in a burgundy leather club chair near the fireplace, while Taylor chose the couch and used a quilt to cover her legs. She kicked off her shoes and sighed with relief.

"Cold?" he asked.

"You try wearing this sad excuse for a dress."

He made a sympathetic face and stood. "I'll turn the heat up."

"No, I'd rather have a flannel shirt or something like that if you have one." She truly wasn't that cold. But the quilt draped over her legs as it was, kept him from getting a view all the way to Outer Mongolia.

"Sure."

"It can wait," she said quickly, frustrated that he hadn't clarified who Maggie was to him. "I'm fine for now."

"It's no trouble…"

"Sit and drink your milk."

One side of his mouth hiked up as he lowered himself to the chair. "Yes, ma'am. You're as bad as Maggie."

"Who's Maggie?" she finally asked. "Your girl-friend?"

He seemed stunned by the notion. "Now, darlin', if I had a girlfriend, would I have been flirting with you all night?"

"Don't call me that." She pulled the quilt up to her breasts when she realized they could use some covering, too.

He eyed her for a long silent moment, as though he were trying to figure her out. "Maggie's my housekeeper. She's been with our family for almost thirty years. In fact, I consider her family."

"Oh. Did you grow up in this house?" Taylor tried to sound more amicable. His tone had changed, part con-descending, part irritated, and she wasn't going to get anywhere antagonizing him.

Besides, she was relieved that Maggie was in the house. Although from the call, it sounded as if she might be in on the scheme. But she'd been their housekeeper for so long, lived in the community with these people. On the other hand, she must be extremely loyal to Clint.

She probably had to depend on him just to live. She couldn't oppose him, she had to—

"Yes."

She frowned at the apprehension in his eyes. "Yes, what?"

"Yes, I grew up in this house. Are you all right? You don't look so hot."

"I'm fine." She waved off his concern. Probably fake, anyway. "I've got a little headache, that's all."

"I'll get you some aspirin."

"That's okay." She got a couple of tablets out of her purse and took them with the water. "So, you actually lived here as a child?" She gazed around the room, spotting eccentric little knickknacks and Indian pottery she hadn't noticed before now.

"For eighteen years. It was a good place to grow up."

"I bet." She couldn't wait for daylight. Her imagination had already painted a wonderful romantic picture of the land.

The defensive thrust of his jaw took her aback. "I suppose this isn't much compared to what you're used to, but—"

She laughed humorlessly. If he only knew. "If I sounded critical in any way, believe me, it was unintentional. I love this house. I can't wait to see it in the daylight."

This time he seemed taken aback. "We have a nice view of the mountains and part of the valley from the front. Out back there's a pool and hot tub."

Taylor sighed. She'd be too embarrassed to take him to the place where she'd grown up. Not that she could. The apartment building had been condemned and torn down five years ago.

"Believe it or not, we're not all that far from the

Swinging R Ranch, as the crow flies, anyway. If we were driving we'd have to take the main highway. On horseback you'd cut across the valley. Do you ride?''

"Horses? I've never even seen one in person.''

His look of disbelief was almost comical. "Not even in a parade or a—''

She shook her head. "Only in the movies.''

"Amazing.''

"Ever see a subway?'' she countered.

"Several, and if I never see one again, that'll be just fine.''

She smiled at the dread on his face, her mind beginning to wander, recalling his reference to Paris. How had a ranch boy ended up there? She knew he'd left and drifted for a while, but one didn't exactly drift to Paris.

Still, a lot of things didn't make sense—like returning to con his neighbors, the same people he'd grown up with. He didn't seem to need the money either, not if he owned a place like this.

Then again, maybe he'd fallen on hard times while on the road, got himself in debt, and now he needed the money to maintain the ranch, keep his employees. So far she'd been wrong about who Maggie was and about Clint being just another run-of-the-mill cowboy.

Of course Taylor was only taking his word that Maggie was his housekeeper. Maybe she was another con artist he'd met on the road and brought back to be his accomplice...

Taylor stopped her crazy thoughts. Clint said the woman had been with his family for almost thirty years. In a small community like Bingo, he couldn't lie about that and not expect Taylor to learn the truth.

And then again, there was someone named Sheila.

Maybe she was his accomplice. Maybe she was somewhere in the house this very minute.

And maybe Taylor's imagination had gotten away from her. She'd already misconstrued some of what she'd heard on the phone.

Or maybe she was just a little too eager to make excuses for him. Max had to be her main concern, not her overstimulated hormones. She had to keep a clear head, find out what was going on so she could keep Max from making a serious mistake.

"Looks like it's bedtime for you." Clint swallowed the rest of his milk and got up.

She looked warily at him. Did he not want her asking any more questions?

"You're zoning out on me," he said. "You didn't even hear the last two questions I asked."

She frowned.

"Unless you did hear, but you're ignoring me."

"No, of course not. You're right. I didn't hear you." She sighed. "And yes, I do need some sleep. Lots of sleep."

He held a hand out to her. She accepted it and let him help her to her feet. Without her heels on, he was taller than her by about five inches, and she'd have to stretch up a tad to kiss him.

The sudden thought stunned her.

She had no intention of kissing him. She just wished her heart would figure that out and quit slamming against her chest.

"You'll have to show me to a room," she said, when they'd stood too long gazing at each other. She pulled her hand out of his grasp. His eyes were darker than they'd been earlier, with no traces of green or gold. His pupils were dilated, making his eyes look almost black.

"Right. Then I'll get you something to sleep in."

"Thank you."

"Taylor?"

She took a step back, her gaze still on him.

"I hope you don't feel uncomfortable being here with me. You're safe. You know that, right?"

"Of course." She gave a small laugh. "Anyway, if I didn't, there's always Maggie."

"Not exactly. She's spending the week with her daughter and granddaughter."

"She is?"

At her anxious tone, he looked somewhat offended. "I could've lied and said she was here. But that's not my style."

She stared at him, several thoughts crossing her mind. Fortunately the sarcasm didn't make it through her lips. "It doesn't matter to me if she's here or not. I just thought perhaps she was the one from whom you said I might borrow a few things."

His expression relaxed and he even smiled a little. "I don't believe Maggie has worn makeup a day in her life."

"Anyway, I can wait until the drugstore opens."

He started toward the back of the house. "That won't be very early, but you'll probably be sleeping in late."

"I doubt that. I have to work on a brief for next week."

"Tomorrow?"

She bristled at the censure in his voice. "Unfortunately, the court system does not operate around my schedule."

He stopped at an open door and gave her a tolerant, almost patronizing smile. "How about this room?"

"It's fine," she said before she peeked inside. "And the bathroom?"

"There's one attached."

"Thank you," she said crisply. He still had that annoying smile on his face. "Oh, by the way, you had another call on your cell phone."

His gaze narrowed and the smile faded. "Tonight?"

She nodded and tried not to look smug. "Sheila is waiting up for you." Taylor slipped into the room and closed the door before he could say a word.

Not that he'd shown much reaction, which really irritated her. Ten minutes later, when she heard his truck start and then he sped off, she punched her pillow.

FIRST, SHE THOUGHT Maggie was his girlfriend, and then she brought up Sheila as if she was another woman he had waiting in the wings. Dammit. What kind of guy did she think he was?

Clint flipped on the coffeemaker switch. He'd already finished one pot this morning while he'd done his morning chores and waited for Taylor to wake up. One thing about horses, they didn't care if it was the weekend, they wanted to get fed anyway.

There were so many things about ranch life he was having to relearn. It still beat the navy, although there were some areas of practicing law that he missed. But if he got stupid and thought about returning to that life, Taylor was a good reminder of the legal profession's downside.

The work followed you, consumed your life if you allowed it. A lost trial meant weeks of second-guessing yourself. Good thing he'd only lost one case in his career. But that had been enough.

Max had shared a little of his fear about Taylor and

how blind ambition had changed her. How she allowed her boss to push her too hard. The guy had already called this morning.

Fortunately Taylor had forgotten her phone in Clint's jacket. He'd been happy to talk to the man. The good ol' boy routine sure worked well with city folk, especially the ones from the east. Clint would bet the ranch old Howard had gotten so frustrated trying to leave Taylor a message, he punched the wall when he got off the phone.

Just thinking about it again made Clint chuckle. Served the guy right for calling early on a Sunday morning. In fact, it was early enough Clint figured it would take him a good four hours before he'd remember to give Taylor the message.

He got some bacon and eggs out of the refrigerator, and then searched the freezer for a bag of hash browns. He couldn't find any. Maggie usually made the dish from scratch. Not him. They were going to have to settle for toast.

He put half a dozen pieces of bacon in the cast-iron skillet and soon after they started to sizzle, Taylor appeared in the doorway. Her hair was down, well past her shoulders, slightly tangled, as though it had been only finger-combed. She looked damn good in his red flannel shirt.

"Good morning," she mumbled and headed straight for the coffeepot. "Mugs?"

"The cabinet to the right. The sugar and cream are over here."

She stared into the cabinet for a moment, as if she'd forgotten what she was doing, and then he realized she was trying to decide on a mug. She selected one with orange and yellow hot air balloons on it, poured her coffee and sipped it black.

After letting out an appreciative sigh, she looked at him with a sleepy expression. "It's strong and perfect."

"It's decaf."

Her eyes widened in panic. Free of makeup her skin was amazingly smooth and clear, but pale. Too pale.

"I'm kidding."

"Never joke about caffeine. Not first thing in the morning, anyway."

"I'll try to remember," he said, then added, "in the future."

Her gaze flew to his, her eyebrows raised.

He winked. "How do you like your bacon, crisp or rubbery?"

"Rubbery?"

"Rubbery it is, then."

"No. I don't want any bacon. But what's rubbery?"

"Not crisp."

"Silly me." She took another sip of coffee and leaned against the counter, watching him turn over the bacon. "Thanks for leaving clothes in the bathroom for me."

"No problem. How do you want your eggs?"

"I don't. Coffee is fine. I don't eat breakfast."

"You should. It—"

"Yeah, yeah, I know. It's the most important meal of the day."

"It probably is but what I was gonna say was making it would keep me distracted from those incredible legs of yours."

She blinked at him, then looked down. His shirt's hem hit her at thigh level, but the rest of her legs were bare. She cringed and set down her cup. "I'm not much of a morning person," she mumbled and started to back away.

"Come back. You're not showing any more than your dress did last night. I shouldn't have said anything." He concentrated on the bacon. "See? I'm not paying any attention."

"The sweatpants you left for me last night were too big and wouldn't stay up." She shrugged. "You were probably in too big a hurry to realize they wouldn't fit."

He didn't get her meaning at first, and then comprehension dawned. Last night she'd heard him leave, and she wanted him to explain about Sheila. Tough. If she wanted to know, she had to ask—although she'd already tried and convicted him in her mind. Her tone of voice last night had told him that much.

"Probably so," he said indifferently. "I'll find something presentable that will get you to the store."

"What time do they open?"

"Around noon or one o'clock."

"Which is it?"

He gave her an amused look. "Hard to tell around here. Whenever the owner wakes up, I suppose. The stores around here only started opening on Sundays two years ago. They haven't gotten into the swing of things yet."

"How quaint."

She thought he was pulling her leg. He shrugged. Let her find out for herself. "You want your eggs fried or scrambled?"

"I don't eat breakfast."

"Well, hell, dar—Taylor, it's almost lunchtime."

"It is not. I never sleep…" She stared at the hand-carved oak clock over the doorway. "That's impossible."

"That's right." He chuckled as he broke four eggs in a bowl and scrambled them with a fork. "I changed the time just to trick you."

"You don't understand. I have calls to make. I

have—'' She pushed her hands through her hair, genuinely agitated. ''Let's see, it's two-thirty in Boston...''

''Taylor?''

''I could call now, and then—'' She frowned vaguely in his direction. ''Do you have a fax machine?''

''Taylor.'' He left the eggs to cook and put his hands on her shoulders and guided her toward the kitchen table. ''It's Sunday. Whatever you have to do can wait.''

''You don't understand—''

''I understand more than you think I do.'' He gently forced her to sit. ''Look, you haven't even finished your first cup of coffee. You were too groggy to remember you weren't wearing any pants.'' At her murderous look, he added with a smile, ''Not that I mind. But wake up a little more before you conquer the world.''

She glared at him, but it was clear his logic was sinking into her pretty head. Just when he figured she was going to give him the silent treatment, she muttered, ''I need another cup of coffee.''

''Coming right up.'' He got the pot and poured her another cup.

She yawned, then sipped. ''What time are we supposed to be at the Swinging R?''

''I don't think Max and Abby will get there until early to midafternoon, so I guess we should show up around then.''

''There's no set time?'' Before he could answer, she held up a hand. ''Wait. Let me guess...'' And in a darn good imitation of him, she drawled, ''Darlin', this here is Bingo. We don't abide by a clock.''

Clint made an exaggerated show of admiration. ''Honey, you're wasting your talent in the courtroom. I'm calling the Leno show today.''

''Honey?'' She sighed and sank back in her chair. Her

long, bare legs snagged his attention. Without nylons they were pale but incredibly toned and shaped and he...

A hideous burnt odor singed the air. And smoke...

"Ah, sh—" He grabbed a pot holder, picked up the skillet and headed for the sink. Taylor jumped up and had the faucet turned on before he got there.

Water hit the charred grayish eggs and steam erupted into their faces. She started coughing, and Clint used a dish towel to disperse the smoke.

"You okay?" he asked, stepping back and swatting at the fading haze.

"Peachy." She coughed again. "Really, I'm fine."

"You don't look it." He grabbed her arm when she tried to duck away. Tears streamed from her eyes and her breathing sounded irregular. "Taylor?"

She took a couple of deep, calculated breaths. "I really am okay. Or I will be in a minute."

"Let's go into the den until the air clears in here."

She didn't argue, a testament to her weakened condition. Instead, she allowed him to guide her by the arm to the couch. She immediately sank down, and he used the quilt she'd left there last night to cover her legs.

Her gaze flicked to his face and she looked surprisingly shy. "Thank you."

"Concentrate on breathing."

She nodded and took several more deep breaths. "I'm okay."

Frowning, he got down on one knee so he could see her face better. She sounded okay, but her skin still looked ashen. "Can I get you anything? Water?"

She shook her head. "I had asthma as a child. I've basically outgrown it, but sometimes I have a minor episode."

Clint watched her curl up under the quilt. She looked

tired and young, not like a tough Boston lawyer, and something stirred deep inside him. He stood before he did something foolish.

Lust was one thing, longing was altogether different. Good thing she was leaving tonight. Once she was on that plane, he'd get Taylor, and any crazy thoughts about her, out of his head for good.

6

"WELL, IT'S ABOUT TIME you two showed up." Mona stood on the porch of the Swinging R with her hands on her hips. "Max and Abby have been here for an hour already."

"If you're the welcoming committee, you might want to practice your delivery." Clint grinned and ducked when she tried to pinch his ear. "Good afternoon to you, too, Mona."

"It's my fault," Taylor said. "I slept too late."

Mona's suspicious gaze darted back and forth. "Sure."

"Get your mind out of the gutter." Clint plucked a cigar she was trying to hide out of her hand. "Taylor had a long day yesterday and she needed the shut-eye."

"You give that back to me, Clint Southwick." Mona glared at him. "Can't a body have any privacy around here?"

"Nope. Not in Bingo." He lifted a brow at her. "Hiding your smoking from Rosie again?"

Mona snatched the cigar from him. "That'll be the day that I have to hide anything from anybody." She stomped down the steps and headed toward the detached garage.

Clint chuckled. "I don't know what those two would do without each other."

Taylor watched him as he stared after Mona with genuine fondness. It made Taylor wonder if he could possibly be a snake who'd take advantage of his friendships with these people.

Of course that's how scams worked. Their success largely depended on the charm of the con artist.

He looked at Taylor and caught her staring at him. "Mona and I are just playing. We go way back. She's a good friend of my mother's. When my dad died, Mona was there at the house, night and day, cooking, making sure my mother and little brother ate right. She isn't the gruff old broad she pretends to be."

Taylor smoothed a wrinkle out of her tweed slacks, the ones from her bag that Clint had thoughtfully gotten from the airport while she'd slept. She had to be wrong about him, she decided. Yesterday had been exhausting and she'd probably misunderstood the call. Too many people here knew and trusted him. And Max was a good judge of character. Worldly, too. He'd smell a scam.

When Clint stepped aside for her to lead the way inside, she hesitated. "I haven't thanked you for everything you've done." He tried to shrug it off, but she laid a hand on his arm. "Will you knock it off, and let me thank you?"

Amusement lit his eyes, and there was a suggestive arch to his left brow. "This should be interesting."

To her amazement, heat filled Taylor's cheeks. "What exactly do you think I'd do to you standing out here?"

He shrugged. "You could always give me a rain check."

"You're incorrigible." She laughed softly. "You've really been terrific. You've gone above and beyond, and I can't begin to tell you how much I appreciate you."

"No problem." He seemed embarrassed. "We'd better go inside before Candy sics her iguana on us."

She put the brakes on. "Her what?"

"Just kidding." He touched the small of her back, urging her inside, and Taylor tried to ignore how much his casual touch affected her.

Even a certain look from him got to her, like when his right brow lifted and his hazel eyes bore directly into hers. It made her insides flutter like they had her first day in court. No man had ever made her feel quite that way before. It wasn't a simple case of nerves—more like anticipation.

The door had been left ajar and Clint pushed it open. Raucous laughter came from the back—the kitchen, if Taylor remembered correctly. A turkey was roasting in the oven, judging by the enticing fragrance in the air, and her stomach rumbled.

Laughing, Abby burst into the room, tears filling her eyes. "You're just in time." She gasped for a breath. "Rosie is giving Max cooking lessons."

Clint had already started laughing in reaction to Abby. Taylor headed for the kitchen. "This, I've got to see."

It was standing room only as everyone gathered around Max and Rosie at the stove. Taylor only got a brief view of Max's profile, but she knew him well enough that the set of his jaw meant he didn't find the situation as funny as everyone else.

"Now, Max," Rosie was saying, "if you can't tell the difference between salt and sugar, I suggest you try a little first before you start dumping it in."

That sent everyone into peals of laughter again. About a dozen people were there, most of them Taylor recognized, although she didn't know all of their names.

"And don't forget to turn on the oven. A bird don't cook by itself." A short bald man slapped his thigh and howled with laughter. When he turned to make sure everyone else laughed at his joke, she saw it was Zeke. He'd been in the wedding party.

Max didn't look particularly happy and Taylor was about to jump to his rescue, but Abby intervened first.

"All right, that's enough." She put an arm around Max's waist. "Everyone out of the kitchen or the food won't be ready until midnight."

"I ought to make you all wait, period," Max grumbled, but a grin tugged at his mouth as he gazed down at Abby.

Taylor blinked at how much he'd changed. Although he'd always had a good sense of humor, exposing his weaknesses had never been Max's strong suit.

"Look who's here," Abby said as he kissed the top of her head.

People were filing out to the parlor, and Clint and Taylor had stepped out of the way. But as soon as Max saw Taylor, he came toward them, his gaze skittering between her and Clint.

"Glad you finally made it. I figured you hightailed it back to Boston after last night." He gave Taylor a hug, shook Clint's hand, then narrowed his gaze. "You two came together?"

She nodded. "I spent the night at Clint's house, and before you say another word, he was kind enough to house me when the motel was closed for the night."

"Oh, sure."

"Max!"

"Unfortunately, it's true," Clint said, with dramatic regret. "She made me promise to be a perfect gentleman."

Max gave Taylor a playful nudge on the chin. "If I know Taylor, she was too busy working and calling Boston to have time for any hanky-panky."

For whatever reason, Max's remark stung. "You make it sound like all I do is work."

Max gave her that annoying cocky look. "What else do you do?"

"You guys, leave her alone." Abby gave Max a small push. "You have gravy to make."

Taylor laughed. "This ought to be good."

Clint started to say something, but Abby wagged a warning finger at him. "One word out of you and I'll make you peel and mash the potatoes."

"Don't change the subject, Taylor," Max called over his shoulder.

She folded her arms across her chest. "At least I know how to cook."

Max made a face. "You've got me there." He glanced at Abby and Clint. "Taylor is the best cook I know. I bet she could give Rosie lessons."

Still hovering over the stove, Rosie turned to give him a withering look.

Clint and Abby both turned to her with surprise in their eyes. "Wow, I can only do casseroles," Abby said.

"And cookies." Max patted his flat stomach. "Her peanut butter cookies are a little too good."

Clint still stared at Taylor, clearly amazed, and smug pride washed over her. Here he thought he had her so pegged.

"How did you learn?" He poked around the bowls on the counter and then put one of them on the table. "Some fancy French school?"

"Yeah, that's right." Taylor sighed. "I only make puff pastry and escargot."

Max snorted. "Taylor's been cooking since she was in grammar school—"

Clint had gone to the sink to wash his hands. He glanced over at them. "Really?"

"We don't have time for all this chitchat." Abby tried to look stern. "We have a bunch of hungry people out there. Now, either make yourself useful, or get out of the kitchen."

When Max started to leave, she grabbed his shirt sleeve. "Not you. This little get-together was your idea, Buster. You're working."

"My idea? I thought it was yours."

Abby narrowed her eyes in suspicion. "Are you serious?"

After a brief silence, they both frowned. "Mona," they said at the same time.

"Wouldn't surprise me none," Rosie mumbled as she stirred something in a huge pot. "You two were so busy making goo-goo eyes for the past three months, you were ripe for the pickin'."

Clint chuckled. He'd quietly sat down at the table and started peeling potatoes.

Abby and Max continued to grumble about Mona and her manipulative ways, but Taylor wasn't listening. She watched Clint work, intrigued by the way he'd assumed the task without being prodded, and performed it without looking for attention.

She took a chair beside him. "Need some help?"

"Nah, easy stuff. You go spend time with Max and Abby." He smiled. "But thanks for offering."

Her gaze wandered toward Max. His attention was centered on Abby, as well it should be. They'd gotten bags of green beans and asparagus out of the refrigerator, and she was showing him how to trim and wash them.

A pang of longing hit Taylor. She missed being part of a busy kitchen, everyone laughing and talking while they shared the chores. It had been like that when she was growing up. Although she'd done most of the cooking, everyone participated in some way.

Now, living alone and working such long hours, she didn't bother to cook much anymore. Usually she had sandwiches or salads delivered to the office.

"Why the long face?"

She met Clint's curious gaze. "I feel so useless just sitting here."

"Isn't the word *relax* in your vocabulary?"

"Excuse me, but who slept half the day away? If I'd been any more relaxed, I'd have slipped into a coma." She sighed. "I still can't believe I fell back to sleep like I did."

"Maybe your body is trying to tell you something."

She nearly choked. Oh, her body had had a lot to say in the past twenty-four hours, thanks to him. Even sitting casually next to him, while he peeled potatoes, for heaven's sake, made her skin feel different. Prickly almost. Alive.

"The only thing my body is telling me is to get back to eastern standard time." She glanced at her watch. "What time will I have to leave for the airport?"

"You leaving out of Las Vegas?"

"I didn't know I had any other option."

"There's an airstrip not too far from here. It caters to small private planes, a couple of commuters and one that takes people over the Grand Canyon."

Taylor frowned. "So I could've taken a commuter from Vegas or Phoenix and saved some time."

Clint put the last peeled potato on a cutting board, and looked at her. "Saved time for what? Working on your laptop?"

She thought of an acerbic remark, but in the interest

of keeping peace for Max and Abby's sake, she merely gave him a warning look. "Why would commuter or private planes be landing out here?"

"The silver mines."

Her attention sharpened. "I thought they were all mined out, closed down, whatever you call it."

"Mostly they are." He shrugged. "A few are still operational. Besides, silver isn't the only precious metal mined near here. There are even a couple of gold mines still around, but for the most part, this area of the state has been depleted."

"How do you know so much about it?"

His mouth curved into an amused smile. "Mining is what put Bingo on the map, and at one time, put food on everyone's tables. Folks here make it their business to know what's happening with the mines. Even ranchers."

She wouldn't bet on that. "Who owns the mines? Companies or private citizens?"

He gave her an odd look, but before he said anything, Rosie brought over an empty bowl and set it in front of them. "Since you're doing such a good job, you wanna cut those potatoes up to be mashed?"

"Now, Rosie, you know I can't deny you a thing." Clint grinned as he positioned the bowl closer to the cutting board.

A smile tugged at the older woman's lips as she rolled her eyes, and headed back to the stove, muttering, "There's more silver coating that tongue of his than there is in all of Bingo."

Taylor stiffened. Rosie was right, and Taylor needed to remember how smooth Clint could be when it suited him. As much as she'd like to believe she'd been wrong about him, she wasn't totally convinced yet. And until she was—

"Oh, by the way." Clint shook his head and exhaled. "I almost forgot to tell you. Howard called."

"Howard?" Taylor stared dumbly at him. "Howard, as in my boss?"

"I believe that's who he said he was."

"When?"

"This morning, when you were asleep."

"This morning? He called this morning and you're only telling me now?" Taylor scrambled for her purse and started rooting through it.

"I said I forgot. I apologize." He didn't look apologetic, not one bit.

"Dammit." Where the hell was her cell phone?

"I did point out to him that there's a three-hour time difference and that it was a Sunday morning."

She winced. "You didn't."

He reared his head back in mock surprise. "Why, darlin', I just…uh, sorry." He glanced at Rosie and Max and Abby who all suddenly seemed very interested in Clint and Taylor's conversation. "She doesn't like me calling her darlin'."

"Cut it out, Clint, this isn't funny." She stared into the contents of her purse, and then at him. "Do you know where my phone is?"

He shrugged. "Probably still in the pocket of my tux jacket you left on the couch."

"If Howard called, and you answered it…"

"I put the phone back where I found it." He kept dicing potatoes. "You didn't expect me to stick it in your purse while you were asleep."

She slumped back in the chair. "I don't believe this."

Another headache was swelling in the center of her forehead and she pinched the bridge of her nose. "Didn't it occur to you that…"

"What?"

"Never mind." Taylor gritted her teeth. This laid-back good ol' boy act of his was wearing thin. He hadn't forgotten to give her the message. He'd deliberately withheld it so she wouldn't spend time working. "Max, lend me your cell phone."

Max lifted a shoulder. "Sorry. I don't keep it on me much these days. No need for it around here."

"Don't worry." Clint had the nerve to pat her hand. "We'll stop and pick it up on the way to the airport."

She glared at him. "Which won't be a moment too soon." Out of the corner of her eye, she saw Max and Abby exchange grins. Taylor's already strained temper heated up a few hundred degrees. "Rosie, may I use your phone? It'll be a quick call, and I'll leave you a twenty to cover it."

"Howard won't be there," Clint said.

Taylor turned back to him with a menacing look. "Excuse me?"

"I told him that since it was Sunday, and you'd be back tomorrow anyway—"

"You're a pig!"

Rosie gasped. "Taylor."

Clint grinned. "Now, that's okay, Rosie, I've been called worse. Let her get it out of her system."

"A chauvinist pig. That's what you are." Taylor quickly looked at Max and Abby. She didn't want to ruin the day. Apparently, she hadn't. They looked amused more than anything. "I'm sorry, but he has no right interfering with my career."

"Hold on there. Your career?" Clint's brows shot up. "If your career depended on one phone call not being returned, then you've got a bigger problem than me."

Rosie promptly turned toward the stove and started

stirring again, but not before Taylor caught the smile curving her mouth. These people didn't understand. None of them did. But Max should, and that he didn't defend her hurt.

"Let's just forget it, okay?" She lifted a hand to push back her hair and was horrified to see it shaking. "Everything is fine."

Or would be once she got on the plane and got the hell out of Bingo.

"Gee, Taylor..." Abby stepped forward, giving Max a small shove from behind. "We're only going to be gone a week. I'm sorry you won't be staying longer."

Silence filled the room. It was obvious Abby was trying to make peace, even change the subject, but she couldn't have made a more ludicrous comment.

"Yeah, too bad," Taylor finally said, and everyone laughed.

"She'll come visit us again, and we'll be making trips to Boston." Max dried his hands on a towel. "Kitchen duty is over for me, gang. Clint, I need to talk with you a minute."

"I'm done." Clint put the last diced potato into the bowl. "I'll leave this for some other lucky person to do the mashing."

Taylor gave Max the eye. He'd better not be discussing her with Clint.

On his way out, Max whispered, "Don't worry, it's only business."

Business? Without another word or a glance her way, Clint followed him out of the kitchen. Warning bells went off in her head at Clint's somber expression. She wondered what kind of business had him suddenly looking so absorbed. Unease knotted her shoulders.

After staring at the empty doorway for a minute, she turned to find Abby watching her.

Abby smiled. "Clint is buying some of the Swinging R land. I'm sure that's all they're talking about."

"Why would he do that?"

"He wants it for his cattle. Max told him he didn't need to buy it, to go ahead and let the cattle graze since the Swinging R doesn't use the land, but Clint insisted." Abby shrugged. "He said it wouldn't be right since he makes money off the cattle."

"Why all of a sudden?"

Abby frowned. "He needs it. There's not much grazing land around here anymore."

Taylor regretted her sharp tone. She shrugged and tried to sound casual. "Did he increase his herd or something?"

"I don't think so. But he hasn't been back all that long. His mother and brother had been running the ranch until three months ago."

"Oh." Taylor smiled. Inside, her brain turned cartwheels trying to think of an easy way to eavesdrop on him and Max.

"Abby, you mind taking this tray in to the men?" Rosie finished pouring coffee into the mugs. "Max has been waiting for this to get done brewing."

"I'll take it." Taylor stood, smiled.

The other two women looked startled, and then they exchanged a knowing glance. If they thought her interest had to do with Clint, she didn't care. This was the perfect way to butt in.

Rosie added cream and a glass sugar bowl to the tray. "Here you go. Max made himself a den out of the second bedroom on the right."

"I'll find it," Taylor said cheerfully, ignoring the amusement on Abby's face.

The rest of the guests had gravitated toward the parlor, and Taylor slipped down the hall without being waylaid with small talk. When she got to the second door, she found it slightly ajar, and she hesitated at the sound of Clint's voice.

"We'll have to wait until you get back to sign everything and get the deed recorded," he said, with a trace of impatience. "I'll schedule a time with the land office. I'd like to do it as soon as possible."

Okay, so she already knew he was buying the land. But why the urgency?

"The day after I get back is okay with me," Max said. "I doubt Abby will have a problem with that."

"You'll both have to sign the addendum waiving your claim to any mineral rights. I hope you explained that to her."

"I did. She's fine with it."

"Good," a strange voice said. "The sooner we get this deal underway the better."

"I was just thinking," Clint said. "If Taylor is a notary, maybe you could sign them today and I can go ahead and get started while you're on your honeymoon. Mabel Hopkins is the only notary in Bingo and she's in Tucson for two weeks."

Taylor almost dropped the tray. She saved it from toppling but it banged the door. Immediately, Clint opened it.

He frowned, his gaze roving from her face to the tray and back again. "You want something?"

His displeasure at seeing her was obvious. That, and his rush to get the paperwork signed, sent up more red flags. "Rosie asked me to bring you some coffee."

He gave a curt nod and opened the door wider. Besides Max, there was a stocky blond man, but he promptly averted his face and busied himself with a briefcase he had sitting in the corner.

An awkward silence fell while Taylor set the tray on a messy teak desk. "I'll have to get another cup," she said. "I guess Rosie didn't know there were three of you in here."

"Uh, don't bother. I was just leaving," the man mumbled, but still, he didn't turn around.

She glanced at Max. Didn't he think the guy was acting oddly?

"Taylor, you're a notary, right?" Max asked, and she nodded. "I have some papers I need to sign and have notarized."

She arched a brow. "I'm also your attorney. Is this something I should know about?"

Max shook his head. "Nah, it's just a transaction among friends."

Friends, her fanny. She wouldn't look at Clint. "Still, I think I..."

"Taylor." Max smiled as though he were placating a child. "I do have a law degree. I think I can handle this."

Great. She'd always encouraged his independence from his family's money and connections, and urged him to rely on his own considerable talent. *Now* he listens to her.

Clint looked relieved, and all her instincts went on alert again. Something wasn't right, and Max was too lovesick to figure it out. Or Clint was that good at hoodwinking people—a likelihood she understood too well. Even she'd tried to talk herself out of believing he had nefarious intentions.

But she wasn't fooled any longer. It was up to her to

protect Max and Abby's interests—not as their lawyer, but as their friend—no matter what means it took.

"Taylor?" Max frowned at her.

She'd clearly been too preoccupied to hear what he'd said. But now she gave him her full attention and smiled.

"Would you notarize those papers for us?" Max asked.

"I don't have my stamp with me. But no problem…I can do it when you get back."

"You won't be here."

"I've just decided to stay another week."

Clint's jaw clenched.

Taylor smiled.

7

CLINT SAT BEHIND the wheel of his truck, drumming his fingers on the seat and wondering what in the world he'd done so wrong to deserve this kind of torture. He watched Taylor walk into the motel office, her small curvy hips swaying gently, her long blond hair streaming down her back, making him shift uncomfortably, making him want to loosen his jeans.

What in the hell was she staying another week for? Max and Abby weren't even going to be here. And Taylor was supposed to have all this work to do. So what was the deal? Why her sudden change of heart? The entire afternoon had been shot after she made her announcement. He couldn't think clearly enough to get the land purchase paperwork in order. Although his business with Max could wait, the sting he was working on for the state attorney's office couldn't. The sooner Clint helped put that no-good con artist Banes behind bars the better...before the scumbag bilked any more ranchers out of their land or mineral rights.

But he had to keep Taylor out of it. Like he promised Max he would. Not that Clint could concentrate worth spit. The real problem was, as much as he wanted to get rid of her, he also wanted her to stay.

Taylor was exactly his type of woman, both physically and intellectually. And she couldn't be more wrong for him. He wanted a simple life, and he needed a simple woman who wanted simple things. Taylor was high maintenance, every which way you looked at it. She wore expensive, fashionable clothes, the kind of clothes required in the finer places she likely frequented—places she wanted, maybe even emotionally needed, to be.

That life wasn't for him. It wasn't a matter of not wanting a tie binding his neck, he didn't want the unrelenting pressure, all the pretense. Yet when he listened to Taylor talk about briefs and trials and court dates, a pang of envy found its way into his gut.

He couldn't afford to get nostalgic. It would be easy to convince himself the courtroom was where he belonged. He'd been a damn good lawyer, but unfortunately, only a mediocre rancher. The lure to go back could be great, if he let his ego rule.

A few minutes later, Taylor stepped out of the motel office, no key in her hand, but a murderous expression on her face that could drop a jackrabbit a hundred feet away.

She hesitated, eyeing him irritably. Probably because she'd told him not to wait, that she would check into her room and be fine. Obviously everything wasn't hunkydory and now she was trying to decide if she should come to him.

After a short deliberation, she marched with purpose toward the driver's side of the truck. He slid down his window.

She set down her bag and shoved away a lock of hair that had the nerve to cling to her cheek. "The guy behind the desk said they have no rooms."

"Hector?"

"I don't know. He said he was the owner."

"Yeah, that's Hector." Clint frowned. That didn't seem right. True, it was starting to get dark already, but the place never sold out. "Did you tell him you had one reserved?"

"Of course I did," she snapped, and then briefly closed her eyes and sighed. "I'm sorry. I don't mean to take this out on you."

Clint glanced around the lot. Only three cars and a trailer were parked. Lights shone from two of the twelve motel rooms. "Well, if he's supposed to be full, not everyone is here yet."

"He claims he has half a dozen rooms out of order because of a leak, and two more that he's been renovating."

"Hector is renovating?"

"That's what he said." She sagged against the truck. "I called Mona and asked if I could stay there for a night but Rosie has family coming in to visit and they don't have any room either."

He drew his head back in surprise. "Rosie has family?"

"That's what Mona—" Taylor blinked at him. "You think I'm making this all up?"

"Of course not. Why don't you get in? It's too chilly to stand out there."

"You don't believe me."

"I didn't say that."

"You don't have to." Her eyes blazing with indignation, she stepped away from the truck. "Your expression says it all."

"Don't be ridiculous. It's just that none of this makes sense. But it has nothing to do with you."

Her hand went to her hip. "You think I want you to offer me a room at your house, don't you? Well, don't flatter yourself."

"That never crossed my mind." He shook his head.

She'd been prickly ever since they'd gotten to the Swinging R this afternoon. Well, too bad. He wasn't happy about this situation either. "Come on, Taylor, get in the truck."

"No, thank you." She picked up her bag. "I'll call a cab and find another motel."

"That'll be a good trick."

She ignored him and turned away. He had a good mind to let her hoof it for a while and find out on her own that there wasn't a cab or motel for another seventy miles.

Damn stubborn woman. Stewing, he watched her in his rearview mirror until she got to the corner and headed in the direction of Main Street. She probably thought the diner was open on a Sunday. She was in for another surprise.

Cursing under his breath, he started the truck and followed her. Her long legs had eaten up a good distance of Main Street and he didn't see her at first. But then he spotted her at a pay phone across the street from Edna's.

He coasted to a stop alongside her. She ignored him. "Taylor, get in the truck."

She buried her nose in the phone book, then fished her wallet out of her purse.

Main Street was completely deserted. No surprise at dusk on a Sunday. He wondered how the hell she thought she'd find lodging. "I'm tempted to leave your fanny here."

She gave him a withering look over her shoulder and then dropped some coins into the phone. Maybe he really should leave her here alone. It was safe enough, but it might be a good lesson for the little hothead.

Maybe he was partly responsible for her attitude. He hadn't exactly been the picture of joy when she'd announced she was staying. Last night, he'd flirted outrageously with her. But that was because he thought she was leaving today.

The truth be told, she scared the hell out of him. She tested his resolve, messed with his concentration, made him stupid. And for the next two weeks, he needed to keep his wits about him, or the land deal could go down the tubes.

"Taylor, I'm giving you one last chance." He'd already shifted out of Park. Better she told him to kiss off. He could leave and go about his business without guilt. Mona or Rosie would see to it she was housed for the night. "Don't say I didn't offer."

He started to pull away from the curb, but she grabbed her bag and hurried to the truck. A host of conflicting emotions rushed him as he leaned over to open the passenger door. Anticipation, apprehension, excitement, wariness, they all converged to make him crazy.

"Thank you," she said sheepishly, as she set her bag between them and climbed in. She wouldn't look at him, but kept her gaze straight ahead. "If you have any suggestions, I'd appreciate it."

"You can stay at my place."

"That isn't necessary. I'm sure there is another motel somewhere between here and—"

"And who's going to drive you there?" He'd started to pull away, but stopped, rested his wrist on the steering wheel, and turned to look at her. Warily, she met his gaze. "You're staying at my house because it's convenient for me. It is not convenient for me to chauffeur you around southern Nevada looking for a motel."

She blinked. "Of course. I just didn't want to put you out."

Put him out? He grunted to himself as he turned back to the wheel and pulled onto Main Street. He was so out of sorts it wasn't funny. How the hell was he supposed to concentrate with her in the house? He had work to do tonight, phone calls to make, legal papers to draft.

"I promise I won't be in the way," she said, as though reading his mind. "I have a lot of work to do on my laptop. I'll stay in my room."

Yeah, and what was she going to do about her scent? Even now the essence of strawberries and cream filled the cab of his truck. Not because she was heavy-handed with the perfume bottle. He wasn't even sure if she wore any fragrance. Maybe it was her shampoo. Hell, he didn't know.

A stony silence accompanied them back to his ranch. When they arrived, they both reached for her bag at the same time, but she managed to snatch it first. He didn't argue, just led the way in through the kitchen.

"Don't you lock your door?" Taylor asked, when he pushed it open without using his key.

"Nope."

"Ever?"

"I suppose if I were going out of town I might."

She frowned as she closed it behind her.

Clint tossed his keys on the counter near the ceramic cactus cookie jar. "Go ahead and lock it if it makes you feel better."

She hesitated briefly, indecision furrowing her brows. "Is it all right if I keep the same room I used last night?"

"Be my guest." He gestured toward the hall, and then opened the refrigerator and poked his head inside. What he wanted, he had no idea. His mind was on Taylor. He was being a jackass. There was no need to be inhospitable just because he was an idiot when it came to her.

He needed to apologize, or at least offer her something

to drink before she disappeared into the room. He straightened, and backed right into her.

"Ouch!"

He spun around. "Sorry. I didn't know you were there."

"That's all right." She flexed her foot. "I didn't mean to startle you."

"Did I get your toe? Or did I manage to fracture your entire foot?"

She smiled. "Neither. I'll live."

"Take off your shoe and let me have a look at it."

With a nervous laugh, she took a step back. "You're not looking at my feet."

"That ugly, huh?"

"Yes."

That surprised a laugh out of him. "Honesty is an admirable quality. But now you've got me curious."

She gave him a wry smile, a smile that told him, "Fat chance." "I wanted to apologize for seeming ungrateful earlier. I do appreciate you putting me up."

"I wasn't exactly the epitome of grace myself," he said, and she gave him an odd look. "For that, I apologize."

"No need. You were put on the spot. It's not easy having a houseguest as it is, much less an unexpected one." She looked genuinely contrite. "If you have a phone book, I'll work on getting out of your hair by tomorrow."

Clint slowly exhaled. She still didn't get it. This was Bingo, a far cry from Boston. There wasn't anyplace else, unless she wanted to stay in a motel that was halfway to Las Vegas. "You're not going to find another motel. Tomorrow maybe we can figure out how to get in touch with Abby or her grandmother. Estelle went Christmas shopping in Albuquerque with Candy. There's a chance you can stay at Abby and Max's place."

"They offered yesterday." She made a wry face. "Now I wish I'd taken them up on it, but I was counting on the motel."

He got a beer out of the refrigerator, and was a little surprised when she nodded to his offer of one. She seemed more the wine and champagne type. He set both their bottles on the table and pulled out two chairs.

She seemed reluctant, but she finally sat while he got her a glass. To his greater surprise, she didn't use it. Like him, she drank straight from the bottle. She wrinkled her nose. "It's been a long time since I had one of these."

"I might have a bottle of wine if you prefer."

"Oh, no, thanks. I don't drink much at all. The beer is fine. It's just been a long time."

He took another sip, studying the way she picked at the label, using her fingernail to lift it from the bottle, as though she were nervous. "I have a question for you," he said. She looked up, her expression somewhat wary. "Why did you decide to stay?"

She blinked, and then looked totally blank. "I explained earlier that I hadn't seen enough of Max. I'd also like to get to know Abby better."

"Yeah, but they're gone."

"They'll be back by the end of the week."

"So what? You'll see them for one day, and then you leave?" He took another sip, his gaze staying with her. "I don't buy it."

Anger sparked in her blue eyes. "And I should care about what you do or don't believe?"

He grinned. "Shoot, and here I was hoping you'd get flustered and confess you stayed because of me."

Her eyebrows went up. "Oh, right."

"Go ahead. Admit it."

She laughed. "You're too much."

He took another slug of beer and leaned back in his chair, nice and comfortable-like. "All I know is that you complained about how you had that brief to write and how your boss wanted you back in Boston. And then all of a sudden, you're staying."

Mirroring him, she leaned back, too, and tilted her head to the side. "Okay, you caught me. I'm staying because I want to screw your brains out."

Clint nearly spit out a mouthful of beer. She looked so calm and composed and serious. Of course he knew she wasn't. He quickly pulled himself together. "Well, darlin', why didn't you tell me sooner? Time's a-wastin' sitting here."

She rolled her gaze in annoyance. "Why do you use that country-boy routine?"

"What are you talking about?"

"Darlin', time's a-wasting," she said in a mimicking tone.

"I *am* a country boy."

"Who also uses terms like 'epitome of grace.'"

"Careful, your nose might get stuck in the air. Living out here doesn't necessarily make us all hicks."

"You know what I mean."

"All I know is that you're mighty good at changing the subject. Let's get back to the screwing thing."

She took a big sip of beer, and then her tongue slipped out to lick some foam from her lips. He was pretty sure she hadn't gotten him hot and bothered on purpose, but that didn't lessen the way his body tightened. Or the way his thoughts raced toward the bedroom where he had a big four-poster that could take a lot of rockin' and rollin'.

"Okay," she said sighing, "it's time for me to disappear. I have a lot of work to do and I'm sure you do, too."

"Taylor, wait." He touched her hand when she started to stand and she immediately sank back again. "All kidding aside, we have to get something straight."

She didn't respond, just watched him with curiosity and an odd vulnerability, her eyes so clear and expressive, he started to lose his nerve.

Dammit.

He cleared his throat. "You must need clothes."

"I figured I'd pick up a few things tomorrow. Surely there's a store in town that sells things like jeans."

"Yeah, that would be Virgil's place, but you won't find much more than jeans and T-shirts."

"That's fine. I don't need anything fancy."

He rubbed his stubbled jaw. She had a habit of surprising him. "I have flannel shirts you can use. They'll be too big but warm. Also, a couple of sweaters that are too small for me."

"If it's no trouble…"

"Of course not."

She smiled, but not her usual one. It was strained, slightly timid, and he wondered if she'd guessed what he really wanted to say. "Was there anything else?"

"Yeah." He cleared his throat again. "About this thing between us…" Oh, for cripes' sake, what was the matter with him? He pushed a hand through his hair, wondering when his backbone had gone soft.

She sat there expectantly, not offering one bit of help.

"Look," he began again, "we have to at least acknowledge the…problem."

"What problem?"

He slumped back. "*What* problem?" She couldn't be

that naïve. "If you don't consider the urge to jump between the sheets together a problem, then maybe—"

Her eyes widened. "I was kidding before."

"I'm referring to last night. The heated looks, the wet kisses—the way you felt in my arms."

She shook her head and looked away. "That was..." She cleared her throat. "That was just playing around."

"Really?" He stared at her until she met his eyes. "You always kiss like that on the first date?"

Rosy pink flooded her face. "That wasn't a date."

"That makes it worse."

She stood. "A gentleman would simply ignore any..." she waved a flustered hand, "any indiscretion."

He pursed his lips in thought. "Indiscretion, huh? That's a nice way of sugarcoating it, I suppose."

She narrowed her gaze. "Well, it wasn't one-sided."

"No kidding. I was so hard last night, you'd have to be a total ice princess not to have felt it."

Again, her face flooded with color and she looked truly taken aback. Every time he thought he had her figured out, she surprised the heck out of him.

"Look, Taylor, I didn't mean to sound crude." He sighed. "You're right. Ordinarily I wouldn't bring this up, but we have mutual friends, and I don't want any bad blood or hurt feelings to come out of this."

Gingerly, she returned to her seat. "I don't quite follow."

"Max is your best friend. I look at Abby as if she were a sister. Anything that happens between us, good or bad, is bound to affect them."

"I understand, but other than staying away from each other, I still don't see what you're getting at."

He smiled to himself. At least she'd finally admitted there was something heating in the kitchen. "That's one option, although not easy with all these busybodies around here. There is another option."

Her brows rose. "I can hardly wait to hear it."

Their gazes touched. "You could crawl into bed with me right now and break the suspense."

The color still hadn't faded from her cheeks, but her eyes stayed steadily on his. Was she actually considering his suggestion? His heart slammed unmercifully against his chest and blood rushed to his groin.

She moistened her lips. "That is another option." She visibly swallowed. "And then again, we could be adult about this, and just be friends. Right?"

He smiled, thought a moment, then got up. She watched with wary eyes as he came around the table to pull her to her feet. Ignoring her sharp intake of breath, he wrapped his arms around her waist and pulled her against him. And then he lowered his mouth and took possession of hers.

A brief jerk was all the resistance she gave, and then she hungrily met his tongue, pushed her breasts against his chest, her hips against his arousal.

They were both breathless by the time he drew back. He pulled in air as he stared into the blue desire in her eyes. "Is that answer enough?"

8

TAYLOR WANTED TO HATE HIM for making her feel this weak, for making her yearn to do exactly what he wanted—to crawl between warm sheets, naked, her breasts touching his chest, his hands gliding over her skin. But she couldn't hate him. Not when he looked so earnest, so hungry, and to her utter amazement, so uncertain.

His gaze dropped to her mouth, and the pulse at his neck beat wildly. She had the inconceivable urge to look at his fly, knowing what she'd find there, wanting the empowerment of knowing she was the cause. But she was on dangerous ground. She'd always been fairly indifferent about sex, but now, with this man…

"Taylor?" He moved closer again, and put a hand on her waist, gently stroking and massaging. "Kiss me."

"We just did that," she said, and wanted to kick herself for the inane remark.

A smile tugged at the corners of his mouth. "I kissed you. Now, I want you to kiss me."

She swallowed and tried to look away from his hypnotic hazel eyes. The light specks gleamed like polished nuggets of gold in a jeweler's case, and lured her with an intensity that made her want to abandon reason, to let her body experience the pleasure Clint would surely lavish.

She shouldn't give in, not when she didn't know who

this man really was, or whether he was a threat to Max and Abby. That was why she had decided to stay—to ensure they didn't get ripped off. She figured she could handle her caseload long-distance for a week. In the meantime, it wouldn't hurt to be nice to Clint. In the interest of fact-finding, of course.

Oh, how pathetic could she be?

Still, she moved an inch closer. One lousy kiss wouldn't hurt a darn thing, she told herself.

Tentatively, she put a hand on his chest. She hoped he couldn't feel her fingers trembling. Her entire quivering body was reacting, as if it had a will of its own, as if she could do nothing but touch her lips to his.

He offered no assistance. He let her take the lead, responding only when she applied pressure, her lips firming, and then parting, her nails digging lightly into his chest. She lifted her other hand to cup the side of his neck.

He groaned and hauled her against him, slanting his head for better access, his tongue plunging deep and sweeping the inside of her mouth. His invasion was thorough and mind-numbing. Dangerous. Her body was primed to take over, ignore rationality.

Then he broke the kiss, but nipped the corners of her mouth. "Taylor?"

"Hmmm?"

"We'd be more comfortable in bed."

She opened her eyes, reality slowly seeping into her consciousness.

"Remember when I said I'd bet you didn't respond this way to every first date?"

She nodded.

"I don't either. I don't sleep with every woman I can."

He kissed her forehead, and then the tip of her nose. "It's you, Taylor. I can't stop thinking about you."

"You barely know me."

"You're wrong. Max talks about you all the time." His gaze dropped to her mouth, and he brushed it with a brief kiss. "How loyal you are to your friends, your family, how you skip meals and sleep to do pro bono work for people who could never afford you. I'm surprised Max didn't marry you long ago."

Heat stung her cheeks. "I'm not the saint Max makes me out to be."

Clint smiled. "That I know firsthand."

She laughed softly. "Okay, so I have a bit of a temper. You're not exactly a paragon of virtue either."

He kissed the side of her neck, and she could feel his smile on her skin. "I know."

The reminder sobered her. She was supposed to find out what he was up to, not what color his sheets were. "Clint." She moved back, immediately missing the feel of his mouth on her flesh. "I'm not ready to make that decision yet."

Disappointment flashed in his eyes. "All right," he said slowly. "I'm not crazy about it, but I understand." He brushed some hair away from her face. "You never asked me about Sheila."

She stiffened and tried to disengage herself, but he wouldn't let her go. "Why should I? It's none of my business."

"I figured that might contribute to your reluctance."

"Not really. I'd actually forgotten."

He grinned as if he didn't believe her. But the truth was, she actually had forgotten. So much else had gone on in such a short time that her brain was too frazzled.

Now that he'd brought up the woman, though, Taylor felt like a bigger fool than she had a minute ago.

"Sheila is Maggie's granddaughter."

"So?" That didn't mean he couldn't be...

"She's seven years old."

Taylor narrowed her gaze.

"Maggie's daughter, Beth, called to let me know that Sheila was waiting up for me to read her a good-night story."

Taylor didn't know quite what to say. It was none of her business, yet admittedly, she was pleased.

"Beth recently separated from her husband. He took off unexpectedly and naturally Sheila is taking it hard. They live in the next town and occasionally I go over and read her a story or take her for a pony ride." He shrugged. "The kid got it in her head that I was going over last night and wouldn't go to sleep. That's why Beth called my cell."

He seemed a little embarrassed. Did he think it ruined his tough-guy image to care about the feelings of a little girl? It made Taylor like him more. Friendship and loyalty were important to her, important enough to risk her boss's wrath by staying. Bottom line, Max was more important than her job.

She smiled at Clint, wanting more than ever to believe the simple explanation meant the other call she'd intercepted was equally innocent. "You didn't owe me that explanation."

"Yeah, I did." He ran his hands up her arms. "I asked you to make love with me. You have every right to know if there's someone else in my life."

By the time he'd gotten to her shoulders she'd already weakened, but as he framed her face with his hands, his mouth drawing closer to hers, she knew she had to make a decision before she was totally lost, rendered incapable of doing the smart thing. A possibility to which she was dangerously close.

"Clint?" Her voice came out garbled against his mouth. She couldn't resist kissing him back. Once. Briefly. And then she pulled away. "I'm glad you told me. But I—"

The phone rang a few feet away. It might as well have been a sonic blast. They both jumped apart, like two teenagers caught by a sudden porch light.

Clint reached for it, glanced at the clock and then stopped. "I'd better take it in my study."

She nodded, but he didn't stick around long enough to see her response. He quickly headed down the hall. The click of the closed door bounced off the walls.

The temptation to hurry after him and press an ear against the door was almost too great. Her gaze went to the wall phone. Did she have the nerve to pick it up and listen? What if the call was personal and had nothing to do with her suspicions? She'd feel like a heel.

She picked up her bag and headed toward her room. It was just past his study. She slowed as she neared his door, and then stopped, pretending to fiddle with the lock on her bag. It was of little use. All she heard was a murmur, a muffled laugh.

Giving up, she made it a few steps when she heard him curse. It was a vicious word she wouldn't expect from him. His voice rose, not enough to make out every word, but she did catch mention of the Swinging R. She edged back toward the study door and leaned her ear against the wood.

"You impatient bastard. You blow this scam, and I'll rip my share out of your worthless hide." The phone slammed, abruptly ending the call.

Taylor didn't care. She'd heard enough.

CLINT RUBBED HIS EYES, section IV in the law book he was studying starting to blur. He glanced at the digital clock on his crowded desk. He hadn't seen Taylor since he'd gotten that miserable phone call from Nathan. Her door was closed by the time he'd left his study.

It was for the best. He had too much on his mind. Or at least he should have. The timing was perfect to catch Nathan Banes. The guy knew Clint wanted to buy some of Max's land, and that he and several of the townspeople were making a bid on the old mine outside of town. What Banes didn't know was that Clint's interest had nothing to do with silver, or conning people out of their life's savings.

That little secret was staying between Clint and Max and the state attorney's office, until cuffs could be slapped on Banes's wrists. In the meantime, Clint had to make sure Taylor kept her cute little nose out of things— not just because he promised Max but because one more person involved would only complicate matters.

He sighed. Steering her clear may not be so difficult, after all. It was already midnight and he doubted he'd see her before morning. She probably was trying to avoid any more bedroom talk.

Maybe he'd been too pushy. Maybe he'd read her signals wrong. God knew that was entirely possible. It had been ridiculously long since he'd been with a woman. That was part of the problem with living in Bingo. You grew up with everyone, and even if you hadn't, everyone knew your business. He wouldn't be surprised if the small community library had the words *discretion* and *privacy* banned from their dictionary.

He took another sip of stale coffee and grimaced. It wouldn't keep him awake, not at this point. He'd be better off hitting the sack and getting up early. Nevada mineral rights laws weren't likely to change overnight.

He cleared away the crumbs from the chocolate chip cookies he'd had for dinner, and then straightened his desk. When he could at least see wood again, he turned out the light.

From the crack under Taylor's door, light fanned out into the hall. He figured she'd probably fallen asleep reading, but then he heard the clicking of her laptop keys. What the heck was she doing up this late? She had to be exhausted.

For a second he thought about knocking and offering her something to eat. But the furious pace at which she was typing told him she wouldn't welcome the interruption. Shaking his head, he kept on going toward his room. The woman worked too hard. He was going to have to do something about that.

NINE-THIRTY!

Taylor blinked at the lighted red numbers on the bedside clock, and then threw off the sheet and blanket. That made two days in a row she'd overslept.

Beyond her room, something was ringing. An oven timer? The phone? She rubbed the sleep from her eyes. The sound didn't go away. She tried to concentrate.

Another ring, more of a chime.

It was the doorbell.

Wondering where Clint was, she quickly pulled on the tweed pants she'd worn yesterday. She'd slept in Clint's green flannel shirt and it would have to do for now. She left the bedroom and made a wrong turn. Retracing her steps and muttering to herself, she finally made it to the front door. Just as she flung it open, she realized she should have at least peeked out the window to see who it was.

"It's about time." Mona bustled past her into the house. "A body could freeze to death waiting for someone to answer the door around here."

Behind her, Herb followed with a large brown grocery sack in his arms. He didn't look particularly thrilled to be there, but he mumbled a good morning as he passed Taylor.

"Where's Clint?" Mona's gaze roamed the room, then came to rest on Taylor, dropping to Clint's shirt with avid interest. "I hope we didn't interrupt anything."

"Oh, please." Taylor yawned, then plowed her fingers through tangled hair. "I have no idea where he is. I just woke up."

Mona frowned. "You East coast people sure sleep late. Max never got his sorry rear end out of bed before noon the first week he was here."

"Is that what you came here to tell me?" Taylor asked sweetly.

"Y'all have smart mouths on you, too." Mona took the sack from Herb, who stared down at his scuffed black boots. "I ought to not give you what I brung, but I'm not that kind of person."

"I sure could use a cup of coffee," Herb said, glancing over his shoulder toward the kitchen.

"Well, go get you some." Mona waved a hand. "I don't need you standing here looking at your watch as if you have someplace to go."

Taylor pressed her lips together. Mona was certainly an original, bossy and annoying, but Taylor remembered what Clint had said about how much Mona helped out when his dad died and that weighed in for a lot.

"The girls and I threw together a batch of clothes for

you for the week." Mona sized Taylor up. "It wasn't easy. You're too tall for my clothes, and too thin for Rosie's." She glanced around as if someone might overhear her next words. "There are a couple of things in here from Candy. I love her like a sister but the woman's got no taste."

It was hard to keep a straight face, but Taylor tried to look gracious. "You shouldn't have gone to the trouble. I planned on picking up a few things today."

"Clint going to take you?"

Taylor slowly shrugged. She'd assumed he would, although she shouldn't have. "I'll ask to borrow his truck. I have to look for a motel, anyway."

"A motel?" Mona frowned as she pulled out something red and frilly. "What for? He's got more than enough room right here." She shook out the garment. It was a nighty, short and sheer. "This here is one of mine. It'll be too short, but good enough for sleeping." She gave a broad wink. "Easy to take off, too."

Taylor used all her power to keep her mouth shut. She didn't even trust herself to thank Mona for the bag of clothes and ask her to just leave it. Instead, she started counting silently, and when she got to ten, she continued to twenty.

"Ah, now here's what I'm talking about. This is Candy's contribution." Mona rolled her eyes. Only midmorning and she already had on false eyelashes. "Look at these ruffles. She thinks wearing these schoolgirl clothes will make her look young again."

Taylor laughed. She couldn't help it. Schoolgirl clothes? The ruffled V dove all the way down to the waist of the white negligee—again, the fabric was sheer.

Mona looked up with a smug smile. "What'd I tell you?"

Taylor shook her head and tamped her mirth down to a grin. But when the other woman pulled out yet another black negligee, Taylor groaned. "You think I'm going to be spending the week in bed? How many of these do you think I—" Taylor cut herself off at the mischievous glint in Mona's eye. "What?"

"I didn't say a word." Mona pretended to inspect the black nighty.

Taylor glared. "Get it straight right now. There is nothing going on between Clint and me."

"Someone call?"

Taylor spun around. Clint walked in from the direction of the kitchen, while pulling off black leather work gloves. His jeans were worn and faded and hugged him in all the right places. With his Stetson pulled down to shade part of his face, he looked mysterious and dangerous. If he were doing a commercial, he'd have a swarm of women waiting to buy the product he hawked.

"Hey, Clint." Mona waved him over. "Come see what me and the girls rounded up for Taylor."

Taylor grimaced. "I doubt he's interested."

"No wonder you're not married yet." Mona shook her head in dismay. "Young lady, you've got a lot to learn about men."

Clint grinned.

Taylor rolled her eyes at him.

His gaze went to her hair, and then to her mismatched clothes. "Did you just get up?"

She sighed, certain she had mascara smudges under her eyes. "The doorbell woke me. But I should've been up hours ago."

An odd smile of satisfaction curved his mouth. "I was worried the men would wake you when they started work at daybreak." He turned to Mona. "So, what you got there?"

Taylor groaned again and headed for her room. She was going to wash her face, brush her teeth, and then drink a gallon of strong black coffee.

"Hey, where are you going? We're not through here," Mona called out.

At Clint's low rumbling chuckle, Taylor kept right on going.

"Is THIS IT? All you want are underwear and two pairs of jeans?" the clerk at Bingo's only store asked. "I thought you were staying for an extra week."

Taylor stared at the woman—short brown hair, brown eyes, glasses, bright red lipstick slightly smeared, but no distinguishing features except a dimple on her left cheek. Taylor didn't recognize her from the brunch at the Swinging R.

"She *is* staying a week." An older, familiar-looking man walked up. His western-style shirt was too tight across his belly and a cigar stuck out of his breast pocket. "But Mona already fixed her up with a few things. Ain't that right?"

Taylor passed her credit card to the clerk. Mona had just left an hour ago. How quickly word spread around here. She smiled politely at the man, and his name suddenly popped into her head. "Virgil, right?"

"That's right. We met at the wedding." He seemed pleased she remembered him. "I own this store, so if there's anything I can do for you, you be sure and holler."

"I'll do that." She felt someone behind her and quickly turned.

Clint moved in beside her, his shoulder meeting hers,

his hand pressed familiarly at her back. He dropped it, though, at her pointed glare. As if these people didn't have enough wheels turning in their busy little heads.

"Afternoon, Southwick." Virgil puffed out his chest, and Taylor winced, waiting for his shirt snaps to pop. "You find everything you need?"

An odd smile lifted one side of Clint's mouth as he met the older man's gaze. A silent communication passed between them that made Virgil's left eye twitch and his brows draw together in a straight line.

"I did just fine, Virgil, but I do appreciate your concern." Clint's tone was polite, but stern. Even the clerk seemed to notice the tension, judging by the way her gaze darted back and forth between the two men.

"That's it for me. I'm ready." Taylor picked up her credit card off the counter, and then her sack of purchases.

Clint smiled at the clerk and touched the brim of his hat. "Nice seeing you, Teresa. You give that new baby of yours a hug for me, you hear?"

The woman blushed. "Well, thank you for remembering, Clint."

Taylor wanted to gag. The way he slipped into that country-boy routine really irked her. Though if she didn't know better, it might be a tad charming, she supposed.

Virgil stepped away from the counter. "Southwick?"

Clint had already started for the door but he stopped and met the other man's annoyed gaze with raised brows.

His chest puffed out again, Virgil hitched up his pants. "I'll expect your call."

Clint's only response was a slight smile as he continued out the door.

"What was *that* about?" Taylor hurried to walk alongside him toward the truck.

He gave her a sideways glance. "You've been here only forty-eight hours and you're already getting as nosy as the rest of them."

Indignation simmered in her veins, and she was about to give him a piece of her mind when it occurred to her he was right. She groaned softly. Indignation felt so much better than humiliation. "You're right. I had no business asking. I apologize."

"That wasn't so hard, was it?" He grinned as he opened the passenger door for her.

"I have no problem admitting when I'm wrong. It just so happens I'm usually right." She climbed into the truck, ignoring his grunt of disbelief.

He got in and started the truck. "Virgil's nephew wanted me to do something for him last night, but I refused and now Virgil will be salty for a day or two. He'll get over it."

"You didn't have to explain."

"I didn't want you losing any sleep over it."

"Ah, such a comedian. I'd stick to ranching if I were you." She sighed, and stared out the window. "Hey, this isn't the way back to your place."

He gave her an exaggerated look of surprise. "By golly, you're right again."

"You said we'd go straight home. I've got work to do."

His wrist was bent and relaxed over the wheel, and he shrugged a shoulder. "I lied."

9

"TECHNICALLY, THIS COULD be considered kidnapping."
Taylor folded her arms across her chest and glared out
the window.

About ten minutes outside of Bingo the landscape gave
way to a troop of cactus, standing like little soldiers in
haphazard rows. She seriously considered telling Clint
what he could do with one of those suckers. A particular
spindly prickly-looking one made her smile devilishly.

"Kidnapping, huh?" He thought a moment, then
pulled off to the side of the road. "You can get out if
you like."

She widened her eyes. "In the middle of nowhere?"

He shrugged. "I wouldn't want to be accused of keeping you in my truck against your will."

"You're really something," she said, shaking her head
and sighing in disgust.

"Does that mean you'd like a ride?"

She gave him her haughtiest look in answer.

"If you do, you're going to have to ask me outright.
I don't want any misunderstanding."

The amusement in his eyes tempted her to get out and
walk back to Bingo, but she hadn't gone that far off the
deep end yet. "Yes, I'd like a ride."

"Oh, come on. You can ask me nicer than that."

"Must you play this childish game?"

"You brought up kidnapping, darlin'." He put the

truck back into Drive. "I just wanted to set the record straight."

She stayed stubbornly silent as he pulled onto the highway, wondering what it was about him that made her so crazy. She usually got along with everyone. Even her firm's more difficult clients eventually became her responsibility. So why the friction between her and Clint?

Fatigue was the culprit, she suspected. Most of his comments she'd normally let roll off her back. But she wanted to pick a fight over everything he said. It wasn't even about her suspicions that he was possibly scamming Max and Abby, and God only knew whom else. Ordinarily she would be able to handle herself more professionally.

She sneaked a look his way, letting it linger on the hand he rested idly on the gearshift. His nails were trimmed and clean. He had a small cut that was healing on his thumb, but that was the only blemish she could see.

Odd for a rancher, or anyone who worked with their hands. She remembered how awful her father's hands would get, with dirt and black grease embedded so deep beneath his fingernails that no matter how hard or often she tried to scrub them, they were never truly clean.

As a young teenager, there had been a time when she resented that he was a janitor, that he didn't wear a suit and tie and carry a briefcase like her friends' dads. That's when she'd started sitting at the foot of his recliner as he read the evening paper, scrubbing his nails with a vengeance.

It ended up a turning point in her life.

Holding down two jobs, her dad had little time for her or her brother and sister. But one day he'd put down the newspaper and asked about her dreams. She hadn't understood, and he explained that everyone should have a dream and a goal in life. That if they truly put their mind to it, anything was possible.

Taylor had admitted that she wanted to go to college even though she knew they couldn't afford it. That very night they started playing "what if" and by the next year she'd obtained a scholarship. At her college graduation ceremony, Taylor hugged her dad with pride. She hadn't even noticed if his hands were clean or not.

Her only regret was that he'd died six months before she completed law school. But her mom and brother and sister had been there, and so had her dad in spirit.

As she reflected on the past, she yawned, her gaze returning to the road and the desert landscape. There was still so much undeveloped land. Even though it was horribly arid, it still amazed her Boston sensibility.

She yawned again. Between lack of sleep and the hypnotic sameness of the scenery, her eyelids were getting almost too heavy to lift.

CLINT OPENED the passenger door and stared at Taylor's relaxed face. She hadn't budged or made a peep for the last fifteen minutes. He was almost sorry they'd arrived so soon. The sleep was good for her.

He just about talked himself into climbing back into the truck and driving around for a while, when Taylor's nose wrinkled and she made a slight whimpering sound. At the same time, Sheila came running out of the house, hollering his name.

Taylor's eyes opened. He expected her to jump, startled that he was practically in her lap. But she only smiled lazily, a sensual smile that made his insides quiver.

"We're here," he said gruffly, then turned to scoop up Sheila as she flung herself at him.

"Uncle Clint, I didn't know you were coming!" She rubbed her nose against his, a greeting ritual they'd started a couple of years ago.

"Well, Pumpkin, I didn't know either. I hope your mom won't be mad that I came without calling."

Sheila wrinkled her upturned nose, her green eyes solemn. "Of course she won't, silly. It always makes her happy when you come over."

Clint set her on the ground. The little squirt was getting heavy. "Is your grandmother home, too?"

"She's next door talking to Mr. Zigdorf." She adjusted the straps of her coveralls and shook her head. "I don't know why, though. He smells funny."

Clint sighed as he noticed that Taylor was fully awake and watching them. He picked a fine time to remember how outspoken and honest Sheila could be in her observations of people. He couldn't wait to hear her first crack about Taylor.

"Hey, Pumpkin, think you can keep quiet long enough for me to introduce you to a friend?"

"Uncle Clint." Darting a look at Taylor, she planted her hands on her narrow hips. She was so much like Maggie it made him smile. "I haven't been a chatterbox since I was a kid."

"That's right. I forgot. What are you, six now?"

She stamped a foot. "You know I'm seven and a half."

"Ah." He grinned, and offered Taylor a hand out of the truck. She barely touched it as she climbed out. "Say hi to Ms. Madison. Taylor, this is Sheila."

Taylor smiled and extended her hand to the little girl. "Hi, Sheila. You look much older than seven and a half."

Sheila's eyes widened as she shook Taylor's hand. It

was an adult gesture the girl hadn't expected. Neither had Clint. He kind of liked that Taylor did that.

When Sheila finally withdrew her hand, she glanced at her grimy palm, and then at Clint. Taylor had to have cringed inwardly at the feel of the greasy dirt, but to her credit, she hadn't so much as batted an eye.

Instead, she said, "If your mom doesn't mind, you can call me Taylor."

Sheila rolled her eyes. "My granny would mind."

"Well, then let's not make her unhappy."

"You talk funny. Where are you from?"

"Boston." Taylor chuckled. "And we think people out here talk funny."

Sheila made a face, and Clint knew an argument was brewing in her head. "Okay, let's all go inside," he said, motioning them ahead of him. "It's getting nippy out here."

"But I wanna know—"

"Inside." He pointed toward the house. "Run ahead and warn your mom."

Sheila didn't like being ordered around like that, he knew, but she scampered ahead of them without another word.

Clint blew out a breath. "I should have warned you about the miniature dictator."

"She's adorable."

"Let's see what you think in an hour." He pushed open the white wooden gate and motioned her down the short walkway that led to Beth's modest pink adobe house.

The place was old and in disrepair, but the young woman kept it neat and spotless, her pride further evident in the two clay pots filled with pink and purple pansies, still flourishing here in early December.

Sheila had left the door ajar and Clint gave a courtesy knock before pushing it open the rest of the way. Beth came from the kitchen, an apron around her slim waist, a broad smile on her heart-shaped face.

"What brings you around? You must've smelled the oatmeal raisin cookies I'm baking." She gave him a brief hug and smiled at Taylor. "Hello, you've got to be Taylor. I'm Beth."

"Hi." Taylor promptly extended her hand. Obviously surprised, Beth hesitated and then accepted the handshake.

Sheila tugged at her apron. "She shook my hand, too," the little girl whispered loudly.

Beth sighed. "I hope it was a clean hand, young lady."

"Sort of." Sheila slid a sheepish look at Taylor, and then at Clint. "Should I go call granny?"

Clint shook his head. "Don't disturb her. Taylor is staying the rest of the week and I figured maybe you could lend her some things."

Beth frowned slightly and looked at Taylor, who was at least a head taller than her. "Like what?"

Taylor chuckled, looking at him for an answer.

"I don't know. I just thought—" He shrugged. "I don't know."

"I could have saved us the trip if you'd told me where we were going." Taylor's patronizing tone annoyed him.

"Oh, Clint." Beth's cheeks pinkened as she sized up the other woman's finely tailored blouse and slacks. "She wouldn't be interested in any of my things."

Mortification darkened Taylor's blue eyes. "I only meant that I'm too tall to borrow your clothes."

Beth shrugged self-consciously. "I don't have anything you'd want, anyway."

Clint stood there silently, feeling like the biggest idiot

this side of the Colorado River. Both women were right. Taylor was tall and slim and wore expensive clothes, whereas Beth was petite and curvy, and now they both felt badly because of his stupid thoughtlessness.

"Actually…" Taylor's eyebrows furrowed in a thoughtful frown, "I bought two pairs of jeans today but if you have a couple of T-shirts…I like the one you have on. The hearts on the sleeve are cute. So if you have a couple more like that to spare…?"

Beth perked up.

"That is, if you don't mind…" Taylor added.

Clint opened his mouth to remind Taylor he had shirts for her to borrow, but she gave him a look that had him clamping it shut again.

"Of course I don't mind." Beth untied her apron and tossed it over a chair. "Clint and Sheila, how about you two go get us some iced tea or lemonade?" She looked at Taylor. "Unless you'd prefer something hot? Coffee, tea?"

"Water would even be fine."

Beth waved her off. "Clint, there are pitchers of tea and lemonade in the fridge. Surprise us. We'll be in my room."

"Yes, ma'am." He saluted her, and Sheila mimicked him.

Beth laughed and led Taylor down the hall toward her room.

"What are you doing?" Sheila asked when Clint stared after the two women instead of heading toward the kitchen.

He glanced briefly at the girl, and then toward the room when the sound of Beth's laughter floated out to them. It had been a long time since he'd heard her sound so young and carefree. Even before her husband had walked out, Beth hadn't been happy.

Of course Clint knew the reason now. The self-centered, controlling bastard had never had time for his family. He'd been too busy chasing the bright lights and false promises of the Las Vegas strip. Beth was better off without him. But she had a ways to go in repairing her self-esteem. That Taylor had handled her so sensitively really touched Clint.

Sheila sighed with disgust. "Come on, already."

"Okay. Let's go." He followed her to the kitchen. "Tea or lemonade?"

"Let's have root beer floats!"

"I don't remember that being an option."

A mischievous smile curved her pink-tinted lips. She'd obviously had a strawberry treat of some kind already. "We could have that if *you* wanted it."

"Nice try, kiddo." He got down glasses and took out both pitchers of tea and lemonade.

Sheila sulked for a minute, but as soon as he got the drinks ready she offered to help carry them. He let her have a glass of tea, then finally gave in when she insisted she could carry another one.

Just outside Beth's room, Clint heard the two women giggling. It stopped him, literally. Taylor didn't seem the giggly type and it had been so long since Beth had cut loose. He hadn't really thought about whether the two of them would get along, but they were so fundamentally different he was surprised that they seemed to connect so well.

"Uncle Clint," Sheila whined from behind him, "these glasses are getting heavy."

"Sorry, Pumpkin. You go on ahead of me."

Sheila edged around him and he noticed that the

glasses were too big around for her small hands. Luckily they hadn't had far to go.

"We've got both lemonade *and* iced tea," she sang out as she entered the room. "Take your pick."

Clint entered right behind her. A stack of T-shirts sat on the bed, and Taylor held a red-and-white striped one up to herself. Both women turned.

"You get to pick first, Miss Taylor, because you're a guest." Sheila held up both glasses.

Taylor set the shirt aside and wrinkled her nose in thought. "Hmm, they both look yummy. How about—"

The glass of tea slipped from Sheila's hand. It hit the edge of the bedpost, and Taylor jumped back, but not in time. In what seemed like slow motion, the muddy brown liquid splashed across her cream-colored blouse. Like giant freckles, it spotted the front of the silk fabric as she stared down in horrified silence.

"Sheila!" Beth's hand flew to her mouth.

"I'm sorry, I didn't mean to..." The girl's frightened eyes began to well with tears.

Taylor wiped her expression clean. "Of course you didn't." She gently took the remaining glass of lemonade from Sheila's wobbly hand. "It was an accident. That's all."

Clint set down the glasses he'd carried in. "It was my fault. I should never have given her those tumblers to hold."

"It doesn't have to be anyone's fault," Taylor said, her sympathetic gaze staying on Sheila. "It was simply an accident. That's why they have a word for it in the dictionary, right?"

Sheila shrugged her slim shoulders, and a tear slipped down her cheek.

"Oh, honey." Taylor immediately dropped to Sheila's

level and braced herself with one knee on the threadbare tan carpet. "It's okay. Honest." She put her arms around the child and hugged her. "Know something?"

Sheila leaned back and eyed her in wary misery.

"If your Uncle Clint told me before we got here that I was going to meet this sweet little girl and her very nice mother, but that I'd probably have my blouse totally ruined, I would have come anyway."

A frown creased Sheila's face. "Really?"

"Really." Taylor smiled. "I can buy a new blouse any old time. It can never replace friends."

Sheila smiled tentatively, and the floor shifted under Clint's feet. The compassion on Taylor's face alone was enough to make him want to steady himself. He knew she had only one other change of clothes besides what she was wearing and the jeans she had just purchased. Most people in that situation wouldn't have reacted so magnanimously.

That her concern for the little girl's feelings ruled over her own predicament was admirable. It also scared the hell out of him.

With her blond good looks and clear blue eyes, Taylor tempted him on a physical level, no question about that. She was also smart and competent and independent, so clearly she appealed to him on an intellectual plane. But when he weighed those positive qualities against her obsessive career ambitions, it was easy to convince himself that they weren't right for each other.

However, seeing this new side of her—this tender, caring, maternal side—made her more dangerous to him than a six-month drought.

10

"YOU'RE GONNA HAVE TO move it more to the right."
Mona folded her arms and frowned at the picture. "Let
me think about this a minute. Set it down, and you two
kids take a break."

Clint and Taylor exchanged glances.

She sighed. He grunted in annoyance.

Mona ignored them both and left the room. She didn't
say when she'd be back, but Taylor had gotten to know
the routine after two days of either Mona or Rosie fab-
ricating some excuse to get Clint and Taylor together.
Crazy excuses like helping the women move a television,
or picking up a painting in another town that they swore
required two strong backs. Taylor alone could have
picked up the print and hung it on the wall.

She didn't know for sure if Clint was on to the women,
or simply thought they were having "senior moments,"
but she suspected he was aware of their matchmaking
efforts. They just never discussed it.

In fact, ever since they'd gone to Beth's house two
days ago, Clint had changed. He talked less, stayed out
at the stables more. It was fine with her. It left her free
to intercept any phone calls that would tell her what was
going on with Clint. Not that she'd received any, but at
least she was getting a good deal of work done.

But it was not enough to satisfy Howard. Her boss had
called four times in the past two days. He wanted her

back in Boston—now. She wasn't sure how much longer she could put him off without jeopardizing his goodwill toward her.

"I'm not sticking around here much longer." Clint wiped his forehead with the back of his arm and moved toward the couch where Rosie had left some lemonade on a table. "None of this stuff needs to be done now. Max liked the way this place was just fine, and I seriously doubt he even picked out this ugly print."

Taylor glanced over her shoulder and shushed him.

"Well, look at it. What a sorry piece of western art. I don't know a cowboy on this continent that would dress like that dandy."

She stepped back and smiled at the picture of a man on a bull. He did look more like a Hollywood version. Her gaze slowly drew back to Clint. He should have been the model for the print. He had to be the perfect image of what any woman who'd ever fantasized about a cowboy wanted—the strong jaw, the wide shoulders, the slightly weathered features that made him look rugged and adventurous and maybe even a little dangerous.

"Do me a favor, will you?" He turned to her, the golden flecks in his eyes warm and inviting, and her heart did an annoying little tap dance. "Next time Mona calls for us to help her do something, tell her we're busy in bed bopping like bunnies."

She blinked. "Excuse me?"

"You know what this is about, don't you?"

"I'm not sure I follow you."

He snorted. "Mona keeps calling and asking us to do crazy things that could wait another century. She's matchmaking."

"I'm already staying at your house. If that were the case, what more could they want?" She knew he was right, but made a dismissive gesture, annoyed by his obvious disgust.

"Yeah, but every time she calls, you say I'm out at the stables or outside somewhere, and that you're working in your room. She knows we're staying clear of one another and she aims to change that."

"That's ridiculous. She knows better. We're too different. We're like oil and water."

"No kidding," he snapped. "Did you hear me say I approve?" He muttered something else under his breath.

"Oh, no, it's quite obvious you don't."

He gave her an odd look. "And what, you do?"

"Want to be hooked up with *you?* Of course not."

"Well, it seems to me I'm the only one thinking of ways to keep her off our backs."

"By telling her we're bopping like bunnies? Oh, that should do it." She straightened her spine and pretended an intense interest in the handmade lace doily on the end table.

"I get it," he said after a moment's silence. "You're sore because I've been ignoring you."

Her gaze darted to his face. His expression was a mixture of dawning comprehension and smugness that she found extremely irritating. "Are you insane?"

"That's why you're so quick to offer our services."

She glared at him. "I haven't offered anything. I've merely passed on messages. You're the one ready to hop in your truck and drag me along."

"That's not how I remember it."

"Then I suggest you do something about your pathetic memory."

He stared back at her, a look of genuine surprise on his face—enough to make Taylor doubt herself. It had bothered her that he'd suddenly started treating her like she was contagious, especially after all the flying sparks earlier in the week. Was he right? Had she been too eager to do Mona's bidding?

No. Absolutely not. He was merely being defensive. She sized him up, the way his arms were folded across his broad chest, the way he put more weight on one foot. His posture was definitely defensive.

"Like what you see?"

At his smug tone, her eyes met his. "You're amazing. Even more astonishing is that Bingo is big enough for your ego."

"You were the one giving me the old once-over like I'm up for auction."

"Ha! That's how astute you are. I was thinking how defensive you look because you know darn well who's been the one so hot to run over here three times a day."

He shook his head, his gaze not letting go of hers for a second. "You must think I'm an idiot. You said it yourself, darlin', we're like oil and water."

"So were Abby and Max." Mona smirked as they both turned to look at her. They'd been too busy getting in each other's face to hear her come back.

"What is that supposed to mean?" Clint's tone was almost a snarl.

"Nothing, I suppose," Mona said, with a slight smile and a shrug of one shoulder.

"Yeah, right." Taylor grabbed her purse off the couch. "I hope you heard enough to realize your little scheme is not going to work."

"Scheme?" Mona blinked her ridiculously made-up eyes.

Clint picked up his hammer and level. "If you want any more work done, I suggest you call Herb."

"But he's in Vegas for the next few days."

"Tough." Clint walked past the older woman and headed for the front door.

Mona planted her hands on her hips. "Well..."

Taylor followed Clint but slowed long enough to give Mona her best stern lawyerly look. "It's not going to happen, Mona."

Instead of looking disappointed or expressing denial, Mona smiled. "We'll see about that," she murmured as they headed through the door.

CLINT WASN'T SURPRISED Taylor gave him the silent treatment most of the way home. In fact, he was enjoying the peace and quiet—until her cell phone rang.

"I believe that's your line," he said pleasantly, knowing she didn't want to talk in front of him.

"Thank you for pointing that out." She sighed and dug into her purse.

It had to be Howard, her boss, Clint thought with disgust. It was always him. The guy had no conscience, or maybe he had the hots for Taylor. He called her constantly over trivial matters and badgered her to return earlier. Not that Taylor often shared that kind of information with Clint. She generally moved to the privacy of her bedroom when she answered a call. Now she had no choice.

Clint smiled.

"Hello?" Her entire body language changed. Tension radiated from her voice, lines bracketed her mouth, and Clint had an overwhelming urge to get on a plane to Boston and punch Howard right in the kisser.

The protective instinct she stirred in him was annoying as all get out. She wouldn't welcome the concern. She was too independent, competent, her own champion, and

Clint reminded himself he didn't want or need that kind of woman.

Nothing was wrong with any of those qualities, and in fact, he admired them, but he needed a partner who'd be content to stay on the ranch, and not challenge the difficult decisions he'd already made for himself.

"Yes, Howard." Her evenly controlled voice belied the frustration on her face. "I've already told you my secretary will fax the information to me, and I'll either e-mail or fax a response."

She slid a glance toward Clint, then angled away and faced the passenger window, as if it granted more privacy. He could still hear every word, see every flex of her jaw, feel the stress that was mounting by the minute.

"Howard, stop." She took a quick breath. "It's unfair that you'd think for a second I'd jeopardize this case." She paused and listened. "For God's sake, I know he's our biggest client. Obviously you're confident in my ability or you wouldn't have assigned him to me."

Assertive, no-nonsense, ambitious—this was the Taylor with whom Clint was most comfortable. The problem was, two days ago at Beth's house, nearly every belief he'd had about Taylor got knocked so far out of whack that he was still recovering from the blow. That she'd treated Beth with respect and kindness didn't surprise him. He'd have expected nothing less from Taylor. That she'd treated her as a complete equal touched him in a way he couldn't explain.

"Howard—"

Clint watched the impatience and frustration grow on her face, making her look all the more exhausted, and he itched to grab the phone and tell her boss where to go.

"Slow down, Howard." Her jaw tightened. "Look, if you're that concerned, pass on the case to Sam Hoskins."

She briefly held the phone away from her ear, and Clint could hear the man ranting.

"I do have everything under control," she said, speaking into the phone again. "But if you're uncomfortable, I'll understand if you—"

He'd obviously cut her off, and she waited in angry silence for a moment, and then said, "No, I'm booked to return home on Sunday. That hasn't changed."

She disconnected the call without saying goodbye. Although Clint suspected Howard probably had been the one to hang up on her. She dropped the phone into her purse and then stared out the window.

Clint tried to ignore the slight slump of her shoulders, the defeated way she laid her head on the glass. This was none of his business. He'd gotten past the desire to interfere, to try to get her to take a time-out. Involvement with her was not an option. She was simply a friend of Max and Abby.

He turned on the radio and pressed buttons until he found an oldies station. One of his favorite Eagle songs was playing and he hummed along, throwing in a word or two as he remembered them.

Taylor continued to stare out the window, oblivious to him and the music.

"You don't like the Eagles?" he asked.

She turned and stared blankly at him. "What?"

"The Eagles?"

She frowned in confusion.

"The group." He gestured with his chin toward the radio.

"Oh." She nodded. "I haven't heard them in a long time."

Because she didn't have a life, he thought but managed to keep to himself. The conversation stalled and he drummed his fingers on the wheel as she turned to stare out the window again.

"Anything you want to talk about?" He turned down the radio volume. Of course he was going to regret asking, but when she turned sad, tired eyes his way, he suddenly wanted very much to be her sounding board, to help get rid of the tension that was eating at her.

"Thanks, but…" She looked uncertain. "Don't take this wrong, but I'm not sure you'd understand."

He smiled to himself. Maybe he should tell her about his other career. The one that had once resembled hers so much it gave him the willies to think about it.

"Maybe not," he finally said, "but it may make you feel better to say it out loud."

She smiled a little. "I don't know anything about ranching but I'm sure you have your own kind of deadlines. That's all this is. I'm preparing for a trial and Howard thinks I can't do that as well here as I can back in Boston."

"And you disagree?"

Her gaze flickered away. But not before he saw her uncertainty. "It's not that simple. It's a fairly big case."

He gave her a moment of quiet while he dove into his own thoughts. From what he knew of Taylor, it didn't make sense that she'd jeopardize a case in any manner, or antagonize her boss over a few days off that she was using to work anyway.

Clint didn't get it. Max and Abby weren't even here. And she'd ended up stuck at his house—something she hadn't counted on, and wasn't particularly happy about. Unless…

His gut tightened, and he felt funny inside.

Nah, Taylor wasn't the sort of woman to risk her career

over some guy, much less a cowboy. It was his ego talking. But then, what?

"So, this guy, Howard, finally got to you, huh?"

She swung a confused look at him.

"He probably snapped you up out of law school and prodded and molded you, and as much as you've appreciated his tutelage, he hasn't figured out it's long been time to lay off."

A stunned look crossed her face. "That's partly true. But he isn't so domineering now. In fact, this case will determine whether I'm offered a partnership."

Clint let out a low whistle. "Not bad."

Her left brow arched in amusement. "Not bad?"

"Figure of speech, darlin'. I mean, Taylor," he grinned unrepentantly, "my guess is you've been out of law school about five years. If they're already offering you a partnership, then you must be damn good."

"I am."

"I never met a modest lawyer yet."

She chuckled. "Really? How much do you know about law?"

"I studied it."

"Right."

"You don't believe me? Didn't you see all those law books in my den?"

"Yeah, but I thought maybe—" She broke off and narrowed her gaze. "Have you actually read all of them?"

"Careful, counselor, you're sounding like a snob."

"I am not. I have a lot of books I haven't read yet myself."

"Okay," he admitted. "I concede the point, but let's get back to the partnership issue. I don't get why you're willing to hang around Bingo and jeopardize a career-making case.''

She stiffened, her shoulders recoiling against the seat back. "I would never jeopardize a case entrusted to me.''

"I phrased it wrong.'' He sent her a pointed look. "But you know what I mean.''

Her chin came up and she turned toward the window again.

"Fine. You don't have to answer. It's your business.''

"I have my reasons.''

"Like I said, it's your business.'' He turned up the radio again and tried to get in the spirit of the Rolling Stones.

She continued to stare silently out of the window.

Another two miles and Clint wanted to tell Mick Jagger it was too damn bad he wasn't getting any satisfaction. Who the hell did, anyway?

"Okay,'' he finally said, "since you're intent on shooting your career in the foot, how about we go dancing tonight?''

She slowly turned to glare at him. "I am not shooting my career in the foot. Besides, what happened to the lectures about me working so hard? I finally take some time off and suddenly everyone's worried about it.''

"Take it easy.'' He reached for her hand. "I'm the last person who'd be critical of you taking a breather. The thing is, you may not be in Boston but you're still working like a dog.''

She stared down at his hand covering hers but made no move to withdraw. "Sorry for snapping.''

"No problem.'' He squeezed a little and some of the tension in her stiff fingers relaxed. "Is tonight a date?''

"I'd really like to but—''

"No 'buts' allowed. I haven't taught you how to two-step yet."

She snorted. "That isn't going to happen."

"You're right."

She tilted her head to the side in question.

"I've got a confession to make. I don't know how to two-step either."

That startled a laugh out of her. "What kind of cowboy are you?"

"I know. Sad, but true." He had to withdraw his hand to hold the wheel when they came to their turn. "We can learn together. Tonight."

"Wish I could. But I really do have to work. I just lost three hours thanks to Mona's wild goose chase."

"How about I help? I can even type."

She gave him an amused look. "Is there no end to your talents?"

"Darlin', that's just the tip of the iceberg." He winked, and her eyes narrowed warily. "By the way, I've tried losing the 'darlin'. I truly have. Guess you're going to have to put up with it."

"I suppose I can...for two and a half more days."

"See there? We've got to go dancing tonight. We don't have much time left." He glanced over, and she shook her head. "Come on. There's a great steak house, with live music and dancing after nine near Saunder's Bend. And since I've got a little business to take care of in the area anyway, I figured—"

"Tonight?" Her eyes widened with an odd alertness. "I didn't realize you had to go out there anyway," she said, shrugging. "Maybe I could squeeze in a couple of hours."

He didn't know what to make of her sudden change of heart. It sure as heck had nothing to do with his convenience, but he wasn't going to ruin things by asking questions. Maybe tonight he'd find out the real reason why she was hanging around Bingo.

Fool that he was, he hoped it was for him.

11

FOR A MAN WHO was supposed to be up to no good, Clint sure didn't act like he had anything to hide. Taylor climbed out of the truck to follow him into the bar, the toes of the new boots he'd surprised her with, pinching her feet. She'd tried to turn down the gift, but he was so darn insistent, that in the end, it was easier to accept the pointy black-and-tan cowboy boots.

She'd had more important things that required her energy—like worrying about whether she was throwing her career away on the mistaken notion that Clint was a crook. It was clear she was the only one in town who believed it of him, and now she wasn't so sure herself.

He'd actually invited her into the bar while he took care of his business, although what sort of legitimate dealings were conducted in a dump like this she couldn't fathom.

"Had your tetanus shot?" One side of Clint's mouth lifted when she hesitated at the steps of the boardwalk.

"I wish I had."

In most cities, the shabby stucco building would have been condemned. It stood at the edge of the tiny town, a good several yards from the closest building as though it weren't even welcome to join the others. A piece of rotting wood had apparently once stated the name of the bar in black letters, but the paint was peeling and impossible to read.

"For the record, I didn't choose this place, but I know it's okay." He motioned her ahead of him.

She refused to budge. "After you."

"Okay, but I'm wounded that you don't trust me."

"I can live with that." In spite of his light teasing, the way his jaw had tensed and his eyes narrowed when they pulled up, had already told her that he wasn't keen on the place. Made her wonder why he'd agreed to do business here.

A pair of muddy motorcycles were parked so close to the door that Clint had to step around them to go inside. She followed, resisting the silly urge to tuck her hand inside the back waist of Clint's jeans. She normally wasn't timid about rough-looking places. Heck, her old neighborhood where she'd learned to walk had also taught her how to run like hell. The local college had actually used the area in a study of urban blight.

But this was different, unknown. And besides, having Clint's broad shoulders in front of her just seemed to make her want to do foolish, whimpering, female things—disgusting as that realization was.

At the threshold, Clint stopped suddenly. He must have sensed her fear because he slipped an arm around her and brought his face close. She gave him her ear, expecting him to whisper something, but instead he kissed her. On the mouth. Rough. Possessive. His tongue dove in between her lips and his arm curved tighter around her until her left breast crushed against him.

He released her mouth slowly. His arm didn't budge. "Now everyone will know you're with me," he whispered, then slanted his mouth over hers again before she could breathe.

This kiss was brief, but her heart still pounded and the quickening of his ragged breath pelted her cheek. She hoped he regretted it. She hoped he had a hard-on that embarrassed the hell out of him.

She hoped he kissed her again, soon.

"Was that necessary?" she asked through gritted teeth.

"Probably not, but it sure was fun."

She half groaned, half laughed. "What am I going to do with you?"

"One suggestion comes immediately to mind."

"Keep it to yourself, thank you." She pulled away and advanced into the dimly lit shoe-box-shaped room.

Only four customers sat at the bar, all men, all looking at her. Two of them, one with a scruffy beard, the other with long greasy hair, had actually turned in their seats to stare. Before she could stop herself, she reached for Clint's hand.

He squeezed it lightly.

"I'm doing this for you," she whispered. "So don't get any ideas."

"For me?"

"Prevention. So you don't get your sorry butt into a fight or something stupid like that."

He laughed out loud. "Not only is that vain, but you've obviously watched way too many movies."

Heat stung her cheeks. "I'm not vain. I meant that since I'm the only woman in here…" She glared at the amusement curving his lips. "Oh, never mind."

"Hey, Clint, good to see you, buddy." A guy sporting a short ponytail slid off a stool at the end of the bar and came forth with an extended hand. His little finger was missing.

"Nathan." Clint nodded, unsmiling, as he briefly shook the older man's hand. "I assume you brought the papers."

The man's gaze slid over Taylor. "What's the hurry? Let's have a drink first."

Clint scanned the room, his expression blank. "No, thanks. You have the paperwork here, or is it in your car?"

The man mumbled something derogatory but Taylor barely listened. She was too preoccupied with studying Clint. Gone was the easygoing, laid-back guy she knew. He was focused, serious and, if she wasn't mistaken, a little tense. A couple of times his carefully noncommittal gaze slid to hers. He knew she had to be curious. So why had he brought her inside?

"I don't want to do business in here," Clint said. "Let's go out to my truck."

Nathan's chin jutted. "I like it here just fine."

Clint shrugged and put an arm around Taylor. "Suit yourself."

When the other man realized Clint intended to leave, he muttered a curse. "Come on, Southwick, let's get the damn papers signed." He turned back to his drink, downed the amber liquid in one gulp, and then picked up a briefcase he'd had stashed against the bar.

Clint urged Taylor out the door, neither of them looking back to see if Nathan followed. "I'm sorry about this," Clint said in a low voice. "I didn't mean for you to go inside but I didn't want to leave you out here alone either."

"No problem." Well, that answered a couple of questions. "Who is he? Doesn't seem like someone who'd be a friend of yours."

"He isn't. He's strictly a business acquaintance."

"He doesn't look like a rancher to me."

Clint thoughtfully pursed his lips. She knew what he was thinking. Exactly what she wanted him to think—

that he'd dragged her into this and now he owed her an explanation.

"Nathan isn't a rancher," he finally said, no elaboration offered.

She mentally sighed. "He looks like a drug dealer."

He gave her a sidelong glance that could freeze a hot skillet. "Which would make me...?"

"Don't get touchy. I didn't mean that at all. Just making an observation."

They both clammed up when Nathan got closer, and Taylor slipped off to the side when he set his briefcase on the hood of the truck. She hoped Clint would forget about her if she stayed out of the way, but not far enough away that she couldn't see what was happening.

Just as Nathan unsnapped the briefcase, Clint looked over at her. He dug in his pocket, then tossed her the keys. "Why don't you sit inside the truck? It's warmer."

"I'm fine out here."

"Taylor."

She didn't like his warning tone and stayed planted right where she was by the corner bumper.

"Just a minute," he told Nathan with a grim expression and then took the few necessary steps to relieve her of the keys and open the passenger door.

When she still didn't budge, he cupped his palm over her fanny. That got her to move, and she might have smacked him if he hadn't done some quick footwork.

"Work with me," he murmured. "I'll explain later."

Without giving her a chance to respond, he practically shoved her inside, slammed the door and rejoined Nathan. Taylor could almost feel the steam coming out of her ears. He'd better believe he'd explain, and answer every darn question she asked.

She tried to tamp down her temper so that she could

observe the men objectively, maybe even detect what was going on. But all she saw was a stack of papers that Clint glanced at for a minute, then shoved into a manila envelope.

They exchanged a few words. Nathan signed what looked like a blank piece of paper several times, and Clint added that to the rest of the stack in the envelope. She was sure looking forward to an explanation for *that*. Not that she assumed she'd get it.

One way or another she'd find out what this was about. Maybe he'd forget to lock his desk. She thought it was odd that he locked it at all, unless he knew she'd snooped in his den while he was out. She'd been horribly torn about doing such a rotten thing, but thinking about Max and Abby and what could happen to them had cinched her decision.

Nathan headed toward a dusty dark blue sedan parked on the side of the bar, and Clint got in the truck. He tucked the manila envelope under his seat before starting the engine.

"Well?"

He frowned at her. "Well, what?"

"What's going on?"

"For cripes' sake, cut me some slack, will you? You're as nosy as the rest of the people around here."

"So you've told me once before." She folded her arms. "You also told me to work with you and you'd explain."

He let out a long frustrated breath. "I'm doing some work for someone. It's no big deal."

"What kind of work?"

"It has to do with mineral rights. You wouldn't understand."

She snorted. "I'm an attorney. Try me."

He glanced at her before pulling onto the highway, his expression wary. "This isn't the kind of law you're used to."

"What? The criminal kind?"

He gave her a sharp look. "You're better off staying out of this, Taylor."

Suspicion rekindled and flared in her chest. It slowly gave way to disappointment that settled around her like a dense fog, and she realized how much she'd hoped for a reasonable explanation. Something that would prove she was wrong about him, and that everyone else was right—that Clint truly was the great guy they all seemed to think he was.

"Getting hungry?" he asked when the silence stretched out too long.

"Not really."

"Too bad, because I'm going to buy you the best steak you've ever sunk your teeth into."

She managed a smile, but nothing more. The disappointment was stifling, making it hard to think, difficult to gauge how hard she should push for information.

"Hey, you."

At his playful voice, she reluctantly met his gaze.

"You okay?" he asked, and she nodded.

"Good. I need to ask a favor."

Curiosity made her straighten a little. "What is it?"

"I may need your legal opinion."

Hope revived her. "Regarding?"

"Of course I expect to pay for your services."

"You will do no such thing. What if I insisted on paying you rent?"

His mouth lifted in a wicked smile she couldn't mistake. "I'd think of something you could do in trade."

"That's illegal."

"Not in this county."

"Very funny." She remembered the Swinging R, and his remark brought heat to her face and an extra beat to her heart. "Let's get back to this favor you wanted."

He chuckled. "It's this land deal I'm working on. It involves one buyer and several sellers, which in itself isn't a problem, but because of the potential for silver or other minerals that might be…" He gave her a wry smile. "I'm boring you."

She blinked. "No, of course not."

"Then why are your eyes glazing over?"

At his teasing smile, she winced. Her mind had wandered. He wouldn't ask her to review anything illegal, which meant her suspicions about him were wrong. Never in her life had she so hoped to be wrong.

"I'm sorry if I seemed disinterested," she said. "I'm really not—just a little tired."

"Hey, forget it." He pulled the truck off the road in front of a rustic-looking building. A large sign identified it as a steak house. He turned off the ignition, and then reached over and squeezed her hand. "We're supposed to be out having fun."

"No, tell me, or I'll feel terrible."

"Later, or tomorrow. But tonight, we eat, drink and dance." He brought her hand to his mouth and kissed the back of it. The look in his eyes promised more. Much more. And God help her, she just might be ready.

"TRY A SIP OF THIS." Clint offered her the glass of Bordeaux. It didn't take a psychologist to know what he was doing, he thought wryly. She thought he was a bit of a hick and he didn't like it.

At first, it had amused him. His attitude had been one of go to hell if you don't like it. Not just with her, but anyone who judged his decision to return to his roots. But now, he wanted to prove to her he was an equal, or at least that he recognized the finer things in life.

She made a face. "I'm not much of a wine drinker, and when I do, I prefer white."

"What do you normally have?"

"Diet cola." She shrugged. "I don't drink much alcohol at all, but I prefer beer."

"That's right. I remember. Is there some kind of new yuppie micro brew that's the hit in Boston?"

She laughed. "I wouldn't know. Whatever light beer is on draft suits me."

He sat back in the worn leather booth and thoughtfully sipped his wine. It was his favorite and came from a special bottle the owner of the steak house kept privately for Clint in gratitude for some legal advice. A place like this wouldn't ordinarily carry this expensive a wine. They served beer mostly, and shots of tequila.

He glanced around the crowded room. Lots of scarred wood, tacky posters, faded jeans and cowboy hats. Nope, this wasn't the Ritz. The funny thing was, Taylor looked right at home here. Not just because of the jeans and flannel shirt she'd readily donned at his suggestion. It was more than that. It was the way she good-naturedly joked with the waitress, the way she dug into the basket of rolls and, later, the steak and baked potato. She looked totally at ease.

Clint studied her as she peered intensely at a couple fumbling through the two-step on the dance floor. "How did you come to appreciate the finer taste of draft beer?"

"Easy." She brought her gaze to his and grinned. "That's all I could afford in college. Well, that's not quite true." Her smile faded and her gaze wavered for a moment. "Even tap beer was beyond my budget. But I'd sometimes drink it from a keg at parties."

Stunned, he set down his glass, aware that she carefully observed his reaction. He cleared his throat. "Didn't you go to Harvard with Max?"

She nodded. "I was on a scholarship."

Confusion clouded his brain. "But you were a part of his crowd..."

A knowing smile touched the corners of her mouth. "Not exactly. We met our first year in law school and became friends quickly so I had occasion to socialize with some of his friends. But was I ever accepted as one of them? No way. Not only did I come from the wrong side of the tracks, but I doubt any of them would have set foot in my neighborhood."

Her voice held no bitterness whatsoever, and his admiration for her climbed a few notches. "I've got to admit, I had you pegged wrong. I just assumed you were one of..." he shrugged, "Max's kind."

She laughed softly. "Even Max isn't one of Max's kind. He was always kind of a loner. So was I. Guess that's why we got along so well."

"Your family still live in Boston?"

"My mom and brother do. My sister just moved to Maine. Dad passed away while I was in law school."

"I'm sorry. Too bad he didn't get to see you graduate."

"Oh, I'm sure he did." She smiled self-consciously. It was a shy and endearing expression that reached her eyes, and made his heart light.

"Everyone must be really proud of you."

She thought for a moment. "They are, and I'm proud of them. They're all successful in their own right. But the thing is, my dad always taught us that we could do anything we truly wanted to do, so it wasn't a big surprise that I became a lawyer and my younger brother is studying computer science. We followed our hearts.''

Clint smiled. She was modest, too. Fulfilling a dream was one thing, getting into Harvard was something else altogether. He knew. He'd tried for a scholarship there, as well, but he'd screwed off one too many times in high school.

He set the wineglass out of the way and reached for her hand. It was soft, warm, and she didn't seem to mind when he intertwined their fingers. "What are your other dreams, Taylor? Where else is your heart leading you?"

She sent him a wary look, and then her eyes became impersonal. "To the dance floor. I decided I want to learn to two-step before I leave."

He cocked an eyebrow. "Right."

"I do."

He stared at her for a long moment, and then he got out his wallet and left several bills on the table. "Okay."

She eyed the money with a frown. "What are you doing?"

He got up and pulled her to her feet. "I thought you wanted to two-step."

"Oh." She smiled and relaxed. "Yeah."

They got to the dance floor and when she stopped, he pressed his hand to the small of her back and urged her toward the door.

Her eyes widened. "I thought—"

"We are," he said, smiling. "But I have a more private two-step in mind."

12

TAYLOR HADN'T BOTHERED to ask where they were going, and when they turned into the drive to his ranch, she wasn't the least bit surprised. Excited, breathless, a little frightened, but not surprised.

From the first moment she'd seen him again at the wedding, sparks ignited, and their relationship had been building to this night. To the moment when the only thing she wanted was him inside her, filling her with his energy, his need. Fulfilling her need.

That he'd asked for her help earlier and was going to let her look at the paperwork was reassuring. More evidence that he wasn't the swindler she'd imagined.

She jumped when he opened her door. So lost in thought, she hadn't realized the truck had come to a stop and he'd already gotten out.

"Take it easy," he said, offering his hand. "I promise I will bite."

She frowned as he helped her down. Had he said...? She stared suspiciously at him, and he laughed.

He held her hand as he led her into the house, and she didn't even think about protesting when he steered her down the hall toward his room. She was nervous but she knew tonight was inevitable. At this point she didn't think she could even get on that plane without knowing the feel of his body against hers, without letting their hearts beat as one.

"Taylor?"

They stopped at the door to his room, and she met his eyes. The tenderness she found there made her knees weak.

He smiled and brushed the back of his hand across her cheek. "If you have any doubts, now is the time to voice them."

She slowly shook her head, careful to keep their gazes fastened so he'd see the certainty in her eyes. "And you?"

"Darlin', I still remember what you were wearing the day I met you on Main Street." He reached out, and she thought he was going to draw her closer, but he yanked the hem of her flannel shirt out of her jeans.

Using the fabric bunched in his hand, he pulled her toward him. "After tonight, I'll remember what you weren't wearing," he whispered before he hungrily took possession of her mouth.

She clutched his shoulders and kissed him back with equal fervor. So much, that her enthusiasm caused him to stumble back. He managed to hold onto both her and his footing until they reached his king-size bed. And then he fell backward on the thick burgundy quilt, bringing her with him.

Their mouths broke contact and they laughed. Taylor tried to roll off him, but he banded his arms around her and kept her atop him, his hands pulling out the rest of her shirt from her jeans.

Her throat was bared to him and he licked a trail to her chin, along her jaw, to the sensitive spot below her ear. She shivered with delight, and the awareness that he was growing rock-hard beneath her.

"I've got a secret for you, counselor," he whispered, his warm breath on her skin, sending shock waves to her nerve endings. "The boots definitely have to come off first."

She half gasped, half laughed when she realized she'd freed his shirt and was already working on unfastening his fly. Swiftly, she withdrew her hand. The aggressiveness she displayed in the courtroom ended there, and this forward behavior surprised the heck out of her.

"Now, don't be so hasty," he said, returning her hand to rest on the growing thickness beneath the denim.

Tentatively she traced his arousal with her fingers, finding satisfaction in his low groan, and then nearly jumping out of her skin when he slid his hand under her shirt. He cupped and kneaded her breast through her lacy bra, and then with a grunt of impatience slid his fingers beneath the underwire. Her nipple had already beaded, and he lightly pinched it between his thumb and forefinger.

She whimpered and arched her back, filling his palm with her flesh. He rolled her onto her back and unfastened her buttons with dizzying speed. He pushed the front of her shirt aside, unhooked the front of her bra, then sucked her nipple into his mouth with such raw hunger, it robbed her of breath.

He'd wedged one leg between her thighs and she feverishly wondered if he could feel the flood of moisture pooling there, making her embarrassingly wet and hot, and dangerously close to losing complete control.

"I thought you said the boots came off first." Her voice was ragged, barely a whisper.

His lips curved in a smile against her skin, his teeth slightly rough over her nipple. "Darlin', when you're right, you're right," he said, then slid down her body, his tongue doing magical things along the way.

When he got to the edge of the bed, he dropped to the

floor on one knee, and grasping her thighs, pulled her toward him, keeping her legs slightly parted. She ended up in an undignified but tantalizing position, and her breath stalled in her chest.

He kissed the inside of each of her knees, then moved up to kiss her inner thighs. The layer of denim between them did little to dull the sensation. His heat branded her as though nothing separated his lips from her flesh, from her...

A phone rang, either in her purse or his jacket. Both had been tossed on a chair.

He didn't stop for a second, and she relaxed against the quilt and closed her eyes.

But the phone didn't stop ringing either.

She struggled to a sitting position. "Whose line is it?"

He brought his head up. His pupils were dilated, his eyes hungry. He unsnapped her jeans, pulled down her zipper. After pushing the fabric apart, he kissed her belly. "Does it matter?"

Closing her eyes again, she wilted against the bed. He was right. Screw the phone.

He moved up to take a nipple into his mouth, biting lightly, licking, sucking. And then he stopped suddenly, and she nearly whimpered out loud at the loss. He sat back on his haunches. "Sorry. You wanted to get the phone?"

She blinked. His face was a tad blurry but she didn't miss the teasing glint in his eye. "You rotten son-of-a—"

Laughing, he pulled one of her boots off. The speed with which he got rid of the second one amazed her. It had taken her five minutes to get them on.

When he reached for the waist of her jeans, she said, "Your boots. Let's get them off."

He quickly complied, then went back to her jeans. She unsnapped his, and he sucked in a breath. He was already so hard freeing the zipper was tricky. After she got it down halfway, she started unbuttoning his shirt.

Her gaze swept over the sprinkling of hair on his powerful chest, just the right amount for her to push her fingers through the coarse silkiness. He felt good against her palm, the taut muscle and smooth warm skin, the way his nipples immediately distended. She stretched up to take one into her mouth, but he shifted away.

"Taylor, don't."

The pleading in his voice, the unevenness of his breathing, urged her forward. She'd obviously found a touchy spot, one that could help push him over the edge, just where she wanted him.

She touched her tongue to the hard nub and he groaned. Her limited experience had never elicited that kind of reaction before and she went back for seconds.

Clint was quicker. He pulled away and tugged off her jeans. There was an underlying animal-like urgency to his movements, a wild glint in his eyes, which set off a yearning in her belly that shocked her. She wanted him inside her. Now.

She moved to help him but he almost had them both naked. Her skimpy black lace panties were all she had left on. He stared longingly at her nude body as he shoved down his jeans and boxers, then kicked them aside.

She tried not to stare back. But it was almost impossible. He was so thick and hard and ready, and she craved him like a junkie desperately needing her fix. She touched him, and they both seemed to fall apart with need.

He crawled onto the bed with her and found her wetness. Embarrassingly close to climaxing, she was relieved to see the foil packet in his hand. She didn't know where it came from, didn't care. She was too enthralled with the way he sheathed himself. And then, in the next moment, he entered her and within moments she fell into an abyss of pure pleasure.

EVEN WITH HER EYES CLOSED, Taylor knew it was morning—early though, before the sun was too bright. The reassuring heat of Clint's body beside her made her smile lazily. Slowly she opened her eyes.

He was lying on his back, his head sharing her pillow. Stubble darkened his jaw and chin, and contrasted his thick black lashes. His mouth was relaxed, making his lips part slightly, innocently. Except she recalled all the devilishly wonderful things he'd done to her with that mouth and there wasn't a darn thing innocent about him.

It was so tempting to kiss him awake because she knew what would come of her efforts. But she supposed his many encore performances last night earned him, at the very least, another hour of sleep.

She shifted a little to her side so she could watch him breathe. Watch the way his strong chest rose and fell, the way his nipples were slightly budded from the cool air. The sheet had settled at his waist and she thought seriously about inching it down so that she could get a full view of him.

But that wouldn't be fair. She'd probably get too worked up to let him continue sleeping.

To distract herself, she looked around the room at all the things she'd been too busy to see last night. The oak dresser was old, probably an antique passed down through his family. So were the armoire and two overstuffed gray chairs. A pair of pictures sat on the table between them and made her curious enough to slip out from under the covers for a look.

She had this sudden and insatiable desire to know everything about Clint—about his family, his childhood, his dreams. She wanted to crawl inside of him until she understood everything about what made him tick. Not just because he was an incredible lover, but because he made her feel so at ease. For the first time in years, she was beginning to feel like the old Taylor, the one who remembered that her life had other dimensions outside of the courtroom.

She was halfway to the table when one of the cell phones rang. Unsure which one it was, she scooped up both her purse and his jacket and hurried out of the room before it woke him.

No surprise, it was hers. She answered it as she got to her room and closed the door.

"Where the hell have you been?"

She sighed. "Good morning, Howard."

"Morning? It's noon already."

"Not here." She cradled the phone with her shoulder while she slipped on her robe.

"Where have you been?"

"Is that why you're calling? To find out where I've been?" There was a long silence…long enough for her to regret her sarcasm. Howard had quite a temper. "I've been here, but I was having trouble with my phone."

"I don't know what's gotten into you this past week, Taylor, but you've greatly disappointed me. I've tried to be patient," he said, and she wanted to laugh. "But I've had enough. Either you get on a plane today, or I pass on this case."

She stiffened. Of course she'd offered that option herself, but it had been a bluff. She'd kept on top of things.

It wasn't necessary. "Look, Howard, I'm leaving day after tomorrow, and I've—"

"Today, Taylor."

Her own temper ignited. She never took time off. "You're being unreasonable."

"Today, or I pass on this case."

She took a deep calming breath. "Fine. I understand."

"No, I don't think you do." Howard paused, but she could hear him breathing—fast, furious, irregular breaths that told her she was walking a fine line. "It's going to be one hell of a long time before we consider adding another partner again."

She briefly closed her eyes. Howard didn't make idle threats. "Look, Howard, let me call you back, okay?" she asked in a soothing voice.

"Only if it's from the Boston airport."

The disconnecting click sounded like a sonic boom.

She tossed the phone on the bed and then sank to the mattress herself. Was she insane? Putting her career on the line like this? Clint was no longer a threat to Max. She was fairly certain of that, so it wasn't necessary to stay any longer.

Of course there was Clint. But he'd understand that she had to leave. They could make plans to see each other again, as soon as her case was over. Maybe they could even take a vacation together. The thought sent a shiver of anticipation through her. It almost made her forget she was about to blow a career she'd nurtured with blind dedication for the past five years.

She twisted around to check the digital clock on the nightstand. She'd have to hurry in order to get a flight out today. It was a shame she'd miss Max and Abby's arrival tomorrow evening, but they'd understand.

Her gaze caught on her suitcase sitting in the corner,

and an unexpected sadness swept her. She didn't want to leave Clint. Ridiculous, she knew. It was inevitable that she had to return to Boston, but she hadn't anticipated it would be so damn hard to say goodbye.

She pushed off the bed just as his cell phone rang from his jacket pocket. For a second she thought about letting it ring, but it wouldn't hurt to take a message for him. Okay, so she was a little curious, too…

"Southwick?"

Nathan's sharp, tobacco-roughened voice slithered through the line before she could say a word. She recognized it immediately. In fact, she realized now that he'd been the one to call the night of the reception.

"He's not here. Would you like to leave a message?" she asked as pleasantly as she could.

"What do you mean, not there? That's why I called his cell. Did he look at the papers?"

"You'll need to talk to him about that. I can only take a message."

"Are you that hot blonde that was with him last night?"

The leer in his voice made her want to slap him right through the line. "I'll give you one last chance to leave a message."

He cursed. "You tell him he better not be stalling. I expect a phone call by noon. If I don't get the answer I want, I'll go straight to Bennett and blow the whistle."

Taylor calmly removed the phone from her ear and disconnected the call. Uneasiness crawled down her spine. She dismissed the sense of foreboding that made her palms clammy. Clint had already asked her to look at the papers. If they referred to anything illegal he wouldn't involve her, especially since she was Max's friend.

Nathan was just a jerk. She'd had past clients to whom she'd have gladly given the boot had it been within her power. This was probably just business. Reviewing the papers would explain everything.

The sudden knock at her door made her jump off the bed. "Taylor?"

"Clint?" She shook her head at herself. Of course it was him. "Come in."

They opened the door at the same time. He wore only his navy blue boxers and his hair was tousled. The sexy smile curving his lips made her heart melt.

"I missed you, baby." He pulled her into his arms, and she readily slipped hers around his neck. His chest hair brushed her bare breasts where her robe parted, and she arched against him. "What are you doing in here?" He nuzzled her neck. "Come back to bed."

God, it was tempting to give in. But she had to call the airlines, pack her clothes... "Clint?"

"Hmm?"

"I can't talk when you're doing that to my—" She gasped when his hand slid down her belly, his fingers probing her hidden curls. "Clint..."

"Come on back to bed, darlin'." His lips trailed her throat, worked their way up to her jaw.

"Nathan called on your cell phone." She figured that would slow Clint down. She hadn't expected such an abrupt withdrawal.

He frowned at her. "This morning?"

She nodded. "Both phones rang. That's why I came in here. So they wouldn't wake you."

He dragged a hand down his face, then blew into his palm. "What did he want?"

The sleepy, sexy man who'd come looking for her was gone. Vigilance now sharpened his eyes. Annoyance thinned his lips. Uneasiness again slid like a preying snake down her spine.

She shrugged. "For you to call him."

His gaze bore into hers, as though he were cross-examining her. "Did he say anything else?"

"He expects a return call by noon, and if he doesn't get the answer he wants, he's going to Max and blowing the whistle."

Clint swore under his breath, then looked off into space, his brows furrowed in concentration, or maybe anger. When he finally met her gaze, he seemed distant. "I've got to go take a shower and then go out for about an hour."

"Okay." She pulled the robe tighter around her so the front didn't gap. "I'll review those papers for you while you're gone."

He'd started to leave, but turned to her, clearly puzzled. "What papers?"

"The ones Nathan gave you last night. You wanted me to—"

Clint shook his head. "Never mind. It's not necessary."

"What do you mean?" She caught his arm when he started to leave again.

"I'm sure you have enough of your own work to do." His tone was even, almost soothing, but his eyes issued a warning.

She stared back, feeling smaller by the second. "You had no intention of showing them to me. You only said that to sleep with me."

He drew his head back, the stunned look in his eyes almost convincing. "Taylor, what are you talking about?"

"What's the big secret, Clint?"

"There's no secret. I told you this is business." He narrowed his gaze. "Why? What else did Nate say?"

"Nothing," she said sadly and turned away. It looked as though she'd been right about Clint all along. Denial was a strong foe, and she'd foolishly let her guard down.

But she wouldn't let Max down. Even if it meant blowing her career, she'd expose Clint. From the call, it seemed the heat was already on. She'd just have to turn it up.

13

"MONA CALLED TO REMIND us about the party they're planning for Max and Abby tomorrow night." Clint waited for Taylor to at least look up from her laptop.

She nodded, barely sparing him a glance.

It had been like this ever since he'd returned home shortly after noon, even after he'd explained why his one-hour errand had turned into three. Granted, his explanation had been a lie, but she didn't know that, and she seemed to accept his excuse easily enough. So why was she so uptight? Selfishly he hoped it had something to do with her boss, and not because she regretted their lovemaking.

"Taylor?"

With obvious reluctance, she lifted her gaze to his.

"Are you going to work all day?"

"I'm really behind," she mumbled, and returned her attention to the computer screen.

He drummed his fingers on his desk. Damn Nathan's impatient hide. Plans had to be stepped up, and everyone involved in the sting had been notified, but the timing sure was rotten. He'd hated leaving Taylor like he had this morning. Unfortunately, he'd have to do it again in two hours.

"Can't you take a break?" He got up from his chair and circled behind her, pushed the hair away from the back of her neck and kissed the spot he knew drove her wild.

She tensed, and abruptly closed her laptop. "I'm going back to my room if you don't knock it off."

He moved his hand away and came around to look her in the eyes. "We have to talk."

She averted her gaze. "Why?"

"Come on, Taylor. It's obvious you regret last night. The least you can do is tell me why."

She looked at him then, denial leaping into her eyes, and giving him hope. "Of course I don't." Her gaze skittered away again. "It's just that I have so much work to do."

"I see." He took a step back. "I guess last night meant more to me than it did to you."

Her shoulders slumped and she looked utterly miserable. "That's not true," she said quietly. "My boss called this morning. He's given me an ultimatum. He wants me back today."

The onslaught of relief should have shamed him. "Or else?"

"He'll pass my case on to the second chair. And my chance at making partner goes out the window."

"Ah, baby, I'm sorry. You should've told me sooner." He took the computer off her lap, set it aside, and then pulled her to her feet and into his arms.

She tensed at first, and then she relaxed and leaned into his chest. He held her tighter.

Damn, he didn't want her to go. That she was even still here was a good sign. Or maybe she simply couldn't get a flight out.

Panic thundered in his chest, and he pulled back so she couldn't feel his fear. "So what's the verdict?"

"I haven't called him back yet." She put more distance between them and wandered toward the window.

He glanced at the clock. "Obviously your flight choices are slim. You must have made a decision."

"I still have business here."

Clint frowned and then his heart started to pound harder. Him? Is that what she meant? "I thought this trip was strictly social."

She turned sad eyes on him. "It started out that way. But Max wants me to—" She stopped, cleared her throat. "I understand you're buying some of the Swinging R land."

He shrugged. "Yeah."

"As Max's attorney, I'll be reviewing the documents."

"Okay," he said slowly. "But I'm surprised he asked you to do that."

"Why?" She stared at him with too much intensity, as if this were a test. "I *am* his attorney."

"But Max has been doing his own legal work." Clint noticed a small twitch at the corner of her right eye that she tried to blink away. "Besides, the transaction is a no-brainer."

"Good. It won't take me long."

"You're risking your partnership for that?"

She crossed her arms and hugged herself. "You sound anxious to get rid of me."

He stared in disbelief, and then he went to her. "Ah, Taylor, that couldn't be farther from the truth." He put his arms around her but she didn't respond.

Despite her assurances to the contrary, maybe she'd felt hurt and abandoned this morning. Maybe he should explain about Nathan and the sting. By tomorrow it would all be over anyway. But dammit, Clint had given his word...

"It doesn't matter," she said flippantly and backed away from him. "We both knew I had to return to Boston eventually."

The coolness in her gaze deflated him. Made him angry and melancholy at the same time. He was such a chump for harboring the slightest hope things could work out for them, especially after what Taylor had told him last night.

Although her modest background gave them more commonality, it also put her further out of reach. She had come far, earned and appreciated the good life her hard work provided. It would be difficult to give any of it up now. He knew too well what it felt like to prove yourself, and how agonizing the decision was to climb back down the mountain.

TAYLOR WAS A MESS. She couldn't work. She couldn't eat. She couldn't stop thinking about Clint. And holing up in her room had done little to ease her pain.

Earlier, she'd wanted to distract him by telling him about Howard. But as soon as Clint had put his arms around her, her ploy backfired. It had felt so good to be comforted by him, to have his breath warm her skin, believe his strong arms promised everything would be all right. She'd almost forgotten he was a crook, and not her confidante. It made her boiling mad, and at the same time, incredibly sad.

How could she have been stupid enough to fall in love with him? Who was the real Clint, anyway? She'd come to learn that he was a kind, funny, even-tempered guy—just the kind who could con everyone.

It really galled her to think she'd still been hoping—and worse, willing—to deny he was up to no good until an hour ago. But when he told her he had an emergency meeting to attend, she knew the pretense was over, that she'd forced his hand. He obviously didn't want her involved in the land purchase. She might catch something Max had missed.

She heard the door to his den close and she took a deep breath before leaving her room to face him. She caught him in the hall, the back of his broad shoulders and tapered waist making her chest ache.

"Hey." She forced a smile.

He turned to her, clearly surprised she'd finally resurfaced. "Hey, yourself."

"You headed out now?" she asked casually.

He nodded. "I shouldn't be long."

"You wouldn't happen to be passing through town…"

"Yup. In fact, that's where I'm going. Why? You need something?"

She moved closer, and he looked even more surprised, but pleased. "I wanted to go to the general store and I thought I'd catch a ride with you." She dusted a piece of imaginary lint off his collar, letting the back of her fingers brush his skin. "Maybe when you're done with your business we can have a drink."

At her coy tone, his eyes narrowed, but already they were darkening with desire. He clamped a hand around her wrist as she was about to withdraw, and then planted a kiss in her palm. "Can you be ready in five?"

"I'm ready now."

His gaze dropped to her mouth. It was clear he wanted to kiss her there, as well. And dammit, in spite of everything, she wanted that, too.

"Look, I'm sorry if I was snippy earlier. I hadn't expected Howard to—"

He stopped her with a finger to her lips. "I shouldn't

have left so abruptly this morning. Let's start the day over."

She nodded, her gaze hopelessly locked with his, and she wanted to do something she'd done rarely in her life: sit down and cry. She'd finally fallen in love. And it was with the wrong man. How could life be so unfair?

"We'd better go," she said while she could still speak. "I don't want to make you late."

He smiled and slid an arm around her shoulders. They walked all the way to his truck before he released her, and she immediately missed his warmth. They said nothing during the short ride, only listened to the radio. A country-and-western singer crooned about a lost love which made Taylor feel all the more miserable.

"Shall I drop you off at Virgil's?" Clint asked when they approached the small town.

"Don't go out of your way. Go ahead and park wherever you're headed and I'll walk from there. I need the exercise, anyway."

"It's not out of my way at all. Here it is now." He slowed to a stop in front of the store. "Since I can't say what time I'll be done, why don't we meet at Edna's Edibles? You can have a cup of coffee while you wait. Maybe she still has some of her cherry cobbler."

Taylor lifted the door handle, her brain scrambling for an excuse to stay with him, or at least find out where he was headed. "Or I could walk over to wherever your meeting is."

"Edna's place is better. You can have something warm to drink and stay out of the cold." He leaned across the seat and touched his lips to hers. "Until I can warm you up myself."

Her breath caught. She cursed herself for allowing him

to have this effect on her. She pulled away and quickly got out. "Where are you going to be?"

He frowned. "The other side of town. Why?"

"No reason." Luckily, the town consisted of only a few blocks. "See you later." She smiled, closed the door, and then immediately entered the store.

She watched from the window until he'd gotten a block away, and then she eased back outside, ignoring the suspicious stare from the clerk at the register. It felt weird skulking around a town like Bingo, sticking close to the buildings so she couldn't be easily seen. Fortunately, Main Street was fairly deserted so there were no curious stares. Unfortunately, she'd be easy to spot if Clint thought she might be following him.

His truck made a sudden turn after the bank and she stopped in her tracks. As soon as it was clear, she dodged across the street and jogged toward the alley he'd turned into.

She was pathetically out of breath by the time she reached the white stucco church where Max and Abby had gotten married. Behind it, she saw Clint's truck parked next to a dusty maroon sedan. She didn't recognize the car, and the rest of the small lot was empty, but then she saw a stocky man coming from the opposite direction on foot.

Slipping between a pair of Palmetto palms, she watched as the man got closer. It was the store owner, Virgil. She thought back to the day she'd bought her jeans, and the odd silent exchange between him and Clint. Were they in on the scheme together?

She briefly closed her eyes. Poor Max. It was going to break her heart to tell him about how he was being conned. She'd never seen him so happy as he'd been since moving to Bingo.

And what about her shattered heart? She swallowed hard. She couldn't think about her and Clint right now. Replaying what might have been would divert her focus and she needed to be sharp. She hoped Virgil would lead her to the meeting spot.

He glanced around before entering the front of the church. She hesitated, unsure how she'd make it across the lot without being seen when she saw Virgil exit the back and slip inside another small brick building she hadn't noticed before.

Craning her neck for a better look, she realized it wasn't an independent building at all, but part of the community center where Max's wedding reception had been held. She gritted her teeth and wove through the shadows toward the door. That the slimeballs used a church and a community center as a cover chafed, but at least she'd know her way around somewhat.

She used a side entrance, quietly slipping into the dark hall. Laughter floated from a room off to the right where a light shone. Only one other area was lit. At least that narrowed her choices.

Briefly closing her eyes, she took a deep breath, then hurried toward the next alcove while the coast was clear. She ended up across from the first room and got a glimpse of a table with several empty chairs. A foam cup sat on one edge of the table. She chanced a better look and saw that the room was empty.

When she heard a voice coming from behind, she had little choice but to seek cover. She found it in a corner closet inside the room. It was small, dark and cramped with a broom and two file cabinets, but she squeezed in between them, left the door slightly ajar and held her breath.

"Where is everyone?" Irritation marked Clint's voice.

"I ought to start charging you guys. Bet we'd start on time."

Another man snorted. "Can't imagine why you're so anxious to get back home." It was Virgil. "It wouldn't have anything to do with a blond lady lawyer?"

"Watch it, Virgil."

"Ah, hell, Clint, I'm just funnin' you. I don't mean anything disrespectful."

"Yeah, I know." Clint sighed. "Here come the others."

Taylor pressed her lips together. Even the sound of Clint's voice got her all worked up. He'd sounded protective. It put a lump in her throat, but it didn't mean anything. He was still a criminal.

A general low murmur made it difficult to guess how many people were out there. Definitely more than Taylor had anticipated and she experienced her first real pang of fear.

"Come on, everyone, save the chitchat for later. Let's get down to business." At Clint's no-nonsense tone, the murmur immediately ceased.

Chairs scraped the tile floor, and then silence fell until Clint spoke again. "As I explained on the phone, we're going to have to move up our plans. Silverado Mining wants to sell before their fiscal year-end. If we don't act fast, they could exercise their option and sell to a private party."

Someone cursed, and then apologized.

"What if we can't come up with the money fast enough?" Virgil asked, while someone else grunted. "Can't you tell them we're good for it? We all got homes or businesses to use for collateral. We just need a little time."

Taylor put a hand to her throat. This was worse than

she thought. He was bilking all of his neighbors and not just Max.

"I understand," Clint said in a disgustingly smooth voice. "But we're talking about a large corporation. Frankly, they don't care about any of us. They want to sell, and that's it. If we don't have the money, they'll go somewhere else."

Taylor felt a stirring near her feet. She glanced down and saw something move. She clamped a hand over her mouth to keep from giving herself away, and luckily caught a sneeze. Her eyes immediately began to water as if she were having an allergic reaction. But there was nothing that would cause...

A soft meow cut through the darkness.

A cat.

Taylor nearly groaned aloud. She stifled it and breathed a sigh of relief. Then she sneezed. A loud, obnoxious sneeze that silenced the entire room.

The cat yowled and leaped from the closet. The door swung open, and Taylor let out another horrific sneeze. Watery eyes blurred her vision, but not enough that she couldn't see the slack jaws and five stunned faces staring back at her. Two men she didn't recognize, Virgil and Clint of course, and...Beth.

She felt sick. How could he do this to her?

"Taylor?" Clint appeared the most astonished of all, as well he should be. He knew he'd been caught. "What the hell are you doing in there?"

She stepped out of the closet, sadly shaking her head. "How could you do this, Clint? I just don't understand."

A puzzled frown furrowed his brows. "Do what?"

Her gaze drew to Beth. The young woman looked flabbergasted...and awfully naive. Taylor caught her lower lip.

Clint turned to the others. "Would you excuse us for a few minutes?"

"Sure." The two men she didn't recognize exchanged confused looks. One of them immediately left, followed more reluctantly by Virgil and Beth.

Distracted by the second man who hovered near the door, she almost missed the one who lurked in the far corner. He looked vaguely familiar...

She remembered. He'd been at the Swinging R the day after the wedding. He was the stocky blond guy in Max's den who'd tried to avoid her when she'd taken in the coffee.

He came forward, his expression grim, and fear surged up her spine. Automatically she stepped back.

"Come on, guys." Clint gestured with his chin toward the door.

Neither of them moved right away, and Taylor reached into her purse and whipped out her cell phone. "I'm dialing the police."

Clint reared his head back. "What?"

The big burly man near the door straightened. "Well, I'm the sheriff, ma'am. Can I help you?"

Taylor snorted, and started pressing numbers. "Right."

He calmly withdrew a leather billfold and showed her his badge. It looked authentic.

She blinked. A crooked cop in Bingo?

"Sorry I'm late, but our plane—"

At the sound of Max's voice, Taylor's eyes widened. "Max?"

"Taylor?" Max gave Clint a stern look. "I asked you to keep her out of this."

Her knees nearly buckled and her head grew dangerously light. Was Max a victim, or a...? "Max, tell me you aren't part of this scam," she whispered.

"Scam?" He frowned, and looked from Clint to the blond man. "How much does she know?"

Clint muttered a curse. The other man simply shook his head.

"I didn't tell her a thing." Clint sighed. "But she obviously overheard something."

Max scrubbed at his eyes. "Honestly, I don't know much about the sting. That's between Clint and the government."

"The government?" Taylor held the cell phone limply at her side. "Which government?"

The three men stared back at her with blank expressions. The sheriff closed the door and joined them.

"Why don't you tell us what you think is going on?" Clint suggested and pulled out a chair for her.

As much as she preferred the advantage of standing, she readily accepted the seat. She didn't trust her legs to hold her up. "Where does Nathan come in?" she asked, and the blond man swore again and glared at Clint.

"He's a separate issue," Clint said grimly. "Sort of...ah, hell." He shook his head with disgust, then gestured toward the blond man. "This is Agent Gerard. He works for the FBI. I'm helping him expose Nathan Banes for fraud. Obviously I'm doing a shitty job."

"You're helping the FBI? You mean you're not—" Heat stung Taylor's cheeks when she realized what she was about to say. What a horrid deed she'd been so ready to accuse Clint of.

Quickly, she averted her gaze from his. But it was too late. He knew the awful belief she'd harbored about him—obviously not the details, but he suspected enough that disappointment and hurt clouded his eyes.

"Clint is a lawyer, Taylor," Max said quietly. "An ex-JAG lawyer. He was with the Navy for seven years."

It was a darn good thing she was already sitting. She let the information sink in for a moment and then stood. "Max, may I speak with you for a moment? Privately."

She couldn't bear to meet Clint's gaze as she led Max out of the room. With any luck, she'd never have to look him in the eye again.

14

"TAKE IT EASY, CLINT, you aren't thinking straight." Max helped himself to a beer from Clint's refrigerator, then offered him one.

Clint shook his head. Damn right he wasn't. He was too flabbergasted and hurt to see straight. How could Taylor have believed he could con his own neighbors and friends?

"She was in a tough position." Max took a chair across the kitchen table. "She'd only just met you, and then overheard something incriminating she thought could hurt Abby and me. I told you once that if I had to describe her in one word it would be loyal. What would you have expected her to do?"

Clint rubbed his tired eyes. Intellectually he understood that rationale. It was his heart that had trouble understanding. They'd made love only twenty-four hours ago. It hadn't been a mere physical act—not for him, anyway. She'd inspired hope for their future with her sweet moans, the soft looks, the way she'd completely trusted him. Apparently her faith in him went no further than the bedroom.

Had her attentiveness and pillow talk simply been a means to get information from him? To stick close and find out what he was up to? Did she have any feelings for him at all?

Taylor wasn't like that. This was his wounded pride

needling him. He wondered if she'd admitted to Max that they'd been intimate. Clint wouldn't reveal anything now, of course, but if Max knew, he wouldn't be wasting time on this pep talk. Making love had changed every-thing, at least for Clint.

"Besides, part of this is your fault." Max yawned and stretched. "Man, I need another vacation."

"What do you mean, my fault?"

"You should have told her about yourself from the beginning instead of doing the country-boy routine."

"I am a country boy, dammit."

Max gave him a slow patronizing grin. "Who happens to have one of the sharpest legal minds I've run across—barring Taylor, of course."

Clint cursed and slumped back with a heartfelt groan.

"She's in love with you."

Clint stared dumbly at Max, who tipped his head back and slowly drank his beer, as if he hadn't just dropped a bombshell. "What the hell are you talking about?"

"Don't tell me you haven't figured it out."

Clint's heart slowed again. So this was only specula-tion on Max's part. Taylor hadn't actually said anything to him. "Well, Max, old boy, I'm going to say something that will probably shock the hell out of you."

"I'm listening."

"I wish you were right."

Max frowned. "Why would I lie?"

"I'm sure you know her pretty well," Clint said, shak-ing his head, "but I think this time you're reading her wrong."

"Reading, hell. I got it from the horse's mouth. She told me herself."

Clint's gut clenched. "Max, so help me, if you're just trying to patch things up—"

"Damn right I am. Just like Abby and Beth are doing with Taylor right now, but that doesn't mitigate the truth. She's fallen hard and fast." Max shrugged, a grin tugging at his mouth. "Personally, I don't get what she sees in you."

Clint had already gotten up and pulled on his jacket, and then he grabbed his cell phone.

"She's at the airstrip waiting for a commuter flight."

He nodded, and hoped he wasn't too late.

"I CAN'T BELIEVE how awful this turned out." Abby stood beside Beth, running her hands distractedly through her hair. "This is just so wrong."

Beth shrugged and sniffed. "Somehow I feel as though this is my fault. I should have told you about Clint. How wonderful he's been to all of us, making sure our rights were protected when the mining company started buying and selling land. Heck, he's even bailed Virgil's idiot nephew out of jail twice."

"Knock it off, you two." A sob caught in Taylor's throat and she had to swallow quickly. "It's no one's fault—except mine, of course." She tried to laugh, sounding more like a sick frog. "Now, would you please leave? I'll be fine. Abby, you're supposed to be on your honeymoon still."

"Why don't you spend the night at our house?" Abby sat beside her again and took one of her hands. "You probably won't get out of Las Vegas tonight, anyway. After a good night's sleep, things won't seem so bad."

Taylor squeezed her hand and smiled. "Max finally did something right. He chose you."

"Then you'll stay?"

Shaking her head, Taylor withdrew her hand. "I can't. I really can't." She stared down at her tennis shoes. She hadn't even taken the time to change. "I hope you won't be offended, but I'd really like to be alone now."

She looked up to find sympathy and understanding in both women's eyes. "You promise to keep in touch?" Abby said.

"Of course."

Abby nodded. "I know. We're going to Boston next summer. We'll see you then."

"I can't wait." Taylor stood and smiled at Beth. "Give Sheila a big hug for me, will you?"

Beth dabbed at her eyes and nodded.

After a round of hugs and promises to call, the two women left. Taylor sank back into her seat feeling totally drained. She didn't even care that the small waiting room was poorly heated, in the middle of nowhere, or that all five wooden chairs were as hard as rocks. All she wanted was to get on a plane and get as far away from Bingo as she could.

Away from the humiliation of what she'd done. Away from Clint Southwick.

God, that thought hurt.

She took several deep breaths, glad she was alone to wallow in her misery. It astonished her that she could have fallen so hard so fast. And she'd lectured Max not that long ago to be careful he wasn't merely infatuated with Abby.

Until this past week, she hadn't believed it was possible to love someone that quickly. But there was no helping it when you found someone who met all the criteria for a life's partner you hadn't even known you'd subconsciously compiled.

When she thought about Clint within the context of other men she knew in Boston, it totally floored her how there simply was no comparison. She had a number of male friends, but none she could think of who were as considerate or kind or good-natured as Clint. And the clincher was, he was every bit as accomplished as all of them put together. She knew. She'd gotten quite the earful about him from both Max and Abby.

As much as she wished he'd told her about his JAG career, perversely she was glad he hadn't spelled out his successes. That was yet another one of the many qualities she admired about him. He didn't feel the need to impress.

She sighed and stared miserably out the window at miles of desert. She couldn't say the same thing. An uptown address, designer clothes, invitations to the A-list parties had all been important for her. That lifestyle had never been her major goal, but she'd be a liar if she denied its significance in proving she'd made something of herself.

It didn't matter now. She was never going to make it back to Boston in time for Howard to forgive her. He could be harsh that way.

She heard a noise from behind her and realized someone had entered the waiting area. A tall man with thinning hair who looked vaguely familiar nodded politely to her, and then sat one chair away.

A moment later, his cell phone rang and he withdrew it from his denim jacket pocket.

He answered it, then turned to her. "It's for you."

She jerked when he tried to pass her the phone. "You must be mistaken."

"You're Taylor Madison?"

She nodded, a creepy feeling churning in her stomach. "Who are you?"

He laid the phone on the vacant chair between them and then left the room.

The temptation to ignore it couldn't hold a candle to her curiosity. She slowly picked up the phone. "Yes?"

"Hello, darlin'."

At the sound of Clint's deep voice, Taylor went boneless. Blessedly, there was no hurt or anger in his tone. "Hi."

"I thought we were supposed to have a drink."

Her heart started to pound. "We were?"

"I distinctly remember you saying that if I gave you a lift into town we'd have a drink afterwards."

She didn't say anything. She couldn't. Her throat had gotten too clogged up.

"You can't leave, Taylor," Clint said softly. "I need you."

Emotion overwhelmed her and she quickly covered the phone to hide her unexpected sniffles.

"Come on, darlin', the town needs you, too."

She smiled. "How does the town need me?"

"Nobody's had such a good laugh since old Milton Cleghorn forgot to wear his pants to church two years ago."

She frowned, confused at first, but when he started laughing, his meaning sunk in. "You—you—" She let out a piercing shriek, and fumbled with trying to disconnect the call.

Her only regret was that she couldn't slam the phone in his ear, she thought as she tossed the phone onto the vacant seat. She glared at the phone. Why could she still hear him laughing? She'd turned the damn thing off.

Slowly she twisted around when she realized the sound came from behind her. Clint lounged against the door frame with a big grin on his face.

She glared at him. Hadn't she suffered enough humiliation? Did he have to rub it in? She was willing to take responsibility for her hasty conclusions, but not right now. She couldn't. It hurt too much to think about how she'd damaged their relationship, how she'd hurt him.

He moved away from the door, jarring her to reality. She jumped up from her seat. The unisex rest room was only several yards away...

He caught her before she reached the door and held her tightly in his arms. "Taylor?"

She wouldn't look at him.

"Come on, baby, don't do this. Look at me."

Reluctantly she lifted her gaze to meet his and found a tenderness she didn't deserve.

"How could you even speak to me again?" she said quietly.

He smiled. "The next forty years are gonna be one hell of a long haul if we're not even talking to one another."

She shifted to get a better look at his face, but he wouldn't let her go. "Clint, don't play with me. I can't take it right now."

"I'm only playing for keeps. I love you, Taylor. I want you to stay here in Bingo and marry me."

The entire universe shifted beneath her. "You want me to marry you?"

He nodded slowly, his eyes locked on hers. "And have my babies."

"But..." she moistened her lips, "how could you after what I thought..."

With his thumb, he dabbed at her cheek. A tear had slipped without her being aware of it. "The real questions is, how could I not respect your loyalty? You were willing to make an enormous sacrifice to protect a friend. I love you, Taylor, and I want you to stay. If you make the decision to marry me, I know I can count on you to always be there for me…for our future children.''

The earnestness in his face nearly unleashed a whole slew of tears, and she had to swallow hard. "My job's in Boston."

"I know." He briefly and gently kissed her lips. "If you want to stay with your firm, we'll work something out."

"But the ranch…"

"Will always be home to me. But it can't replace you."

She smiled. "I can't believe I fell in love with a cowboy."

A lazy grin curved his mouth. "What was it that got you, the hat, the boots, the darlin'?"

"This." She wrapped her arms around his neck and kissed him so hard they both heard bells.

Epilogue

"WHO'D WANT TO WEAR that poor excuse for a garter? There's not an inch of real lace on it." Mona wedged herself between Candy and Taylor. "This teddy is perfect." She smiled at Taylor. "It's blue and it's borrowed."

Candy lifted her chin. "No wonder Herb won't marry you, you bossy old broad."

Taylor sighed. Good thing the temperature was cool outside. The white stucco church hadn't gotten any bigger since Max and Abby's wedding and it was just stuffy now. Of course she doubted any place was big enough for Mona and Candy to coexist.

"Ladies, please don't start," Taylor pleaded. "You're not supposed to give the bride a headache on her wedding day."

Mona turned to Candy. "See what you've gone and done. I'll go get you some aspirin, Taylor."

"She doesn't like aspirin. She likes the other stuff." Candy quickly followed Mona out the door.

Taylor and Abby exchanged looks and started laughing. "It's reassuring to know some things never change," Taylor said as she turned to pick up the wide-brimmed white hat she'd chosen to wear instead of a veil.

"Thank goodness Bingo has." Abby fussed with the back of Taylor's hair. "Before you know it, your new office will have more business than you want."

Taylor groaned. "I've only been here a week and I already have too many clients, especially now that Chester Southby has retired. I wanted to take it easy for a while. Commuting back and forth every other month has me whipped. I'm glad it's over."

"Clint always complained about having to take a suit when it was his weekend to go see you."

"Yeah, as if we ever left my apartment." Taylor blushed when she realized what she'd said.

"Gee, I wouldn't have the slightest idea what you mean." Abby grinned. "Max and I still spend most nights at home, old married couple that we are."

"I can't believe tomorrow's your anniversary already."

"It's gone quickly. I'm not sure Max knew what he was getting into as co-mayor. The job keeps us both hopping."

"It's the best thing that's ever happened to him."

The door creaked open and they both turned. It was Beth. "Taylor, Clint wants to see you."

Abby shook her head. "Tell him it's bad luck—"

Clint poked his head above Beth's. "It's important."

Taylor hurried to the door. "What's the matter?"

Beth got out of the way, and Clint grabbed Taylor around the waist. Hauling her against him, he kissed her breathless. "We can still elope."

She smiled. "The wedding is in thirty minutes."

"I can't wait," he said, and kissed her again.

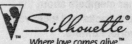